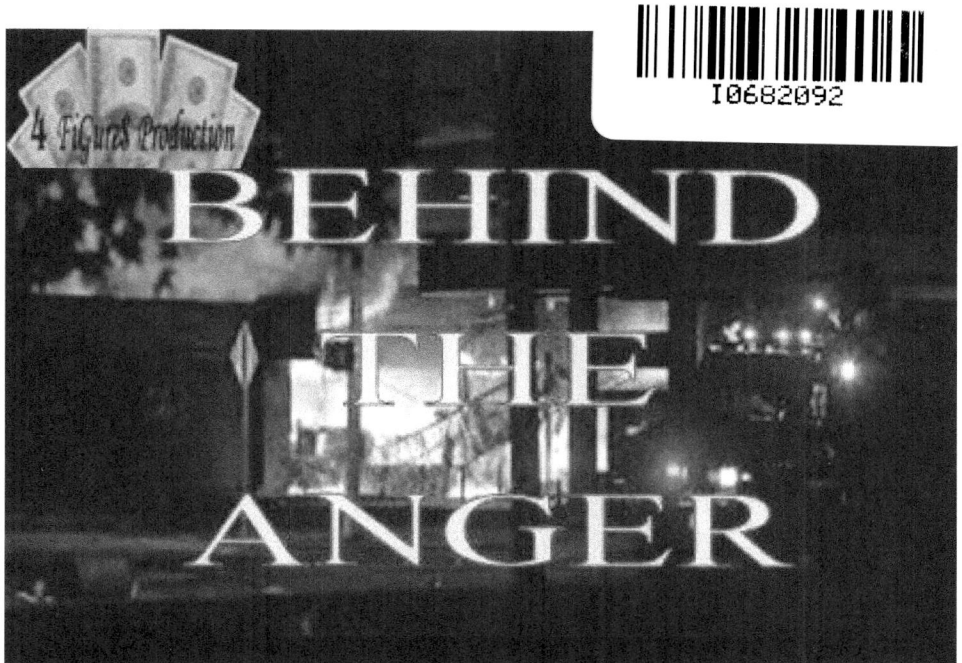

4 FiGureS Production
BEHIND
THE
ANGER

THE YEARS OF FRUSTRATION

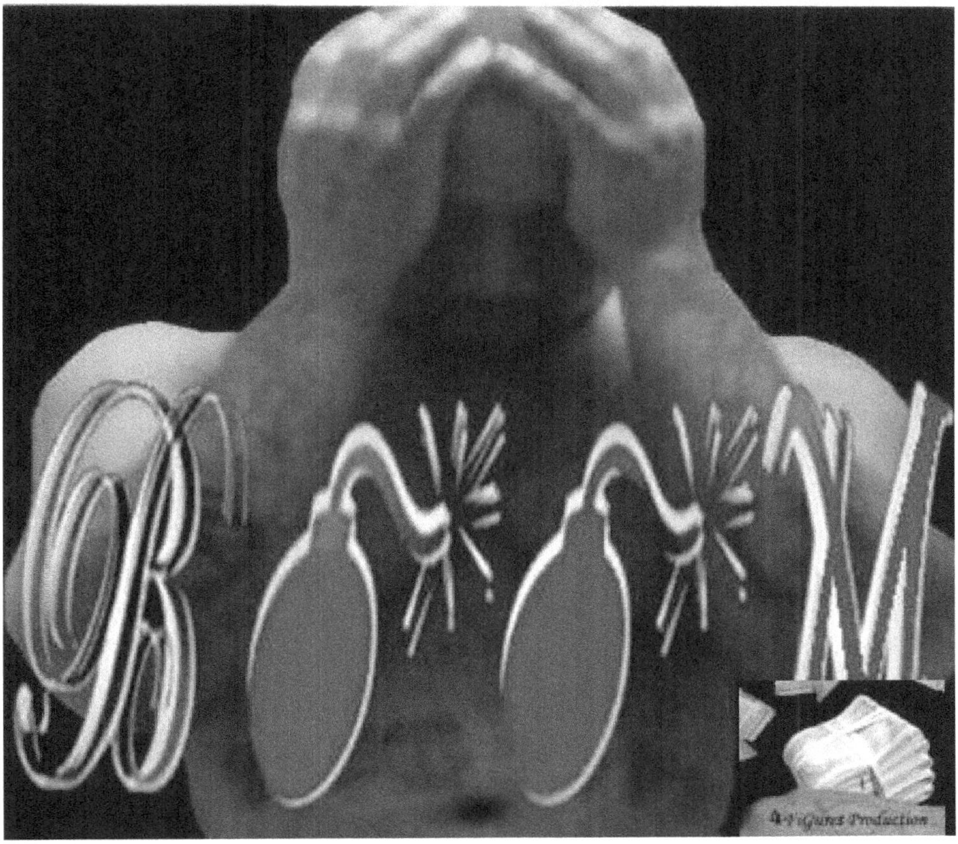
BOOM
4 FiGureS Production

Behind The Anger: The Years Of Frustration

Happens to be a: *4 Figure$ Production L.L.C.* Product.

Created By: Willie James Evans Junior
Illustration By: Willie James Evans Junior
Written By: Willie James Evans Junior
Edited By: Willie James Evans Junior

4 Figure$ Production L.L.C.
5050 Clayridge Drive Suite 213
Saint Louis, Missouri 63129

PRINTED IN THE UNITED STATES OF AMERICA

For information regarding special discounts for bulk purchases, please contact a *4 Figure$ Production L.L.C.* Special Sales Representative
At 314-585-5733 or at  *4figuresproduction@gmail.com*

4 Figure$ Production L.L.C. Can arrange for authors to appear live at your special events. For more information or to book an event, please contact a *4 Figure$ Production L.L.C.* Live Speaker Bureau Representative at 314-585-5733 or email us at *4figuresproduction@gmail.com*

<u>*Prologue*</u>

*M*y name is Tj Green; but I'm also known as Boom. The story I'm about to tell is not only for you common folks, but for every individual whoever had dreams to get rich legal or illegal. Due to unwise decisions that I made as a youth, I ended up losing my freedom time after time after time. In the process of all the years I spent incarcerated, it overall affected my way of thinking and changed the way that I lived.

I grew up in poverty on the streets of Saint Louis, Missouri. I have an older sister who is physically attractive to whomever eyes set upon her, male or female. Although she is physically beautiful, mentally she is immature. Eventually, my bigger sister decided to run away from home; and never again have I seen her.

My mother was only twenty-two years old when she gave birth to me. Due to the stress that we caused her, as a single parent, she gave up on life. My mother later on fell in love with a pimp; who not only turned her on to tricks, but drugs as well.

As conditions became worse in our unsteady house hold, my own mother ended up abandoning me on a couples' porch; who decided to raise me as their own, instead of giving me to the state. Shortly afterwards, a fatal accident occurred; leaving me stuck without a place to go.

As far as my birth father, I never had a chance to meet him. By me never meeting him, I decided that he was the one person that I didn't want to be like in life. So with no father figure or mother in my life, I ended up looking up to those selling drugs and packing guns in the communities I grew up in.

When I was small growing up, I never imagined some of life's struggles that I would go through. I can recall when we were doing bad, going from place to place just to sleep. I even remember sleeping in car-shop garages during the winter just to keep warm; not knowing that the hard parts of life were just about to start.

Chapter One

*I*f you never experienced having to do without, you couldn't possibly imagine how life was for me growing up. I was raised by my momma, Sparkle, in a one bedroom apartment in the projects with my bigger sister, Precious. To say we had different daddies, we looked alike; just like both of our fathers had nothing to do with either of us growing up.

My mother worked days at a fast food restaurant getting paid three dollars and twenty-five cents an hour. While at night, she would leave us alone in the apartment and tell us not to open the door for anyone or she would beat us to death. My bigger sister and me would never know what time our mother would come home; but every morning she faithfully would wake us up, even if we didn't have to go to school.

Precious would always ask momma where she was going, but her only reply was, "I'm grown! I don't have to tell you nothing; but for your information, I'm going to work. So watch your brother and ya'll bet not mess up my damn house!"

My sister would always be mad, so most of the time we would fight after mom left. Normally I lost, and then my sister would make up with me and talk about how she felt. "Momma always saying she's going to work and don't never take us nowhere. Ever since you came along, she makes me sleep on the floor with you; and the lights stay getting cut off. If you wasn't here I'll probably have my bed by now."

"It's not my fault we got to sleep on the floor. That's why you got a bug crawling on you."

She would kill the bug and then say, "I hate you! I wish you would die just like these roaches." Then we would begin fighting again.

I think we use to fight with each other just to take our minds off the roaches and rats that might as well been family since they always crawled on us and ate just about anything we had. It wasn't always bad for us at first. Momma use to take us places and cooked for us all the time. But as time went along, I didn't know what seemed to be worse; momma sending us next door all the time to get food to eat, or having to wear the same clothes three and four times a week.

I hated to go to school because all the children would make fun of me for wearing the same clothes every other day. So I stayed getting into fights and sent home with a note for my mother to come back to school with me. Momma would punish me at home, and then hit me in front of the class for having to bring me back. The whole class would laugh at me and as soon as she would leave they would start back picking on me and I'd be right back in trouble. So I started skipping school.

If I wouldn't have started skipping school, I would have never known my sister was skipping school too. "Boy, why you not at school? You going to get in trouble." she replied.

"I hate school. Everybody always messing with me. Anyway, why you not at school?"

"I'm going by my friend's house."

"I can go with you?"

"No and you bet not tell momma!"

"Forget you. I don't want to go with you anyway." I would be mad because I didn't have anywhere to go. I knew I couldn't go home; and if momma would have found out that I was skipping school, she would have beaten me until I seen Jesus. So I would just hang out at the park until school was over.

After missing so many days at school, my teacher started asking for a note from my mother explaining why I was missing so many days. When that happened I started making up excuses on how I kept forgetting to get the note from her until that story got worn out. After that, I had to talk my sister into writing letters for me and signing momma's name on them. At first, I didn't think the letters would work; but it did for awhile. At least until report cards came out.

"Tj, bring your ass here! Why you have all these damn D's and F's? Better yet, why you have so many fucking absents? You better tell me something got damn it!" my momma snapped.

I would be scared to say anything because I knew I was going to get punished and if she found out I was lying to her it would be even worse. So I would say, "I don't understand everything in class. Then everybody be picking on me all the time."

"Why do you have so many absents then?"

"I don't know. They must have made a mistake on that."

"I'm going to see. I'm taking ya'll to school tomorrow."

I knew I was going to get a beating. I was just hoping it wouldn't happen in front of the whole class; but I knew it was coming. When momma left Precious started going off on me, "Now look at what you done did. Because of you I'm going to get punished too! At least I was going to school. You missed damn near three months straight. Momma going to beat the shit out of you!"

I knew she was right even though I didn't want to admit it. All I could say was, "I don't care. I'm still not going back."

"Oh you going to go when momma finish whipping your ass tomorrow!"

"You going to get a whipping too; or I'm going to tell her you wrote them notes and be with that boy."

"Oh you little motherfucker!" Precious would say before we would start fighting. By the time we would finish fighting she would then say, "I wish all of ya'll would just die!"

That use to hurt my feelings because I still loved my sister and mother even though they both treated me like they didn't want me around and called me stupid all the time.

When momma brought us to school the next day, I was hoping my heart would just stop because I knew we were in for it. "Hello Tj; and you must be Mrs. Sparkle Green. I've been waiting to meet you!" my teacher said in a tone of seriousness.

"Oh really! Any reason in particular you wanted to meet me?" My mother responded.

"To be frankly honest, yes Mrs. Green!"

"Please call me Sparkle."

"I'm majorly concerned with all the days Tj seem to be constantly missing. Is there some kind of personal problem you are having at home causing him to miss so many days?"

"Excuse me! I don't understand what you are talking about. I was coming to find out how could you possibly say my child done missed a hundred and seven days when I send him to school everyday."

"Well Mrs. Green, excuse me Sparkle. I'm afraid you might be sending him; but he's not making it here. I haven't seen him in bout three months until today!"

"Tj, you mean to tell me you haven't been coming to school?" my mother angrily snapped, but I didn't even get a chance to say anything before she hit me three times.

"Sparkle! You can't hit him like that in here."

"What you mean I can't hit him? This is my child!"

"I understand you are upset; but you can't hit a child on school property ma'am. The only thing I can do is to allow him to make up his work so that he won't fail."

"Thank you so much ma'am. He will do all of it too. When I'm finished with him, he will not miss anymore days either. Isn't that right Tj?"

"Yes ma'am!" I said on the verge of crying. Then we went to meet my sister's teacher. Along the way there, I caught a few more hits across the head while she cursed me out.

When we met my sister's teacher, I knew momma was really mad and we were going to get beat like it wasn't a tomorrow. "Hello Precious, and you must be her mother." my sister's teacher said.

"Yes I'm Precious mother. Just call me Sparkle."

"Since you insist Sparkle. I don't know where to begin. I've been having problems with Precious all year!"

"What type of problems are you having with her?"

"She refuses to stop talking in class when she comes! And I'm ashamed to say it, but we had no other choice but to send her home a few times because of the way she dresses."

"What is wrong with the way my child dress?"

"Today she is dress fine; but some days, she comes to school with short mini-skirts on revealing just too much."

When the teacher said that, momma eyes turned red as a demon. I could already feel the beating we had coming. Somehow momma controlled her temper and said, "I'm sorry for any disturbance Precious has caused; but after today she won't give you anymore problems. Isn't that right Precious?"

"Uh-huh."

"It's yes, not uh-huh! You understand me?"

"Yes."

Normally it would have taken us almost thirty minutes to walk home, but not today. Momma was cursing us out and smacking us all the way home, so we made it there in a little bit over fifteen minutes. As soon as we made it home, one of my cousins that just moved from California seen us and asked, "Can ya'll come out and play?"

I was wishing we could, but I had to tell him, "Not today, we about to be on a punishment!"

He just stood there with a blank expression on his face, then ask, "Well can I come over?"

"I doubt it! But you can ask my momma and see what she says." Precious said.

When he asked momma could he come over, she blew on him. "Didn't they just tell you they on a punishment? No you can't come over! They can't have company or come outside for a month!"

He got the picture when she finished talking, and then ran off without anymore questions. As soon as we stepped in the door momma said, "You motherfuckers get out them damn clothes! Ya'll think ya'll can do whatever the fuck ya'll want to do! I'm going to show ya'll, ya'll can't outsmart me!"

Once she started whipping me with her favorite leather belt, I was screaming hoping Jesus would stop her from hitting me again. I mean she hit me so hard so many times, that the belt broke. I thought my prayers were answered until she grabbed an extension cord and begun whipping me all over. By the time she was finished, I was bleeding with red extension cord marks all over my body. That was the first time I really felt like I hated my momma and wished she would've died; but it wasn't the last time.

Chapter Two

*T*hat evening when my momma went out like usually, my sister asked me, "Are you alright?"

I really didn't want too answer her because I felt like momma took it easy on her compared to the whipping I received. Then I said, "Momma make me sick! She be beating on me like she don't love me. She beat on you too, but she don't beat on you like she do me. Why?"

"I guess because you a boy she figure she don't be hurting you."

"She don't be hurting me! Look at all these marks she put on me! You think they don't hurt?"

"I know they hurt. I got some too. Well you better go to sleep before momma get back."

That's exactly what I did. When I did wake up, all I heard was momma cursing. I thought I was dreaming at first; until I seen that boy my sister be with running out the door. When I realize who I just seen, I knew we were going to get another whipping so I kept my eyes closed until I fell back asleep. All of a sudden, momma woke me back up, "Where is your fucking sister at? You knew that boy was in my house? Precious, where the fuck are you?"

I didn't know what to do or say. I knew momma was real pissed off even more than she was earlier. So I didn't say anything and acted like I wasn't all the way awoke.

"Got damn it, I know you hear me talking to you! Where is your sister at?"

"I don't know. She ain't in the bathroom?"

"You mean to tell me you didn't know that man was in my damn house?"

"What man was in the house? What are you talking about momma?"

Before I knew it, I was getting another whipping for something I didn't even know about and I wasn't even lying this time. By the time my mother realized I didn't know what she was talking about, she broke down crying. I never saw my mother cry like she did that day. The way she broke down crying, made me start crying and it wasn't because I just gotten a whipping.

I was telling her everything was going to be okay, even though I didn't really understand what she was crying for. Precious and me always talked about leaving home, but I never figured she would leave for real. "Tj, you don't have an ideal where your sister might have gone?"

"No ma'am. She's going to come home though."

"You don't know who that boy was? He looked like he could have been grown."

"I don't know who you talking about, but Precious going to come home."

I was trying to put things together in my mind why Precious had left without telling me. At first I couldn't come up with a clue. Then when I thought about seeing that boy running out of the house, I knew why Precious had left. Momma would have damn near killed her if she wouldn't have left.

For the first time in about a year, momma sat down on a crate that we used as furniture in the living room and began talking to me. Half of the time I didn't know if she was speaking to me, or just out loud while she was rocking back and forth. All I really knew was that momma was hurt; and if my sister would have walked through the door somebody would have died that night. After sitting there for hours rocking back and forth, momma realized I was still up watching her and said, "Tj. You know I love you, don't you?"

"I know you love me momma and I love you too."

"It's just I don't know what to do with ya'll anymore. I bust my ass to make sure ya'll have; but somehow I seem to fail. I'm sorry for taking my anger out on you. I hope you don't hate me. You my baby and I love you. I just don't know what I would do if I was to lose either one of you."

"You not going to lose us momma. Everything is going to be alright."

"I hope so son. You can go sleep in my bed."

I knew something had to be seriously wrong when momma told me I could go sleep in her bed. As far back as I could remember, momma never allowed me to sleep in her bed. So I said, "That's alright momma; I'll sleep on the floor like I normally do."

She started crying again when I told her that. I didn't know if I did something wrong or not; so I just grabbed my blanket and went in the corner where I normally slept and went to sleep.

The next morning when I woke up momma was already up. When I looked at the clock, it was ten-thirty-three. Since I was old enough to go to school and tell time, momma never allowed us to sleep past eight o'clock in the morning; so I knew she had to have a lot on her mind. Once I gotten all the way up I asked momma how she was doing, but I could tell she hadn't slept a wink when I seen how red and swollen her eyes were. She just looked at me and said, "When you finish brushing your teeth, get dressed so we can go."

I didn't know where we were going, but I didn't ask any questions. I just did what momma said because I couldn't take another whipping. I was already hurting from yesterday and I had enough extension cord marks to last me for a month. As soon as I gotten dressed, I told momma I was ready to go. Then we left.

We stopped at a pay-phone where I thought momma was calling the police until I started paying attention to what she was saying. "She still haven't came home. I don't know. He right next to me. Uh-huh. No. Okay, I'll see you then." then she turned to me and said, "I'm sorry I got you out here without eating. Let's go get something to eat."

I was expecting us to begin walking back home thinking about how much butter and sugar I was going to put on my rice, but we wasn't walking towards the house so I asked, "Where we going? I thought we were going home to eat."

"I'm going to take you to White Castle's. I know you haven't had that in a long time."

I couldn't believe she was actually taking me to White Castle's. The hamburgers were only thirty-six cents, but we only ate there about three times a year unless our neighbors had leftovers or extras. When we arrived there momma ordered me three castle burgers and asked me, "What kind of soda do you want?"

I didn't want to push my luck, so I said, "None! I'll drink some water!"

Once we sat down, I couldn't believe I was really about to eat some White Castle's at White Castle's. I ate them as if I hadn't ate in a week. When momma seen how quickly I at them, she said, "You must have been hungry. You want some more?"

"Yes ma'am if I can!" I replied.

She went back to the counter and ordered me three more castle burgers. When she came back she said, "Now you sit right here and eat them slow while I go make a phone call."

"You don't want none momma?" I asked because I realized that she didn't order herself anything to eat. She just shook her head and walked out of the place. I didn't know what else to expect out of the day. To say we didn't know where my sister was, momma was actually treating me like I was her child instead of someone she couldn't stand.

When she came back I was finish eating the castle burgers. She said, "You didn't save me any. Not even one!"

I just knew I was going to get a whipping. I said, "I thought you were shaking your head no when I asked you if you wanted any."

"It's alright. I'm not hungry." Then momma finally asked me the big question, "Be honest with me Tj. You know where your sister would have went or who that man was that was in my bed?"

When she asked me that, it took me a second to catch on that she said in her bed. That right there explained to me why my sister really left and haven't came back home. I said, "Momma I really don't know where Precious might be or who was in the house. You woke me up last night. I had went to sleep a little while after you left, and Precious was still in the house with me then."

"Where do you be going when you skip school then?"

"To the park."

"Well lets go, our ride is here." I didn't even know we had a ride coming or waiting. When we went outside, momma walked up to a clean Lincoln Continental and told me to get in the back.

Inside was an older Black man. He introduced his self as Mr. Wayne. To me he looked like an old high roller and spoke as if it wasn't a thing in the world that could get him upset. Right off the back I could tell he was the type of man that wanted his presence to be known; but it was something about him that I just didn't like.

He rode us around for a long time looking for my sister as if he was really concerned. After a few hours of just riding around, he offered to buy us something to eat. Momma said, "I'm not hungry, just get him something to eat."

"Well lil' man, what do you want to eat?" Mr. Wayne asked me.

I didn't know what to say because momma always told us not to take food from folks we didn't know. Then again here was my chance to get anything I wanted to eat and momma was right here so I couldn't see it being a problem. I replied, "White Castle's."

"You sure that's what you want?"

I looked at momma and she seemed to be in her own world so I answered him, "Yes sir, Mr. Wayne."

"You don't have to call me Mr. Wayne. Just call me Money."

"Okay Mr. Money." He didn't say anything about me calling him Mr. Money. He just smiled as if he was turned on by hearing the word money.

He drove us to the same White Castle's that we went to earlier then said, "Sparkle, you sure you don't want anything to eat?"

"I'm alright!" she answered in a low tone.

"Look Sparkle, you have to eat something! I'm just going to get enough so if you get hungry later you will have some."

She didn't say anything. She just remained looking spaced out.

After we gotten our food, he brought us home. I said, "Thank you Mr. Wayne. I mean Mr. Money," then got out of his car. Momma stayed sitting in there for a minute before getting out. I guess they had something to talk about that they didn't want me to hear.

Once we opened the door to the apartment, I knew things were back to normal. Bugs were crawling all over the place as if they lived there and we were visiting them. I use to hate coming inside because I knew they were going to crawl all over me eventually and that use to drive me. I shook a sheet free from roaches that we used to cover a box in which we used as a table,

then placed the food on it. After I did that, I asked momma, "Are you going to come eat with me?"

This time she came and ate two burgers; and then said, "You just eat what you want and save me some." Then she went into her bedroom and closed the door behind her.

When I finished eating, I realized I didn't have nothing to do since Precious was gone. I asked momma did she want me to put the rest of the food in the oven or in the refrigerator. It took her a few moments to tell me in the refrigerator, but I didn't pay it no mind. I thought she might have been laying down until she came out of her room and went into the bathroom.

When she opened her bedroom door, it smelt like she was smoking crack in there. I couldn't help but noticed that smell being that I smelt it all the time in the building we stayed in. I thought it was just coming through the window being that the window was cracked; but I just didn't know, my momma was really getting high.

Chapter Three

*L*ater on that night, momma came out of her room and said, "You can warm up them burgers; and then take a bath. When you finish you can go to sleep in my bed. I have to go to work tonight. While I'm gone you can answer the door, but you bet not open it for anyone but your sister; if she comes back. Do you understand me?"

"Yes ma'am."

When momma left I was really lonely. It felt strange being in the house by myself. I didn't have anything to do. I couldn't watch television because we didn't have one; and I didn't want to mess with the radio on the clock because I might have messed up the time and momma would have known it was me. So I just laid in the bed and listened to the neighbors until I fell asleep.

The next morning momma woke me up like usual for school. Once I got ready, momma said, "Don't tell anyone your sister ran away. You understand me?"

"Yes."

"And, you better go to school and come straight home afterwards. Is that clear?"

"Yes."

It felt real funny going to school without my sister. On the way there, I bumped into my cousin and we began to walk to school together. "Say *cuzz*, what did ya'll do to get on punishment? Your momma was mad!"

"We just been getting into a lot of trouble at school; and momma just got sick of it."

"She really going to keep ya'll on punishment for a month?"

"I don't know. She might!"

"Where Precious at?"

Now when he asked me that, I thought about what momma said; but she didn't tell me what to say. So I asked him, "What you said?" trying to buy some time to come up with an excuse.

"Where your sister?"

"Oh, she sick so she got to stay home today." and that was that.

Once we arrived at school we went our own way and the day went on normal. By lunch time I was ready to go; but I knew I couldn't skip a few classes without it really being noticed; so I just went to all of them. By the time I went to gym, my normal day made a sudden turn. The gym teacher told us, "Change into ya'll gym clothes." When I took off the long sleeve shirt I was wearing, the tee-shirt under it came up revealing some of the extension cord marks that I had and he pulled me to the side, "Tj, are you having problems at home you want to talk about?"

I thought he knew my sister had ran away, but he couldn't have known. I didn't tell anybody! I said, "Why would you ask something like that?"

He said, "You don't have to be afraid to tell me if you are having problems. I saw the marks on your side. Are you getting beatings at home?"

"No sir. I just got a whipping because of my report card."

"I can understand you might get a whipping or some type of punishment; but looking at how many marks you have on you, that's considered child abuse! Now I don't want to put Family Service on your parents causing more problems for you, but I will have to suspend you until those marks heal on you."

"Suspend me! If I get suspended I'm really going to get punished. Please don't do that, I'll participate in class!"

"I'm sorry, but it's not about participating in class. If any other teacher here would happen to see all of those marks on you, they would call Family Service; and nobody could stop them once they step in."

I just dropped my head. How was I going to explain I just been suspended to my momma? I knew momma wasn't going to give me a chance to say anything or explain. I just made my last plea of hope to the teacher, "Since you going to suspend me, can you at least write me a note explaining it's not my fault this time?"

"I'll tell you what, I'll call your parents and talk to them."

"That sound good, but we don't have a telephone."

"Oh, is that so? Well I'll write you a letter, and then you can go ahead and leave before anybody else sees you."

Once he gave me the note he wrote, I left. I already knew I was going to get in trouble; so I figured I'll go straight home and deal with it. But on my way home, I saw Mr. Wayne. From where I was standing at, it looked like he was arguing with four women. Then all of a sudden, I saw them all taking money out of their bras and pocket books and hand it over to him. I guess that's why he called his self Money.

When I got close enough that they could see me, I recognized that the four women were neighborhood prostitutes. I was wondering why they would have been giving Mr. Wayne money; but when I really looked at the picture it didn't take a genius to see that Mr. Wayne was a pimp.

"Hello Mr. Money." I said walking by.

"Oh, how you doing Tj?"

"I'm alright. How about you?"

"Just fine! Where are you going this time of day?"

"Home."

"Well come on, let me give you a ride." Once I got in the car he asked, "Are you hungry?"

"No sir, I'm alright."

"Have you heard from your sister yet?"

"No. She didn't even come to school today."

"She'll come home sooner or later."

"I hope so; I actually miss her!"

"It's going to be okay! I'll see you later on." then he dropped me off.

I wasn't expecting my momma to be at home when I got there, so I figured I'll have enough time to get my story together on how I was going to tell her I gotten suspended. When I opened the door I thought somebody must have broken in because the whole house smelt as if someone was smoking crack cocaine; and I knew for sure it was crack I was smelling.

"What the fuck are you doing home early?" momma snapped.

"I got suspended and they sent me home."

"What your dumb ass get suspended for this time?"

I didn't bother to say anything; I just handed her the note my teacher wrote for me. When she finished reading it she said, "Motherfucker you going around telling people I'm beating on you! You my motherfucking child! If I feel I want to whip you until I get tired, it ain't a motherfucker that could stop me!"

I knew she was going to find some kind of way to make it seem like I had gotten suspended on purpose; and the way she was looking, I knew she was smoking that stuff. When she cooled down, I told her, "I saw Mr. Wayne. I guess he's going to come over because he said he'll see me later."

"Where you seen him at?"

"On the way home; he the one who brought me home."

For the rest of the day I was drove. I was hoping Money would come over, but I guess I wasn't that lucky. Around seven o'clock momma cooked some rice and warmed up the left over White Castle's we had. When she finished she said, "Eat all you want, and then go to bed. I'm about to go!"

In a sense I was happy she was leaving. I couldn't stand the thought of knowing that my mother was turning into a dope fiend. I wished I knew where Precious was; I would have left and went by her.

It was three eleven in the morning when momma returned home. I noticed she was wearing: a short skirt, a shirt revealing her stomach, and some red lip stick. At first I thought I was dreaming because I knew that wasn't how my momma left. I soon realized that I wasn't dreaming, when I heard her running some bath water and smelt crack burning again. I just covered my head up and made myself go to sleep.

Chapter Four

*B*efore I realized it, I haven't been to school in just about two weeks and we haven't heard a word from my sister. I don't know if momma got fired from her job or if she just quit. I knew one thing, she haven't been going to work during the day and we just got an eviction notice. Momma seemed not to care a bit about the eviction notice, but I guess that was because she knew the electric was getting ready to be cut off again. All she said was, "Get you and your sister clothes together, we going to be moving soon."

I knew we really didn't have a place to move to, but what was bothering me was how we were going to move and we didn't know where my sister was. So I asked, "If we move before Precious come home, how is she going to know where we moved to?"

I didn't think I was asking anything wrong, but momma snapped, "If Precious motherfucking ass not here when we get ready to fucking move, then she don't need to know where we stay! I'm not the one that told her to leave. You just do what I tell you to do damn it!"

Within the next two days, we moved in with a lady name Samantha. I didn't know Samantha was one of Mr. Wayne's whores. To me she looked attractive. I just couldn't understand how a woman could sell herself for another's pleasure. Even my own mother was attractive, but she wasn't any better than Samantha. I didn't know much about Samantha, but I could tell she was living better than we were.

After we got settled in, momma sent me back to school. My gym teacher pulled me to the side and asked me, "Are you doing better now?"

"Yes sir," I replied. You still could see the marks from the extension chord, but they were healed up just about as good as they could get.

When school was out, a girl named Michelle came up to me and said, "Your sister want to see you."

I just looked at her at first. Then I asked, "Where she at?"

She just said, "Follow me," and then began walking towards the school student's parking lot.

I was following behind her when my cousin stopped me and said, "Where you going cuzz? I haven't seen you in a couple of weeks."

"I have to do something right now. I'll catch up with you later on," then walked off. He just stood there as if it I had just played him before he began walking off. When I got to the parking lot I still didn't see my sister. So I asked Michelle, "Where my sister at?"

When I said that, she opened the door of a light-green Oldsmobile and said, "Get in."

I wasn't sure about getting in the car. Then again, how things been going for me, it couldn't hurt me anymore I thought. When I open the backdoor I seen Precious was ducked down, but she quickly replied, "What's up ugly?"

I was actually happy to see her, so I didn't mind her calling me ugly in front of her friends. "Where the hell you been? Don't you know you got momma going crazy?"

"I told you I was going to leave one day. What momma said when I left?"

"Oh you could have told me you was leaving. I got a whipping and I didn't even know what happen. We moved yesterday. We stay with some lady name Samantha, but I don't know how long that's going to be. So are you going to tell me what happened?"

"That's a long story. I just wanted to see how you were doing. So take care of yourself ugly!"

"You not coming back home?"

"I'm afraid not."

"Well can I come with you?"

"No, you have to stay with your momma. I'll see you every now and then, but I have to go. I love you."

"I love you too." After that I never saw my sister again. Every time I would see Michele I would ask her about Precious, but she would just say she haven't heard from her.

After staying with Samantha for two weeks, Samantha and momma fell out. Before I knew it we were moving again. This time we didn't have anywhere to stay. We started off sleeping in abandon apartments in the projects. Then by different family members until they got tired of putting up with momma's shit. One bad winter came along and we had no choice but to sleep in a car-shop garage just to keep warm. When that happened I couldn't stand my momma because all she wanted to do was get high every chance she could.

Things were getting so bad for us, that we had to eat scraps of food that were other people waste. We couldn't even take a bath. We had to wash up in restaurants' restrooms. When I became ill, that's when momma through her hands in on me and decided to leave me on a couples' porch.

I could never forget that day. It was in the middle of the winter, ten degrees above zero to be precise. I was coughing up blood and had caught pneumonia. I was sweating buck-shots, but was colder than it was outside. Momma and me had stolen some medicine from a store; but it seemed not to be working, and my coughing was getting worse. Finally momma just clicked, "I can't stand you. Why I had to have you? If only I could get another hit, but I can't even turn a trick cause I got you here," then she broke down crying.

I didn't know what to say. I just thought all the problems we were having were my fault. After listening to what she had said, I knew she loved crack more than she loved me and I was her baby even though she didn't want me. I was feeling so bad, that I couldn't see us making it through the whole winter on the streets. I began coughing until I spit up nothing but blood. When that happened I asked, "Am I going to die?" because it damn sure felt like it.

"You going to be alright; first put on some more clothes to keep warm. I'm bout to take you to your new home."

I already had on all of my clothes that I could fit over each other, including a couple of Precious' sweaters that I was using as a coat. When I thought about momma saying she was about to take me to our new home, I just knew she was lying. If we really had a place to go, we would have been there I thought.

When the wind died down momma said, "Come on. It's time to go." We were walking out and away from the projects. I had the slightest ideal where we were headed; I just kept walking trying to keep up with my momma. We must have walked about a mile before we reached a white and red brick house. That's when momma said, "Go knock on the backdoor."

I didn't think about it twice. I just went and knocked on the door because I was happy to be at our new home. When I knocked on the door, nobody answered. I thought I might wasn't knocking hard enough, so I knocked a few more times until my hands started hurting. After nobody still didn't answered the door, I went back around the house to the front; but momma was nowhere in sight. I thought she might have gone in through the front-door while I was knocking on the backdoor, so I began knocking on the front-door. I mean I knocked and knocked and yelled out momma, but nobody answered. That's when reality hit me. Momma just left me.

Chapter Five

I sat on that porch crying at first, because I couldn't believe how my mother just played me. In the back of my mind I was hoping my momma was playing a game on me, but as it got later I knew she wasn't coming back. I actually hated her with a passion now and wished she would have died or never gave birth to me.

After what seemed to be hours past by, a red Ford Escort pulled up in front of the house. I was so cold, that I couldn't even lift up my head to see who all was in the car. I heard a man's voice saying, "Who is that up there?" but I couldn't say anything back. So he asked again, "Who is that up there on the porch?"

I finally lifted my head up and said, "I'm Tj."

"Tj! Who are you? Better yet, why are you sitting on our porch?" the man questioned.

"My mother told me to knock on the back-door. When I came back around the house, she was gone."

"Who is your mother?" the woman with him asked.

"Sparkle. Ms. Sparkle Green."

"You mean to tell me, you don't know where your mother went? Where do you live?" the man asked.

"No sir. I don't know where my mother could have gone. We used to stay in the projects, but we been staying on the streets for awhile now."

"How long have you been sitting here?" the lady asked.

"For awhile now. It was still light outside."

"Oh that's a shame. Honey lets get him inside. I know he has to be freezing." The lady said while I guess the man was her husband opened the door.

Once we had gotten inside their house, I asked, "Could I use the bathroom?"

"It's right there sweetheart." The lady said.

Inside the bathroom I could hear the couple talking about me. "Honey get the telephone so I can call the police." the man said.

"You can't call the police. They'll take him and put him in some kind of home."

"We can't just keep everybody's child we find sitting on our porch."

"I understand that, but we can at least keep him until someone reports him missing. Lets give it a try!"

"I don't know."

When I heard him say he didn't know whether to keep me or not, I put it in my mind to get ready for the streets. I took a face towel that was hanging up, and stuffed it in my pocket. I figured if I had to go back in the cold, I could at least keep the wind from hitting me across my neck some with it.

Once I opened the door they stopped talking. I didn't know whether I should have waited on them to tell me I had to leave or just left. Before I could make up my mind, the lady asked me, "Would you like some hot chocolate?"

"If it's not any trouble Mrs."

"Of course it's not a problem. My name is Mrs. Walton and that's my husband Mr. Walton."

"Thank you Mr. and Mrs. Walton for allowing me to come in and warm up instead of running me away."

"Oh don't worry about that son; we're not the kind of folks that would do something like that. We want to try and help you if we can." Mrs. Walton said while warming me some hot chocolate. When she finished she asked, "Tj, you sure you don't have any idea where your mother might have went or be?"

"No ma'am. All she told me was to knock on the back-door, and when I came back around the house she was gone."

"Do you have any other family that might know where to find your mother?" Mr. Walton asked.

"No sir. We been living on the streets for the past few months sleeping in abandon buildings and garages. The only other person who was close to us was my sister, and she ran away before we got evicted."

"What did your mother do about that?" Mrs. Walton asked.

"We looked for her, but after awhile momma just gave up looking it seem like."

We went on talking for awhile. After a few hours went by, Mr. and Mrs. Walton went into a different room. I didn't know what they were talking about, so my mind was wondering. I just kept picturing all the ways they were going to tell me I had to leave, so I was mainly just thinking of where I was going to go. When they came out of the room, Mrs. Walton asked, "How would you like to stay with us? We have an extra bedroom so you will have a place to sleep."

I couldn't believe she had just invited me to stay. I just knew they were going to tell me I had to leave. I was so shock that I could barely get the words to come out of my mouth. "Oh, thank you Mr. and Mrs. Walton! I would love to stay with you."

"Well don't get too excited, this is only temporary. If anyone reports you missing, you would have to leave. Until then, consider this your new home."

Mr. and Mrs. Walton just didn't know how much it meant to me for them allowing me to stay. On the inside I felt bad because I had just stole a towel from them thinking they were going to put me out, when in reality they were being more courteous to me than my own family. Without a doubt in my mind, I knew I had to put that towel back before they noticed it was missing. I asked, "Can I use the bathroom again?"

"You don't have to ask if you can use the bathroom; I told you to consider this your home." Mrs. Walton replied.

"Its just I'm not used to doing whatever I want in anybody else's house." I replied then went inside the bathroom. Inside, I took the face towel out of my pocket and placed it neatly back where I got it from. After I did that, I looked in the mirror and said to myself: I can't mess this up, no matter what I do. Then I left the bathroom.

Mrs. Walton showed me around the rest of the house, including where I would be sleeping. The room itself was bigger than my mother's bedroom. The first thing I noticed was that the room was absent of roaches. It had a large bed, a desk with a computer on it, two dressers, and two nightstands, one on each side of the bed.

When she finished showing me around, she said, "We don't have any clothes that will fit you, but I'll bring you one of my husband's t-shirts for you to sleep in tonight. Tomorrow we will go buy you some clothes. How does that sound?"

"That sound like a winner, but what about school?"

"What do you mean what about school?"

"I still have to go, don't I?"

"That would be a wise decision if you want to make something out of your life. What school do you go to anyways?"

"Gunlock. If I pass this year I can go to Roosevelt."

"What do you mean if you pass?"

"I missed a lot of days, so in order for me to pass I'll have to work really, really hard."

"As long as you try, that's all that matters. Just give it your all. Anyway, let me go get that t-shirt for you. Have you eaten anything today?"

"No ma'am. Now that you mention it, I haven't eaten anything today besides that hot chocolate that you gave me."

"Oh baby, you have to eat something. I'll warm up a bowl of chili for you. It'll be good for that nasty cold you have. I'll be right back." When she left the room I looked around in amazement. A few moments later she came back with the t-shirt and said, "Your food is ready. It's sitting on the table with a nice big cup of juice for you."

"You're not going to eat anything with me?" I asked her.

"No, I already ate. I'm about to go to bed. I'll see you tomorrow." then she left out of the room.

I took off a few of the sweaters and shirts I had on, then I went into the kitchen and ate. The food tasted good and was well seasoned. Right then, I knew I didn't have to worry about not having a good meal to eat. When I finished eating, I made some dish water and began washing the dishes I used. Mr. Walton walked into the kitchen and when he saw me he replied, "What are you doing? You don't have to do that."

"My momma always made us wash the dishes when we were finished eating. That way the bugs wouldn't get too bad. I haven't seen any here, and I don't want to be the cause of any coming."

"I understand. Well you don't pay me any mind. I'm just about to turn the heat up a little."

Before he left out the room I asked, "Mr. Walton, can I take a bath before I go to bed? I feel real dirty."

"I don't see any reason why you can't. Let me get a towel for you."

After he gave me the towels, I went and got the t-shirt and began taking my bath. It felt strange taking a bath in these complete strangers' tub, but at the same time it felt good. When I finished, the tub had six big black rings around it. I didn't know I was that dirty. I hurried up and cleaned the tub.

When I finished I was exhausted. I was ready to go to sleep, but my mind kept thinking about how my momma did me. I laid in the bed for hours thinking about how she just left me and didn't come back. The more I thought about it, the more I hated her. I eventually fell asleep.

Chapter Six

*T*he next day Mr. and Mrs. Walton took me shopping to get me some new clothes. I must have thanked them a hundred times in thirty minutes. They actually bought me clothes I wasn't ashamed to wear.

When I started going back to school, my classmates stopped picking on me. They were like, "It's about time you got some new clothes." I even got motivated to start paying attention in class, so I could pass. After school, I even brought home my books so I could make up the work I missed.

Before I realized it weeks and weeks were going by. Thanks to Mrs. Walton I was doing good in school now, and would be able to graduate with my class. That's something I didn't think I would've been able to do. I still hadn't seen my sister, but after a while that didn't matter to me anymore.

For the summer my new parents took me on vacations with them. That was something I never experienced with my mother. The only places we ever went together was the store so that we could steal food, or when she brought me back to school after being suspended.

Time was going by fast. I made three birthdays in Mr. and Mrs. Walton's house. Every now and then, I would feel as if I didn't belong there, but they kept showing me love; lifting me up when I felt down. I didn't know how long they were going to let me stay, but they didn't seem like they wanted me to leave so I wasn't going to push the issue.

Every now and then I would go hang in the projects with my cousin from California, but before school started again he moved back to California and we lost contact. Hanging in the projects, I thought I would have ran across my mother, but I never saw her or Mr. Wayne. Even the neighborhood prostitutes that I knew were nowhere to be found. I guess they all ended up getting locked up or moved out of the hood, but I didn't know where they went. When I started Roosevelt, it wasn't comparable to Gunlock. You could tell who had money and who the trouble makers were right off the back. Some of the folks attending were old classmates, but most of all the students were new to me. There was a whole staff of security guards to protect the school, but as the year went on I found out most of them were there just to get a paycheck.

After a while I started hanging with Terral and Tina. I knew them from Gunlock and the projects, so we got along well. Tina and I were closer to each other than Terral and I because half the time he would be with his gang; but that didn't stop us from being cool. We just had our boundaries.

We all had the same classes, so we would just exchange answers after classes. Tina was good in language, so she would do all the assignments in that subject. Terral knew his history, so we just went along with whatever he wrote. I knew math like I knew the projects. When it came down to science, we all had to participate.

I was staying out of trouble at first. I wasn't skipping school or anything. Slowly but surely I started hanging out with Terral and his gang. I didn't even realize they considered me family. The next thing I knew I was breaking into houses and stealing cars with them just for kicks. After almost being caught one day, I decided that wasn't for me and slowly pulled away from them. We were still cool; I just didn't hang with them so much.

When my sophomore year came around, I was still hanging with Tina, Terral, and sometimes my folks in the hood. The three of us ended up having the same classes, so we cheated all year long and kept the teachers trying to separate us; but that didn't stop us from acting a fool in class.

The gang fights were getting worse, mainly because there were folks from the north, west, and south sides all in one place. To say we had security guards at school, they didn't really matter because guns and knives were all through the school. If you were caught slipping, that was your issue. All you could do was hope somebody would help you out if they didn't kill you. I mean, some got beat so bad, they were lucky the paramedics would arrive quickly.

Half way through the year, I would have to say I started maturing. I started looking at females differently. I started spending a lot of time with Tina. She would ask me to hook her up with different dudes I knew, and in return she would hook me up with her friends. We never messed around with each other, but when we caught each other flirting with someone else, we would act like whoever got caught was trying to cheat. To say we were just friends, if you didn't know us you would've thought differently. The only thing I found sexy about Tina was the way she stood. Other than that I didn't see what other cats saw in her.

By the time we were juniors, you could really see the difference in us. Terral became involved in all the school programs and was what we called the teacher's pet. I used to trip off how much he became involved with different programs at school, because I knew him. If it was your first time meeting him, you would swear he was a nerd; but if you caught him in the hood, he smoked weed and got drunk like it was legal.

On the other hand, Tina changed too. She became involved in the school's drama class. So she spent most of her time practicing and performing in school plays. I can't deny it, she was good at acting. I could see her making it in the future as an actress.

Myself, I became popular, but that's about as far as things got for me in school. I was ready to drop out personally. It was like I wasn't learning anything; for one it was all about who I could fuck and where at. So much shit was happening at school that I felt safer on the streets at times, but Mr. and Mrs. Walton kept on supporting me to finish school. I always remembered what Mrs. Walton told me about giving it my all, so I didn't want to become a quitter and let her down.

I became involved with this chick named Patricia. She was the first girlfriend I had that I took serious. The thing that I liked about her was the fact she accepted me for me. Even when we had our differences she stood by me like no other and tried to keep me headed in the right direction.

It seemed like every time a new day came, new problems came with it. One particular day I had to make a choice that not only caused me to get suspended, but I could have lost my life in the process.

It was second lunch when I saw my homies, Terral and G-Dog, fighting against a gang from the north side. By them being my homies and I hung with them, I began fighting with them. The more we fought the more folks began jumping in, but that didn't mean anything to us. They had locks and pocket knives but the only bad thing was we didn't know if anyone as strapped with pistols. We knew guns were in the school, but that was a chance we had to take. After about seven minutes of battling the guards finally came. Folks were breaking out running in all directions. At least those that were able. Only four people had to go to the hospital due to stab wounds. Everybody else was either in the principal's office waiting on disciplinary actions or in the nurse's office getting ice packs. I ended up in the principal's office. I didn't know what kicked the fight off, but it wasn't over. One of the dudes from the north side was in the office talking shit, and before anyone could stop me I ran on him. The guard that broke us up was from the hood. He said, "Look you little motherfuckers. Ya'll want to fight? I got a place for ya'll and I'm not going to stop it."

Without thinking I said, "Got damn me, it don't matter to me. These motherfuckers ain't gone come around here trying to run shit."

"Fuck ya'll. Ya'll ain't running shit." The dude I just ran on said.

"Alright, ya'll still want to fight, come with me." The guard said leading us to a closed door. Behind the door was a small room, a little bigger than an average size closet. Inside he said, "Ya'll can fight until ya'll get tired, but ain't nobody going to jumping on anybody except for me." then closed the door behind him.

The door had barely closed when I ran back on your boy. He was pissing me off even more because he didn't swing back after he was talking cash money shit, but I didn't stop swinging on him. I knew we were going to get suspended either way it went, if we didn't get expelled. After I hit him a few times he fell. What he did that for? I began stomping him until he yelled. Once he started screaming like a little bitch, the guard opened the door again and said, "That's enough."

Altogether, forty-two of us got suspended that day, but they were smart about the situation. They didn't let us all leave at the same time, and they had so many police at the school at the end of the day that it would have been crazy to do anything. Just to be on the safe side, when they finally let us go, we all clicked back up, but the police quickly escorted us away.

When that happened I decided to go to Patricia's house. I chilled over her way for a few hours until I got tired of hearing her tell me about unwise decisions I be making. Even though I knew she was right, I just didn't want to hear anymore about the things I was doing. It was bad enough I was going to have to explain I've been suspended for exciting a riot to Mr. and Mrs. Walton.

When I got close to home, I could smell something had been burnt. I didn't have any idea what it could have been, but the smell was loud. The closer I got to home, the louder the smell was. Then I saw the unimaginable.

Chapter Seven

*W*here what I used to call home was, was nothing but a burnt-up building with yellow tape wrapped around it. I couldn't believe what I was seeing. My first thought was: "Where was Mrs. And Mr. Walton?" I seen the car was parked in front of the house, but they were nowhere in sight. After everything I had been through that day, I wasn't expecting this.

Mr. and Mrs. Walton were the only folks who treated me like family. I didn't know where I was going to go now or what I was going to do. I was assed out; and for the second time, I was stuck on stupid.

I saw one of the neighbors sitting on their porch just watching, so I walked by them and asked, "Do you know what happened or where Mr. and Mrs. Walton are?"

"I'm sorry baby, but Mr. and Mrs. Walton died in that house fire. Are you related to them?" the neighbor asked.

"They died! That can't be! I just saw them this morning."

"I can't believe it either, but you never know when it's someone's time to go."

I just walked off. I didn't know where I was going, I was just walking. My mind drifted back to the times I spent with them. I just couldn't accept they were really dead. I was hoping I was just having a real bad nightmare, but the fact remained they were really gone.

I didn't even realize how far I had walked. By the time I really paid attention to where I was, I was at Dakota Park where Terral, G-Dog, and the rest of the gang hung. Nobody was there at the time, so I just sat on a bench in my own world. I just sat there, homeless and without a clue as to what I was going to do. I was so far gone in the mind that I didn't even notice it started raining. Once I was soaked, I pulled myself together and started walking towards some apartments.

The first apartments I came to, I went inside its hallway and sat on the steps. Out of the blue, a man walked inside the building. I guess I must have startled him; at least I could tell by the expression on his face when he saw me. I stood up to let him pass by, but instead of just passing he asked, "Are you waiting on someone?"

I just looked at him, hoping he would go about his business. When I realized he was waiting on an answer, I replied, "Not really. I'm just waiting on the rain to stop."

"I don't blame you. The rain is coming down pretty hard right now, but as soon as it lightens up, you will have to leave. I don't allow loitering." He said, then he walked into his apartment.

I couldn't believe he had the nerve to be telling me about loitering. If only he was in my shoes, and knew I didn't have a place to stay or go; and the only place I could call home had just been burnt down. I wondered what he would have done. I knew he wouldn't have been worrying about no damn loitering, but I had to respect what he had just said. I didn't want to be bothered by the police behind no bullshit.

I sat back down on the steps trying to figure out where I was going to go when it stopped raining, but I was clueless. I knew I couldn't go to Patricia's house because her parents weren't going to allow me to stay there. My mind drifted back in time, to when I lived on the streets with my real momma. I guess you can say she actually taught me something that was going to help me out at a time like this, whether I liked it or not.

From all of the stress I was dealing with, I ended up passing out. I didn't have the slightest idea how long I was asleep before the man I had previously met woke me up, "I thought I told you, you had to leave when the rain lightened up! What you still doing here? Don't you have somewhere to go?"

"Honestly I don't. My home burned down yesterday."

"I saw something about a house fire on the news last night. Didn't two people die in that fire?"

"Unfortunately, I'm afraid so. I'm sorry if I caused any problems." Then I began to leave.

"Hold up! Where are you going?"

"To get something to eat. Why?"

"Well, I'm about to do the same thing. I can give you a ride if you want. Other than that, I can offer you a job whenever it's not raining. It doesn't pay much, but it's easy money."

I really didn't want to work, but I knew I had to do something. I asked, "What kind of job can you offer me?"

"I have my own business selling balloons, bears, and roses. I'll pay you twenty percent of whatever you make. So do you want to work or not?"

"I'm afraid not. Maybe in the future if I need work, I could come work for you." I said while thinking to myself what the fuck I look like making him a hundred dollars just to get twenty of it?

"Do you want me to give you a ride or not?"

"No thank you. I don't mind walking right now."

"Suit yourself."

When he left, I started walking down the street looking to see what apartments were abandon. I kept a reminder of them just in case I needed to sleep in one of them. That was something I just picked up when I stayed on the streets with my mother.

After I went down a few blocks, I finally made it to the local grocery store. I didn't plan on spending a penny if I didn't have to. When it came to stealing food, my momma made sure we knew how to do that, being that we did it so much. I grabbed a shopping cart and began putting what I wanted to eat in it. After I got everything I wanted to eat and drink, I began walking down different aisles eating and drinking everything I could. Afterwards, I left as if nothing had happened.

I wanted to know when and where Mr. and Mrs. Walton were going to be buried, but I didn't know how that would've looked if the police was to do an investigation and found my fingerprints on just about everything and decided to question me. What was I going to tell them. I was a stranger to them at first, but they decided to let me move in with them. They had been taking care of me for years due to the fact that nobody ever reported me missing. Then all of a sudden, they ended up dead in a house fire and I'm the only survivor because I wasn't there. I didn't want to take my chances on finding out what they would have thought.

I decided to go back to the projects, despairingly hoping I would find my mother. The more I searched for her, the more my hope of finding her seemed to fade away. I couldn't even find Mr. Wayne. I went by Samantha's house hoping she could tell me how to get in touch with Money, but she didn't even stay there anymore. It seemed like everybody I knew from the projects was moving out if they hadn't already moved.

I had thirty-two dollars and seven cents to my name. I knew that wasn't going to last that long on the streets, so I had to be extremely careful about what I spent it on. It wasn't like I was guaranteed to get some more money without working and I wasn't ready to work. The only clothes I had were the ones I had on, and I wasn't about to be wearing the same clothes everyday.

I went to the mall and went straight inside Dillard's. The first thing I picked up was a Black duffel bag. I removed the price tags from it, then began filling it up with: a pack of boxers, socks, about four shirts, and four pair of jeans. Once I got it filled up, I had the feeling someone was watching me. So, I continued walking through the store until I saw my chance to make it out of the door.

As soon as I got close to the doors, the store alarms went off. All I saw were two guards running towards me. I didn't know where they came from, but I didn't waste any time hanging around. I broke out running. For a split second, I thought I was going to get caught. I was running between moving and parked cars and trucks and was just about to throw down the duffel bag, but I needed them clothes. Once I made it to the street the guards stopped chasing me , but I kept running anyway.

After I knew I had gotten away safe with the clothes, I went to one of the abandoned apartments I had seen earlier. That's when I began removing all of the alarm detectors that were on the clothes. The only things I didn't have were: a toothbrush, some toothpaste, and a different pair of shoes I could change into. I wasn't really worried about the shoes, but I was going to get the toothbrush and toothpaste before the day was out.

Chapter Eight

*W*ithout a doubt, I knew I had to get back in school. I didn't know how I was going to pull it off, but I had to. I decided to go up to the school and talk with the principal, hoping he would allow me to come back on my own behalf.

Before I made it to the school, I stopped at a store. I already knew what I needed, and once again I wasn't going to pay for it. I unzipped my duffel bag just enough to drop the few items I needed in it: a bar of soap, a toothbrush, and a tube of toothpaste. Once I got the items, I headed to Roosevelt.

The same guard that allowed us to fight in the lil' room stopped me as soon as he saw me. "What are you doing here? Don't you know you are trespassing right now?"

"Hold on sarge! Before you even jump to conclusions, I came to see the principal. That's it."

"You came to see the principal? Someone came with you?"

"No. I came to see the principal by myself."

"Well you have to sign in, then I'll take you to the principal's office."

"That's no problem." I replied. After I signed in, the sergeant took me to the principal's office just like he said he would.

I still didn't know exactly what I was going to say. I just sat there until he said, "I'll see you now." then walked back into his office. The way he looked at me, I didn't know if he was in a good mood or not. I mean, by his facial expressions, he looked like he was ready to snap at any second. That's when he asked, "How can I help you Tj?"

"Mr. Brown, I'm one of the students you suspended the other day behind the fight that took place."

"How could I forget? I thought I told you the only way you could return is with your parents."

"Sir you did, but my parents are unable to bring me up here."

"Why is that?"

"They're dead! They died in a house fire the day you suspended me."

"I'm sorry to hear that Tj. Where are your legal guardians?"

"I'm afraid I don't have any. I'm on my own now. That's why I came up here by myself, hoping you would allow me back in on my own behalf."

"I don't know if I can do that. Give me one reason why I should let you back in."

"Mr. Brown, I might not be one of your favorite students, but I'm not one of the dumbest either. I know I done made some stupid decisions here, but I don't think dropping out of school would be a very wise decision. Especially because I don't have anybody to bring me back to school. Besides that, I only have one more year left, sir."

"I see you've given this a lot of thought. If I was to let you come back, could you guarantee me you are not going to get into any more trouble?"

"No I can't guarantee you that I'm not going to get into any more trouble, but I can try my hardest not to. You never know what the future is going to bring. I've had to learn that the hard way."

"I tell you what; I'm going to allow you to come back this time, but if you get in any more trouble Tj, you are out of here. Do we understand each other?"

"Yes sir, and thank you Mr. Brown for giving me a chance. Can you give me a pass so I can go to my class?"

"Just wait until the bell ring. This period is just about over. You only have a few more minutes."

Right before the bell rang, I asked, "What period is this about to be anyway?"

"Fourth." Mr. Brown replied. Then the bell rung.

Instead of hanging in the halls like I usually would have, I went straight to class. I really couldn't wait to get there, because that was the class Patricia and I had together. The teacher was shocked to see me in class before the bell rung again. The first thing she asked me was, "Are you alright? I can't recall a time this year, you been here this early."

"I'm alright. I'm just trying not to get in trouble."

"I don't know what happened to you or what you had, but whatever you done did got you in the right direction." my teacher replied.

By the time the bell rang, there were only ten of us in the class. Slowly, one by one, more students started coming to class. Almost twenty minutes went by before Patricia came inside the class. For a moment I didn't think she was coming, but I guess that was normal to the teacher because she didn't say anything.

When Patricia sat down next to me, I said, "Damn, I didn't think you was coming for a minute. What took you so long?"

"You know I wasn't in a hurry to come in here. Anyway, why have you been dodging me all day? This is the first time I done seen you today?"

"Now you know it ain't like that. Mr. Brown just let me back in. Anyway, I need to talk to you about something that's important later. What you doing right after school?"

"I don't have anything planned. What you need to talk to me about?"

"Don't worry, we gon'na talk."

When class was over, I went straight to my next class. Once again, another one of my teachers was surprised to see me on time. This time though, instead of asking if something was wrong with me, the teacher exploded, "What are you doing here? You are on the suspension list Tj!"

"The principal just took me off of suspension."

"I'm sorry Tj, but you will have to go get a note from him before I can allow you back in my class."

"That's no problem." I said before walking out of the class. Now you know damn well I didn't go straight to the principal's office. I went by Tina's drama class first.

It was something about seeing Tina acting that made me feel like I was mesmerized. I just stood in her class door way watching her practice for a few minutes. If it weren't for the tardy bell, there's no telling how long I would have stayed there watching her.

When I finally made it to the principal's office, Mr. Brown looked at me in disbelief. He snapped, "Tj Green! Tell me my eyes are deceiving me! I know you are not back in the office already!"

"Cool down Mr. Brown! The teacher said I had to get a note from you before she could allow me back in class because my name is still on the suspension list."

"Oh! That's it? Let me hurry up and give you a note so you can get back to class."

After that the rest of the day rolled on smoothly. As soon as school was out, Patricia and I met up. We went to a public library, and that's where I told her about everything that was going on with me. She thought I was playing at first, but before it was all over, she knew I was serious.

I didn't know how long Patricia was going to stick with me, but she said she was going to stand with me through this struggle. She didn't beat around the bush though, telling me I needed to get a job whether I wanted one or not. She told me that as long as I was trying to better myself, she would do all that she could for me.

By it being close to winter, I knew I had to get some winter clothes and boots, in order to deal with the snow and cold. You already know how I was planning on getting it.

Over the next few weeks I started stealing a few sweaters here and there. I stayed in different abandoned apartments just to keep up with which ones were abandoned. Every now and then I used to sneak and stay at

Patricia's house. A few times I almost got caught. If it wasn't for me hiding in her closet or jumping out of her window, we would've been busted.

Before the winter came into full bloom, I swallowed my pride and went back to the apartment where I met the man who offered me a job and asked to work.

"Oh, you changed your mind about working?"

"I guess I did. I had to realized I had to start some where, even if it's not the best pay in the world. By the way, my name is Tj. Tj Green."

"Well Tj, my name is Rafael. Let's get down to business. Don't think this is the worst job because I told you it don't pay that much. Twenty percent don't sound like a lot, but when you are making twenty-five to thirty dollars for yourself in a few hours, you are actually making more then you would be if you were getting paid minimum wage."

When I thought about it in that way, I knew he was telling the truth. The on y catch was I had to sell something to make anything. We ended up going on the corner of Kingshighway and Natural Bridge. As soon as we got there he showed me how to sell the merchandise. There was nothing to it. The more I thought about the possibility that I could make more than a minimum wage job pa d, the more I tired to sell. At the end of the night I made twenty-five dollars for myself, but Rafael gave me an extra five plus brought me something to eat. After that night, I worked for him just about everyday until it got too cold.

I accumulated eight hundred and fifty six dollars after working forty-four days. I had a reasonable amount of winter clothes along with the summer clothes I had stolen. I was still kicking it with Terral, Tina, and G-Dog every so often, but most of the time I just tried to stay off the streets as much as I could.

The winter didn't start off too bad, but eventually the snow came. With temperatures below zero, water pipes were freezing, some even burst. If it wasn't for a dope fiend choosing to come to the same place where I was planning on staying, I would have never learned how to steal electricity, nor how to tap into telephone lines.

When Christmas came along, I became unexplainably depressed. It was the first time I was actually alone by myself for a holiday. I thought about my mother, Precious, Mr. and Mrs. Walton, and my cousin just about all day. I couldn't believe there was no way I could get in touch with any of them.

After being sad so long, I decided to call Patricia. She sounded happy to hear from me and asked me to come see her. I felt bad by not having her a present, being that she was my girlfriend and been sticking with me, so I didn't really want to go; but I eventually did.

When I got to her house, she was there by herself. That's when she told me she wanted to see how I lived on the streets. I didn't want to show her that, but she insisted. So I figured fuck it and we left.

I decided to take her to an abandon apartment by Dakota Park. They were the cleanest ones I knew that we could get into. On the way there Rafael rode by. He stopped and asked, "Where are ya'll going?"

I replied, "I'm about to show her how I live on the streets."

"You mean to tell me you still don't have a place to stay?"

"I told you I was on my own. It's not like I have anybody looking out for me."

"What you been doing with the money you been making?"

"Just letting it build up until I can afford a place to stay. Other than that, I get the lil' things I need."

"You want me to rent a room for ya'll?"

When he asked that, I looked at Patricia but she just shook her head. That's when I said, "I would, but she really want to see how it is on the streets."

"Well look, when you get time come see me. I might be able to do something for you. Until then, take care of yourself and be careful out here." then he pulled off.

When he was just about out of sight Patricia asked, "Who was that?"

"That was Rafael, the man I been working for. He cool folks."

When we made it to the abandon apartment that we were going to, I could tell Patricia got nervous. She didn't want to admit it, but I told her, "That's how it feel everyday out here. You never know what's going to happen. When we get inside, first thing you do is lock all the doors and windows. Then make sure ain't nobody else is in there. So check all the rooms well and keep down the noise because other people stay in the other apartments."

"You sure it's safe to go in there?"

"That's the chance you have to take, but it's only one way to find out."

Once we got inside, I found out the electric was cut off. First I checked the breaker-switch inside, but it didn't do anything. That's when I said, "Come on. Now I'm going to show you how to steal electricity."

"How are you going to steal electricity?"

"I'm going to show you." Outside I could see the electric meter was already in place, so all I had to do was lift the switch up. That's when I said, "I guess we are lucky this time. All I had to do was lift the switch, but it's not always that simple."

We made small talk while the apartment warmed up. Then slowly began feeling on each other. It felt strange at first because all we ever did was kiss before. This time we didn't have to worry about her parents busting us, and we didn't have any boundaries. After feeling on each other and kissing, we began having sex.

We fucked from one side of the room unto the other. When we finished, we both were soaked in sweat. We just laid in each other's arms catching our breath. Once we both caught our breath, we began fucking again until we both were satisfied.

Chapter Nine

The next day when we woke up, we didn't realize it was going on twelve o'clock in the evening. We fucked again. This time when we finished, I went into the bathroom, washed off, and took care of all my personal hygienes. After I got dressed, I walked Patricia back home and left my duffel bags by her house. We said our good byes, and then I went straight to Rafael's house.

As soon as I knocked on the door, he opened it. "I was wondering when you were going to pass by. Where's your friend?"

"I just walked her home. Anyway, what was you talking about yesterday?"

"You know, I didn't think you were really living on the streets until I saw you yesterday. I have an available apartment I could rent to you for a little of nothing. It's not really ready to be rented out, but if you want it you can get it."

"Exactly how much is a little of nothing?"

"Two hundred dollars a month. You want to go see it?"

"4-sho!" I replied.

We took a ride to the apartment. It was right off of Arsenal. Inside the apartment, I noticed paint and carpet were still needed in some of the rooms; but at least it would be mines. I asked, "If I move in today, I have to pay you two hundred dollars?"

"Just give me thirty dollars since we're more than halfway through the month. Next month you start paying me the whole two hundred dollars until I finish fixing the apartment."

"That's cool with me." I said. After that, things began to change for me.

Things were never the same again after I got that apartment.

I remember when I was about seven or eight years old, I used to dream that one day I was going to be balling out of control; living in luxury, not having to work hard, if at all. At least that's what we used to call it. I always wanted a four door Cutless with hydraulics, sitting on Daytons and low profile vogue tires. Instead of getting it, I ended up working for a man selling stuffed balloons, all different sizes plush teddy bears, and silk and real roses. I felt embarrassed because all the hustlers and folks who were doing good would ride past me in their fancy cars and trucks with their jewelry shining and all I could think about was: I want to be like that. Not knowing that life would change even more than I could imagine. So I jumped off the porch and into the game. Even though I now had an apartment, I just wasn't satisfied.

Nobody told me that selling drugs would be easy, but looking at movies with Al Capone, John Gotti, and Scarface in them, I figured there was nothing to it. The deeper I was getting involved with selling drugs, the more I learned. I started off breaking even and falling short at first, but that's all in the game. I had to learn somehow, especially since I didn't have anyone to give me the game. I wanted it so bad that I kept on trying until I finally learned how to use a triple-beam scale to weigh the product; how to cook the dope; and most importantly, how to bag it up so that I would make a profit instead of falling short or breaking even. By the time I finally started making a nice amount of money, I didn't even realize what I was getting myself into.

I started to do what we called flighting: staying out all day and night and coming home when the sun was coming back out for a few hours of rest. I did this for a lil' minute trying to get paid in a major way, but was only getting petty change compared to big time drug dealers. I learned, but I didn't learn. I learned what it meant to be failing in school due to the lack of sleep, having to run from the police, and jumping fences. I remember the saying, "When you have money, you have friends." However, I had to learn that when you're broke and don't have shit, you can't get shit. All of a sudden, everybody started trying to be cool with me, hanging around me all the time. I was able to have two and three hoes; cousins, sisters, aunts, moms, and best friends at one time. Not realizing that it was all because of the money, and everybody wanted some of it, if not all of it. By me recognizing this, I built an invisible wall around me to keep back vultures who were trying to use me because of my ignorance of what they were really after.

Somehow veils seemed to still cover my eyes. What I didn't realize was the more I continued hanging out slanging (distributing illegal narcotics); the more I was burning up my name and any future chances I might have had to do something positive with my life. But that didn't stop me because I was coming up, and that's all I saw in my mind. Never did I realize the people and families I was hurting, taking their rent, gas, and electric money. If they had food stamps, I wanted that too. If they owed me, I didn't give a fuck! If they had children and they were in front of them, that didn't mean shit to me. They better had turned a trick to come up with my money. Personally, I didn't give a fuck how they came up with my money, as long as they came up with it. Besides, why should I? I had to learn the hard way.

I wasn't worried about anything. I was making a profit every shipment, able to buy clothes and jewelry that I wanted, and cars before I was even old enough to get a drivers license. So you would think I was doing good, huh? But then trouble came...

Chapter Ten

*H*ard working folks always told me, "What comes fast don't last," but I really didn't understand or get the meaning of what they were trying to tell me. Instead, I used to tell them, "It might not last long, but I'm going to enjoy it before it's gone." I guess that's when greed started kicking in.

Everybody started claiming dope sets and gangs, so now a lot of things were starting to get cut throat. You have jackers pulling armed robberies that we call two elevens; and you have what we call stunters selling get'ems and dummies, whichever you want to call it because it's all the same: fake drugs. By everyone doing their own thing, I didn't know who to trust. So who do I turn to now?

You've probably guessed it. Mary, Tec, and Nina. I know you probably wondering who Mary, Tec, and Nina are, and where they came from, but don't panic. Mary is the one I turned to, better known as marijuana or weed, whatever you want to call it. Tec and Nina are actually my guns: a Tech-nine and a Glock-nine. Now Mary kept telling me not to leave without Ms. Nina, and when I roll make sure I had Tec on my side. I never questioned her and always did what she said because Mary been in the game. No sooner than I answer my pager, a car came speeding from around a corner filled with jackers trying to get me.

I didn't even see it coming until it was too late, but when that jacker put that pistol in my face, he had my full attention. My first thought was, ain't this a bitch. I couldn't believe someone had the heart to try to rob me in broad daylight, but greed had me so blind that I refuse to give it up. Instead, I broke and ran, praying to God that bullets wouldn't hit me as I bust shots back. But two problems occurred: I ran out of bullets while they were still coming for me; and second, a bullet hit a baby as soon as a lady stepped out of a taxi cab holding her. Damn, all of this occurred over some paper!

You would have thought that would've changed my mind about trying to get it right, but it didn't. I didn't pay the signs no mind. It was like I had invisible veils over my eyes again. What hurt even more, was when I found out that baby had died. It was my lil' homie Terral's new born child's first day home. Tears rolled down my eyes, but I couldn't tell my lil' homie why.

I went to the funeral because I had to pay my respects, even though some would say I shouldn't have been there at all. The casket was so small I couldn't believe that it was real, but it was. I saw them lowering the casket into the ground, and of course it was closed. You know how much bullets can mess up an adult, so just picture what they did to a new born baby who was only six pounds and seven ounces. My homie and his girlfriend were crying, barely able to stand up, and the emotions of regret mixed with the shock of reality were starting to take its toll on me. I couldn't even begin to express how sorry I was, but it couldn't have compared to the hurting pains that they were feeling.

I have to move on now, because no sooner than the funeral was over, I was back on the wrong path. This time I had revenge on my mind. You might say, "That's cold.", but that's how it was. Greed, revenge, anger, and lust for the money just don't mix, especially when all you know is how to get it.

I went from just wanting it, to toting two Tech-nines and a Glock-nine; slanging, shoot outs, and smoking weed trying to cover up the pain I was going though. But I still didn't realize what the reality was of what I was doing. Two weeks later I caught up with them jackers that were trying to get me. How did I know it was them? That was simply because I recognized the name plate he was wearing, so you can imagine all hell broke loose...

Chapter Eleven

*T*hey must have been at a block party or something, but I waited until everyone went into the house and that's when I made my move. I hurried and grabbed a gas can that I had in my trunk, half filled with gasoline, and ran around the house pouring it out all across its sides. That way the only way anyone could have escaped was by the front-door, and that's where I would be waiting. Next, I hurried and put the gas can back in my trunk and grabbed my two Tech-nines. When I dropped the Black and Mild I was smoking, the flames rose and about six seconds later, the bullets started flying.

As they were running out of the house in shock, wondering where the fire came from, they caught or should I say they felt hot lead hitting them as they were falling looking me in my face. I wondered what was going across their minds, but I guess I'll never know.

After I shot down the ones I was waiting on, I put my Glock-nine to the middle of their heads and put a slug in them. "That's for my lil' homie's baby, cause you're the cause of this." I replied, then jumped into my ride and went by my girl Patricia's crib and took a shower.

She didn't notice that I had blood on me, and I wasn't about to tell her what just happened. Instead, I made it seem like something was wrong with my car, so I was just going to chill with her for the rest of the day. She was so happy I was going to spend time with her that day that she was willing to cook for me, but instead of letting her cook I told her, "Just chill."

I remember we ordered pizza that day and watched Eddie Murphy Raw. I couldn't get into it like I wanted because I was waiting on the ten o'clock news to come on. When it did come on, they said that they had no suspect or motive. So I thought that I had made a smooth get away, but notice I said, "I thought." until the next day came.

I saw one of my home-girls, Tina, who was telling me that some detectives were asking if anyone knew who drove a white car described like mines. So I knew one thing, someone said something but I didn't know who.

I should have known something like that was going to happen because it was daytime, but revenge was on my mind so I didn't care who saw me. I just wanted those jackers in that house.

You know, I might do some dumb things, but this is one time that I thought I was doing the right thing by following my mind. Something told me I had to leave, and when I say leave, I mean get somewhere and quick. I didn't waste any time. I packed up my clothes and hit the highway.

Before I got too far, I stopped on the side of the highway and waited for traffic to clear up, then threw my guns in the Mississippi River and drove off. After that, I stopped at Dakota Park, where I used to hang and slang at, and that's where I burnt the clothes that I was wearing that day.

Lil' homies from the neighborhood saw me and started asking, "What are you doing?"

I just told them that I was on a mission to kill the conversation. Instead, they all just looked at me because they all knew that when we say we're on a mission, something done happened or something about to happen. Then as if all of them were thinking the exact same thing at the exact same moment they asked me if I needed their assistance. I knew I could count on them, but instead I told them, "Naw!"

By my folks knowing me they just nodded their heads, but you best believe before they allowed me to leave one of them told me, "Hold down this pistol just in case!" I took it because I figured I'd rather be strapped with it, than be caught without it. Then I rolled out...

Chapter Twelve

I was driving on the highway for about twelve hours just thinking about all the shit that I got myself into. How it all started and what I was going to do once I reached my destination. All I knew was how to get it, and that's by hustling. I never asked myself what I really wanted out of all the hustling I was doing. You would think that would have been the first question I would have asked myself before I went and started hustling.

At first, it was just for the clothes, jewelry, and cars, but I never thought beyond that. I even had all the things you could have wanted for a house, but not a house to call my own.

I ended up in a lil' town they called Marrero, on the outskirts of New Orleans, for those of ya'll who didn't know. The town was too slow for me. When I say slow, I mean I couldn't compare it to the Lou (St. Louis).

Everything was different. Folks were friendly and speaking to me, even though they didn't know me, and I wasn't used to that. It amused me how they spoke; it was like they had their own language. To this day they still get a kick out of the way I talk, just like I get a kick out of them when I hear them talk.

I ended up meeting a young lady at Popeye's named Keisha. At first she played me off and told me I was too short to holla' at her, but I had to respect her mind on that. At least she knew what she wanted and didn't want. But by me being me, I had to be a player about the situation. I made Keisha feel like she wasn't shit to me, and talked to another lil' chick that was working there. Her name was Natashia.

Now, Natashia had a nice lil' figure. She had a light-brown complexion and two gold teeth in her mouth at the top. We hit it off good, but by the manager, Tyrone, liking my style, he filled me in on her and told me she didn't have any money like talking about and would just be an easy fuck. He went on to say that if I wanted someone who had something going for herself, then holla' at Keisha.

I was like, "4-sho. Thanks for letting me know," but I knew I had to find another way to get her if I wanted her. After awhile, Tyrone and I became real good friends. In a way he was like me, but older and loved to chase women.

I started hanging at Popeye's because I didn't know where everybody else chilled at, and the malls weren't hitting on shit. I mean you could damn near count all the folks in the mall and most of them worked in there.

So one night Tyrone asked me to count some money for him while he did some paperwork. I was like, "4-sho," and started counting the money.

That's when Keisha asked me, "What are you getting into tonight?" while she was waiting on her ride home.

I told her, "I don't have anything to do. It ain't like I know my way around, or anybody. Why?"

She was like, "I see you're always in here, I thought that I'd get to know you."

I couldn't help myself and replied, "That sound good, but didn't you tell me I was too short to holla' at you?" She started smiling, that's when I knew I had her. I asked her, "Can I take you home?"

"My ride should be on the way."

"Call and see if they left. If they haven't, I don't mind taking you home. I could at least spend a few moments with you."

She made the call. After a few minutes, she came back and said, "I'm ready whenever you are."

"I've been ready." I gave Tyrone the money in stacks, telling him exactly how much it was, and then pushed with Keisha.

I must have spent about four to five hours with her that night. We talked about some of everything, getting to know each other on a different level than when she was at work. After a couple of weeks, Keisha and me started getting involved on a sexual level, going to the mall, just chilling as if we were more than just friends. What I didn't know, was she ended up getting pregnant.

I had moved out of that town and moved to what they call the A-L-G, but the real name is Algiers. It was only about a ten minute ride from Marrero, but it felt more like I was actually in a city then. The only problem that I had was that I was trying not to get into any trouble. Yet now all the temptation in the world seemed to be surrounding me. Through it all though, I tried my best to resist temptations and do the right things.

Chapter Thirteen

I started going to a school in Harvey, Louisiana, but even the schools weren't the same. I was used to being patted down before they would let me into school, metal detectors, everybody hanging in the hallways, wearing hats doing whatever you felt like, whatever! But not here. You couldn't wear hats to school: everybody had clear book-bags, and was going to class before the bell would even ring. I mean, everything was different.

My first day at school I felt out of place, but I had to peep my scenery. I didn't see anybody who even looked like I would've fucked with, but I ended up meeting a Spanish looking dude from Honduras named Daniel. Now trip off how I met him.

I had a hat on that I had gotten customized with the letters B. ✡ .S. written across the front, and B💣*💣*M written across the back. Daniel started questioning me about it. I figured he was trying to test me or check me on the slick, how the conversation was going, so I asked him, "What you claim?"

He said, "V L."

"What's that supposed to mean?" I replied mean mugging him.

"Vatos Locas."

"All right," I said, ending the conversation because I didn't believe him nor did I trust him.

So the bell rang and everybody was going about their way when Daniel and some dudes came walking towards me. The first thing that came across my mind was they must be planning on jumping me, so I'm on my guards watching them close. They came up to me and one of the dudes asked me, "What's happening?"

The first thing I thought was he wanted to do something. So I was like, "What you want to be happening?" mean mugging them all.

By the look on my face, they knew I was about fighting or taking it farther. So Daniel hurried up and made it clear to me that when they say, "What's happening?" it's the same as saying, "Hello."

I was like, "My bad. What's up?" but still watching them just in case though.

Daniel then asked me, "You want to blow a Joe?"

Without a second thought I asked him, "What the fuck you say to me? I want to blow a what? You trying to play me like a hoe?"

"You tripping! You want to blow a Joe?" and showed me a cigarette.

When I seen it, I was like, "A square. I don't fuck with them. I blow Blacks and Blunts," now they were looking at me stupid. I didn't bother to explain it. I just said, "I'm fixing to push. I got to go get on that level." (Meaning I'm about to go and smoke some weed.)

Before I left Daniel said, "You need to come around my way, I'll show you what's happening down here."

I took it the wrong way again. I forgot when they say "What's happening?" they not talking about doing anything concerning violence. It's the same as if I was to say, "What's up?"

Anyway, I ended up going by Daniel's house to see what was up with him. Daniel, his brothers, and friends were shocked when they seen my car and heard the music. They were like, "That's yours?"

I was like, "Ya'll see me driving it don't ya'll?"

I guess they never knew anyone with hydraulics. So they kept on asking me to, "Hit your switches."

I figured fuck it; let me show them what I'm working with. At first, I didn't know he stayed on what I call a million dollar dope set. Off top I was peeping out my scenery because I'm a hustler. I got to seeing they had cluckers (people who are strung out on drugs) all around their way, and they were the only people trying to slang.

To me their rocks and bags of weed were so small, it just didn't make sense. I figured as long as they were getting away with it, they suppose to been balling. Especially, since it wasn't anybody else really hustling around their way. So you can imagine, I really started hanging and coming around a lot.

It wasn't even a month later and I was back to being the old me, hustling. I guess it runs in my veins. I didn't intend to, but shit happens. I seen the chance to make more money and the folks that were around me seemed like they didn't want any of it. I always believed in the saying, "If you see the opportunity take it; besides, you only have one life to live." So there I was flipping and flipping my money until I got caught up. Somebody snitch!

Chapter Fourteen

I was at school one day, taking my final exams. I figured, I only had three classes so afterwards I was going to get high, and then hit the set. I calculated I would have been out there before 12:00 p.m. and it would've been all good. Notice, that's what I thought I was going to do.

It was still early in the morning when I bumped into this lil' cat named Brandon. Brandon knew that I be rapping and had that work (drugs). So he asked me, "Say Boom, you got some weed?"

"Yeah! What you need? I only have a couple of zones left."

"I just need something to blow on for now."

I was like, "Fuck it! How much you got?" thinking he at least wanted a dub (A twenty dollar bag.).

"Man I got five on me."

"Five! What the fuck I suppose to do with that? Cause I fuck with you, I'm gone do that for you plus give you some extra. You got something to put it in?"

Brandon said, "Naw."

So I ripped a piece of the sand-wish bag that I had a zone in and put it in there. Then I gave it to him and told him, "I'm gone holla'."

I walked down the hallway and a lil' cat that be trying to rap with me was like, "You got some herb?"

"What you need?"

He was like, "I only have a bill on me."

Instantly I said, "I got you," and gave him an ounce. Then we pushed to class.

While I was sitting in my last class for the day taking my final exam, the principal walked in the classroom. He mumble to the teacher, "I need to see Tj Green, right now."

"He's in the middle of his final exam!" she protested.

This time he was direct when he said, "I need to see him; now!"

Listening to them talk, all I could think about at first was, I got to get rid of this weed in my pocket. I couldn't pass it to anyone because the principal was standing right next to me now. I got to thinking maybe he just wanted to talk to me about all of the days I been missing at school, which could affect me at graduation time. So I was playing it cool.

"Make sure you get all of your things Tj." He said.

"Alright," but by now I'm not feeling too comfortable because I still didn't know what he really wanted exactly.

As soon as we walked out of the classroom, there were two detectives standing on each side of the door. Off top I was thinking, *this fucked up.* I knew I was caught right then. So I started thinking ahead and planned on throwing the weed behind the next set of doors we were about to walk through, since we were in a hallway with no exits. As soon as we went through the next set of doors, that plan was out of the question. There were two more officers waiting just incase I tried to run from them.

I couldn't help but wonder how the fuck did they find me because I knew I been on top of my shit. All that kept running through my mind now, was the murders that happen back in the Lou. *Damn! How did they find me?* I kept thinking.

As they walked me into the room that was at the end of the hall, the two officers stopped and waited outside of the door. While the principal and the other two detectives came into the room. That's when all the questions started.

The principal kicked it off by asking me, "Do you know about any drugs being sold here at school?"

"Drugs being sold! At school? I don't know what you talking about." I replied

So one of the detectives asked me, "How can you afford the car you drive?"

After a quick thought I replied, "I saved all the money I worked for, plus my father looked out for me," with a fuck you smile.

The other detective then asked, "How many gold teeth do you have? I know they had to cost you a nice amount of money."

"Simply," I said. "I have four for your information. I always wanted them, so I got *'em.* Is this what we are here to talk about?"

The principal interrupted, "No; but we have a number of students here that said you are selling drugs at our school."

"Could you tell me who said that?"

"Numerous of students." The principal harshly said.

I didn't believe him though, because I never put anybody into my business that I wasn't doing business with. Second of all, all the transactions I made, I made when it was only me and whomever I was dealing with present. So I just said, "Numbers huh?"

He went on and asked me, "Do you have any drugs or weapons on you?"

I was debating on telling the truth because I knew I couldn't beat them at least not today. So I was like, "No! I don't have any weapons on me."

"Well, would you empty your pockets out? We have to search you regardless."

So I started pulling things out of my pockets. Everything except for the weed. When I finished, the principal and the two detectives said at the same time, "That's it?"

I was just looking at them and said, "Do you see what ya'll are looking for?"

All of a sudden, the principal just walked out of the little room without saying a word. Seconds later, he returned with a bag of weed in his hand. When I seen the bag of weed, I knew exactly who I gave that to. Brandon.

I was like that motherfucker got caught up and like a fake as informer he ratted on me, and I broke him off some extra. The principal asked me sarcastically, "Do you recognize this bag?"

"I never saw it before." I quoted. Just my luck, I had already sold the bag that I had ripped the plastic from to make the bag he was showing me.

He stated, "The person you sold this to, said he gave you five dollars. We can see you have all twenties and one five dollar bill. You care to explain why you have all this money on you?"

"I don't know who said I sold them that bag, but that's a lie. The reason I have so much money on me is because I was planning on buying something when I left today."

The detective asked me, "I s that everything out of your pockets before I search you?"

I knew that I couldn't win, so I pulled out the weed that I still had in my pocket. The principal mouth dropped as he said, "Oh my! How much is that?"

Before I could reply, one of the detectives said, "Oh that's about three joints," while looking at me like I know what that is but we not going to tell anyone.

The principal asked, "What were you planning on doing with that?"

I stated plainly, "I wanted to smoke a couple of blunts when I left."

They all said, "What is that?" with a blank expression on each of their faces.

"A cigar filled with weed."

Right then the officer placed me under arrest. Before he escorted me out of the school, the principal told me, "You are expelled for two weeks. If you want to come back, you first must attend a drug rehab program. When you return, you will have to join all of the school's programs. Last of all, you will not be able to graduate until the end of next year." Then we headed to the police station.

On the way to the police station, I was thinking about what the principal said. I said to myself, "Fuck that! I'll go back home first, or fuck school." Then I really thought about it. I knew I had came too far to say I was just going to drop out of school.

Inside the police station, I had to wait about three hours before they told me how much my bond was. When they finally did tell me, I thought I was stuck in jail. I didn't have ten thousand dollars to give them. I talked to a bails bondsman and he explained to me, that I only had to give him ten percent; then go to court on whatever day they set for me.

Once I understood that, I was like, "Well what's taking you so long to get me released? I can pay you now!"

Within another hour I was released, with a court date for the next month. I had to give the bails bondsman an extra twenty dollars just to take me back to my car. Then I decided it was time for me to go back to St. Louis.

When I got back in St. Louis, I decided to go back to my old high school Roosevelt. They only had two weeks left before graduation, so everyone was wondering where I been all year. I just told everybody, "I was on some business," to keep them out of my business.

I only had two classes because of my credits, so the rest of the day was mines. During the day, I kicked it with my home-girl Tina, who told me that the detectives were asking about a car described like mine before I left. She told me, "Things have died down some, but why didn't you tell me what happened?"

I didn't answer her; I just looked at her because I knew the beef wasn't completely over. That's something you learn growing up in the Lou. Instead, I let her update me on what's been going on, and then I pushed.

I went to Far Side, that's the hood, by my folks who last seen me before I left. They asked, "Boom, where you been gangster? Better yet, why you didn't tell us them laws was looking for you?"

I was like, "What ya'll talking about?" trying to play it off; but I couldn't bull shit them, they knew what happened by now. So I asked them, "Them laws still questioning the hood, trying to find out who I was?"

They all implied, "They not questioning much, but they got a lot of under-covers in the hood trying to figure out what all happened."

I was like, "Word."

Before I left, G-Dog, the one who gave me the gun, told me, "G, be careful. If you need me, I got your back gangster." I just looked at him and nodded my head; words didn't need to be spoken to understand my appreciation of his loyalty. I blew a few blunts with them, and then pushed.

I knew I couldn't get too comfortable after what my folks told me. There were so many new faces in the hood; that I couldn't tell who the laws were. I just looked at everyone new as under-covers, and decided to keep a low profile. I made my mind up to just finish school and push. So that's what I did. After graduation, I pushed without anyone knowing.

A week after I got back in New Orleans it was time for me to go to court I didn't think they could have done too much so I wasn't worried, but I should have been. It was fucked up. The lil' cat that got caught with the weed in the first place, Brandon, was working with the state. It was bad enough that he ratted on me when he got caught with the weed, but to work with the state and take the stand that to me was below some bitch shit.

I ended up having to take a plea bargain for three years in the Department of Corrections, for distribution of a controlled substance in a school zone.

"Ain't that a bitch," I said to myself. "I graduated high school, and left home to come straight to prison." *What more could go wrong? I thought.*

I guess I should have never asked that question. I only had Tyrone, Daniel, and a few homies from the Lou numbers in my head, so I was limited on whom I could call. Out of all the numbers I had though, I decided to call Tyrone.

When I got in touch with him, the first thing he asked was, "When you got locked up?" We were running it for awhile before he hit me with the most shocking news that I couldn't believe. He said, "What you going to name your li ' one?"

"What you talking about?" I asked dumbfounded.

"You know your girl pregnant?"

"Who?" I asked because I had the slightest idea who he was even talking about.

"Keisha. You know she's about four months pregnant for you. When was the last time you talked to her?"

I was like, "You playing right? I haven't seen her in some months, you sure she pregnant for me?"

"She hasn't been talking about anybody except for you. I have her phone number if you want to call her, but that's on you," he hinted.

I said, "Yeah, let me get her number. I want to find out who she pregnant for."

After Tyrone gave me Keisha's phone number, I didn't know whether to call her or not, but I knew I had to speak to her. I eventually got in touch with her. At first, I didn't know what to tell her because I just wanted to know about the baby she was about to have.

She was running on and on about this and that: where I been, why I'm in jail, when I'm coming home, blah blah blah, but never did she mention anything about being pregnant. So I interrupted her after answering so many questions, and asked her, "Who are you pregnant for?"

After a long silence she said, "For you!"

The way she hesitated, I didn't know whether to believe her or not. So I asked her, "What took you so long to answer that?"

She was like, "I didn't know if I should have told you it was yours or not. Besides, after we started sleeping together you just left, and I didn't know if I was going to keep the baby or not Tj."

I talked her into keeping the baby, even though I explained to her I wasn't going to be there when the baby was born. We kept in touch up until she had the baby, and then shortly after I stopped calling her.

I had a year left to do, but the thought of being a father behind bars was only feeding my hunger to go and get it even more. So I stayed plotting and scheming on things that I was going to do when I was released.

After doing eighteen months, I was released. I thought it wasn't about nothing, but now it was time to ball. It also made me realize that they have what I call "Haters" (people who want to see you fall one way or the other) all around the world. But, I didn't let that stop me; I just looked at it as a minor setback for a major comeback and kept on going.

I can't deny that when I got caught up, that hurt my pockets; but a true hustler, whenever they take a fall, if they are a true hustler, they going to find a way to come back up. How you read me? It might take them a minute, but they gone come back up.

I made my way to Keisha's house, about three days after I was released. Instead of a warm greeting, I received a bitter surprise. Keisha answered the door, "What you want?"

"Damn, that's how you answer the door? What happened to hello; how you doing?"

"I don't have time to play with you. It's obvious you don't care about how I'm doing or your baby. I told you I had the baby and you just stopped calling, didn't write nothing. Now you want to come over here, what you want?"

"Keisha, can I come in so that we can talk?" I replied. She just looked at me for awhile, and then let me in. Once I got inside I said, "I know you mad at me, and maybe I should have kept in touch; but don't treat me like I ain't shit when I'm at least trying to make things right. I stopped by to see you and to see the baby. You haven't even told me the baby's name, nor let me see him."

"You right. I'm sorry. I should have handled this situation differently. By the way, my baby's name is Tiarell James Evans. But tell me something, why after I told you I had the baby why you stopped calling? You didn't even bother to write." Keisha replied.

"You know I was wrong, but at the same time I was skeptical if the baby was really mines or not. Besides, the last time I seen you, you wasn't pregnant and I knew you weren't able to work right after you had the baby. So I didn't want to put you in debt," I responded honestly.

I guess my words were revolving around in her mind as she was trying to decide whether to believe me or not. After staring at me for a few moments, she said, "You want to see our baby?"

Without a second hesitation I said, "Yeah! I been waiting to see him."

Keisha left out of the room and came back holding Tiarell. When I seen him, I couldn't believe what I was seeing. He looked identical to me. Keisha said, "He looks just like you."

I couldn't even say anything while holding him. I was just looking at him in amazement. I didn't have a doubt in the world that he wasn't mine. I said, "Look at daddy's baby!" smiling. "He gone be a threat when he gets bigger."

After holding him for awhile, Keisha laid him back down and we talked for awhile. While talking to Keisha, I was looking around her house and decided I wanted my son to have more of the finest things in life. I just didn't let Keisha know what I was thinking. Before I left, I kissed Keisha on the check and told her, "Take care of my Lil' Threat, and I'll be back."

When I left, I was thinking to myself *I got to get my shit together. I don t have a job. I don't have any income coming in and I just got out of prison. Something got to shake.* All I really knew how to do was to slang drugs, but I wasn't trying to go back that route. As for as a job, I thought who was going to hire me; a young Black convicted felon? So I jumped to another level…

Chapter Fifteen

*A*fter a few days of thinking, I knew it was time for me to do something. I was running out of money. I only had fifty five dollars to my name. The first thing that came to my mind was, *I got to flip this fifty with no ifs, ands, or buts.*

So I headed to what I called, "The Spot." The Spot was actually just a block where everybody hustled at to get quick money. Before I went there, I stopped by Keisha's just to see how her and Lil Threat were doing.

When she came to the door she said, "I'm happy to see you. Your son need some pampers. If you don't mind going to buy him some."

"That ain't no problem, I can at least do that." I said but on the inside I was like, "Fuck! I ain't gone even be able to score a fifty."

After I brought the pampers, I dropped them back off over Keisha's house. She said, "You not going to stay and spend time with your son?"

"I want to, but I really got something I have to do."

"It's more important than your baby?"

"Don't go there. I'll be back, but I got to do something." I said then left without any more delays.

By the time I got to the spot, it was going on twelve p.m. Some of everybody was out there, looking at me as if they were seeing a ghost. "What's happen Boom? Where the fuck you been?" Daniel asked.

"Got damn me, you know I been locked up. I just got out about a week ago."

"How you end up getting locked up?" he question.

"Got damn me, you remember Brandon, don't you? That little punk got caught up and snitched on me."

"That's fucked up!" Daniel replied.

"But fuck all of that. I need a favor from you until I get straight," I said staring at him.

"Boom, what you need? I got you."

"I have a few dollars to my name, but I got to get on my feet and quick. I'm doing bad G. I need some work or let me hold down a strap," I said boldly.

"I don't have no work like talked about it, but I'll put you on a lick if you want it."

I told him to tell me about it, but after he finished it didn't sound too dependable, so I turned it down. By then, Dennis walked up.

Dennis was a young, wild dude compared to the folks that he hung around. His main difference amongst his chosen crowed, was the fact that he didn't slang drugs. He did his own little dirt and kept it to his self. That's what I liked about him. I asked Dennis, "What's up? What you getting into?"

Dennis said, "I'm chilling right now, but it ain't no telling."

Us three chilled for awhile blowing blunts, while Daniel and a few other lil' dudes made crack and weed sells on the block. I was thinking to myself something got to shake and soon. I thought about the lick Daniel was telling me about, but I kept saying no to myself because it sounded like straight jail bait. I got to do something, I kept saying to myself. All of a sudden, Dennis jumped up and said, "It's time, I'm about to push. I'll get with ya'll."

"It's time," I repeated Dennis' words to myself. "Hold up Dennis, let me holla at you," then I walked off the porch and joined him. I said, "Look, I know you do your thing on the slick, but feel me out for a second. I don't need nobody in my business, but folks I'm doing bad. Will you hit a few licks with me until I get on my feet?"

Dennis said, "Damn homie, when you start doing shit like that? You always had work. When you fell off?"

"Got damn me, I just got out of jail. I been down a year and a half. You know I ain't with robbing. I slang, but right now I got to make something shake. You feel me?"

He asked me, "You got a heater?" (Talking about a gun.)

"That ain't no problem," I said.

He then asked, "When you gone be ready?"

"Right now as we speak," I replied as if he thought I was bullshitting.

"You for real? Come on." He whispered.

I said, "Hold up," then ran and told Daniel to let me use his strap. He didn't say anything; he just passed it to me without anyone noticing.

When Dennis and me got into his car and pulled off, he asked, "You ever robbed someone before?"

"No, but if this is what it's going to take I'm all in."

"You know there are two kinds of robbers: stupid ones, and smart ones. The stupid ones don't think. They do a robbery and don't think about the outcome, or the chances they're taking. A smart robber always knows the chances are the same, so they got to be on top of their game at all times. You feel me?"

I nodded my head to let him know I understood what he was saying. Then he pulled up in a grocery store parking lot and parked. Dennis said, "If you was about to rob someone right here, who would you rob?"

After looking at the parking lot, I pointed at a man in a red Yukon truck and said, "Him right there."

"Why?" Dennis asked.

"Because he have an up to date truck, so I know he have to have some money to push that. Besides, he's the closet to the exit."

"You might get away with it now, but most likely you will end up in jail before the week is out because you didn't think."

"Why you say that?"

"Many reasons. First, you don't never do a robbery in your own car. Second of all, you don't have anything covering your face, so he could easily identify you. Third, the only way you can get out of this lot is to go through the exit where he's parked at; but if traffic is bad, how are you going to get out? He will have plenty of time to get your license plate number," he schooled me.

"Damn, I never thought about all of that."

That's when he said, "I'm going to show you the right way," then pulled off again. He drove around the corner and parked. "Now we are no more than three minutes from the store," he said while grabbing two black ski masks from under the driver's seat. "Put this on, but don't pull it all the way down yet." After I put it on he said, "Come on."

We were headed back towards the store we just left. When we got there Dennis said, "You ready to get it?"

I was nervous, but I couldn't let it show. So I said, "Hell yeah! Who we gone get?"

"You see the blue car pulling in? As soon as she park we got her. Pull your mask down." As soon as she parked and cut the engine off, we were on her.

Dennis said, "Bitch shut up and give it up!"

I was looking in amazement because I knew shit was real from here on out. The lady looked scared to death, while we had our guns pointed at her. She said, "Take my purse, it's all I have."

Dennis grabbed the purse. That's when he said, "Bitch empty your pockets. You think we're playing?"

She hurried and emptied her pockets revealing about seventy dollars that I quickly snatched. Once we got that money, we ran back down the street towards the car removing our ski masks on the way. Once we were secured inside, Dennis then pulled off.

"I knew you had it in you Boom," Dennis said.

"I told you, got damn me, I got to get it."

Then Dennis said, "Now that was almost a smart robbery. They don't know what we are driving, or what we look like. You just have to move quicker."

I said, "I feel you," while I was going through the purse to see if she had any more currencies.

She had: credit cards, pictures, twenty-five dollars, and some coins in her pocket book. So I said, "We got all together ninety-five dollars, and some change."

"That ain't bad for your first robbery, but it's not always gone be like that," replied Dennis.

So I said, "Well, put the five in your tank and we'll split the ninety. That's cool?"

He said, "Yeah," then pulled up in a gas station.

I told him, "You go pay for it and I'll pump it."

After pumping the gas, we was about to pull off when a young looking white boy pulled in the gas station with his music blasting and beating. I looked at Dennis then said, "Say D, you see him? I'll get him, his car and all."

He just looked at me and said, "Well, what you want to do?"

"You have a spot where I can take the car and strip it?"

"Not right off the back that I could think of."

"Damn! At least I can get him out of his paper right quick," I said devoted.

"Well Boom, what you gone do?"

"G, you pull around the corner and I'm going to get out right here. I'll meet you around the corner; I'm going to get it," I said as I stepped out of the car. I waited until he pulled off, then I made my move. I knew I had to show Dennis I had it in my heart to get it with him or without him. The young male in the car never seen it coming, he was to busy talking on the phone. I approached the car at the same time he was opening the door. I said, "You know what time t is. Break yourself, empty your pockets and give me the stash. I know you got it!"

He must have damn near pissed on his self when reality kicked in on him of what was happening. He said, "What the fuck!"

Then I cut him off and said, "Shut the fuck up. Opening your glove box and you bet not make a fucking move. "

When he opened his glove box, I saw a black thirty eight. So I hurried and grabbed it along with the rest of his money and wallet, then broke and ran. I knew I was taking to long, so I was running like the police was right behind me. When I made it to the car, I jumped in and Dennis pulled off.

We hit a few more licks that day before he dropped me off. At the end of the night, I had right at two hundred dollars in my pocket and a thirty eight.

I sat up most of the night thinking about the arm robberies we pulled off. Although I did them, it really wasn't my thing. I felt played on the slick. It felt more like it went against everything that I believed in as far as seeing the next coming up. If I'm the one causing anybody to stay down and fall off, I feel like

I'm no better than a crooked lawman that's always trying to beat us down, take our money and drugs, then put charges on us and show up to court and say we did whatever.

At first, I didn't even know how to rob any one. I kept on second questioning who I should rob or where I should rob them at. It wasn't nothing like selling dope or carjacking. You have to choose who you think has money. Where you could find them type of people? If something goes wrong, how are you going to get away? I mean you never know what's going to happen, or what can go wrong.

I hit a few more licks with Dennis, but they were pissing me off because we really wasn't getting anything major. We might get a lil' here, a lil' there, but fuck all of that. We were robbing: whites, blacks, drug dealers, customers and all, but it was only coming out to be petty change after we splitted whatever we gotten. I was ready to ball again, but I couldn't go and score no weight with the lil' money I had gotten. So I took it to a more deeper level...

Chapter Sixteen

*B*y me not having a reliable source of income, it was becoming harder and harder for me it seem. I was trying to be a man and take care of my son, but between him and my bills something was gone have to give. I was tired of pulling robberies for petty change, even though I was starting to get good at it.

I went over Keisha's house and told her boldly, "We need to talk."

She asked me, "What's wrong? What we need to talk about?"

I came straight out with it. "Look, I'm in a situation were I need some help and bad. I can barely afford to pay my rent, and I don't have anyone I can turn to for help right now. I know you don't want me locked up, and you want me to be here for my son. But to be honest with you, the way I'm headed right now, there ain't no telling if I'm going to be around without any help."

"What done happen like that? What you mean you might not be around?"

"I need a place to stay as of last week. I'm trying to find a job, but right now I don't have one. I don't want to go back to doing wrong, but if nothing don't shake, you know me. I got to get it! So can I stay with you until I get straight?" I asked with desperation in my voice.

I knew I had her on the spot, and she really didn't know what to say. But she managed to say, "Don't worry about nothing. You can stay as long as you want."

I kissed her and told her, "Thanks! I really appreciate this." But when I kissed her, it was like an electric wave went between us. Before I knew it we were kissing again, but this time passionately. I don't know if it was just me, but it seemed like we both been waiting for that moment.

She started kissing me slowly around my neck, licking and nibbling on my ears, making her way to my chest while removing my shirt. I said, "Hold on, let's do this right if we gone do it," leading her towards the bedroom.

Once we got inside the room, Keisha lit some candles and put on some slow music. Then told me, "You just get ready while I slip into something sexy for you," and went into the bathroom.

` "Don't have me waiting too long, or am I going to have to come and get you?"

She just smile and said, "Huh," looking exquisitely sexy at me.

I pulled the covers back on the bed, then remembered seeing some champagne in the refrigerator and decided to go get it. When I came back into the room I didn't only have the champagne, but some strawberries, grapes, and two wine glasses as well. I sat all of that on the nightstand on the side of the bed, and then removed the rest of my clothes anticipating the moment to come.

When Keisha came out of the bathroom, I poured us each a glass of champagne. She was looking so gorgeous and sexy that I had to catch my breath. I instantly became aroused. She had on some money-green see through lingerie that was showing all of her curves just right. The desire I had to make passionate love to her was like an adrenaline rush that was long overdo.

We began kissing again, but this time her body was against mines and I knew it was right. I picked her up and laid her across the bed while kissing her, then reached and grabbed the two glasses and said, "To us." After a few sips, I began to remove her lingerie, piece by piece, until I had nothing else to remove.

I began kissing her around the neck while caressing her breasts, then took a strawberry and dipped it into some champagne and fed it to her. Seeing the way she licked and ate the strawberry only turned me on even more. So next, I poured some of the champagne over her body and began licking it off her in small circular movements, only teasing her more, causing her not to be able to hold back her desires.

The uncontrollable yearning to be with each other was impossible to resist any longer, so we began to make love to each other. She went down on me, sucking my dick and licking my balls until I started shooting sperm as if throwing darts. I then went down on her, eating her pussy as if I was a professional. I don't know which was better though, the wet warmness of her mouth, or the tight warm moisture grip her pussy had while I was penetrating her. We had sex for hours before drifting off to sleep.

While she was sleeping, I laid back in the bed putting together my next moves. I knew any illegal activity I involved myself in would have to be a major lick and not just petty change. So I just laid back plotting until I drifted back off.

The next day, I awoke early and decided to go fill out job applications after checking in with my parole officer. I guess it was meant for me to go job hunting because I received an interview on the spot, and was later hired.

I worked the job, but was ready to quit after I received my first pay check. I felt played! I was busting my ass and only got two hundred dollars after taxes. I knew I could sell more drugs than that a day, or rob folks and get that.

So I decided to take my hustling to a deeper level. I figured if I hit a lick for some G's, I could get on my feet and wouldn't have to do any more robberies. So I set back and organized the perfect crime.

To pull it off, I had to swallow my pride and stay working to get all the information that I would need to pull it off. Thanks to Dennis, I learned that there are two kinds of robbers, and this wasn't the time to be a dumb one if I wanted this to be my final caper. So I took my time making my decision on what to do. I mean months went by while I was plotting; planning the perfect time, the getaway, how long I had to get in and get out before anyone came. What time the police would ride by; all the way down to what time the street lights turned red and green.

So I finally pulled it off. It was just like taking candy from a baby. I mean it went so smooth, I felt like a big kid in Toys-R-Us. It was so easy, that Lil' Greedy (my conscience) came talking to me telling me, "You might as well do it again, and then you can really sit back."

I got to thinking *yeah, you right*. So I did it again, and thought about doing it just one more time. But I knew that I couldn't do it again, because I was getting addicted to how easy it was. I knew if I tried to rob the places one more time, I would be making the decisions of a dumb robber that was bound to get caught. So I chilled. Besides, I done hit for about eight thousand dollars already. I was just starting to be greedy.

I stayed working for a minute, but you already know that was coming to an end any moment now. Besides, I was sick and tired of all the clocking in and out shit. I was too used to making drops and moving when I felt like it. To top it all off, the money I was getting paid on my checks, I was used to making that in a sale, two at the most. So quitting wasn't shit when it came to the pay. I guess I stayed working for about one more week, and that was a wrap. I called it quits.

I didn't let Keisha know that I quit. To her we seemed just like a content family, but I had other plans. I was ready to get paid. I knew I didn't want all the heat on her house that I would bring once I started hustling heavy; so I found a studio apartment for two hundred and seventy-five dollars a month and rented it. Then I bought a GMC Jimmy for five hundred dollars.

Once I told Keisha, "I was moving," it was like she flipped out.

"Why you leaving me now? You got everything you need, and you're still not happy. What's wrong?" Keisha asked.

I wasn't about to tell her what I was really up to. Besides, I knew she would've really tried to stop me. So I just said, "Come here. You know it's cool being here with you and my son; but I don't feel right here. It's like I'm taking over your place. I know you don't mind me being here; but like I said when you first let me move in, this was only until I got on my feet. Now if you want to move in with me, I don't have a problem with that. That will be cool to me; but I got to go."

She was still bitching when I walked out the door; and I felt bad and all, but I had to do what I had to do. I headed to the spot.

Chapter Seventeen

*W*hen I got there, I ran into Daniel. He was like, "What's up with you? I haven't seen you in awhile. Where you been hiding?"

"I been chilling, trying to do my thing. But fuck all of that, you know who got some weight I can score from?"

"What you trying to score like that?"

"G I'm trying to get ten pounds of weed. At least eight and some coke."

"Well let me call Spanish B to see if he still got it."

"Who's Spanish B?"

"That's this lil' dude named Brian. He's been holding it down for awhile now." Daniel said.

"Well make that call and see what's happening! I need that now." I demanded.

After Daniel made the call he said, "You in luck, he's on his way. You want to smoke something until he gets here?"

I thought about it, but I wanted to make sure this Spanish B cat wasn't trying to sell me some bullshit. So I replied, "I'm good for now. I can wait on your boy. He not going to be long is he?"

"He should be here in about five minutes." Daniel answered.

After a few minutes past, this dark blue truck pulled up. I didn't know who it was. By the way the lil' dudes were looking, I figured it had to be Daniel's boy Spanish B. The one on the driver side got out and nodded his head at me as if saying what's up, then walked towards Daniel. The other lil' cat sitting on the passenger side never moved or said anything. He just watched everything and everybody.

"Boom, come see." Daniel said. Then he introduced me to Spanish B.

Spanish B said, "What's happening with you?"

I replied, "Look, we can skip the chatter. Let's get down to business. I hope you didn't bring no bullshit and its weighting right."

Spanish B said, "Off top its fire and it's weighting right."

"I hear you talking, so you shouldn't mind me rolling a blunt to test it then? If it's fire and weighting right, we gone be doing a lot more business." I stated.

"It's cool! Let me go get it."

He came back with some lime green sticky weed. When I seen it, I knew it was that fire. I rolled up a blunt right quick, and after a couple of hits I said, "Is it all lime?"

Spanish B answered, "Yeah, you want it?"

"Yeah, but I got to weight it."

"It's cool. Let me go get the rest of it." When he came back he said, "It's all there."

"I hope so, but I still got to weight this." When I finished weighting it I said, "You a lil' short ain't you? You missing a whole quarter pound. That's a hundred and twelve grams you were trying to play me out of or something?"

Spanish B said, "Oh, I didn't know. Just give me forty-eight hundred for it." Now I felt he was trying to play me and I guess he must have seen it written across my face because he asked me, "That's cool?"

"No, that ain't cool B; but I tell you what I'll give you forty-five hundred for it, for trying to play me or you can roll with it. Now, what you want to do?"

He looked at me for a moment and seen I was serious then said, "Since I was short, I'm going to do that for you," then left.

After he left, I told Daniel, "It's time to get down to business. I'm about to slang shop."

I went to slanging; half of pounds, whole pounds, and quarter pounds. Either way it went, the money was good to me. Quick because of my prices, and it wasn't all that this person, that person, dealings. I was paying cheaper than up north, but it wasn't the cheapest I could have gotten it for in the south.

I kept on dealing with Spanish B until I finally met the real man behind the weight. They called him, "Amigo." To me Amigo was a scary lil' fellow. He always seemed spook when I came around. I guess when you dealing with as much weight as he was, you have to be cautious about everything and everybody. On the other hand, he was alright with me.

Every-time I dealt with Amigo, I had my own money and didn't want him to give me anything on credit. I felt like this, if I couldn't pay for it right then and there, I didn't need it until I could afford it. I guess it was shocking to him, that every-time he tried to give me anything, I would turn it down. After I told him my reason why, I think he respected me more. Yet he still played on me to see if I would fuck over him, or be his duck if you asked me.

You probably are wondering why I would say that. After scoring from him about a month, Amigo asked me to make a run for him. He was willing to pay me a thousand dollars and give me a pound of weed, but this is why I felt he must have wanted to see if I would be his duck. A thousand dollars to me wasn't shit, when I was making that every sell, two at the most. Second of all, the pound that he wanted to give me would have only been good for my personal use, the way I was smoking at the time. To top it all off, he wanted me to go to Texas to pick up five hundred pounds of weed and seventy-five kilos of cocaine with cash money. I could have fucked over him all around; but I didn't.

I learned that the dope game is always a gamble. You have to learn who to trust and when because you never know when you are going to need someone, or when they are setting you up. Either way this game is always a gamble.

I just stuck to paying for my own work; therefore it wouldn't be any temptation or slick-side crossing. I knew that if I fell off, I already done gained Amigo's trust so I could always make a pickup for him if needed. For the time being I was straight. Besides, he was selling me ten for three. That's ten pounds of weed for three thousand dollars. I couldn't complain at all. That was damn good if you ask me. I could never get ten pounds for three thousand dollars in St. Louis. In the Lou, you are going to spend a thousand dollars or more a pound all day long, and you better hope it's not what we call, "*Drought Season*."

I figured the easiest way to come up, was to go back home and slang quarter pounds for two hundred and twenty five or two fifty. Being that they were sold for three twenty five to three fifty all day long. If I just wanted to hurry up and get rid of the weed, let the QP's go for two hundred dollars. I knew everyone would jump on that because one ounce can cost you a hundred dollars, and I am going to give them four for two. They couldn't beat that! I still would be making eight for the whole and able to buy damn near three pounds for each pound I sold. So that's what I did.

I must have did that about eight times before bad luck blues came along my path again. This time when bad luck blues came to me, it left me in a cell with a million and a half dollar bond with two fugitive holds. So I knew I was through...

Chapter Eighteen

*W*hat happen? I know that's what you are thinking right now. Like the saying goes, "What goes around, comes around" and "What's done in the dark, shall be brought to the light," is about the best way I can explain what happen next.

After selling the last of the weed I had in St. Louis, I came back to New Orleans. I had stacked up close to ninety thousand dollars within a month. I figured it was time to chill for a minute because I been flighting and knew I was getting hot.

I was chilling by my house with Keisha, playing with my son. We had just left a pool party a few hours ago and went shopping for dinner. Keisha had started cooking some fish, shrimp, and spaghetti when my pager went off. It read 20-------500. I forgot what the actual phone number was, but by the code I knew what they wanted. So I call to find out exactly where they were.

When they answered the phone, my first thought was to tell them, "It ain't nothing shaken; get at me tomorrow," because I had just gotten in and really didn't want to go back out. Besides, payday Friday was the next day and I knew that I'd make every bit of six G's in a few hours. But nor, here comes Lil' Greedy talking to me again. This time telling me, "Man, that's five hundred dollars for a fifteen minute ride. You better go ahead and get that money, besides that's an extra five hundred you can play with tomorrow."

I got to thinking, "Yeah, you right," and told Keisha, "I'll be right back" but I didn't tell her that I was really getting ready to go somewhere.

I ran and jumped into my Jimmy not knowing the trouble that I was headed to. I seen this dude name Carlos, which I met before I got put out of school, on the parking lot before I pulled off. We ran it for a minute, that's when he introduce me to his cousin Mike that was out there with him.

I could tell they were high by the redness in their eyes, and the liquor smell on their breath. That's when Carlos said, "You see him right there, (Talking about Mike) he a soldier. He'll go in that water with you."

I said, "Yeah," checking out his cousin with a mouth full of gold teeth, thinking he might just be bout it. I didn't underestimate him and took Carlos's word for law. In the Lou if someone tells you something, you can damn show take it to heart. I then asked them, "What ya'll about to get into?"

Carlos said, "I'm about to duck off with this chick Carla."

"You just gone leave your cousin?"

"He stay back here. Infact, he just moved back here three days ago."

So I asked Mike, "You want to take a ride with me? I got to make a drop. It ain't gone take that long."

Mike said, "Yeah, I don't have anything to do," then jumped in.

Once we pulled off I asked him, "You smoke weed?"

"Off top!" he replied.

"Well light this up, and don't drop no ashes on my floor." I don't know if it was the weed or whatever he had before we hooked up, but he started falling to sleep. I said to myself, "He ain't no smoker. I'm going to use him for my excuse to have to leave when we get where we going because I knew Shelly is going to try to keep me over there."

I know you probably are wondering who is Shelly? Why is she going to try to keep me over there, and why am I going to need an excuse to leave? To answer all of them questions for you, Shelly is a lil' chick that was making me anywhere from a thousand to fifteen hundred dollars every night, and wasn't asking me for a penny. Not even to get her hair done. She just wanted me to come and spend some time with her every now and then, and fuck her like a dog in heat. So you know I couldn't spend a night with her, at least not that night.

When I pulled up on the set, nobody was outside. That right there should have told me something was wrong. It looked like the feds had been out there. I don't know if it was because I was high or just slipping on my game that night, but I told Mike, "I'll be right back," and ran around the corner to the spot.

I went into the house for about three minutes and kept on telling Shelly and one of her friends to come outside because I knew if we stayed in the house any longer she was going to try and keep me there. So Shelly asked me, "Who you got with you?"

I told her, "Nobody," besides she didn't know him anyway. Fuck I barely knew him and I didn't want him to see who I was dealing with.

Anyway, I finally convinced them to come outside. When we got to the bottom of the steps, things still didn't seem right. We must have took about seven more steps, when a reddish looking car rode by. That's when it all happened.

A jacker came running from around the corner, wearing a ski mask with a gun in his hand. It was three of us out there, and just one of him. I thought, "This can't be happening. Not for real!" I had dope in one hand, money in the other, and not a pistol in reach. I didn't even have one in the truck that night. I kept thinking, "I can't believe this shit, on my on set. Ain't nothing like this every happen on my set."

The jacker must wasn't paying attention because instead of taking the money and dope out of my hands first, he tried to take the purse from Shelly's friend first. By then, a dope fiend walked pass and the jacker turned his head for just a second. That second was all I needed. I figured that's my chance to break and run. If he shoots, I got a chance that he'll miss and my lil' homies in the house would come out blasting or I'll just get hit. Either way, I couldn't see me just giving it up like that. Not on my set. So I broke out running.

I ran down one block; turned down another street, turned again, and then finally I made it back to the block that I had my truck parked on. I still had some dope and money in my hands. I said to myself, "I'm tripping! If the laws ride up on me right now, how am I going to explain why I got dope and money in my hands." so I put what I had left in my pockets.

By the time I made it back down there where my truck was, Shelly said, "Let me talk to you. I know you didn't set that up."

I snapped, "Bitch I feel like you set me up! I was at home chilling. You the one that called me over here."

Shelly then said, "Well, the police are on they way."

So I waited just to show them that I didn't have anything to do with that. Then I thought about if they would have searched me, I would've been assed out once they found the dope. So I left.

When I got back into my truck, Mike wasn't in there anymore. Where the fuck was he at? That's what I wanted to know. I rolled around the blocks a few times, but I never did find him. So I said, "Fuck it," and went back to the crib.

As soon as I got back home Keisha asked, "What did you just do?"

"What you talking about?" I replied because I knew I wasn't by the house doing nothing.

Then she went on and said, "I know you didn't just rob anybody!"

She blew my mind when she said that. I told her, "Hell nor I didn't rob anybody!" Then I went on and told her what had just happen. She thought I was lying, because she didn't believe that I was selling drugs again. So I showed it to her.

I could tell Keisha was upset then. She said, "I don't believe you went back to slanging! You haven't learned yet? I hope you don't have any of that stuff in here because the police called about seven minutes ago and said that they are looking for you to question you about an arm robbery."

I thought about what Keisha said, and was like, "All shit!" Then I started grabbing; scales from here and there, bullet shells, weed, and some coke that I had stashed in the house. It looked like I was on a video tape playing in fast forward how fast I was grabbing shit. Then I went outside with everything that I had just grabbed.

If a police car would have just rolled by right then, it would have spooked the fuck out of me. I mean I was paranoid again as if I was in St. Louis. I started seeing folks in cars I never seen before. I mean, I was on everything that moved.

A dope fiend that I knew good, seen me and came by me. The first thing he said was, "What's wrong with you? You need a gun or something?"

Before I knew it, I said, "Hell nor! When I needed one where was you?" at the same time I was still looking for the police because I knew that they should have been pulling up at any moment.

The dope fiend was still talking to me, so I cut him off and said, "Here take these rocks, and go some where away from me." because he was making my nervous even worse. Then I ran over to my lil' homie Jay Dee's apartment with everything else.

Now Jay Dee, he was like my right hand man. I always could count on him to be bout whatever, as long as it contained money and bitches. Besides, he was from Texas; so I knew I could always use him for a connect if needed.

When I got to his apartment, he wasn't there; but his gal Shantay and a few other homies were there. I didn't want all of them in my business, so I called Shantay into what we called *The Smoke Room*. Once she entered, I closed the door and gave her all the: cocaine, weed, scales, and bullets that I had left. Before I could say anything, Shantay questioned, "What is all of this for?"

That's when I told her, "You know how to use everything right here and so does your man; so take it and get on ya'll feet. Ya'll don't owe me nothing; but I might, just might, need ya'll help later on down the line."

Now she was looking at me like, "What's wrong, what happened?" because she knew that I was about putting in work if I had to. Besides, I done went out there head first to get her brother out of a sticky situation before, and he's not even apart of my personal team. So I kind of made her scared because she knew it wasn't no telling what I done did or when I was going to do what.

She was about to ask me something else when I cut her off and said, "Look, I don't have time to talk right now, but that's close to ten thousand dollars worth of dope right there. Tell Jay Dee I said handle his business and ya'll get on ya'll feet." and then we walked out of the smoke room.

The rest of the lil' homies that were over there said, "What's happening? You acting funny."

I just looked at them. By me recognizing the real and the phony out of them, I started leaving out of the door telling them, "You know some fucked up shit done took place. I mean I don't know who to trust or who to turn too. So I'm gone leave ya'll as I came. True." Then proceed stepping out the door.

Once I got outside I took a deep breath, then started thinking, "Damn! Now what am I'm going to do? I done got caught up in the mix of some fucked up shit." But at that moment I thought, "I don't have nothing to worry about. I'm not the one that done it. So fuck it, I can go deal with the laws. Besides, it ain't ro sense in running from something I didn't do."

When I made it back to the parking lot, all I seen was police lights blocking off all of the exits. They had my Jimmy blocked in, as well as my Bonneville. I seen Jay Dee parking across the street, but I couldn't even get close to him. I was like, "Damn! They must really want me."

I called myself walking around a building, thinking that I might be able to make it across the street by Jay Dee. Instead, I walked right into a bigger surprise. Twelve police drew down on me and yelled, "Freeze motherfucker, don't move! Get on the ground!"

"It ain't even got to be like this. I ain't running or strapped!"

They put some handcuffs on me, and then asked me, "Where did you just come from?"

"I was just walking trying to clear my mind." I stated. Then they walked me back to the front of the complex next to my Jimmy.

They were talking back and forth over their radios, and then one of the officers said, "We got him." A couple of moments later, the same officer who said we got him asked me, "Can we search your truck?"

I didn't even get a chance to say a word before I heard at the same time on the cop's radio that they had the search warrant signed, giving them permission to search and seize if need be. So I was like, "Be my guess," because I knew I didn't have anything in there stolen. I had receipts for everything in there; all the way down to the air in the tires.

They started taking my truck apart in front of me. I was like, "Damn," looking at my lil' homies walking by shaking their heads like, what the fuck did you do!

Keisha was just looking as if to say, she couldn't believe what was happening. Then she broke down crying and whispered, "I love you," as the police began to haul me off to Jefferson Parish jailhouse.

Chapter Nineteen

*W*hen they finally booked me in, I was all fucked up in the mind. I was just waiting on them to set me a bond, because I knew I was going to make my bail and roll. Instead, they kept telling me, "No bail! No bail! No bail!"

After the third day of waiting in the holding tank, they finally called my name. "We have a Tj Green in here?"

"Right here," I yelled.

"You are charge with two counts of arm robbery. Your bond is five hundred thousand on each robbery. That's a total of one million dollars. You also are charge with criminal operation of a vehicle, and that bond is set for five hundred thousand dollars. You also have two fugitive holds. One for Westwego, and the other one for New Orleans."

I just dropped my head because I knew I couldn't post my bail. Even if I could, I still had two fugitive holds. They were making sure I wasn't going anywhere. I sat in the holding tank in shock, thinking how am I going to get out of this. I was only twenty years old, but I was facing more time than I done lived. An old timer in the holding tank said, "Well Shorty, you might as well get comfortable. It look like we gone be here for awhile."

I just looked at him blankly but I took it offensively, and then I snapped, "What the fuck you mean, we gone be here for awhile? You don't know me got damn it!"

"Cool your horses down young blood. I didn't mean you no harm. I was just saying, with a million and a half dollar bond, I don't see how you are planning on getting out of here unless you have some pull. By the way, they call me Uncle in here, but my name is Willie. Willie Lostin."

"Well Willie, they call me Boom; but I'm not in the mood to chatter right now. Maybe later we will holla."

He then said, "There's a lot of ways to do time, but don't let it do you."

Later on that day, they called about six of us to go up stairs. It just so happen, that Willie and me ended up sharing cells in the dorm. When we got there, the first thing I did was observe what was going on in the dorm while staring back at everybody that was staring at us.

I noticed that four white boys were sitting on the floor in a group. By the looks of them, I knew that somebody was taking all of their things and beating them up, it looked like at random. That made me look, to see who I might have trouble with. I wasn't worry about fighting because I grew up having to do that, but I damn sure wasn't going to let anybody just fuck over me.

In the cell Willie asked me, "Boom which bed you want? It don't make me a difference."

I told him, "I'll take the top. I had enough dealings with the rats." And that was that.

Willie unpacked his things, and then laid down. I walked out of the cell and just started pacing back and forth thinking I can't believe I'm back in this bitch, when one of the other inmates walked up questioning me.

"Say red, where you from?" he asked in a deep voice, but I didn't pay him no mind and kept walking. He then said, "What, you don't hear me talking to you?"

That's when I stopped and stared at him and said, "You talking to me dog?"

"Who else I'm going to be talking too?" he said as if checking me.

"Man, I'm from St. Louis. You don't know me G." then I started back walking.

"St. Louis! What your dumb ass doing in here? You a long way from home, ain't you?"

Before I could reply, I just went off throwing blows at him. I mean, I was hitting him so hard and quick that when I stopped his face was bloody and he just fell to the floor. I said, "Bitch get up! I told you, you didn't know me and you got the nervous to call me dumb." He jumped up and began to charge me like a bull. I waited until he got close enough, then step to the side and hit him with a few more licks until he fell again. "Bitch that's all you got? You gone have to check up out of here. Matter of fact, where your store at? You don't have no need for that!" I said. He just laid there covering his face so that I wouldn't hit him in it, but I was serious. I wanted his store now. I told him, "You can get up and get it for me, or I'm going to beat the shit out of you and still get it."

He got up and went into his cell while I stood there watching him. When he came out he had a shirt full of zoo-zoos. I took it back to my cell and dumped it on the bed, and then threw his shirt back to him.

Willie just shook his head and started laughing. Then said, "Young gun, I know he didn't see that coming! In the penitentiary he would be for somebody."

"I know. I done been up that road before, so I know how it goes. You want a smoke or something?"

"I don't mind if I do," Willie replied and then started back laughing. He then said, "Yeah, you sure put it on him," and went to sleep.

After awhile, the dorm seen that I was about handling my business big or small, so they knew It wasn't no punking me and tried to become cool with me. I must have seen the dorm change about twenty times. It was only: Willie, and a lil' dude name Robert, and me left that had been in there for awhile now. Everybody else had gotten they time and been shipped up-state.

I just so happen to be thinking one day that I didn't see a single person go home. Not even one since I been there. The white boys and all have gotten time. I started thinking, "Shit! They kept me in here this fucking long; I might not be going home either." They already were talking about giving me a hundred and ninety-eight years on just the two arm robberies.

I mean days turned to weeks, and weeks turned to months. Finally, I was called to see my lawyer, but not knowing the real surprise I was headed too. The guard called me to the door while I was playing dominoes and said, "Get dress. Your lawyer wants to see you."

I was surprise because I wasn't expecting him. Besides, he never came to see me before; so I figured he must have had some good news for me. Once I got dressed, the guard took me down the elevator to the second floor where two detectives were waiting. When the elevator doors opened, the two stocky detectives looked at me and said, "That's our man."

The first thing I noticed was that they had on New Orleans badges. Then I also noticed that, they weren't my lawyer. The next thing I knew, they were slapping handcuffs on me and taking me down to the first floor. So then I was thinking, maybe my lawyer was down stairs. The only problem was when we got downstairs; I noticed they were taking me the same way that they brought me into the jail, except this time I was heading out.

Outside waiting next to the undercovers' car, were two more detectives. Now I'm thinking, what the fucks going on here. They placed me in the back seat, and one of the detectives that was waiting by the car got in beside me, one drove, and one rode in the passenger seat. The other officer drove the regular police car that was following right behind us.

I asked the detectives in the car with me, "Where are ya'll taking me?"

The detective on the passenger replied, "You going to find out."

The detective next to me then said, "You look like a good kid."

I didn't say anything. I just looked at him as if to say, only if you really knew me. That's when the passenger detective said, "Good kid some shit! That son of a bitch is going to get it."

The driver never said anything; he just kept looking at me through the rearview mirror. The one in the backseat with me said, "It's a shame you going to go down for your friends."

That's when I asked, "What are you talking about?"

The passenger cut me off, "Got damn it, you know what the fuck he's talking about. Keep fucking playing stupid and wait until we get there."

The driver still didn't say anything. He was barely keeping his eyes on the road, staring at me as if he felt sorry for me. We pulled up to a brown brick building surrounded by a high electrical fence. The building had in white writing "Detective Bureau."

When we went into the building, the first thing I noticed was it had a lot of doors leading into different rooms. I was looking curiously, without a doubt, trying to figure out what this place was because I didn't have a clue. I was trying to peep into one room when another detective seen me and yelled, "Get that son of a bitch!" but I didn't know that he was talking about me.

As soon as I turned around, two detectives came out of nowhere and grabbed me by the arms and said, "Come this way," leading me pass about six more doors.

I asked them, "Do I still have to wear these handcuffs, since I'm apparently at the place where we suppose to of been going?"

One of them replied, "Shut up!" I thought to myself, this is going to be a long day I can see.

We entered a room that was about halfway down the hall. Inside it contained: three desks, a long brown bookshelf across the back wall, and a chair right in front of the door. The one that told me to shut up told me to, "Sit down right there and don't move." then walked back out of the room.

Moments later, another detective walked into the room and sat in front of me with some papers in his hands that he started to write on. When he finished writing whatever he was writing, he pushed them all in front of me and said, "Sign all of them."

"I can't sign the papers with my hands behind my back."

That's when one of the stocky officers came behind me and unhooked one of the handcuffs, then handcuffed my hands in front of me. I didn't even know he was there. The one at the desk told me, "Now sign them."

After that, I started reading the papers that was in front of me, starting at the top:

State Of Louisiana
Department of Robberies and Homicide
Detectives Bureau

You have the right to remain silent. Anything that you say, can and will be used against you in the court of the law. You have the right to have a lawyer present during any questionings. If you can not afford one, one will be appointed to you by the courts.

Date:

_____

Do you understand these rights? _____   **Signature**:

_____

_____

_____

I signed my name Tj Green, and then turned the page. The next page started off the same way.

_____

_____

State Of Louisiana
Department of Robberies and Homicide
Detectives Bureau

I _____hereby wish to waiver my rights and make a statement.

Date:

_____

Signature:

_____

_____

_____

I stopped right there and asked the detectives. "What do I suppose to be making a statement about?"

In return he said, "Motherfucker, sign the got damn papers!"

"I'm not about to sign no more papers, until I know what I'm signing about."

He raised his voice again, "Motherfucker, you gone sign them got damn papers and now!"

I remember just looking at him for a few seconds. I had a feeling that if I signed the papers, I might as well wrapped up the thought of coming home. He jumped to his feet and nodded at someone behind me. It was another detective.

He entered the room and walked straight to the bookshelf in the back of the room. I thought he was coming to get something and going about his way, until he picked up a big red and yellow dictionary and set it on the corner of the desk in front of me. That's when he said, "You might as well save yourself some trouble and cooperate with us. We got you right."

"Got damn me, I don't know what you talking about." I barely got them words out of my mouth before he picked back up the dictionary and hit me across my head knocking me out of the chair I was sitting in. I couldn't believe he just batted the piss out of me and I couldn't do anything about it. I got back up without thinking and said, "That made you feel more like a man, hitting a man while he helpless."

He said, "You son of a bitch!" and hit me with the book across my head again.

I had no choice but to take that lick then shake it off. I looked at him and the other detective then thought, I'm going to remember you motherfuckers and I hope I catch ya'll slipping. I'm going to get my revenge.

The one that hit me said, "What you want to hit me back? Take the handcuffs off of him." I didn't even know that there was already another detective behind me until, he grabbed me like I was a piece of paper and started unlocking the handcuffs. While he was doing that, the one that told him to take the cuffs off said, "I hope he tries to run or fight back, so I can have an excuse for shooting him."

When he made that statement, I just stood there. He had a look on his face that said, if he could make it look like I was trying to escape, he would shoot me dead without a second thought. So I knew this wasn't a time to be trying my luck. Besides, it was know a total of five of them in the room.

Two of them were tall but solid looking, with black hair. The one behind the desk in front of me looked the oldest out of all of them, with big arms. The last two were about my height. One stocky and the other one looked like he could have been gay.

The one that looked gay closed the door, and all I remember was feeling like a helpless child getting hit every time I took a breathe. They each shouted different questions at me, but instead of waiting on a reply they would hit me and then tell me what I suppose to have done. All the time, I knew that they were talking about robberies Dennis and me did.

After they had hit me so many times and got tired of me saying the same thing every time they hit me. I yelled, "Got damn me, I don't know what the fuck ya'll talking about and I want my fucking lawyer!"

That didn't even stop them. They kept on beating me until they got tired of me refusing to tell them anything; then brought me back to Jefferson Parish jail.

Once I got back in the dorm. I went straight to the toilet and began throwing up. Robert and Willie came to the cell and asked me what happened? That's when I started telling them about the events that took place while I was gone.

Willie then suggested that I go to the infirmary, because he believed that I had a good legal case against the state. Before I could even respond back to him, I began throwing up again. That's when they started bucking, beating on the doors, telling the guard that I needed to go to the infirmary.

By the time I did get to the infirmary, they kept asking questions as to what happened. They observed that I had a few red bruises across my sides and back, along with two knots on my head, but the only treatment they gave me was two Tylenols and an ice pack for my knots. Then they sent me back to the dorm.

Robert said, "You back already! That was a fast x-ray."

I said sarcastically, "Yeah that was a fast x-ray alright. They didn't even do one. They just seen I had a few red bruises on me and gave me two Tylenols and an icepack for these knots I got."

Willie then said, "That's some bullshit! I can't believe these bitches. It's about time somebody do something about them. I tell you what Boom, you got a good case on them and I'm going to help you sue them if you want to."

I didn't even have to think about if I wanted to sue them. I wanted my revenge one way or the other. So I asked Willie, "What are you going to want if you help me with my case against them?"

"Nothing! I'm just tired of seeing them fuck over folks because they are in the system and figure no one can do anything about it."

After I let my bruises heal for a few days Robert, Willie, and me began going to the law library working on my case against the state. The more I started reading the law books, the more I began to see that I did have a good case against them.

Chapter Twenty

ℬefore I even realized it, seven more months had gone by and I was starting to go to court for the arm robbery charges that I had. At first, I didn't know what to expect; but I knew they had me down bad so I wasn't going to worry. Keisha surprised me by being in court every time I went, even though they just kept setting my date back. The last time I seen her in court, she told me to call her she had something to tell me.

I couldn't figure out what in the world she could have wanted to tell me, so I called her. She was telling me about my son and how big he was getting, but I knew she had something else on her mind that she wasn't telling me. So I asked her, "What did you have to tell me in the courtroom?"

"Oh yeah, your boy Jay Dee, told me whenever I got in touch with you, to make sure I gave you his number and for you to call him immediately. I don't know what it was about, but he made it seem like it was important. He also gave me five hundred dollars, and told me that's for Lil' Threat. So make sure you call him." Then she gave me his phone number.

I told her, "Thanks for the information," then we talked dirty until the fifteen minute phone call was up. After that I called Jay Dee.

Jay Dee answered and accepted the collect call and said, "What the fuck took you so long to call me?"

"G you know me. I just been going though some thangs trying to deal with them. Anyway, you handling your business huh?"

"Off top, but man what happened? I seen the laws when they had you shackled up, and then they towed your truck. I was wondering what the fuck you done did, how they were out there."

"G that's a long story, but they got me all fucked up though! Say Dee, thanks for looking out for my lil' one. I miss that nigga'!"

"It's no need to thank me. Besides, if it wasn't for you, I probably wouldn't be able to do that. Anyway, you know Lil' Threat my dog. He looks just like you. Oh yeah, when are you getting out? You know right after you got locked up, about three days later, G-Money Records came through with a contract wanting to sign us and wanted us to play a few roles in a movie they about to make called *The Third Hustler*."

"That's good G. Handle your business, I might be in here awhile. Fuck the way they beat me, they trying to deal with me one way or the other. At least that's how it look G."

"What the fuck you mean the way they beat you? You alright? Matter of fact, don't worry about nothing. I'm about to go buy you a lawyer as soon as we get off the phone."

That's when I told him, "If you can, do that. If not, don't worry; but I go back to court tomorrow at eight o'clock in the morning in division K."

"I promise you, as soon as we get off the phone I'm gone handle that. You got my word G. Infact, when we get off the phone, hit me back in about a hour. That should be plenty of time for me to do that. Hold on for a minute, my girl want to holla at you."

"What's up baby? You doing alright in there? You know you had me worried about you, but I know you can take care of yourself. Just be careful Bcom." Shantay said.

After I got off the phone with them, I was hoping Jay Dee did get a lawyer for me. I called him back about three hours later, just to see if he got a lawyer for me. When I got in touch with him, he said he did and the lawyer's name was Kenneth B. We ran it for a few, and then cut the conversation short.

I laid in my bunk that night mostly awake smoking cigarettes. I thought to myself, ain't this a bitch, out of all the things that could have been on my mind, I'm thinking here I am smoking cigarettes like they blunts and in the world, you couldn't even get in my car talking about smoking a cigarette. Then I started thinking about the night I got locked up. I still haven't seen my fall partner Mike but one time in court, and we couldn't run it like talking about. I didn't even know he was locked up until then. Finally, I dosed off into a deep sleep.

When I woke up the next morning, I seen that Willie had gotten my breakfast and sat it in the cell for me. I felt like I didn't sleep a wink the whole night, but I must have been sleeping hard. I didn't hear them bring in the breakfast. I was about to jump in the shower to wake myself up all the way, when I noticed that Robert was gone. So I asked Willie, "Where Robert at?"

"He had to go to court this morning. You forgot they about to start his trial too?"

I played it off and said, "Oh yeah, you know I just got up and don't have it all together yet," but I really forgot.

"Well you better get it together; they should be coming for you in about twenty minutes." He replied

Once I got in the shower, I started waking all the way up. For some reason though, I kept wondering why Robert really murdered his wife instead of just leaving her. I also knew he wasn't telling me all of the story. At first he said, that he had just come home from work when he heard a strange noise coming from upstairs. So he grabbed a butcher knife out of the kitchen and made his way upstairs. Once he got up there, he heard his wife saying, "Fuck me harder, fuck me harder." then not just one man's voice but two. When he opened the door, he couldn't believe what his eyes were seeing. His wife was tied to the bed sucking somebody's dick, while getting fucked by somebody else he didn't know. So he just clicked. The two men ran and he began stabbing his wife and fucking her at the same time.

Then he said, he guessed the dudes must have forgotten something and crept back in the room. When he seen them, the visible picture of them with his wife came back to his mind and he grabbed for his pistol that he kept under his mattress. Before he got it, one of the men began tussling with him, while the other man was grabbing their personal things. By the time he got control of the gun right, the two men were gone for real. He didn't realize his wife was already shot, so he just finished her off.

As soon as I finished taking my shower, the guards was already there to get me, I had to hurry up and get dressed. Willie said, "I thought you was trying to drown yourself in there. You ready to deal with them?"

"If I ain't ready, I don't know when I'm going to be. You feel me?"

"Well go get them then." Willie said.

Once we got inside the court room, they placed all of us inmates in what they call "the box", then the judge began calling out names. My fall partner, Mike, was sitting next to me. That's when I asked him, "What the fuck happening to you? Where you went?"

Mike said, "Man, when you left some dudes came to your car with some pistols asking where the dope at? I told them I didn't have any dope, that's when they told me to get out of the car and searched me. They took everything that I had, then told me to run. So that's what I did. The next thing I knew the police cars was surrounding me with their guns drew down on me, talking about I'm a suspect for an armed robbery. They brought me back around where you was parked at, but you was gone and some bitches came talking about that's him. So here I am, plus I had five distribution charges."

His story sounded kind of lame, but after that night I could believe that happened. That's when the judge told us, "Be quiet in the box," and sentenced the man sitting next to Mike to eighty years hard labor.

I couldn't believe how much time this bitch was giving out. That's when my public defender lawyer came over talking to me. She said, "The DA is willing to give you twenty years if you take a plea now, which I think is a good deal considering you are a second offender."

"Twenty years! Bitch, you got to be crazy! I just turned twenty," I exclaimed.

"Calm down Mr. Green." She said lowering her voice. "It's either take that, or if we go to trial and they find you guilty, you know you are facing the possibility of receiving one hundred and ninety eight years."

"Look bitch, you take the twenty years and let me do your job, then tell me what you think about that," that's when the judge called my name.

Right at that moment, a man who had just walked in the courtroom said, "Can I approach the bench your honor?"

She allowed him to. That's when the man she just gave eighty years to said, "Say red, you doing the right thing. Make her do her job; that's what she's here for."

I said, "That's real." then began talking to Mike. I asked him, "Well do they have you right on the distribution?"

"They showed me the tapes they got, and I know it was me in about three of them but they don't look like me now."

"Well look, as far as the armed robberies, I'm going to ride with you to the end on them. We can go to trial, or if they come to you with a reasonable deal you can take that. Just let me know what you want to do," was my reply to him before the man who just approached the judge's bench came next to us.

"Mr. Green," the judge said, "we are going to set your case back until tomorrow."

"Tomorrow! I'm tired of this bitch setting me back," I said under my breath.

Right then the man who just came into the courtroom came next to us and replied, "Tj Green, my name is Kenneth B. I'm going to be representing you from here on out. I know that you are ready to go home, but like I told Jay Dee I can't promise you when you are going to be released. I will make sure that you come out with the best deal if we have to make one. So you just sit back and let me see what all they have."

That's when the judge called Mike's name. The DA said, "Your honor, we are ready to proceed with this matter."

His lawyer had already filed a motion to discover, so the judge called, "Recess," while the DA set up the VCR.

The court was still in recess when Mike's lawyer was playing the VCR tape. She printed out a picture and reached it to the bailiff. She asked him, "Is there anyone in this court who looks like this?"

The bailiff looked at the picture twice, then at everyone in the courtroom. After that, he walked straight to Mike and the courtroom was filled too. I whisper to Mike, "I can't make you take no time, but if you go to trial and the DA prints out that picture and someone does the same thing, I don't see how you are going to win."

He was just sitting there because he knew I was telling him the truth. That's when his lawyer said, "It's going to be hard to beat this in front of a jury if that was to happen. If you are found guilty on any one of the distribution, they are going to give you all of them which carry up to thirty years on each of them. The second problem you will have is that you will not be able to speak on your own behalf on the armed robberies you are charged with if you are convicted; which I believe we can beat. So let me go talk to the DA and see what type of deal they are willing to give you or what do you want to do?"

Mike just sat there in shock. He didn't say anything, not one word. His lawyer just walked off. That's when he asked me, "What would you do?"

I told him, "If I knew that was me and they had me right, I most likely would take a deal as long as I felt I could do it and it wasn't to long. But I can't tell you to take no time because I ain't trying to take none if I don't have to. Besides, that's not just numbers, that's your life. Years you will be gone to prison." Right after I told Mike that my lawyer Kenneth B. came towards me smiling. I couldn't help but to ask him, "What the fuck you smiling about? I don': see nothing funny."

Kenneth said, "Cool down! It don't look that bad. We just have to wait to tomorrow. We got this beat."

When I heard the words we got this beat, I felt relief; and then said, "Well, I'll see you tomorrow."

After that, everyone came back into the courtroom and the judge called it to order. They started off calling other people names then sentencing them. I mean out of the whole courtroom, they were finding everyone guilty, sentencing them to forty to eighty years. The least amount of time anyone gotten was fifteen years, as if that was even better. By the time they called Mike's name, the judge said, "We are going to finish this up tomorrow."

Before they brought us back to the jail, I told Mike, "Think about what you gone do. Tomorrow is our day." He just nodded his head, but didn't say anything.

When I got back to the dorm, I seen Robert packing his things so I walked over to him and asked, "How did you make out?"

Robert replied, "Life! Life, they found me guilty and sentenced me to life in prison without the possibility of parole."

I didn't know what to say to him. I mean, what could I possibly say to a man that knew he wasn't ever going home again. So I said, "I'm sorry to hear that, but once you get up that road, you might find a way to give some of that time back. But don't give up on your faith." then I went and laid down in my cell.

Willie walked in and asked me, "Well, how did you turn out?"

"I'm suppose to go back tomorrow but my lawyer said I have a good chance in beating this. So I just have to wait and see." After I told Willie that, I tried to get comfortable and get some rest because I knew tomorrow would be the big day.

Chapter Twenty-One

$\mathcal{T}$he next morning when I woke up, I was stressing already. I had a headache, and I didn't feel like getting out of bed. I knew what lied ahead of me was going to be a long aggravating day in court. I didn't get a good nights sleep because I kept waking up thinking the judge was going to give me one hundred and ninety-eight years after the jury found me guilty.

Finally, I made myself get out of bed to take a shower and got ready for the big day! After I got out of the shower, I realized Robert was already gone. So I asked Willie, "How long has Robert been gone?"

"I don't know, but I'm glad that lying piece of shit is gone, anyway. He was starting to get on my nervous."

"Damn dog, I thought ya'll were cool; what happened between ya'll?"

His response was, "Yeah, we cool and all, but I get tired of hearing him tell all those lies about what he did to his wife."

"I feel you all the way on that. He told me so many different stories, that it didn't make no sense. I knew he was going to be found guilty." I replied.

After that they called for breakfast and told me to get ready for court when I was finished. Since I was already dressed, I decided to sit down and smoke me a cigarette and run it Willie until they called my name.

Willie was telling me something about my lawsuit against the state, but I wasn't paying attention because my mind was set on what was going to happen to me in court today. Then the guard called my name.

It was like déjà-vu walking back into the courtroom, and getting placed in the same seat next to Mike except this time someone else was sitting on the other side of him. The first thing I did was ask Mike, "What did you decide to do?"

Mike answered, "I think I'm going to take a plea, if it's reasonable as long as they don't try to slam me too bad."

"I was thinking the same thing; if that's what my lawyer says would be my best option. But what's so fucked up G, I didn't even do the robbery. I could see if they caught me slanging, I'll take my lick. They got me all fucked up right now." I replied.

I was looking around the courtroom to see if I knew anyone else in there, but so far everybody else was strangers to me. My lawyer wasn't even here yet, but Mike's lawyer just came in. As soon as he seen Mike, he walked up and asked, "What do you want to do?"

Mike hesitated then said, "See what the best deal you can get for me is. If they are not willing to give me something reasonable, then we can get ready to go to trail."

His lawyer said, "Okay, let me see what I can do," then left.

Mike then asked me, "You think I'm doing the right thing?"

"Yeah, but don't just take anything."

The courtroom door swung open and a group of lawyers and the district attorney, along with other people coming to court entered. That wasn't anything spectacular to me, until I seen Shelly and her friend walk into the courtroom.

When we finally made eye contact, I couldn't help but notice how fine she was; and then I asked her, "What's up? You came to help me out?"

She rolled her eyes as if she couldn't believe that I was asking her that question, then looked at her friend, who was mean mugging me. When she finally looked me back in the eyes, I said, "What the fucks going on; what you gone do?"

Shelly looked at me for a minute, and then pointed at me and said, "I want to see you go down," then pointed her thumb down.

Everyone in the box with me was like, who's she pointing at? That's when I told Mike, "She must really think I had something to do with that."

He said, "Who?"

"That bitch that was pointing up here."

"Damn that hoe fine; that's the bitch that supposed to have got robbed?"

"Yeah! Her and the chick sitting on her right."

"You can't get them to help us out?"

"I don't think so. If they were going to help us, they would have by now. Besides, she knows I have money, so if that's what they wanted I would have gave that to them already."

On the inside, I was so pissed off. I couldn't believe how Shelly was playing the game. This was the same hoe I was fucking; and she was making money for me everyday. I was just staring at her as if I was dreaming and was waiting on someone to wake me up. But that didn't ever happen. The more I stared at her, the more furious I became of my reality. My mind was so far gone, that I didn't notice my lawyer enter the courtroom.

Kenneth walked up to the box and said to me, "How are you doing champ?" but I did not reply. That's when he said, "Don't worry about nothing. I just read the police report and according to it, they can not charge you with arm robbery. So cheer up!"

The only thing I could bring myself to say was, "I'll cheer up when I'm free. Until then, I don't have shit to be cheerful about in here! You know how it feels to be accused, betrayed, and thrown away for something that you didn't even do, and don't nobody believe you telling the truth, not even the ones you consider family?"

Kenneth couldn't even reply back. He just stood there as if what I said just amazed him or something, and then walked off. Mike's lawyer walked up as soon as he walked off, and began talking to Mike. I couldn't help but to eavesdrop to find out what was going on.

I overheard Mike's lawyer say, "They are willing to drop one of the arm robberies you are charged with, and give you eight years on the other arm robbery. Plus, eight years on each distribution you are charge with. You can run them all concurrent with the eight years for the arm robbery, if you are willing to take a plea bargain right now. This is a good deal being that if we go to trail you are facing up to ninety-nine years on each arm robbery plus up to thirty years on each distribution. But it's all up to you; it's your life on the line!"

Mike replied, "Eight for the arm robbery, plus eight on each distribution. I thought you said you could beat the arm robberies?"

"Look, you will only be doing one eight year sentence if you take the plea. By you being charged with arm robbery, you will end up doing six years and some months. Plus, you can earn good time if you go get a trade or just go to school. But what do you want to do? Are you going to take the plea or not?" his lawyer said.

Mike replied, "Can I have a minute to think about this?"

He said, "Don't you have kids? Besides, you are young, and still will be young when you get out. I tell you what, think about it for a minute; then I'm going to need an answer."

I know Mike didn't think that he would be making a decision like that today. By the look on his face, he was looking as if he couldn't believe this was real. That's when I told him, "G, eight years may seem like a long time, but being in a predicament where you know they have you at least halfway right, you have to play the cards you are dealt. It might not seem right or fair, but that's life. Especially when you know that you are in a predicament where they can give you way more than eight years. I can't tell you to take that, but I would. Now if you want to, we can still go to trial on the arm robberies. It's been a year and a half almost and I haven't seen anybody win at trial yet. So just let me know what you want to do."

Mike sat there in silence for a moment then said, "Well, I'm going to take the deal. Like you said, I haven't seen anyone go home either now that I'm thinking about it. Plus I know they have me right on the distribution, so fuck it."

I knew that was a hard decision he had just made, so I just told him, "Its not going to be as long as you think, before you know it, you will be on your way home."

After that he called his lawyer over to the box, and told him he was willing to take the plea bargain. His lawyer just smiled as if he didn't have any intentions on helping Mike beat either of his charges anyway and said, "I think you just made a good decision, give me a minute to get the papers together for you to sign."

Once I seen how Mike's lawyer was smiling and looking, I couldn't help but get drove. I then started whistling to get Shelly's attention. When she finally looked at me, I couldn't control my temper any more. I snapped, "Bitch, you ain't gone help me after all we done been through? I'm the same motherfucker that fuck you and lay my head in your bed, and this is how you gone play me? Bitch fuck you!"

After that, I felt like I just released a little tension off of my chest, and she just hurried out of the courtroom as if she was about to cry, but I didn't give a fuck. I wanted her to feel the pain I was going through.

Shortly after that, Mike's lawyer and mine's came walking up at the same time. Mike's lawyer was going over the papers with him, as my lawyer began to say, "Well, I have some good news and some bad news, which do you want first?"

I said, "Want you quit beating around the bush; what more can go wrong?"

Kenneth answered, "They are going to drop one of the arm robberies; that's the good news. The bad news is that they want you to plead guilty to the other arm robbery. If you do, they agreed not to max you out being that you are already a convicted felon. So it's all up to you. What do you want to do?"

"I thought you said that you had this case beat. If you are not going to work for me, you might as well give Jay Dee his money back. I don't need a motherfucker to charge me to sell me out; what the fuck I look like? Anyway, how are they going to charge me with the same arm robbery that he just took the charge for? I didn't have anything to do with that, you all full of shit. So you can take that plea bargain and shove it up your ass, then get ready for trial. You can even ask the victims and they will tell you I didn't do it. They right over there."

"Look Mr. Green, I'm going to go and talk to the DA one more time, but I really don't think it's going to do any good." Kenneth said.

"You need to go talk to someone, because I'll be damn if I'm going to plead guilty to any arm robbery. You said you read the police report, and the victims clearly said I'm not the one that had robbed them. So give me one reason why I should plead guilty!"

Kenneth didn't say anything. He just stood there realizing that I made sense, and then walked off. Mike was finishing up signing his papers then said, "If you want to go to trial, I'll take the stand and tell them you didn't have nothing to do with the robbery if that's what it's going to take for them to cut you loose. Besides, it don't make sense for both of us to go to the penitentiary when I'm already going."

Now I was struck because I didn't know what to do. I had a lawyer that I didn't know if he was working for me or against me. A chick I was fucking, trying to press charges against me, and Mike the only one willing to take the charge, trying to help me. My mind was racing because I knew it was only minutes before I would know what was going to happen.

Kenneth came back shaking his head; then said, "Well get ready to change clothes and pick-out your jury, we are about to go to trial."

By the way he was shaking his head, I couldn't help but get the vibe that something wasn't right. So I asked him, "What, you didn't want to go to trial?"

"I wasn't expecting it to go that far."

"What were you expecting? I wasn't expecting it having to come to this point either, but I'm not about to plead guilty for an arm robbery that I know I didn't do. Especially, when both victims said I'm not the one that did it; and the one that just took the arm robbery charge is willing to take the stand and say I didn't have anything to do with it."

Chapter Twenty-Two

*T*he judge called Mike's name again and his lawyer took the judge the papers he had just finished signing up to her. The judge began reading them, and then said, "Mike C. More, do you understand what you just signed?"

Mike hesitated then said, "Yes your honor."

The judge then said, "Before I can accept this plea, will you tell the court in your own words what you are pleading guilty to?"

Mike hesitated longer, as if debating on if he wanted to go through with the plea bargain, and then slowly said, "I'm guilty of selling illegal substances knowing that it was wrong." He paused for a moment and looked around the courtroom and replied, "And of robbery."

I knew it was hard for him to say that because of the way his voice sounded, but it was just about over in the courtroom for him. The judge held up some papers and asked Mike, "Is this your signature?"

Mike replied, "Yeah," as if regretting it.

"Did anyone force you to sign these papers?" the judge questioned.

"No!" Mike responded.

The judge then went on and said, "I hereby accept your plea of guilty. The DA agreed in your plea bargaining to sentence you to eight years hard labor in the Department of Corrections; and all charges be ran concurrent. I accept that sentence, but Mr. More, I want you to know that this is a very lenient sentence, so don't take it for granted. I hope while you are incarcerated you take time to think about what you were doing and make a change. Next case!"

The judge went on calling names and sentencing people while I was talking to Mike. I could tell he really didn't want to be bothered at the time, so I stopped talking to him and then just stared at the rest of the folks in the courtroom wishing someone out there could break me out, but I knew that was too much wishing.

When the judge finally called my name, my lawyer said, "We're ready to go to trial your honor."

The judge asked the DA, "Are you ready as well?"

The state district attorney replied, "No your honor; I will need a little while longer. We just finished up Mr. More's cases, and Mr. Green and Mr. More are co-defendants, so we just need a little longer your honor."

"Well we are going to skip this case for now, but we are going to finish this up today. Next case!"

Now I was just sitting in the box thinking, well at least I'll know whether I would be going home or not today. As I started listening to other folks' charges and the time they were getting, I was like damn! I didn't realize all the time that I was doing a lot of things, I could have gotten caught, and end up with as much time as they were getting. Listening to half of the cases made my mind drift back in time when I had no choice but to get it how I live.

I started thinking about when I was in St. Louis. All of the breaking in houses, stealing from stores, robbing folks, strangers, even murder, and how it all seems to escalate as if it happened over night. I mean, so many things that I had did in my past was coming across my mind, and I was seeing them as if I was watching a movie that only I could see. I wasn't ready to go back to the penitentiary, but my actions on the streets told a whole different story.

Kenneth came back up to the box with a law book in his hand and said, "First of all, you are right. They can not charge you with the same arm robbery that someone else has already been convicted of; but they can charge you with accessory after the fact, and possibly before the fact even. This simply means you are not the one that did it, but you played a part in it. That carries a five year sentence with or without hard labor. So what do you think of that Mr. Green?"

"You didn't understand me when I said I'm not pleading guilty to any arm robbery! I'm ready to go to trial. If they actually had me right, maybe I would take a plea bargain. But in this case, they don't. So fuck a plea bargain! As far as accessory, how am I going to be accessory to something I didn't have apart of? I almost got robbed that night, but I ran. I was out there with them." I replied.

"Mr. Green, you are not understanding what I'm trying to tell you." Kenneth said before I cut him off.

"I understand clearly. You want me to plead guilty to something that I didn't do."

"At least let me finish telling you what I was about to inform you of. If you go to trial for arm robbery, you have a good chance of winning. If the district attorney drops the arm robbery down to accessory before or after the fact and you decide that you still want to go to trial, you have no chance of winning." Kenneth clearly said.

I quickly asked, "Why won't I win? I'm not the one who did it."

He responded, "Like I previously tried to inform you, that mean you are not the one that did the robbery; but you played a part in it. By Mr. More pleading guilty already, and making a statement that he was with you, that automatically makes you have a part in the robbery."

"What if he takes the stand and tells the court that I didn't have anything to do with it, or had any knowledge that he was going to rob them?"

"They would still find you guilty because he was a passenger in your automobile. So do you want me to try to get you a plea bargain?" Kenneth asked.

I told Kenneth, "No, I want you to just act like we are ready to go to trial and see what kind of plea bargain they bring to you, instead of you asking for a plea bargain."

He just nodded his head, and then walked away and sat down. I made up my mind that I had to take a plea bargain because either way, I was in a no win situation. I figured if they came with two years, I would jump on it. Even five years wasn't too bad. I would only have a year left after I got my good time.

They must have went through damn near forty people before the judge called my name again. When she did, I just knew she was going to set me back until the next day, but I was wrong.

My lawyer said, "We're ready your honor, we're just waiting on the D.A. to proceed prosecuting."

The judge asked the district attorney, "Are you ready to proceed with this matter?"

The district attorney replied, "Your honor, can we just have two minutes, and then we will be ready?"

The judge granted it to him, and then said, "That will be it."

I seen the district attorney walk over and begin speaking to my lawyer. By the way it looked; you couldn't have told me that they weren't working together in some kind of way. The district attorney turned around and looked at me for a second, then back at my lawyer. After that, he began writing on a piece of paper, and then handed it to my lawyer. My lawyer acted as if he was going over the paper, and then walked over towards me with it.

The way that scenery looked, I wanted to tell both of them they could both kiss my ass and die slow. I mean I felt played and it was killing me to bite my tongue.

My lawyer approached me as if he was about to tell me some good news; then said, "They agree not to charge you with arm robbery, and they are willing to give you a plea of five years which means you will do two and a half years with or without hard labor for accessory after the fact. All you have to do is just sign these pages and we can wrap this up."

I just sat there wishing I could strangle him until his eyes just popped out; rocking back and forth. I couldn't even say anything for a few moments because everything that kept coming to my mind was, *this bitch trying to play the piss out of me*. Finally, I said, "That's the best you can do for me? Five years! That's the most they can give me; so what type of deal is that? Then again, I already know. You really don't give a fuck; you already got paid. Plus you can go home when you get ready to. Infact, just let me sign them papers so I can go about my business, and get this shit over with because I can see ya'll don't give a fuck about who's really innocent or guilty. Ya'll just a bunch of lowdown dirty motherfuckers!"

Chapter Twenty-Three

*A*fter I took my time, they brought me back to the dorm. As soon as I enter the dorm Willie came by me and asked, "How did you make out?"

I just dropped my head, and then said, "They just a bunch of low down motherfuckers in there. They don't care who really innocent; all they want is a got damn conviction. All of them motherfuckers work together. I can see if I actually did the fucking robbery, but even Shelly and her friend said I'm not the one who robbed them. But what good did that do? Even Mike was willing to take the stand and say I didn't have anything to do with the robbery; but they wasn't trying to hear that."

"Well how long did they give you?"

"Them bitches threw out one of the robberies; then dropped the other one to accessory after the fact. Then they gave me a five year plea bargain, which I had to take according to my lawyer."

"Five years! You acting as if they gave you the maximum sentence. You only have to do two and a half years, and you already been down a year and a half; so what you bitching about? You short!"

"You don't feel me. It's the point I know I didn't do it, but I still have to do some time. I'm about to lay down. I'll holla' at you later if they don't move me before I get up."

Before I went to lay down Willie said, "Be happy they gave you a roll out date. Least you know you going home."

When I laid down, my mind was all fucked up. I didn't know who really had it in for me. All I could see was Shelly pointing at me, telling me she wanted to see me go down. Then I didn't know if Mike really was the one who did the robbery. What kept driving me though, was when I seen Kenneth smiling with the D.A. then acting as if he was doing me a favor by telling me to take the plea bargain. I was so fed up, that I just went to sleep. It felt like shortly after I fell asleep, Willie woke me up again and asked me, "You gone eat something, young gun?"

"You can have it; I don't want that shit."

"You going to have to eat something. Just because you have to do time, don't let them get the best of you. I know you stronger than that. Besides, you still have your law suit against the state if you proceed with it."

My mind wasn't even on the law suit. I put it in my mind and heart to get justice on the streets, whenever I crossed paths with them detectives. So I told Willie, "Look, I appreciate all the help and work you been doing with me to get a victory on this law suit I have, but I don't even want to go there with it any more. I'm going to get justice my way."

"Are you crazy or something? You have a good case against the state, and you don't want to go through with it!"

He didn't bother to wait for my reply, he just walked off. I didn't really give a fuck. For all I knew, they would find away to win that case too. That's when I decided to call Keisha.

I was wondering why she wasn't in court today. When she finally answered the phone, she sounded as if she was aggravated or up-set, so I asked her, "What's wrong with you?"

"Tiarell took sick last night. I had to take him to the hospital."

"Is he alright? What was wrong with him?"

"He's alright now, but they told me to watch how he sleeps. They said he had asphyxia. That's a lack of oxygen, or excess of carbon dioxide in the body. It is usually caused by interruption of breathing, and causes unconsciousness." Keisha replied.

"What was he doing that would cause him to have a lack of oxygen?"

"I don't know. When I went into the room he was asleep, but looked blue. So I didn't waste any time, I took him to the hospital. They say he's alright."

"Well that's good, but let me tell you what happened to me in court. I had to take a plea bargain for five years, so I won't be coming home for another year."

"What you mean you had to take a plea bargain? I thought you said you didn't have anything to do with that, and you almost got robbed too. What, you lied to me?"

When she said that, I couldn't control my temper and went off on her. "Bitch, you have the got damn nervous to think that I lied to you about a fucking robbery? If any motherfucking thing, you should be mad because I was fucking them, and then sleeping with you at night. Matter of fact, got damn me, you just do your thing, and I'm going to do my time," then I hung up the telephone.

As soon as I got off the telephone, a dude named Kevin said, "You sure told them off."

I jumped to my feet and said, "Bitch, you ear hustling? What, you don't know how to mind your own motherfucking business? You have one mo motherfucking time to disrespect me and it's going to be me and you; and if you want to do something just put your shoes on."

He just stared at me stupid as if he wanted to do something, so without hesitation I punched him in the mouth. We went into a quick mix before the guards came running in there breaking us up. To say we weren't fighting that long, blood was all over us; but I wasn't bleeding.

The guards took us both to the infirmary to make sure we were alright, and to find out what happened. After they seen I wasn't the one bleeding, they asked Kevin, "Do you want to press charges?"

Kevin said, "No, I'm alright. We just had a fight."

That's when the guard asked, "Why were ya'll fighting?"

I just looked at them, and then asked, "Do it really matter what the fuck we was fighting for?"

I guess I made them mad, because they hurried up and threw me in the hole. In away, I think that was the best place for me at the time, besides my blood was already boiling and was just waiting to explode on whomever that up-set-ted me.

I ended up in the hole for fourteen days to be exact. When they let me out, I thought they were about to bring me to a dorm. Instead, they were bringing me out so I could get ready to go to the penitentiary. It was ten of us getting ready to go up that road, and Mike and me just happened to be a part of that ten.

Before we were ready to go, I seen Willie on another chain gang going to court. He said, "You didn't think that you were going to leave without me seeing you did you?"

"To be honest with you, I didn't think I was going to see you. You know, you never know when you going to cross paths with someone in here. Anyway, keep your head up timer."

"I'm going to keep mines up, you just watch yourself up that road. By the way, where you going?

"They haven't told us yet," then Willie was gone and I was still waiting to leave.

I didn't realize until that moment, how much of a liken I token to Willie. Even when we had our differences, he kept me on my toes. To say I was on my way to the penitentiary, I couldn't help laughing to myself about what Willie said he did to be in jail.

He told me that he was out drinking when he decided to go by somebody's house that he was creeping with. He was walking, but didn't realize how drunk he was, or where he was really headed. Before he knew it, he decided to turn back around when he noticed a truck that had lawn mowers and weed eaters in the back of it. The next thing he knew he was taking apart the lawn mower as if it was his, but didn't know the owner was watching him in the window. After he got the lawn mower free, he began walking down the street with it. That was until he had to use the bathroom, and decided to use it on the side of someone's house. He said he was peeing, when he heard what sounded like a woman moaning, so he looked through a window. After watching for a few minutes, he got excited and accidentally hit the air conditioner. That's when all of his troubles came. He was trying to run with the lawn mower and the police was coming up the street. So he was just struck and ended up in jail.

I couldn't control myself from laughing and thinking dope fiends come to jail for some stupid things. Finally, they called us to leave, and I took my last look around me, and then followed the guards out.

Chapter Twenty-Four

Once they had gotten all of us shackled in the van we were riding in, the driver said, "Now listen, you motherfuckers shut the fuck up. Ya'll not on a field trip."

That's when one of the dudes in the back with me said, "If we don't, what you going to do? Give us some more time?" then started laughing.

That really had the driver drove. He just started driving fast and turning the van hard, so that we couldn't do anything but slide into each other and the walls.

When we made it to the penitentiary that we were headed to, I seen that they were still going by the same procedures they were the first time I came into the system. Letting everyone that knew their D.O.C. numbers go ahead, but this time I knew mines so I was able to go. Out of the ten of us that came, only four of us were repeat offenders. Mike wasn't one. So I told him, "You don't have nothing to worry about, we here. It's count down from this point on," then we separated.

After I had gotten processed, I was put in one of the cell blocks, which they called, "Beavers." I knew that we would only be in there up to two weeks, so I was chilling. The only drive was being locked down in a one or two man cell for twenty-three hours with no television or nothing to do; and then having to get out of bed every time the guards would come count.

I ended up sharing cells with an old white man, who looked like he was in there for child molestation. I mean the way he acted, told me he had some sugar in his tank. Besides he never did talk about women, so I stayed watching him because I knew I couldn't trust him as far as I could see him.

Three weeks ended up going by before they called me out of the Beavers. I knew they were about to let me know if I was going to population (What they called the compound. Which only meant I wouldn't be living locked down in a cell.), or getting shipped. They had about sixty of us lined up on the walk waiting to find out where we were going.

They eventually called my name, but I still didn't know where I was going yet. After they finished calling out all the names and separating us, that's when we found out where we were going. I was getting shipped to what was called, "Avoids Correction, or AVC," and Mike was coming along too.

When we arrived there, they made all of us wait in a large room where we were getting the rules of the facility. It was one thing in particular they said, that made me speak my mind and that was, and "Eighty-five percent of the inmates here are HIV positive; if they don't already have full blown Aids."

I couldn't help but questioned and say, "Well why the fuck ya'll ship me here? Ain't nothing wrong with me. I don't have Aids."

One of the guards there said, "I understand that everyone here doesn't have Aids, but it's in all of the facilities. As long as you are not doing anything that you don't have any business doing, then you will be alright. You can't catch it by breathing."

On the inside I still protested against being there, but knew I would be wasting my breath. It was a situation I had to just deal with along with everyone else, regardless of how I felt. Besides, I done already had enough experience with the cell blocks that I wasn't in a hurry to go back to them.

When I finally made it to a dorm that I would be living in, I knew that everything from that point on was serious. I couldn't trust a motherfucker; not even Mike and I came up here with him. I didn't even make it to my bed before a fight broke out. I just said to myself I got to get me a shank because I wasn't trying to fight anybody with Aids. I just was going to kill them.

After I got settled in, I was still watching everybody else. The only person I spoke to, was a lil' dude that slept next to me. His name was Murphy. He put me on top of my game and showed me around.

About a week passed, and I had gotten settled in before I had to start working. When the judge sentenced me to hard labor, she wasn't bull shitting because that field was getting that noise out of me until I caught on. They had us walking about four miles one way, before we even started doing any work. I couldn't wait until my year was up.

The first weekend I had off, seemed like all my problems hit me at once. I couldn't get over how I ended up in prison over some bullshit, and how Keisha had the nerve to accuse me of lying about the fucking robbery. Then I was missing my lil' one. So I decided to write her and let her know how I really felt. Afterwards, Murphy and me ran it.

Murphy ran the story down to me on how he ended up in prison. He was from a small town in Georgia. Him and his cousin decided to come to Louisiana to meet some chicks that they knew that stayed out here. They ended up kicking it with them for a few days like they planned, but ended up spending all of the money they had. In the process, they decided to pull a couple of robberies to get them back home; but things didn't go right. They were robbing a corner store when a group of people walked in while they were in the act so they ran out of the store and jumped into their car and pulled off, but didn't get any money. Next, they tried to rob someone at a club, but couldn't catch anybody slipping, so they gave up on that. Finally, they were about to run out of gas so they said, "Fuck it! We are going to steal some gas, and rob the next gas station we come across." So that's what they did. They were almost out of the state when they decided to rob another gas station, but they didn't know that the police had already gotten their license plates number along with their pictures. So while they were robbing the second gas station, a police car pulled up and recognized the car; and then tied them back to the other robberies. So here he is, doing eight and a half years on a ten years sentence.

About another week passed by before I heard from Keisha. She was telling me how sorry she was for not believing me, but she didn't want anything else to do with me because I kept coming into her life, and then leaving her. I was mad a lil' bit, but I had to respect her mind because I never did plan on doing right by her. Even though she didn't want anything to do with me, she kept sending me letters and pictures of my son so I couldn't really complain.

Mike and me kicked it at times, but to say we were fall partners you wouldn't have been able to tell if you didn't know it. I heard stories that he had supposedly done the robbery, but I didn't know for sure because I heard a lot of stories about things he was supposed to have done and I knew some of them stories wasn't all true.

Again, to say Mike and me were fall partners, I didn't know he knew how to rap until we were kicking it in the field one day. After that we became even cooler and started writing raps together. Next thing I knew, we were doing penitentiary concerts together at random. Other than that, we didn't kick it at all because I didn't trust him.

Over the next few months, I passed my time by lifting weights, and doing push ups. I was getting big and quick, but I kept pushing myself so that when I would come home I knew I would be right. I kept writing Keisha over the months as they went by, but she slowly seemed to stop writing back. Every now and then she still would send me pictures, but I told her to stop after a guard and me got into it over a picture she sent me.

I felt he was not only disrespecting me, but lusting off my pictures even though I told him that she was my wife. He didn't give a fuck about what I was saying, so I took it to his ass. I was beating the fuck out of him, until his backup came. Then they got the best of me.

I ended up going to the cell blocks for that for six months. I thought they were going to take my good time from me, but they didn't so I guess I got off lucky. By the time I made it back to the compound, the guard that I got into it with apologized to me saying he was out of line. I accepted his apology, but I really didn't want to hear that shit he was talking.

Before I knew it, my year was up and it was time for me to come home. I said my byes to those I'd gotten cool with, and then departed the Aids and HIV infested facility. I couldn't be any more happier to be leaving that place, and I damn sure didn't want to go back either.

The guards ended up taking me to the nearest bus station where I had to wait about four hours for the next bus going to New Orleans. To say that I was free, the only thing I was seeing was fields. As much as I hated them now, I didn't mind seeing them now that I didn't have to work in them any more; but I couldn't wait to see some city.

Chapter Twenty-Five

I ended up doing two and a half years on the five year sentence I gotten. The outcome was good compared to how many other crimes I had gotten away with. Over all, the whole situation left me pissed though.

I had already put it in my heart that when I came home, nobody could get shit from me. Besides, they had done all left me struck out. My aces, my dogs, my associates, my folks, my whole lil' click seemed to have just vanished, as if they didn't exist. The only two folks that kept it real with me was my baby mama and Jay Dee; and again I was in need.

I needed a place to stay. I called over to Jay Dee's house and an unfamiliar woman's voice answered the telephone. At first I thought I had dialed the wrong phone number, but then she told me, "Jay Dee is not here; who's calling?"

"This Tj; I can speak to Shantay then?"

"Tj; isn't you the one locked up that they called Boom?"

"Yeah, but who is this?"

"My name is Sandra. I done heard a lot about you. When are you getting out?"

"I don't know what all you done heard about me, but it couldn't have been too good being that I never heard of you or from you unless you have a man, which could explain why."

"It's not like that. I wouldn't even know how to write you or what to wr te about."

"I can understand that, but you are doing a good job in talking to me now to say you still don't know me. Let me ask you something, when would you like for me to be getting out, and if I was too, what then would you do?"

"If I could have it my way, you would be out now. Right now, and what I would do with you words couldn't say. But, it would be all good!"

I couldn't help letting my mind drift off in a sexual fantasy for a split second, then said, "If it's gone be all good, what if I tell you all I need is a ride right now, and we can make that happen. But that's up to you."

"Quit playing with me, because I would come and get you if I thought that was possible, and that's not all I would do!"

"You know it sounds good, but I'm from the Show-Me-State; and seeing is believing. Further more, I'm not about playing games anymore, I done passed that stage in life. If you want to make that happen, all you have to do is come pick me up at the bus station. If not, let me talk to Shantay." I said in a serious tone.

"You serious? What bus station you at?"

"I don't know the name of this bus station. But I do know that if you are coming, it won't take fifteen minutes to pick me up, and be back where you are. So what are you going to do? You can be on your way by now, and we could be doing all them things you said words can't describe, if you not stunting."

"Well let me quit playing with you, here is Shantay and you take care of yourself in there." Sandra said then gave the telephone to Shantay.

Now I felt played on the slick. I didn't even know who Sandra was, but I felt like she just played the fuck out of me. When Shantay got on the phone, the first thing I asked was, "Who the fuck was that?"

Shantay said, "Oh, that's my girl. I told her about you. I know if you were here you would like her."

"Where's Jay Dee at?"

"Oh, he's gone right now, but he should be back in a little while. How are you doing? You need something?"

"Actually, I need two things. First, I need someone to come pick me up from the bus station. Are you going to come get me or what?"

"For real, where are you?"

"Why everybody think I'm playing or something? I'm at the bus station."

This time she knew I was serious and said, "I'm on my way right now."

I didn't know what I was going to do next, but I did know whatever I decided to do it was going to have to keep me out of jail. I was so excited to be out and see women, that I started flirting with every woman that passed by.

Finally, a lil' chick approached me named Angela. Angela was about five feet eight inches; light complexion as if she was half Spanish and half African, with long silky Black hair, and was just about breath taken gorgeous. We talked for a few minutes before she gave me her phone number and told me to call her anytime, but she just didn't know I was going to make it my business to call her.

A couple of minutes later, Shantay pulled up in a dark blue Park Avenue, sitting on what we called Fifties and Vogues, with the music just beating. I didn't even know that was her, until she jumped out of the car and started running towards me, as if I was her best friend in the world.

I couldn't deny it, her greeting made me feel very important and missed, but I couldn't wait to meet her friend, Sandra. I had to let her know, that I don't be faking when I say something, but to my surprise she was there too!

We all chattered on the way back to Jay Dee's crib. Shantay was filling me in on what been going on, while Sandra just sat there as if she couldn't believe they had just picked me up. As bad as I wanted to tell Sandra a thing or two that was on my mind, I couldn't because I knew if I told her off, I wouldn't have been able to fuck her afterwards and I wasn't about to let that happen. But you can damn sure bet I was going to make sure I told her a thing or two afterwards.

When we reached Jay Dee's house, I heard music coming from inside and folks talking as if a party was going on. I couldn't wait to see who else was there. Everybody stared at me as if they had seen a ghost when I walked in. They then asked Shantay and Sandra, "Who is that?"

I can only imagine that I was looking at them the same way. I mean, it was nothing but females in the room, and I was the only male; fresh from prison. In the penitentiary, a man would go broke just to be in my shoes for a few minutes.

They all started introducing themselves to me, while Shantay yelled in the back room to Jay Dee and told him to come see, she had a surprise for him! Out of all of Shantay's friends, the ones that caught my attention were: Rachel, Brenda, Monica, and of course Sandra. Knowing me, I figured in due time, I'd get a chance to be with each one of them.

When Jay Dee walked in the room, his eyes got big, then he said, "Damn, when you got out?" and hugged me.

"You know they couldn't hold me forever. I just got out today."

"You want to smoke something? As a matter of fact, baby, go get that bottle of Hennessy and bring it to him. I know it's your favorite drink."

"I'm surprised you remembered what I liked, as long as I've been gone G."

"Now how you expect me to just forget what you like? You're the one that got me on this shit! Oh yeah, James is in the back!"

I made my way to the backroom with the bottle of Hennessy in my hand, and a joyful feeling to be back home. When I got in the room, I seen James was weighting some weed but he didn't look back to see it was me that entered the room instead of Jay Dee so I asked him, "Is it weighting right?"

He turned around quick as a motherfucker when he heard my voice; and then said, "Man you spooked the fuck out of me. When did you get out?"

"I just got out today; but I can see since I've been gone you done changed a lot. When I left you maybe blew a blunt or two, but other than that you were chasing behind your girl. Now you are hustling. What happened like that?"

James replied, "You know how it is. Everybody was doing good out here, and I was just settling for less. It was time for me to come up. Besides, you've been gone."

"Well, do your thang and handle your business," I told him, and then walked back out of the room.

I don't know if it was the Hennessy kicking in or by me just getting out, but I felt out of place in a sense. I mean before I went upstate I was the man with the dope, but now I see my folks been handling their business and I got to turn to them for assistance. That's how it be happening though. You ball until you fall; then while you're gone, you got to respect the next man's game when they balling and let them do their thang.

Finally, Jay Dee walked up to me and said, "You not finished with that bottle yet? I got some weed that's so good, you going to have to smoke it by yourself though G. When you finished with that bottle, you got another one in there to get you right."

"G, you trying to get me fucked up for real! I just got out. My systems not ready for all of this. Plus, as bad as I want to smoke me some weed, I can't even do it. I haven't gone to see my parole officer yet, and you know how that is. But check this out; I need you to do me a favor."

"G, name it and consider it done. What you need?"

"Folks, you know I just got out, and right now I need a place to stay. I don't want to intrude on you and your family, but you're my only hope right now."

"I can't do nothing for you, so you just assed out on that!" After he told me that, he just looked at me for a moment and then just busted out laughing and said, "G, that's all you wanted? I don't even know why you standing there asking me something like that for. You know off top you can stay here. You didn't even have to ask that. What's mine is yours. What ever you need I got you!"

When he said that, I knew he was serious. I was just grateful he was keeping it real with me unlike others whom seemed to turn sour when they got a hold of a lil' change. That's when I told him. "I ain't forgot what you did for me while I was down; and I'm damn sure ain't gone forget this."

"G, I told you whatever I got consider it yours. If it wasn't for you, I wouldn't be doing this good now more than likely so drink up. I know you want to fuck something and all of them hoes in there are freaks! You can fuck any one of them hoes, if not at the same time. So handle your business, and tomorrow after you go see your P.O. I got something for you."

I had the slightest ideal what he could have had for me, but that wasn't important to me right then. That Hennessy had kicked in and I was ready to fuck somebody's daughter and it wasn't a secret. I asked Jay Dee, "Which one of them you think I could fuck right now without that extra bull shit?"

He just laughed at me and replied, "Which ever one you pick. I told you, you probably can sleep with all of them at the same time they ain't nothing but some hoes. But look, just chill with them for a minute and let me and James finish handling that business."

I said, "That's cool with me, but you never did tell me how you got James from chasing behind his girl."

He just laughed and walked back into the back room and laughed some more as he said, "I got it from you; you taught me everything I know!"

I went back in the front where Shantay and her friends were and clowned around with them. They were smoking blunt after blunt and drinking, but what was fucking me up was before I left Shantay didn't smoke weed, now here she was talking about, "Blow me a charge."

I was like, "Damn, when you start getting down? Before I left, we were barely able to smoke around you."

She just blushed and said, "I can't believe you not smoking! You want some more to drink, or something to eat?"

"I'm alright, but I do need some Blacks."

Rachel said, "I got you," and gave me a Black.

I told her, "Thank you," and sat back looking at her and the rest of her friends, but only now all of them looked like they could fulfill any man's sexual needs.

I mean hours went by while we were just kicking it, listening to music, and talking shit before we started watching a movie. I was so fucked up that it felt like the room was spinning and I couldn't stop it. I went to the bathroom about twenty times already, but still I had to use it again. This time when I went in, Brenda walked in while I was pissing.

I done became so use to having folks always around me, that when she came in I just looked at her but didn't say anything. I thought she was going to walk back out and close the door, instead she closed the door and said, "That's a shame your dick sticking up like that."

When Brenda said that I said, "What can I say? I'm in a house full of girls and I ain't had sex in damn near three years; plus I been drinking that Hen."

She barely let me finish that statement before she just grabbed my dick and began kissing me. I thought I was going to nut right then and there as good as it was feeling to have a woman playing with my dick while kissing me. I stuck my hand under her shirt and began playing with her breasts until her nipples began to poke out. Then I lifted up her shirt completely and began sucking them.

All of a sudden, Monica just burst into the bathroom on us. She said, "That's a shame," but she didn't leave out of the bathroom nor close the door. She just stood there watching as if seeing us was turning her on.

Finally Brenda told Monica, "Come in and close the door."

I didn't know what to expect. In my mind I was saying, "Ain't this a bitch! At least I could have nutted." But to my surprise, Brenda and Monica must have been messing around on the low, because as soon as Monica closed the door they began kissing. I just knew it was about to go down then.

They stopped kissing and looked at me as if they were about to rape me, but I was all for it. This time Monica kissed me while Brenda began licking me on my ear. Before I knew it they both were sucking and licking my dick and balls. As soon as they started doing that I came instantly, and like some professionals they sucked and licked me dry. I thought I was going to pass out or fall, that's how good it was feeling. When they finished they began kissing again. I said to myself, "They should be getting paid for shit like that.

Now I was completely lost of time. I don't know how long we were in the bathroom, but I knew I was satisfied. When we went back into the living room Sandra stared at me as if to say, I know you didn't do what I think you just did. Shantay looked at me smiling, and then said, "Tj, you feeling good now?"

"Got damn me, I can't complain at all, but I need to go to the store. I got to get me some Blacks. I'm ready to blow and I can't."

"You don't have to go to the store for that, I keep plenty of them." Shantay said. She got up and walked towards the kitchen and I followed behind. When we got in the kitchen she said, "You handle your business with my girls?"

"Got damn me, what you think?"

"I know your sexy ass was going too. Welcome home! You want something to eat while I'm in here?"

"I'm straight. I just want some Blacks and your girls." I said, and then we both laughed because we both knew I was serious.

When we went back into the living room Jay Dee and a few more homies were all in there with bottles of liquor and weed. That's when Jay Dee said, "I know you didn't think we wasn't going to celebrate you coming home G. Drink up, this for you. Oh yeah, I didn't know if you had any Blacks, so I got you a case. It's in that bag on the sofa."

I don't know if it was the loud music beating or all the drinking I was doing, but I had caught a bad headache. Rachel must have seen something was wrong with me because she asked, "What's wrong with you? You was just kicking it a minute ago, now you acting as if you don't want to be here."

"I have a real bad headache, and it's driving me."

"That's all? I thought you wasn't enjoying yourself. I have some medicine that will make you forget all about that headache, let me get my purse." When she came back she told me, "Take it with beer it will knock it out quicker."

By the time I finished my beer my headache was gone and I guess I must have passed out. I think!

Chapter Twenty-Six

*T*he next morning when I woke up, I was lost. I didn't have on any clothes, didn't know where I was at, and there were three hoes in the bed with me that I didn't know. I mean I was trying to figure out what was going on and where I was at, but I didn't want to move because I didn't know who else was in the room. Besides, my dick was halfway in one of the hoe's mouth and I guess it was one of her friends laying across me with her breast almost touching my lips. While the other lil' chick's head was between my legs. All I could think was, *I must have had a good night,* even though I didn't remember it.

Finally, I made up my mind on what I was going to do. I woke up the chick that was laying across me. When she woke up she started to kiss me, but I pulled away from her and said, "Hold on lil' momma, who is you? Better yet, where are we and who the hell are they?"

She looked at me and said, "That's fucked up! You forgot my name already? I'm Nicole."

"I'm sorry if I offended you Nicole, but got damn me I got the slightest idea who the hell you are, or how I ended up in here with ya'll."

"You really don't remember last night?"

Before I could answer her back, the chick that had my dick in her mouth woke up damn near biting my shit. She kissed my dick then said, "I'm sorry about that; you alright? What time is it?"

She fucked me all the way up how she was acting. I mean she just woke up as if it was nothing to have a stranger's dick in her mouth. Nicole answered her saying, "Girl it's just eleven thirty."

"Damn! Get up Rose, you supposed to drop your momma off at work before twelve." She replied.

Finally Rose woke up, "Girl, fuck! What you want?"

"Bitch you better get your ass up, it's almost twelve o'clock and you suppose to bring your momma to work," the chick said while getting dressed herself.

By the time we all got dressed I asked Nicole, "Where are we?"

"We in the Hilton Inn, but we got to check out by twelve and it's damn near that now. What you gone do?"

"I got to go check in with my parole officer before I do anything else today. Why, what's up with you? What you getting into?"

"Well, me and Gold Dee got to make a run to Pensacola, but we should be back by tonight. You want to hook up with us?"

"Who's Gold Dee?"

"That's me!" the one who had my dick in her mouth said.

"Well that's on ya'll. Holla' at me when ya'll get back." Then I thought about it, I didn't want to give them Jay Dee's home number so I asked them, "Ya'll have a number I can get in touch with ya'll?"

Nicole pulled out a piece of paper and wrote three phone numbers on it then said, "Call whenever you want because we have to do this again."

I took the phone numbers then asked Rose, "Where do your momma work at?"

"In the state building on the other side. Why do you ask?"

"If you don't mind, that's the same building I have to go check in at, and I needed a ride there so I wanted to ride with you if that's cool with you."

"Well come on, I don't want to hear my momma mouth about why I'm late."

Before we left she told Gold Dee and Nicole to, "Make sure ya'll call me when ya'll get back."

Rose and me made small talk on the way to pick up her mother, but I was still trying to figure out how I ended up with them across the river. Once we got to her mother's house, I got out of the front seat and jumped into the back. Her mother said, "You didn't have to get in the back for me. What is your name anyway?"

"My name is Tj, and I was just showing you my respect," I stated.

I guess she could hear the accent in my voice because the next thing she asked me was, "Where are you from? I can tell that you are not from here."

"St. Louis."

"St. Louis? Where is that at?"

"That's in Missouri. Two states north from here."

"What are you doing down here? Never mind, it's none of my business." Rose's momma said.

I just left it at that because I didn't feel like making up a lie to tell her. We arrived at the state building at exactly twelve o'clock. I got out and opened the door for Rose's momma, then told Rose, "Thank you for bringing me up here too."

"It wasn't a problem. Are you going to need a ride when you are finished with what you have to do here?" Rose asked.

"Naw; thank you anyway. I can make it from here." I replied, and then asked, "Am I going to see you tonight?"

"Most likely you will, if you are not too busy."

"Well, I guess I'll see you tonight. So let me let you go so I can get this bullshit over with and get out of here."

I went into the building to see my parole officer. Once I got inside of the Parole and Probation office, I had a feeling something was wrong. I guess it was because it was the second time I was coming to get a probation officer that I didn't want to be bothered with.

Finally, an older man called me, and then lead me into a smaller room which was in the back. He introduced himself as Mr. Cromer, and then told me, "I will be your parole officer until further notice." After that he began asking me questions that he already knew the answers too, so I just nodded my head in agreement to everything he said.

I was in his office going on three hours now, so I knew he should have been wrapping it up. That's when Mr. Cromer said, "I need you to do one more thing for me. It shouldn't take no more than five minutes."

I quickly asked, "What's that?"

"I need you to give me a urine sample for a test before you leave." And then he handled me a container.

I took the cup and asked him, "Where you want me to take the test at?"

"Right here."

So I pissed in the container to complete the test, and then reached over the desk and handed him the cup. After that I asked him, "Is that it?"

He said, "Wait one minute, I have to get the results." He sat the container on its side, and then asked me, "What are the results going to tell me?"

I already knew that I had alcohol in my system so I said, "It's going to show you that I had a drink when I got out, but that's it."

"Well there's nothing wrong with a drink every now and then, but your sure that's all I'm going to find?"

"That's it, and to be exact I was drinking some Hennessy if you care to know" I responded.

He picked up the container and studied the results. After a moment he said, "You sure you don't have anything else you would like to tell me before I tell you the results?"

"Not that I can think of, besides when is the next time I have to come and see you?"

"We are going to get to that. But first, I want to let you know the results of your urine test. You turned out to be negative on all substances except for two of them. Alcohol, which you explained. But, if you don't mind would you care to explain why the results are also showing that you are positive for codeine in your system?" Mr. Cromer asked.

"Codeine in my system! Unless it's in Hennessy, I don't know what you are talking about Mr. Cromer."

That's when he said, "You know that I can violate you right this moment and have you back in the Department of Corrections before the day turns to night don't you? So why don't you try telling me the truth."

"I'm telling you the truth Mr. Cromer, you must be reading the results wrong. All that should be in my system is alcohol. Honestly." I replied looking at him in his eyes.

That's when he asked me, "What all have you done since you been released?"

I started telling him all that I remembered which wasn't much. All the way up to the part of me walking into his office. When I finished telling him about my night he asked me the same question that I had been trying to figure out, "How did you end up with three women in a hotel that you don't know?" I still didn't have an answer. I just sat there looking dumb. That's when he said, "I'm not going to violate you this time, but I want to see you next week. If you are dirty then I will violate you and send you back to prison. Get out of here!"

He didn't have to tell me that twice, I hurried up and left his office. On the inside, I was pissed off. I couldn't wait to get in touch with Jay Dee. The first pay phone I seen open, I stopped and called his house.

Chapter Twenty-seven

*I*t was just my luck that Shantay answer the phone. The first thing I asked was, "Where is Jay Dee?"

Shantay said, "He not here, who is calling?"

"I been gone that long that you don't know my voice?" I replied.

"Oh, what's up baby? You know I know who you was. Where are you?"

"I'm at the state building. Can you get in touch with Jay Dee and tell him I'm waiting on him?"

"That's not a problem. Do you want me to come pick you up?"

"No, but thank you anyway. I really need to see Jay Dee."

After I got off the phone with Shantay, I was trying to recall what all happened last night. I was only able to recall up to the point when Jay Dee and some homies came over. After that I was lost.

I was so fair gone in my own thoughts, that I didn't even hear Rose's mother talking to me. "Tj. Tj, you alright baby?"

"Oh I'm sorry; I didn't even know you were talking to me."

"Your name is Tj isn't it?"

"Yes ma'am."

"Whatever you were thinking about, I hope you figured it out. Anyway, what are you doing up here? Rose outside already?"

"I really don't know. I had to take care of a few things myself up here. I can check to see if Rose is here for you if you want me to."

"Oh you don't have too. I'm not ready yet anyway. You take care of yourself and I guess I'll see you again."

"The same to you Mrs.... I didn't catch your name," I replied.

"Mrs. Smith," she said.

"Well, Mrs. Smith, you take care of yourself and I will see you again." I replied.

I was hoping Jay Dee would pull up soon; I was ready to get away from the state building before my parole officer changed his mind about violating me. I knew if Shantay had gotten in touch with Jay Dee, he would be on his way.

I pulled out a Black & Mild and started smoking it, when a black F-150 pulled up in front of me. The windows were tinted, so I didn't know who was inside of it. I started walking back and forth thinking where the fuck Jay Dee at. I was just about to walk back in the state building when Jay Dee let down the window and said, "What, you want to get in?"

I looked at him for a second, and then said, "Why didn't you let me know it was you? Who's this truck for anyway?" I asked as I climbed in and shut the door.

"This mines, but I thought you seen me."

"Now you know can't nobody see you behind that tint, what you trying to be funny? Anyway G, what the fuck happen last night? The last thing I remember, I was at your house. When I got up this morning I was in a hotel across the river, with three hoes in the bed with me. Then I almost got violated today for having codeine in my system, and you know damn well I ain't trying to go back up that road. Tell me something! I didn't smoke no weed; but I can't tell you what happened?"

"Cool down G! You ate anything?"

"Cool down! Got damn me, if I would have gotten violated, there ain't a motherfucking thing nobody could have done for me. I would be the one doing the time."

"Look," he said while driving, "I don't know how you ended up with codeine in your system. Last night, I brought you out. I knew you wanted to fuck something, so I introduced you to Gold Dee, Rose, and Nicole. They were digging on you, so I figured what the fuck and got a room. I knew you would be alright, because they work for us. I told them not to give you anything but a good time, and something to drink. So how you got codeine in you, I don't know."

I thought about what Jay Dee said, and it sounded like something he would do, even though I didn't remember leaving with him. Finally I said, "You said they work for us?"

"Yeah, I got them doing drops for us. That way if something goes wrong, we won't be in the mix of things. I learn that from you." Jay Dee said then pulled into Copeland's parking lot.

We went into Copeland's, and then Jay Dee said, "Get whatever you want to eat, but I think you would enjoy the fish and shrimp platter. In fact, that's what I'm going to get."

I said, "That sounds good right now. I haven't had that in a long time."

After we ordered our food Jay Dee said, "I told you I had something for you yesterday, if you remember or not." Then he made a phone call. When whoever it was on the other end answered, he said, "Bring that, we waiting on you," then hung up the phone.

I couldn't help but ask, "Who was that; and what are they suppose to be bringing?"

All Jay Dee said was, "Be cool! I told you I got something for you. Trust me. I know you going to like it."

"You know I don't like surprises and I damn sure don't like being in the dark on things. Whatever you got coming, I hope it's worth it G."

"Damn, Boom! Don't get uptight on me now. What you want some Hennessy? Better yet, let me get you a bottle of Moet. You straight with me G." he replied then ordered the Moet.

My mind was racing trying to figure out what he had planned. I couldn't help but to be curious because I knew Jay Dee was like me so I had to be prepared for anything at any given time regardless of the consequences that came with it; and that's what I didn't like, but I played it cool anyway.

When the bottle came, Jay Dee said, "Drink up G! Maybe that will help you relax."

I took a nice swig then said, "Oh yeah, when did you get that truck G? That bitch clean."

"I got that a few months before you got out, but don't nobody know I got it except for you. That's my duck off ride."

"Yes indeed!" I said. "You learned from me. Tell me something, and be real with me. I know you are doing your thing right now, but have you ever thought of investing your money in something else as well?"

Jay Dee sat there for a minute as if thinking about what I asked him, and then said, "Really, I haven't. I wonder how it would have been if we would have signed that contract with G Money Records. Then I ask myself, what do I really want from slanging, but I don't have a clue. Its like I'm addicted to the lifestyle."

I knew that he was falling victim to greed, because I done been down that same road. What made it bad though, I didn't know how to help him with me being broke. What I did know, was at some point he was going to have to choose when to give it up. So I told him, "Think about another way we could get paid G. I know this might sound funny coming from me, but we could be getting paid and wouldn't have to worry about the laws being on us. You feel me?"

He said, "I don't know about that G, but right now I'm bringing in a hundred G's a week at ease. So I can't see giving up the game." I was about to ask him something, when he cut me off and said, "Your surprise is here. Meet Paula and Delia."

I said "Hello," but I was staring at them as if they worked for the laws.

I guess Jay Dee was able to read my mind, because he said, "G, it's cool, they work for us."

I just looked at him as if to say don't involve me with these hoes. I don't know them and don't trust them. Besides, how could I? They walked up wearing business suits, carrying two suitcases, and I had never met them before. For all I know they could have been the F.B.I. and Jay Dee just told me he was making a hundred thousand dollars a week. I told them, "Excuse me for a second, I'll be right back," then looked at Jay Dee with death in my eyes.

I walked as if I was headed towards the restroom, and then walked clean out of the building. I looked around to see if I recognized any laws or undercovers watching, because at this point I didn't trust anybody. I put it in my mind if anything went wrong, I was going to kill Delia, Paula, and if it came down to it, Jay Dee with no hesitation.

After a couple of minutes I went back into the restaurant. Jay Dee asked me, "You alright G?"

I looked at him, and then said, "I'm straight."

That's when Jay Dee said, "Lets get down to business then. This is Delia and Paula. Paula is in charge of making sure all of the money is right when workers bring it in, and Delia's job is to bond any of our workers out if something was to go wrong," he began before I could cut him off.

"How many workers do you have all together?" I asked.

Paula answered, "It's ten of us all together, twelve if you count you and Jay Dee."

I said, "I hope you all don't mind, but before we go any further, I need to know for a fact I can trust ya'll. Paula and Delia come with me for a second," then I lead them to the restroom.

Jay Dee just sat there as if trying to figure out what I was about to do, but he didn't say anything.

Delia asked, "Where are we going?"

When we got to the restroom I said, "In here," then waited on them to enter it.

When we got into the restroom I locked the door, and Paula and Delia asked at the same time, "What's going on?"

"Before we do any business both of ya'll have to strip. Get out of everything. If this is a problem feel free to leave; but don't return." They looked at me like are you serious, then began undressing. After I seen that they didn't have on a wire I told them, "Get dressed. I hope you understand; but I can't take any chances with just anybody. You feel me?"

Delia said, "It's cool, I understand."

Once they got back dressed, we went back to the table where Jay Dee was waiting. He said, "Is everything cool now?"

"4-sho! I just had to make sure you wasn't slipping. It can't hurt to be cautious. You feel me?"

"I told you, I learned everything from you. But anyway, let me give you your surprise, but before I do that, Paula and Delia, I'll get in touch with ya'll later on." They excused themselves, and then he went on, "I never did find out what all happen, that caused you to go to jail. At the same time, if it wasn't for you I wouldn't have shit. Therefore to show you my life I'll give it, and love I have plenty. I remained loyal to you for blessing me with the gift to understand the game G. When I came home that night I didn't know what all you done got into, but I felt bad because I wasn't there. When my girl told me what you gave her. I knew it was serious. What I found amazing was, you the only mother fucker I know that would give it to me and say I didn't owe you anything. Everybody else would've tried to tax me, but you kept it real with me from jump. In them suitcases right there, is a hundred G's a piece, and that's all yours G. Just say your money was well invested. So what you want to do now?"

I was all fucked up now. I didn't expect for him to break bread with me like that, and just to think I was willing to make his blood spill a few moments ago. I had to remain silent for a minute, then I said, "Love, you done shown it, and loyalty you done proved it. Even your life you done gave it, so in exchange my life you done earned it. As for what I want to do, I want you to slow down. If you can afford to give me two hundred thousand like this, you got to be straight. Besides, you already making a hundred G's a week, you can afford to chill. If you are going to stick with the game, at least wash your hands and name. Meaning, run it; but don't have any direct hand dealing in it. Just think about what I'm saying. You have too much to lose G."

"I can feel you on that G, but I can't just stop. As for me washing my hands and name, I don't know anybody that will run it right or like I would, so that's not going to be an easy thing to do. Maybe in time, but you mean to tell me you don't want to do nothing?"

"Well check this out, I want you to take me shopping, I need some gear anyway. Besides, I had this on since I got out, and you know that ain't me. After that, you can take me to see my son, if you have time."

"I tell you what I'll do, when we finish eating, I'll take you shopping and pay for it. That way you can invest your ends however you want to. When we finish that, you can either go buy you a ride or just drop me off and we will hock up later."

"That's cool with me."

After eating, Jay Dee took me shopping at the mall. When I tell you he got me every kind of outfit and shoes that I wanted, I mean he went all out. I remember when I was able to do that, but now my lil' partner the man.

When we were done shopping he told me, "Drop me off at the storage on Manhatten, and when you are done doing whatever else you going to do, bring my truck back up here and call me. I'm going to come and get you."

"4-sho," I told him, then proceeded to take him to the storage.

On the way there I stopped to purchase a cellular phone at Radiotelephones. It was at that moment that I realized that I didn't have Jay Dee's cellular phone number. So I asked him for it, but instead of writing it down I told him, "Just call my phone, that way I'll know that I have it," then gave him my phone number. After that I dropped him off at the storage, and headed to Keisha's house.

Chapter Twenty-eight

I didn't really want to see Keisha; I just wanted to see my son because I was missing him. Besides, I knew he was getting older, and I knew from first hand experience how it felt not to have my father in my life. That was something I didn't want him to experience in life. I really didn't know what I was going to say, so I figured I'd just go with the flow and see what happens.

When I got to her house I knocked on the door, but was surprised when a man answered the door. "May I help you?" he asked.

"Is Keisha here?" I replied.

"Hold on one second," he said and then went and called Keisha. Now I didn't know who the fuck he was. He had me waiting outside as if I wasn't welcome there, so I couldn't wait for Keisha to come to the door.

When she finally did come, the first thing I asked was, "Who is that?"

She hesitated, then pulled the door close and said, "That's my fiancé. I'm about to get married in a few months."

"Damn! That's your fiancé, and your about to get married? What else done change around here? Better yet, congratulations; I wish you happiness if that's what you want. By the way, what's his name?" I said in shock.

"His name is Tony. My friend at the Kingdom Hall hooked me up with him."

"The Kingdom Hall! What's that?"

"Oh, I didn't tell you that I gave my life to Jehovah. I'm a Jehovah Witness now. You should come along to the Kingdom Hall and change your life."

"Look, its good you found God and about to get married; but I don't know nothing about no Jehovah Witness. I tell you what though; I am trying to change my life because I'm tired of going to prison. I might just go there with you if your fiancé don't mind. Now I don't want to be intruding on ya'll, I just want to visit my son if you don't mind."

"Sure you can see your son; that boy getting bad. Let me go and get him for you," and then she went into the house and called him.

When he came to the door, I saw that he had grown a lot. I didn't know what to say to him or where to begin. I was just looking at him thinking damn he look just like a little me. Finally Keisha broke the silence between us and said, "Say hello to your daddy."

He just looked at me like who are you? That's when I said, "Hello Threat, I'm your daddy. How are you doing?"

"That's not my name. My name is Tiarell and you're not my daddy. Where is Tj at?"

When he said I'm not his daddy I was so hurt; but then to hear him call me Tj didn't make the situation any better. I looked at Keisha like, *Bitch; you got him calling me by my name.* After that I told him, "I know that your name is Tiarell James Green; and I am your daddy. I'm Tj!"

"You not Tj. How you know my name?"

I tried to explain to him who I was, but I knew that would take some time. Regardless of how long it would take me to get my son to understand who I was, I wasn't going to stop until he knew me without a doubt.

When I finished talking to him I told him he could go play. That's when I started telling Keisha what was on my mind. "How are you going to have my son calling me by my name? What the fuck did you do with the pictures I was sending him? I know he couldn't have gotten them if he don't know who I am. What the fuck, you got my son calling your fiancé daddy?"

"No, I let him know that you are his daddy."

"I can't tell!"

"As far as the pictures you were sending, me and Tony got into it over them, so I got rid of them."

By this time, Tony came outside and asked, "What's going on?"

That's when I said, "Got damn me, I don't give a fuck about what you and Keisha do, but when I send my son any motherfucking thing, he better damn sure get it or we gone have problems! You feel me? I don't have a problem with you being with her, but don't interfere with me and my son because I'll go all out for mine," then stared at him so that he'd know I was serious.

Tony said, "I understand where you are coming from. I was just making sure my baby didn't have a problem out here."

"I'm alright." Keisha said, "You can go back in and I'll be in there in a minute."

I could tell that he was uncomfortable with me being present with Keisha alone so I said, "Oh yeah, Tony that's your name right?"

"Yeah."

"Congratulations on your wedding to come. You got a good woman if you don't know it."

He just looked at me and said, "Thank you. I know I got a good woman, at least I look at her like a blessing" then walked in the house.

Once he was gone I told Keisha, "Look, I'm going to let you get back to your family. I just wanted to see my son, and I'm going to be coming to get him so let your fiancé know it. Other than that, I don't have anything else to tell you except that if my son needs something let me know. I got a phone number you can reach me at, but I don't have any paper to write the number on."

"Hold on, let me go get a piece of paper and pencil," then she walked in the house and I jumped in the truck. When she came back, she didn't see me inside the truck so I stepped out. She said, "That's a nice truck. That's for you?"

"No. This is Jay Dee's truck. He just let me use it. Anyway, let me write this number down for you. You can call anytime. That's my number" after I wrote down the number I told her, "Take care of yourself and if you still want me to go to the Kingdom Hall with you, just let me know when," then I left.

Chapter Twenty-nine

I didn't know what I was going to do next. For some reason, this day seemed to have more surprises than I could deal with. I still hadn't taken a shower or changed clothes, and that's something that I should have been and done. I just wanted to be by my self for awhile to get my thoughts together.

I started thinking of all the things I could remember that had happened since I got out, but there was still one thing bothering me that I couldn't figure out. How I'd ended up with codeine in my system? I felt like in a sense, that somebody was hoping I would go back to prison, but I didn't know who it was, or why. That's when I called Jay Dee.

Ring. Ring. "Hello!"

"You ready for your truck G?"

"You finished doing what you wanted to do already?"

"Personally, I just want to get a room, take a long hot bath, and gather my thoughts in peace."

"Everything alright with you; huh?"

"I'm straight. I just need to be by myself for a little while; I been having a long day. You feel me?"

"I feel you. Well check this out, go ahead and keep the truck and we'll hook up tomorrow. I'm gone holla' at you."

By the time we hung up, I was pulling up at the Marriot Hotel and decided that was where I was going to rent a room for the night. As I walked into the lobby and was looking around, I figured this was going to be the best spot for what I was looking for. As I approached the desk clerk, I noticed that she was looking at me as if I didn't belong in here, then she asked me, "May I help you?"

"If you can, I'll like to get a presidential suite for tonight."

"Are you sure? It cost four hundred and fifty dollars a night, plus a three hundred dollar deposit."

"That's it? Well, let me get that and have a bottle of Crystal and Aliza' sent up."

"Will you be paying cash or using a credit card?"

"Cash!" then I realized that I didn't have that much money on me so I said, "Can you hold on one moment? I forgot my bag," then I ran back to the truck and removed a stack of money from the suite case, and grabbed one of the bags of clothes I had. I then re-entered the lobby. I told the desk clerk, "I'm sorry for having you wait. How much did you say the room was?"

"For a presidential suite like you wanted, it will cost you four hundred and fifty dollars a night, plus a three hundred dollar deposit. Are you sure you want it?" she asked sarcastically.

"Yeah, and don't forget to send the bottles up like I requested," and then I gave her a thousand dollars and told her sarcastically, "You look like you could use the change, so keep it!"

When I got into the suite, it was more than I could ask for. I started running me some bath water while I was waiting on my requests to come. In the process I found Angela's phone number in my pocket and figured I'd call her to see what she was about.

When I got in touch with Angela, she didn't have the slightest idea who I was. So I said, "Damn you must have a lot of friends or do you just give your number to anybody?"

"You take it the way you want to take it. Who is this anyway?"

"This Tj."

"I don't know a Tj. Where do I suppose to know you from?"

"Damn, you don't remember me? I just met you the other day. Infact, you came on to me."

"Oh, you the one I met at the bus station. I'm sorry. How are you doing? I was wondering when you were going to call."

At that moment I started to hang up because I knew she was lying and I didn't like dealing with a lying ass bitch. Instead of hanging up on her I said, "I'm glad you remember me, but anyway. I'm alright I guess."

"You guess! What's wrong with you?"

"It's been a long day, and I wanted someone to chill with. What's up with you?"

"I'm sorry to hear you having a bad day. Mines not going all that good either; so I was just chilling."

"Well since you are not dong anything, why don't you let me come and get you? At least then I'll be able to get to know you better."

"That sounds cool, but how are you going to come and get me?"

"Don't worry about that. When will you be ready?"

"I'm ready now."

"So what's your address then?"

"2974 Manhatten Blvd."

"You said 2974 Manhatten Blvd.? That's right down the street. I'll be there in fifteen minutes."

"Is that water I hear running in the back ground?"

"Yeah. I was about to jump in the tub. Hold on a minute," I said and then I went and answer the door. It was just the bellboy bringing my requests. I threw him a twenty dollar tip, and then jumped back on the phone, "Hello."

"I'm still here, but like I was about to say, why don't you put that bath on hold, come get me and let me wash you?"

"Check this out, you don't have to say no more. I'll be there in six minutes; just be ready." Then I hung up and left.

On the way out, I bumped into a fine white girl that I thought I recognized from the restaurant today. She gave me her room number, and then told me, "Come by if you like, I'm going to be alone."

I thought about it, but decided to go get Angela as planned. When she had told me her address, I knew exactly where she lived, so I found her house with no problem. When I pulled up she was standing outside, and invited me in. I told her, "I don't want to go in your house with me smelling bad. I told you I was getting ready to take a bath."

"It's cool; let's push then."

Once we pulled off I asked her, "Is there anything you need before we get where we're going?"

"Something to drink would be nice. Anyway, I thought you just got out; how you get a new truck?"

"Be cool on that, it ain't for me." As soon as I answered her, I could have swore I'd seen a ghost. I mean I just seen someone that looked like a person who I knew was doing thirty years at least and had to do half of it. But that couldn't have been him especially not around here. I just let that go, when she broke my concentration by placing her hand on my lap. I removed her hand and told her, "Chill out, we're almost where we're going."

When we pulled up at the hotel, she said, "What are we doing here?"

"This where I'm staying for now."

When we entered the room, she was tripping off how luxurious the room was like I did when I first entered. Then she said, "I know you have something to drink in here."

I pointed to the mini bar and said, "Help yourself, but I got some Crystal and Aliza' in that bucket; that's what I'm going to drink on."

As I started to undress, I was thinking of all the ways I was going to deal with her. Then I told her, "When you done fixing our drinks, help yourself out of them clothes and into the bathroom; unless you want me to help undress you myself." Then I walked into the bathroom butt naked, feeling her eyes on me. I knew I was going to have a hell of a night.

When she came into the bathroom, I couldn't help but think to myself that this was one fine ass bitch, and I had to keep her on my team. I felt like I was in a dream when she passed me my drink and stepped into the tub then begun to scrub my entire body. My dick was on hard and I was ready to go with this bitch, but I had to take my time with her and show her that no other man was going to satisfy her the way that I could.

As she finished washing me down, I took the sponge from her beautiful hands and asked her, "Mind me returning the favor?"

She told me, "I'm yours for the night baby, so do as you please."

I had to smile, and then told her, "You won't be sorry Angela. I'm going to make you wetter than you've ever been."

I washed her fine ass from head to toe, and kissed her in every spot that my lips could reach. I had to stop when I caught myself eating that beautiful pussy longer than I had planned on. Anyway, when we finished taking our bath, we stepped out of the tub. As we were drying each other off, I got down on my knees and began tonguing that pretty ass pussy of hers again. As soon as I knew for sure that she was caught up all into the moment, I stopped. Then I asked her, "Have you ever had this much pleasure before?" Then begin to slowly tease her body. She claimed that no one had ever ate her pussy before. I stopped and asked her to turn around for me and started to kiss her neck, ears, and caress her nice firm tits as she started to jack me off.

I couldn't take it any more, so I gently pushed her towards the counter and made her lean over it. She just stared at me through the mirror and I couldn't help but notice that she appeared to be a bit nervous. That's when I told her, "Don't worry boo, I'm not going to hurt you. I promise you that this is going to be pure ecstasy for you." She closed her eyes and let out a big smile and nodded at me, giving me the green light to go ahead and fuck her for everything she was worth.

She looked back up at me at the same time she arched her back and tilted her big ass up at me. I grabbed my dick and rubbed the head all over her soft ass wet pussy. She just trembled, and the let out a moan of pleasure and pain as I penetrated her slowly inch by inch. I then was definitely sure that I was going to have to make her my permanent girl because I knew I had just entered a virgin pussy; and I loved it.

I was ready to cum, but I held it back. I had to please this girl. This was her first time, and it was with me. That pussy was first class, and I was her first man ever. The only thing that was going through my mind was how tight that pussy was, and how fine this girl named Angela was. I stopped to turn her ass over on her back, and then it all began. I put her legs as far back as possible, allowing me the deepest penetration inside her.

When I put my dick in her all the way, she started to yell and moan so loud I couldn't help but to feel like the badest motherfucker alive. She open her legs even more, giving me the best fuck ever. My nuts were slapping all over her big round ass, and it was at that time I couldn't stop myself from cumming, but she beat me to it. She had one of the most powerful orgasms I had ever experienced with any girl. She actually came in gushes and I let my nut go deep inside of her warm vise grip pussy.

When we finished, we laid across the bed as if we were both wore out; then began talking. On the inside I was still tripping off how I just put that dick down on her; replaying what we did over and over. Finally she said, "You know you are the first man I ever been with. Where do we go from here?"

"Just because we had sex, that don't change nothing. You think I would have brought you here if I didn't want you? I could have took you anywhere if I just wanted to fuck. Anyway, tell me about yourself. What you like to do?"

She began telling me about the things she liked and other things she wanted to do. In the process, I fixed us another drink and lit a Black & Mild, while she continued to open up. It was one thing she said that caught my attention, and that was she liked to do hair. So I asked her, "If I was to open a beauty salon, would you work for me? Say you and a few of your friends?"

"Yeah, I would work for you if I was getting paid! But let's be real, you don't have the money to open no business like that. You got to have a license to do hair anyway."

"I'll tell you what, if you and your friends go get ya'll licenses to do hair, I'll get it started and that's on the real."

As soon as I said that, my phone rang. When I answered it, it wasn't anybody but Jay Dee. "You up G?" he asked.

"I'll hate to know I'm talking in my sleep; of course I'm up! What's up?"

"I need you to meet me at the storage."

"When?"

"It's one seventeen now. If you can, by one thirty."

"I'll be there." After I hung up the phone with Jay Dee, I said, "Angela, I'm sorry but I got to drop you off. I've got something to do that's important, so get dress so we can go."

When I got dressed Angela said, "Damn, you getting all dressed up for other bitches!"

"Got damn me, don't start that bull shit! This is how I dress! You just saw me in some old prison clothes. Anyway, are you ready?"

"I guess so since you putting me out."

"It ain't like that. I'm going to make it up to you later," then I gave her a kiss and we left.

I got her to her house at one twenty two. I could tell she was mad, but it was something she would get over. By the time I pulled up to the storage, Jay Dee was already there. He said, "You right on time. Just give me a second to put the car in the storage, and then we'll be ready."

I didn't have the slightest idea what Jay Dee had planned, but I knew it had to be something important. I just had a feeling that I wasn't going to like what he was getting ready to get us into.

Chapter Thirty

$\mathcal{W}$hen Jay Dee came back I asked him, "Man, what we about to do?"

"Be cool, I got some business to handle. I just wanted you on my side like old times. I want you to see how I'm running things."

"Now you know got damn me, I can't get mixed up in no business right now. If something was to go wrong, them motherfuckers are going to lose me and you know this."

"Be cool! I told you I got everything covered. All we are doing is making sure the exchanges go right. We not touching anything. Infact, they don't even know we watching them."

"Who we suppose to be watching anyway and it's going on two o'clock in the morning?"

"Peep this out G. Rose should be checking in the Hamilton I nn as we speak. Once she get the room my beeper is going to go off with the room number. By that time, we should be getting off the highway on Magazine Street. As soon as we get to the red light, a white Lincoln Town car should be parked on the right hand side. That's Paula's car. If she is still there, that means that Nicole and Gold Dee should be pulling up at any minute. We are just going to go around the block and park down the street. That way we can see them when they make the exchange. As soon as they make the exchange, I'm going to call Nicole and give her the room number where Rose will be. She will know where to go once she sees the number. At that time, Paula will be going to the Shell gas station back on Manhatten, where James is going to make a drop off to her, and we will be across the street watching. After that drop is made, James is going to call me to find out where I want him to meet me at. So just cool down, you don't have nothing to worry about G."

I couldn't say anything. He sounded like he had everything worked out. Even his beeper went off revealing a three digit code, which I assumed was the hotel room number, as we were exiting onto Magazine Street. When we reached the stop light, there was a white Lincoln parked on the right hand side just like he said it should have been. As soon as we made the block and parked, Nicole and Gold Dee rode by us. Gold Dee reached out of the window and handed Paula a book sack, and then kept rolling as if nothing ever happened. That's when I said, "I guess that's your cue to make the call to Nicole."

"I'm already on that."

When I seen how quick and smooth the drop went, I knew why Jay Dee had them doing the transaction there. There wasn't a police car in sight; and the entrance to the highway was right there too, just incase they had to get away fast. I said, "So far I can't lie, you on your shit. That's good! I hope the next drop goes that sweet."

"It will, don't worry about nothing. Besides, we're not riding with anything. We not dirty. Right now only Paula is riding with money, besides the money James about to give her. When he make that drop, we all going to meet up in the hotel room Rose got. Oh yeah, you never did tell me did them hoes treat you right?"

"Shit, to be honest, I couldn't even tell you. I just remember waking up with my dick in Gold Dee's mouth, Nicole's breast damn near in my mouth, and Rose had her head between Nicole's legs. I was all fucked up. We supposed to hook up and do whatever again tonight, but I don't know what's up yet. Besides, I just finished handling my business before I came by you."

"With who?"

"This lil' chick named Angela. I can't even lie, she got that come back. I'm ready to go back already and I just left her."

"Don't tell me she whipped you. I ain't even hearing that. Out of all folks not you."

"G, you can call it what you want, but I got to keep her."

Jay Dee just laughed and said, "You still my dog," while shaking his head.

When we exited the highway onto Manhatten, we were able to see there were four police cars surrounding a car on the Shells lot. I thought to myself, "I hope that's not James car. When we finally got across the street from the Shell station, I asked Jay Dee, "What time is James supposed to meet Paula over there?"

"He should already be there. I'm going to give him a few minutes. If he's not there, I'm going to call him to find out what's happening. Oh, there he is now."

I was trying to figure out how he was going to make the drop without being noticeable, when he jumped into the car with Paula and she pulled off. Jay

Dee said, "What the fuck is going on? That's not part of the plan." Before he could pull off, we seen that Paula went to the Tastee Doughnuts, right there next to the Shell station, and that's when James got out and she went on her way.

James called just like Jay Dee said he would, and asked, "Where you want me to meet you at?"

"At the Hamilton Inn, I'll be there when you get there." Then we drove back to the storage, and swapped rides.

It was going on three o'clock in the morning by the time we made it back to the hotel. We hooked up with James on the parking lot. He was surprised to see me out there and said, "What you doing here Boom?"

"Now you know when business take place you can find me around. I'm still tripping off you handling your business now. That's something I never thought I would see."

"Well like I said, shit happens and it was time for me to get mine. You feel me?"

"Oh I feel you G. Do your thang!"

Jay Dee told James, "They in room seven twenty. I'll be up there in one second. I forgot something. Say Boom, come give me a hand."

The way he said that, I knew he didn't want James to hear what he had to say. So when James was gone out of the picture I asked him, "What's up? What you got to tell me?"

That's when Jay Dee said, "When we get in the room, I want you to peep out everybody from head to toe. I want them to know you running everything, calling all the shots. If you feel like something wrong with anybody, let it be known."

"I don't know who all is going to be in the room, but if I feel they're a threat you gone know."

"That's what I'm talking about. Let's go in there then."

When we entered the room, it was more motherfuckers in there than I expected. I knew Rose, James, Nicole, and Gold Dee, but it was three more chicks in there that I never seen before. Gold Dee, Rose, and Nicole greeted me before Jay Dee asked Rose, "Where is Kandy?"

"She's not here yet, but you know how she is. Temera said she told her to be here before three."

"That fucking hoe always late. Call her and see where the fuck she at."

When Jay Dee said that, I asked him, "Who is Kandy?"

"Somebody that works for us, but after tonight I might have to get rid of her. She's always late." Right at that moment Kandy knocked on the door. She was fine but had that attitude as if everybody was beneath her. Jay Dee said, "What is it; you can't tell time or something? Why you always late?"

"Just be happy I came when I came. I started not to come at all." Kandy replied.

I could tell Jay Dee was about to say something, but before he got a chance to. I pulled him to the side. "Say folks just chill out and let me handle this. After you introduce me to everybody, I'm going to handle things from that point. By the way, you strapped?"

"Now you know how we roll. I don't go nowhere without it. Why you ask?"

"Just give it here. I got my reasons." Jay Dee just didn't know that I was about to show every motherfucker in the room that I was dead serious when it came down to business; and I wouldn't tolerate any fuck-ups.

After Jay Dee gave me his strap, I saw that it had exactly what I needed on it, a silencer. That's when he said, "Let's get down to business. If ya'll don't know yet, this is Boom, the one I been telling ya'll about. I know ya'll done heard about him, but ya'll don't know him personally. So that's why I asked ya'll to meet up here. If it wasn't for him, neither one of us would be where we are at today. So I want ya'll to respect him like ya'll do me. I want every single one of ya'll to tell him exactly what he wants and needs to know. Are we understood?"

The lil' chick they called Kandy smacked her lips and rolled her eyes as if she wasn't concerned with what was going on so I snapped and asked her, "What the fuck, you don't want to be here or something? You don't like your job? What the fuck you smacking for? Got damn me, this ain't no motherfucking do what the fuck you want to do shit! Better yet, I'm going to show all of ya'll how I get rid of problems." Then I shot her.

Everybody in the room was fucked up. They looked as if they couldn't believe what they just witnessed. That's when I continue taking control of the room and said, "I don't know how much Jay Dee done told you all about me, but got damn me I won't tolerate disrespect and fuck ups at all. Say Jay Dee and James, go throw that bitch in her trunk. I'll get rid of her later. Anyway, back to what I was saying. If ya'll can't be loyal and follow the rules, I will get rid of ya'll. Now starting with you, tell me who you are, what you do for us, and what you do when you not with us."

The lil' chick that I pointed to said, "My name is Chaos. I have the hookup with any kind of guns you can think of. When I'm not doing business here, I'm a lawyer."

"What type of lawyer are you?"

"I do drugs and gun cases."

"What about you? Mrs..."

"Diamond. Everybody calls me Diamond. I normally make the trips to California. Other than that, I'm just me. Is there anything else you would like to know?"

"That's all for now. If anything else comes across my mind, I'll let you know. What about you in the white blouse; what do you do?"

"My name is Temera. I'm an architect in the day, but once I'm off the clock I make drops in Chicago, Illinois."

When she finished talking, Jay Dee and James came back into the room. Jay Dee asked me, "Everything going alright now?"

"So far we straight; they're still introducing themselves to me. I just need to know what Nicole, Rose, and Gold Dee do, and then you can take over if they don't have any questions for me."

"Well look, I'm Gold Dee as you know already, and I'm a stripper and make drops in Pensacola, Florida."

"You know I'm Rose, but I make drops in Highland, Indiana. During the day, I work as a secretary in the state building."

Finally Nicole said, "You already know me. I do pick ups from Texas. Other than that, I might ride with anyone in this room. When I'm chilling, I practice being a hair stylist. Now can I ask you something?"

"Shoot your question." I replied.

"When are you going to let me do your hair?"

Everybody started laughing, and then I said, "I thought it was already done, but I 'll tell you what. You'll get your chance. Is that it?"

That's when Diamond said, "Well, I got one question. When can I get a chance to spend some time with you?"

"That depends on why you want to spend time with me. Is it personal or business?"

"Personal!"

"That can be arranged, but it might be sooner than you think. That way I can find out what else you do besides just be you. Which that's not bad, but I know you have some hidden talents that you aren't telling." She just smiled, so I told Jay Dee, "You can go on now. I'm finish finding out what I need to know for now."

Jay Dee said, "Now that that's out of the way, the other reason I asked everyone to meet here is because I need everyone to get off everything that ya'll have left by next week. I have a surprise for everyone here then. So don't make any plans for the next few weeks. Is that clear?"

"Yeah, but what is the surprise?" Temera asked.

"Everyone will just have to wait and see!" Jay Dee replied. "Until then, if ya'll don't have anymore questions ya'll free."

"Hold on, before ya'll do whatever ya'll going to do make sure I get a phone number where I can get in touch with ya'll at any time of the day or night." I replied.

After everyone gave me their phone numbers I said, "Oh yeah, one more thing. Everything that happens amongst us stays amongst us. Nobody outside this family should know about anything we do. Nobody!"

It was close to four o'clock now, and Jay Dee asked me, "What you want to do?"

I told him, "I'll call you in the morning when I'm ready to hook up with you, but before you leave let me get the keys to Kandy's car. Which one is it by the way?"

"You're going to know it. It says Kandy on the license plates, and its right outside the door. Here," he tossed me the keys, "Be careful; I'm gone."

I took the keys, and then James and Jay Dee left. Diamond was about to leave until I stopped her and told her, "Don't leave yet, I got something I want you to do."

She just looked at me as if trying to read me, then sat down. I told everyone else, "I'll see ya'll again, until then take care of ya'll selves."

When I said that Nicole asked, "Are you going to stay here with us?"

"Sorry, but I got to take a rain check on that. We gone hook up again," then I told Diamond, "Let's go."

In the hallway she asked me, "Where we going?"

"First we are going to the gas station were you are going to purchase some gas and put some in a can. I'll explain the rest on the way there."

"Are you always like this?"

"Like what?"

"Bossy! Well not bossy, but demanding."

"When it's business, yeah. Other than that, I'm not really bossy as you call it, but I can be persistent when I want something. I hope that don't offend you."

"It's okay; Infact that turns me on."

"I'd like to know what else turns you on, but right now I can't afford any distraction. I don't mix business with pleasure. You understand where I'm coming from?"

"It's cool. Can I ask you a question without you taking it the wrong way?"

"Let me tell you something; if you got something on your mind that you want to know, then you got to ask your questions. I ain't telling you to go overboard with it, but ask your question."

"I know you said what happens amongst us stays amongst us, but did you really have to kill Kandy?"

"Look at me; we in a business that can cost us our lives everyday rather if it's on the streets or to the system. I done been to prison twice already, so I can't afford another lick. I take this business dead serious, and refuse to have any motherfucker affiliated to me that don't. In Kandy's case, I didn't feel she was a hundred percent loyal. I know it comes a point in a person's life were they might want to change, but if that's the case say it up front and I can accept that. Kandy made it seem like she didn't give a fuck about what happen, so I had to show her that I did. Is that all you wanted to know?"

"Yeah."

"Well from here on out, don't let Kandy's name come out your mouth.

We never knew her. You feel me?"

"You don't have to worry about me speaking of her again."

"I hope not. You have a gas can in here?"

"Yeah, I got one in the trunk."

"As soon as you get out to pay for the gas, pop the trunk so I can get it out."

When we pulled up to the gas pumps at Clark's Gas Station, she did exactly like I told her to do. After we got the gas and pulled off, Diamond asked, "What are you going to do with that?"

"You are going to see," I replied. "When we get back I need you to follow me on top of the bridge on the highway. When you see me pull over, pull right behind me and pop your hood. Then get out of your car. You got me?"

She answered, "Yeah, I got you."

She didn't sound too sure, so I was hoping she wouldn't turn sour on me. When we got back to the hotel, I jumped into Kandy's car and drove towards the highway. Diamond was following behind me just like I told her. When we reached the top of the bridge on the highway, I pulled over. There wasn't that much traffic on the highway, so I was able to throw Kandy's body and Jay Dee's pistol over the bridge almost as soon as Diamond pulled over. I took a towel out of her trunk, and then wiped the back of her car clean of all the fingerprints that would have been there. When I finished I told Diamond, "Now I need you to trail me close. After that, you will almost be done," then I jumped back into Kandy's car.

I knew a spot where everybody burned cars after they had stripped them down to just about nothing, and decided that would be the perfect place to get rid of Kandy's car. It took us about twenty minutes to get there. When we arrived, I didn't waste any time pouring the gasoline throughout the car. I wiped off the steering wheel and door handle, and then opened the trunk again and poured the rest of the gasoline in there. I made sure I had put the keys back in my pocket, and told Diamond, "Pop your trunk again." As soon as she did that, I placed the empty gas can in her trunk. Then I told her, "Pull up right next to Kandy's car and keep your foot on the brake so you can pull off fast." She did just what I said. Once we were right next to the car, I lit the towel that I wiped the fingerprints off the car with on fire, and then threw it in Kandy's car. *Swoosh* was the only sound we heard before we pulled off.

Chapter Thirty-one

Diamond was driving as if she was in her own world. Then Diamond finally asked, "Where are we going now?"

"Actually you can drop me off at the Marriott Hotel, right off the expressway. Infact if you want to, you can come up with me; but that's on you."

Diamond still didn't say anything. She just smiled as if she could have seen herself doing something she would enjoy. After a few moments she said, "I might just come up."

"That's cool! I'll hate to know that you'll be driving by yourself at five something in the morning when you can chill. Besides, I just got the room tonight and as you can see I haven't been here. But tell me something, are you going to tell me what you was thinking when you were just smiling; or are you going to leave me wondering?"

She said, "You feel like playing games?"

"I'm not really into playing games if they are not physical."

"Well I'm in the mood to play any kind of games, especially if they're physical."

She didn't have to tell me twice. I caught on to what she was saying, and as fine as she was I knew I was going to deal with her. So I said, "Let's play a game. It's called *How much can you take?* I'm going to do things to you, but you have to stay focused on the road and don't kill us! You game for it?"

"Yeah, let me see what you going to do."

I didn't waste anytime touching and kissing her all on her firm breast. I slid her shirt up slowly revealing her smooth peanut butter colored stomach and gently kissed it. Instantly her nipples stuck out like two bullets. When I seen that happen, I lifted her bra and began licking and kissing her perfect round breasts. Her nipples were sticking out even more now. Once I placed her right nipple in my mouth and began sucking it, she let out a moan and placed her right hand on my head. I stopped and said, "You can't do that, you have to stay focused on the road," and began sucking her left breast. Again she placed her hand on my head, so I stopped again.

This time she said, "I can drive with one hand!"

"I didn't say you couldn't, but you supposed to be able to keep both hands on the wheel while I'm messing with you. Once you take your hands off the wheel, you lose. But how do you like the game so far?"

"It's straight, but I think you cheating. I can't touch you back."

"That's the whole point. You have to be able to control your desires. So are you going to be able to control your desires?"

"Un huh."

When she said that, I began kissing her on her ear this time. Then I kissed her again on her neck and made my way down to her navel, and then back to her breast. At the same time, I slid my hand under her mini-shirt and slid her panties to the side. I began rubbing her pussy, then slipped one of my fingers in her wet warm pussy. She let out a loud moan, and then said, "You have to stop!"

I bust out laughing, and then said, "What, you lost focus or just couldn't take it?"

"You ain't right. I couldn't take it, but I'm going to get you back." She said smiling.

When we arrived at the hotel I was still laughing at her. "What are you going to do to get even?" I asked her on the walk to the hotel.

"You gone see."

When we reached the lobby door, the white chick that I seen earlier was coming out at the same time. The white chick just hugged and kissed me, and then said, "You can still come up if you want too. I'm in the same room." and kept walking.

I turned around and looked at Diamond. She had an expression on her face as if she wanted to fuck up the white chick. I grabbed her by the hand then said, "I don't even know her, so quit looking like that."

She snapped, "You mean to tell me bitches just walk up and kiss and hug on you all the time? You probably did fuck that white hoe."

I had to laugh because it was funny to see hoes get jealous. Infact, it turned me on. I knew Diamond didn't find anything funny, so I said, "If I would have fucked her, she damn sure wouldn't be walking out of the door. She would be more like a dope fiend trying to get some more."

"I believe you, but you said that like you sure your working with that fire."

I said, "I can tell you anything, but I'm from the Show-Me-State; and believe in what we call Show & Tell, so we'll see."

"Yeah, we will see."

When we entered the suite Diamond said, "This isn't a regular room. You must have been planning on having some important company or someone special over."

"Actually, I got this to be by myself, but since you are my company I guess that makes you someone special."

I thought she was going to change the conversation, until she seen the glasses that Angela and I drank out of. "I guess you was drinking two glasses at a time. Is this the glass that white hoe drank out of?"

"Look got damn me, I don't owe you no explanation for shit I do. I told you already, got damn me, I don't know that white chick. You know just as much about her as I do, I just seen her first. Anyway, if you want something to drink or eat just order it. I'm about to take me a quick shower. You welcome to come join me if you want, if not just get comfortable and make yourself at home."

I jumped in the shower wondering if she was going to come or not, but she never did. When I got out I just slid on some boxers and lit a Black & Mild up. She was laying across the bed naked listening to R. Kelly's song *Down Low*. When I seen her I said to myself, we got to keep this on the down low. I climbed in the bed next to her and asked here, "Are you comfortable now?"

"Un huh, I'm just missing some twelve play" then rolled over on top of me and began kissing my chest. I started to put the Black I was smoking out when she said, "Un uh, don't you put that down. It's my turn to see how much you can take now." I laughed, and then she said, "I told you I was going to get you back."

She was licking and kissing me all across my chest and stomach until my dick became hard. Once I became aroused, she grabbed my dick then said, "What do we have here?" I wasn't going to stop her from doing anything she wanted to do with it. I just laid back and let her do her thang while I smoked. Once she climbed on top of me and began riding me, I had to put the Black & Mild down. She didn't say anything until after she got her. "I guess you couldn't take it. I see you put the Black down."

"Really you lost because you didn't stop when I first put it down. I guess you couldn't take it, or was it feeling that good to you?"

"What you think?"

"You don't have to tell me, I know it had to feel good to you because you damn sure didn't stop." Then we laid down and went to sleep.

About eleven o'clock, she woke up and said, "I got to get ready to go. I have some business in Cali and have to be finished by the end of this week like Jay Dee said. You don't know what the surprise is he suppose to have for us?"

"If I did know, I wouldn't tell you cause then it wouldn't be a surprise now would it?"

"You don't have to tell me, but I hope you are a part of it," then she left.

Chapter Thirty-two

I laid across the bed for a few more moments before I made myself get up to take a shower. As soon as I was finished I called Jay Dee and asked him, "What's the haps?"

"I'm just chilling, dealing with these crazy ass hoes. Where you at?"

"I'm in the room I got yesterday. What hoes you dealing with?"

"That ain't nobody but Shantay friend's Rachel, Monica, and Brenda. They been asking about you all fucking morning. What did you do to them G?"

"I ain't did nothing. Don't give me no charges. Anyway, come get me or send one of them hoes to come and get me. I got to checkout at twelve."

"Don't worry, I going to send Rachel to come get you. That's straight?"

"It don't make a difference who comes. I just don't want to be waiting, so tell her to come now."

I got the rest of my things together while I was waiting on Rachel to come get me. I didn't realize that I still had Kandy's keys until that moment. I didn't care who was coming to get me, I had to get rid of them keys and soon. When I seen them I couldn't believe how deep I put myself back in the game. Then I had a lot of witnesses. If anyone of them would turn sour, I would be sentenced to death and I knew that. Then I had the nerves to tell Jay Dee to give up the game knowing he looked up to me. I had to explain to him what I did was wrong because I didn't want him to make the same mistake I just did.

I called Keisha while I was still waiting on Rachel. When I got her on the phone, she said, "I'm about to leave and go to bible study. You still want to come or were you just playing?"

"I still want to come, but I can't make it today. I was just calling to see how my son was doing, and if I could spend the day with him."

"When we leave the Kingdom Hall, I will call you or you can come get him tomorrow."

"Call me when you make it back home and I will come get him tomorrow. So say a prayer for me because I know I need it." and then I hung up.

When I got off the phone, I grabbed my bags then went to checkout. While I was checking out Rachel walked in. I said, "You right on time; I thought I was going to have to wait awhile on you."

"I came as soon as Jay Dee told me. Besides, I was about to go get something to eat anyway."

"What was you going to eat?"

"I'm in the mood for some chicken. I'm going to Popeye's."

"That sounds good. I haven't had any of that in awhile anyway."

I would have never figured out Rachel was the reason I had codeine in my system until she said. "I'm happy to see your headache went away. I thought you forgot where Jay Dee lived since I haven't been seeing you around."

When she said that, I could feel my blood pressure rising rapidly. I snapped, "What the fuck did you give me?"

"A Xanex pill. I told you it would make you forget all about that headache you had."

"Yeah it made me forget all about that headache I had, and in the same process damn near made me go back to prison. I went to go see my parole officer and he was talking all stupid to me about having codeine in my system. and I know damn well the only thing I should have had in my system was alcohol. Can you imagine how I would have felt if he would have violated me and I hadn't the slightest idea of how I got dirty?"

Rachel really wouldn't have known how I would have felt if I would have gone back to prison behind the pills she gave to me. She said, "I'm sorry if I almost cost you your freedom. I was just trying to help you out that night. I hope you can forgive me Tj."

I had to accept her apology because she sounded so sincere. As soon as we pulled up to Popeye's and got out of her car, I threw down Kandy's car keys. I figured if anyone found them now, it wouldn't make a difference because we were a long way from where we set the car on fire at. We ordered some food, and then left.

Once we reached Jay Dee's house, I seen Brenda was doing Shantay's hair in the living room and I asked her, "Can you do mine?"

Brenda laughed and then said, "What do you want done to it?"

"Washed and braided."

"I'll do it when I'm finished," she replied, "But why don't you ask Monica to do it? She can braid hair real good."

So I asked Monica if she felt like braiding my hair. She jumped off the sofa and asked, "Are you ready now?"

"I'm ready whenever you are." I replied.

She began undoing the braids I had in my head, and then said, "I didn't know your hair was this long! How long have you been growing it?"

"I've had it for awhile now; I couldn't tell you how long."

When she finished washing and braiding it, I seen that she knew what she was doing and said, "You should be working in a shop. If I open one, will you work there?"

"As long as I'm getting paid, I'll work anywhere!"

"Of course you would be getting paid. As long as you get your license, we can do something on the real."

Right then, I knew I had to put together a business. All the pieces were coming together, just like a puzzle. I started telling Jay Dee about what I was thinking about doing and he was cool with it. He was like, "What all are you going to need and what are you going to call it?"

"I'm going to invest the money you gave me to open it up. I even got a few folks willing to work there already. As far as the name, we can call it *4 Figure$ Production*. Meaning anything for the currency since that's what it's really about."

"4 Figure$ Production huh. Well like you always told me, make it happen."

I knew I couldn't just start it up over night, but I knew I was going to make it happen no matter what. I asked Jay Dee, "You still be writing raps?"

"I have a few, but I haven't been really messing with that since you been gone. James on the other hand, has been doing his thing. The trip part about it is, he been doing gospel rap with some dudes in Forever Records. I'm just not with it, but it sounds good."

"That's cool he doing something. I got a few gospel raps myself."

"You got gospel raps! You need to stop. Then look at what you did last night."

"Oh yeah, that's what I wanted to talk to you about. When things took place last night, what did you see wrong?"

"Nothing! You felt like she was out of place, and you handled your business."

"Yeah I handled my business, but I did it stupid. You never let your right hand know what your left hand is doing. Last night, I could have done that another way. I let my anger control my actions which caused me to make a dumb mistake."

"A dumb mistake!"

"Yeah, a dumb mistake! There were too many witnesses present. If anybody that was in the room would turn sour, I would be fucked with no if ands or buts. You feel me?"

"I understand where you coming from. But like you said last night, we all family and what we do stay between us."

"I said that G, but you can never trust anyone a hundred percent. Remember this, you only know how fast your feet move and what your mouth says. I can tell you anything now, but when I'm not around you I can also say anything. You feel me?"

"Say no more. I understand exactly what you mean. What you want to get into today?"

"I was planning on spending the day with my lil' one, but his mother said they were going to bible study so that was that. I need to find me an apartment so I don't have to keep renting rooms."

"You know damn well you don't have to rent no room, you can stay here. Unless you saying my place ain't good enough for you."

"Don't play me like that. You know damn well I consider this home. I just wanted my own place. I need you to take me to go get a ride today; if you have time."

"What kind of ride you trying to get?"

"Something nice as long as it don't cost too much."

"I know where a Lexus 400 at. All you have to do is dress it up the way you want it."

"Take me to go see it."

"4-sho!"

Jay Dee took me somewhere off Airline Hwy to a car dealership. When we got there, the salesman was talking to Jay Dee as if they were old friends. When they finished talking he greeted me, and then took us around the building and showed me the Lexus.

It was jet black with peanut butter leather interior. I barely turned the key and it started right up. It had less than ten thousand miles on it too. I could just picture me in it, so I asked him, "How much?"

"You like it? Twelve thousand dollars."

"Twelve thousand dollars! I don't like it that much. It don't even have no rims or sound."

"Twelve thousands not that bad. It's only two years old with less than ten thousand miles and one owner."

"I tell you what; I'll take it off your hands for nine thousand cash and not a penny more. What's it going to be?"

He looked at Jay Dee and Jay Dee just put his hands in the air as if to say he didn't have anything to do with that. The salesman then said, "Nine thousand cash is good."

"I said, "Another second longer and you could have kept it. I know you didn't pay that much for it." He just smirked.

To say I had just bought a big body Lexus, I felt like I was driving a raggedy ass beat up car. I told Jay Dee I was going to hook up with him later I had to go do something, but he knew I was about to go buy something for the car.

The first thing I bought was some Vogue tires to match the gold stripe going along side of the car, and the peanut butter color interior it had. When I finished getting the tires put on, I went and got a CD player; a pair of 6 x 9's. and had the windows tinted limo black to match the car.

To say I didn't have any rims on my car I felt like I did. I guess anyone would have felt as good as me coming home from prison having money, and being able to do just about whatever they wanted to.

I called up Angela to see what she was doing, hoping I could spend a little time with her, but she didn't answer the phone so I figured I'd catch up with her later. I drove around a lil' bit, getting use to the car, then headed back to Jay Dee's.

As soon as I got there Jay Dee said, "Let me see what you done did to the car."

"I didn't go all out the way on it. Infact, that's all I'm going to do to it."

"You can tell that bullshit to somebody else, I know you already. You not going to stop till you put some rims on it."

"I'm not about to buy any rims for it. I told you, I got to make 4 Figure$ Production happen and I'm going to do that. Where James at? I want to hear what he working with."

"Let me call that fool, I haven't talked to him all day."

While Jay Dee was making the call, I decided that I was going to spend about ten thousand on just studio equipment so we could do something on our own. When he got off the phone, I told him, "Feel this, if I go get all the equipment we need to open our own studio, will you go get a place we can set up in?"

"Off top! In fact, I know a place that sells equipment cheap. How you read me?"

I had to laugh when he said how you read me, because I use to tell him that all the time. Then I replied, "I read you loud and clear. Before we even get into anything else, let's go get that equipment. We can bring it back here for now, until we get a place to set it up."

"That's cool, let's go."

When we left we rode in my car, and then went to the storage to get Jay Dee's truck, I followed him to a place called Tim's Studio Music Accessories. Tim had everything we needed: Mpx's, keyboards, beat machines, computers, CD burners, etc. All together he charged me twenty four thousand dollars and some change. I was mad at first because I spent more than I planned on, but I knew it was well worth it and I was going to get my money's worth out of it.

After we got everything back to Jay Dee's house and set up, I followed Jay Dee back to the storage to drop his truck off. On the way back Jay Dee called James and told him, "Meet me at my house."

He didn't question Jay Dee, he just said, "I'll be there in a minute."

We pulled up at the same time. When we got out of my car James said, "Damn that car clean! Who's that for?"

"Oh that's mine. Anyway I heard you was doing some gospel rap now. When are you going to let me hear something?"

"Whenever you ready. What you ready to get back into music now?"

"You know we were doing our thing before I got locked up; and I heard about the contract G Money Records wanted to give us but ya'll turned it down. At least I can make up for that. Besides I got some gospel raps too."

James said, "How could you of all people come up with some gospel music? Especially when I know you living just about as wrong as it could get?"

"You know ain't nobody perfect, but when I was down this two and a half years I learned about God and Jesus. So I can relate to rapping about them."

"I still don't see how," Jay Dee said.

"Me neither, but what's up with you anyway?" James asked.

"Uh, come check out this equipment I just got so we can do our thing."

We went into Jay Dee's crib and messed with the equipment for hours recording raps and making beats. Before we realized it, it was going on three something in the morning before we quit. The only reason we called it quits was because Angela called me.

"So that's how it is? I give you some pussy and now you don't know me or want to be bothered?" Angela said sounding very upset.

"Why it have to be like that? I called you earlier today and you wasn't anywhere to be found. Where was you at?"

"I had some things to take care of today. I just thought you was dodging me or something?"

"I wouldn't even play you like that. If I didn't want to be bothered with you, believe me you would know. I don't hesitate to speak my mind about how I feel. Anyway, did you look into what I asked you about?"

"What, getting my hair license?"

"Yeah."

"Not yet. I thought you was just talking to make conversation."

"Angela, feel me for a second. I be dead serious when it comes down to business. I told you to get that because I'm trying to make something happen. I don't be stunting when it involves money, so handle your business baby girl. Anyway, what you doing up this late? You just got in or something?"

"I been home for awhile now, but I couldn't sleep. I wanted to see you, so are you coming over or what?"

"I'll be over there in a few, let me finish recording this beat then I'll be on my way. I should be there in about fifteen, twenty minutes tops, that's cool?"

"I'll be waiting. Where you at anyway?"

"I'm not that far from your house. Infact I'm almost finished so I'll be there sooner than you think. You want me to bring you something?"

"Just you. I'll see you soon."

Angela just didn't know how bad I wanted to be with her. Every since I slept with her, I been wanting her on my side. Even when I was fucking Diamond, I kept thinking about her and Diamond was a bad bitch.

Before James got ready to leave he asked me, "We going to hook up tomorrow and record some more?"

I said, "Look, as long as Jay Dee says it's cool, you can come down when you ready until we find a building to set it up in. Like I said, I feel I owe ya'll that much. We Shut'em Down Records now. Our motto is bring it how you feel. So when you feel it, bring it; but make sure you shut'em down so no matter who is listening to your music they have no choice but to respect your mind. How you read me G?"

"Loud and clear. I'm going to get at ya'll tomorrow then."

Jay Dee replied after James left, "G, you done got colder since you been gone. I mean you just went off tonight. If we get a few chicks to sing for us, we'd really have it made. I'll go look for a building tomorrow so we can set it up all the way right. You want something to drink? I got some Hennessy in there."

"I'm straight folks. I'm about to go by my gal crib."

"Your gal? When you get one of them?"

"Man I told you about that chick Angela. I'm straight digging her."

"Oh yeah, Mrs. Comeback. Well do your thang. I'll call you if I really need you. Keep your head up G."

Chapter Thirty-three

*W*hen I got by Angela's house, I wanted her to know that I was serious about making shit happen and bullshitting around wasn't going to get it. The first thing she did when she saw me was give me a long kiss and tight hug. She then asked, "Who is that car for?"

"Oh that's mines. I just got that today."

"How can you afford something like that?"

"That cost me a lil' nothing; you want to take a ride?"

"If I can drive."

"I don't know about that, but we can go somewhere if you like."

"You don't believe I can drive?"

"I didn't say you couldn't drive; but you not about to drive that." I replied. Before it was all over, she ended up driving while we talked.

"I don't know what it's going to take for you to really believe that I want you to run a hair salon. You know, if that's something you really want like you say you do, then you got to handle your business. What good is it to want something if you not going to do anything to get it?"

"I really do want to work in my own hair salon; I just didn't know that you were really serious. You know how people be saying they going to do this and that, but don't never do nothing. I figured you were just talk."

"Got damn me, play me for something! I know when you first met me it didn't seem like I had shit; but don't let your eyes fool you."

We ended up going to a duck off spot they called *The Level*. Really it's just a mini version of a riverfront. Once we got there, we walked along the side of the riverfront talking until we came to a place where some rocks were piled up.

We climbed on top of the smooth surfaced rocks, and then began kissing under what remained of the moon light.

It was just about to be daybreak before we decided to leave. We both were tired and I knew I had a big day ahead of me. I was planning on spending the day with my son no matter what. After I dropped Angel off, I went by Jay Dee's house to get some sleep.

I woke up around ten thirty. The first thing I did was call Keisha to let her know I was coming to get my son. I took a quick shower, and then got ready to leave. Right before I got to the door, Jay Dee stopped me. "Are you going with me to find a building for the studio?"

"Most likely I'm gone be gone all day. I'm about to spend time with my son. Whatever you chose to get, it's all good. It don't have to be all that big, just have enough room to set the equipment up right. If you need me, just call me," then I pushed.

I made it to Keisha's house right at eleven. When I knocked on the door, Tony answered it. When he seen it was me, you could tell his whole attitude changed. By me seeing that, I just asked for Keisha. When I seen he was about to close the door in my face, I asked, "I can use the bathroom, if you don't mind?"

He let me in, but I knew he really didn't want to. Before I made it to the bathroom, Keisha came out of a room. When she seen me, she looked back and forth from me to Tony as if something was wrong.

"How you doing too? You don't mind me using your bathroom do you?" I said.

"You know where it's at."

After I used the bathroom, I seen Tony was sitting on the couch so I went and sat across from him. That was the first time I realized he wasn't that much older than me, so sarcastically I asked, "How do it feel to be getting married?"

He looked around, and then said, "It's cool. Really it doesn't feel any different than before we decided to get married."

"I hear you. I just never thought about getting married, but everybody got their own thing. Tell me something, you a Jehovah Witness like Keisha?"

"Naw! I been to a few studies with her, but that's about it."

"I told her I'd go; but I ain't went yet." I replied as my son and Keisha walked in the room. "What's up man? You ready to go?"

"Where we going?"

"Where ever you want to go."

"Well here are his clothes Tj." Keisha interrupted.

"We don't need them; I got everything we gone need."

"How long are you going to keep him?" Keisha questioned.

"As long as he wants to stay; I'll call you when I'm bringing him back." I said before we left.

I knew without a doubt, that I had to take my son shopping because I didn't like what he had on. Besides, I felt like he should be dressed like me since he was my son.

We stopped at a store called Urban Fashion. There I purchased a few outfits so we could dress alike. After that, I took him to the mall and bought some more clothes and toys. When we were finished, I let him play some video games at the mall's arcade; and then we left.

We drove to the Holiday Inn afterwards, and I rented a room for a week. After that, I asked him, "Are you hungry? What you want to eat?"

He replied, "A sandwich."

"A sandwich! What kind of sandwich do you want?"

"I don't know."

I didn't have the slightest idea what kind of sandwich he could have wanted, so I asked him, "You like pizza?"

"Yeah, but I don't want no pizza. I want a sandwich."

The only kind of sandwich I could think of was a hamburger, so I asked, "You want some McDonalds?"

"Yeah! I want a messy sandwich with a toy."

I knew exactly what he wanted; then I asked him, "Do you want to dress like daddy before we leave?"

"Un huh."

"What you want us to wear then?"

He picked out an outfit, and then said, "This one right here."

I said, "Well put them on, and then we can leave."

"You not going to put yours on?"

"Of course, I'm going to put mines on. I'm going to be dressed just like you." He just smiled, and then began changing outfits. In the process, I called Jay Dee to see if he had any luck in finding a building to put the studio equipment in.

"Hello," he answered in a deep tone.

"G, get that bass out of your voice; it's just me."

"Oh, what's up G? You must have known I was about to call you."

"For what?"

"I just got a building and the electric on already. All I have to do is move the equipment, but James going to give me a hand on that."

"Where the building at?"

"It's right off of Forth Street and Second Avenue. You want to come check it out?"

"Right now I'm about to take Lil' Threat to McDonalds. After that, we can come check it out."

"How Lil' Threat doing?"

"Oh he chilling! Just changing his clothes. I tell you what, when ya'll finish moving the equipment pass by McDonalds. We gone be at the one right there on Manhatten Blvd. that's cool?"

"4-sho! We gone pass through. Let me start moving this stuff then."

"4-sho!" I replied to Jay Dee before hanging up. "You ready Threat?"

"Yeah, but why do you call me Threat?"

"I been calling you that since you was a baby. All it means is that you're going to be a heart breaker; and by you acting and looking like me, some people are going to consider you a threat to them. You don't like that name; or would you prefer me calling you by your real name?"

"I like it now; I just wanted to know why you called me that."

"Are you enjoying yourself so far?"

"Yes. You going to let me play the game you brought me?"

"Of course! When we come back you can play it as long as you want to. I almost forgot; we need to put on our cologne to smell good."

"What's cologne?"

"That's something you put on to smell good. Come here." I sprayed some on him, and then myself; and then I asked him, "How does that smell?"

"Good!"

"Well let's go."

I drove straight to the McDonalds on Manhatten Blvd. When we went in and order our food, the lil' chick behind the cash register started flirting with me and giving us complements on how we looked. I thanked her; but left it at that because she really wasn't my type.

Once we got our food, I thought everything was straight until I seen how my son was looking at his cheese burger. "What's wrong?" I asked him.

"It's not messy."

"What you want on it?"

"Everything!"

"You like onions?"

"Yes."

"Well hold on; and let me see if I can fix this." I went back to the counter where the lil' chick was that served us, and then asked, "Can you make another sandwich for my son or just fix this one?"

"What's wrong?" she questioned.

"He like his sandwiches messy. All you have to do is put some: lettuce, ketchup, pickles, tomatoes, mayo, mustard, and onions on this; and he'll be straight."

"You sure about the onions?"

"Very! He like them."

She remade the sandwich for me, and then said, "I hope he likes it."

When I gave him the sandwich back and he seen it, I knew it was like he wanted it. I soon found out why he called it a messy sandwich. Almost everything fell off of it before he bit into it, but he ate it all. Seeing him eat his cheese burger, made me think back to when I was around his age.

I was tripping off how far I done came in life. At one time eating White Castle's hamburgers felt like the world. Now here I am with a son and able to buy him whatever he wanted to eat like it ain't nothing. I didn't know what life had in store for me, but I knew I had to be prepared for anything.

We sat there for awhile eating and talking before Jay Dee pulled up. The first thing I noticed was James wasn't with him, but I already had a good idea where he was.

"What's up boss? What's up Threat? Ya'll save me some?" Jay Dee said.

"How you know my name Threat? Who you is?"

"I'm your uncle Jay Dee. You didn't save me no food?"

"No, I ate it all up."

"Tj, he getting big." Jay Dee said looking over at me.

"You see that huh? You ready to roll; or you want something to eat for real?"

"I got the munchies for real! Let me get something to eat real quick."

After Jay Dee got his food, I followed him to the building he rented. It was really just an apartment building. James had just about everything hooked up already, so I helped him finish up. When we were done, James left saying he had some business to handle and that he would catch back up with us later. Right before he walked out, I told him, "Just get in touch with Jay Dee later on. He is going to have a key for you. That way you can come handle your business whenever you ready. You feel me?"

"I read you loud and clear."

After he left, I told Jay Dee, "I need you to get in touch with Monica and Brenda, and make sure they handle they business on getting their license. The sooner they get it, the sooner we can open 4 Figures Production."

"I got you. I'm going to make sure they on top of that. What you and Threat about to do?"

"I got a room for us; I'm going to keep him for a week or so."

"You went to see your P.O. again yet?"

"Naw, I got a couple of more days before I have to see him. Why you ask?"

"I'm just making sure you gone be ready this week."

"Ready for what?"

"I told you I got a surprise for the whole family."

"And I told you, I don't like surprises."

"G, just be cool; everything gone turn out good this week."

"I hope so. I'm going to get at you tomorrow, and don't forget to handle that for me with Monica and Brenda."

"I told you, I got you."

Since I was already close to Angela's house, I was hoping she would be at home and I could pick her up. I called her and just my luck, she answered the phone. "Hello Mrs. Beautiful! What you doing?"

"Nothing; who is this?"

"Damn, every time I call you, you gone ask me who I am?"

"I'm sorry if I offended you. I know who this is. What you doing?"

"I was hoping I could come and get you since I was close to your house. What you doing?"

"I was just chilling, but you can come get me if you want."

"Well get ready, I'll be there in a few minutes. Get a few outfits together as well."

"How long are you trying to keep me?"

"As long as I possibly can! At least for a couple of days."

"That's cool! Well let me get ready."

When I made it to Angela's house, she was still getting ready. "Daddy, I have to use the bathroom." Tiarell said.

"Hold on a second; you can use it over my friend house. We're almost there."

When Angela opened the door after I had knocked, she seen I had Tiarell with me. "I'm almost ready. Who is he?"

"That's my son, Lil' Threat. Let him use your bathroom."

She walked him to the bathroom, and as she was walking back she said, "I didn't know you had a son that big. How old is he?"

"He five going on six. You ain't ready yet?"

"Just about; I got to get one more thing."

After she got her stuff together, we left and went straight to the hotel. Once we got inside, I hooked up the video game system I had bought for Lil' Threat so he could play with it like I told him. While he was playing the game, Angela and me talked for awhile. That's when she told me she was supposed to start a class on Monday to get her hair license.

I was hoping she would handle her business. Then to hear her say she was starting classes at the beginning of next week, I knew I would be able to see my plans go into effect soon. We stayed up a bit longer talking about the salon, and then we all took our baths and called it a night.

Chapter Thirty-four

Over the next couple of days, I made the most of it. I was enjoying the time I was spending with Angela, but being with my son meant more to me than anything. When I went to bring Tiarell back to his mother's house, I let Angela ride with me. I didn't know how Keisha would react, but I wanted her to know that I had a bad ass bitch on my team. When she opened the door, she was acting like she really missed Threat. So I said, "Damn, I can still get that kind of affection?" She just smiled sarcastically so I said, "I guess I can't. Just because you are married, don't forget you still for me though. Anyway, come give me a hand with some of Threat's bags."

When I opened my car door and Keisha saw Angela, her whole face expression changed. She rolled her eyes towards me, and then said, "Oh, I didn't know you had someone with you. How you doing? I'm Keisha."

"Hello Keisha, I'm Angela. It's nice to meet you."

When we finished getting all of the bags out of the car, Keisha said, "Let me talk to you for a minute."

I knew it was going to be some bullshit so I replied, "Check this out, I'm in a hurry right now; just call me," then Angela and me headed out.

I didn't waste any time dropping Angela off. I had to be in my parole officer's office at eight thirty, and I didn't want to give him any reason to violate me. Besides, he done already gave me one chance when he found me dirty.

As soon as I entered Mr. Cromer's office, he began asking the same routine questions that he already knew the answers too. I just went along with anything he said to save myself some time in his office. Before it was all over, he still made me take an urine test. Once he seen that I was clean, he told me I could leave and didn't have to come back until next month. Once he said that, it was on and popping.

I called Jay Dee to find out where he was. He just so happen to be at the studio, so I told him I was on my way. When I arrived, I seen someone done put a whole living room set up in one of the rooms, along with a big screen television, and a video game system hook up to it. The first thing I asked was, "Where did all of this come from?"

Jay Dee replied, "James brought all of this in a couple of days ago. Anyway, you checked in with your parole officer yet?"

"I just left there. Everything straight until next month. What's up with the surprise you suppose to have for us?"

"Oh, don't worry about nothing. Everybody is going to meet up with us at Copeland's at noon. Then we're going to make our move."

"4-sho! You ever handle that for me with Monica and Brenda?"

"Yeah, they said something about starting a class Monday. Where Lil' Threat at?"

"I dropped him off earlier. Speaking of him, let me call his momma. She wanted to tell me something."

Once I called Keisha, she didn't hesitate telling me what was on her mind. "You got a lot of nerves bringing one of your bitches by my house!"

"Hold on got damn me, don't even start that shit. The same way I have to respect you moving on with your life and done got married, got damn me just respect what I do. As long as I'm taking care of my son, don't question who the fuck I'm with. But if that's all you wanted earlier, I'm gone holla' at you."

When I hung up the phone, Jay Dee asked, "What you did that I missed?"

"You ain't miss nothing. She tripping cause I had Angela with me when I dropped off my son."

"You brought that girl by her house?"

"You fucking right I did, and I'll do it again! She's the one that got married. Anyway, fuck that shit; let me beat your ass in this game right quick until we get ready to go."

After playing a few games of Madden Football and talking shit to each other, we left to go to Copeland's. We drove our own cars up there. As soon as we pulled into the parking lot, I noticed Diamond's car so I assumed everybody else was there except for James. I could have sworn I made it clear that I wouldn't tolerate any fuck ups amongst our family. Just to give James and whoever else that wasn't inside the benefit of the doubt, I sat inside my car giving them a few more minutes since it wasn't exactly twelve o'clock yet.

I guess James must have known I wasn't going to go for any excuses, because he pulled into the parking lot before twelve. I stayed sitting inside my car just watching the scene. Something didn't seem right, but I couldn't quite put my finger on what it was. At eleven fifty nine, I went inside the restaurant.

I noticed Jay Dee and everybody else as soon as I walked through the door. I took the seat at the end of the table between Diamond and Temeka. After

I greeted everybody, Jay Dee said, "I know ya'll all been waiting on me to tell ya'll what the surprise is, but believe me it was well worth the wait."

"Well what is it?" Nicole interrupted impatiently.

"Be cool! I'm about to tell ya'll. You know if it wasn't for everybody here staying loyal and taking care of business, we wouldn't be here today able to buy whatever we want. Just to show ya'll my appreciation, we all going on a vacation today. Infact, our cruise departs at three."

"Where are we going?" Rose questioned.

"To Puerto Rico. It's only going to be a five day vacation, but it's the least I could do. If everything goes okay, we'll be able to go on a cruise every month. How does that sound?"

"It sounds good to me." Nicole replied.

"Me too." Gold Dee joined in.

At that moment, I noticed the same lil' white chick that I seen before at the restaurant and the hotel. I said, "Excuse me for a minute," and then I walked up to her. "I don't know if this happen to be a coincidence, but to me it seems like I might as well get to know you since I keep seeing you. My name is Boom; and yours?"

"Jennifer. Oh, I remember you! How are you doing?"

"I'm doing alright, but the question is how are you doing Jennifer?"

She just blushed, and then said, "I'm doing pretty good. Can I buy you a drink?"

"I'm afraid not. Maybe if I see you again we could have a drink then or do something else. You have a way I can get in touch with you?"

"Of course I do."

After Jennifer gave me her phone number, I walked back to the table. Nicole, Rose, Gold Dee, and Diamond was looking at me as if they couldn't believe I just got that white chick number in front of them. All I heard as I sat down was Temeka asking, "Why we can't bring that much?"

I asked, "What's going on? What I miss?"

Jay Dee answered, "You didn't miss anything. I was just telling them that they don't need to bring a lot of stuff." Then he went on and said, "Now that we got that clear, let's order something to eat before we leave."

After we finished getting our food and had ate, Jay Dee told everybody, "Ya'll can park by my house, so ya'll won't have to worry about ya'll cars while we are gone," then got up to leave.

I stopped him and asked him, "Man, where you about to go?"

"I have to meet Paula, to pick up some money. Just meet me by the house, and don't tell Shantay where we are going."

"You know I ain't gone tell her nothing about what we do. Just handle your business G. Don't let me hold you up."

I already had enough gear, so I didn't need to go shopping for clothes. I just had to stop and pick up a traveling bag. I didn't know what the weather was going to be like in Puerto Rico, but if I needed anything else I was gone have to get it once we got there. I stopped at a K-Mart to get the traveling bag, when I had the feeling I was being followed. I thought I had seen a white Toyota follow me all the way from Copeland's, but I guess I was tripping because nothing happened and nobody approached me. After I found a bag that was suitable for what I needed, I headed back to Jay Dee's crib to meet up with everybody.

When I pulled up on the parking lot, I saw that everyone was there except for Jay Dee. As soon as I parked, Gold Dee and Nicole came up to my car. I told them to get in while we were waiting on Jay Dee to get there. Gold Dee asked me as soon as she got in, "How have you been doing stranger? You've been too busy to see us?"

I had to laugh to myself because it was funny to me how she was coming at me. Every since the morning I woke up with them in the bed with me, I haven't even thought about them any more. That's when I said, "You know it ain't even that type of party. I had to handle my business, just like ya'll had too. What's up anyway?"

"I was just wondering, well we were just wondering when we gone hook back up? You know we're all going to be together this week. That's five days we can get to know each other better, if you like too." Nicole said.

Now they just put it on my mind how it could go down, and I knew they were game for it. I probably could have even got Diamond to join in, but I wasn't going to expose my hands to them. I just said, "We going to see what's gone happen."

By then Jay Dee pulled up with a limousine following behind him. I knew it was on and popping then. Everybody climbed into the white limo carrying a duffel bag a piece. On the way to the dock, we were all just kicking it and running it. It seemed like we just got in the limo when the next thing I knew we were pulling up to the dock.

Once we all got out and made our way over to the cruise ship, I was amazed at how much larger it was up close than how it seemed to be on television. As we were walking up the gang plank, I noticed the word Fascinate was written in large blue letters on the side of the ship. It was then that I knew this was going to be an interesting trip.

Chapter Thirty-five

*A*fter we all got settled in our rooms, I began walking around the ship to see what all it had on it. I was amazed by how large it really was. It had: a pool, pool tables, video games, and other things for our entertainment. I decided to go to the lounge and get something to sip on, as I had noticed where it was a few minutes ago.

When I entered the lounge, the first thing I noticed was a beautiful lady walking behind the counter. I couldn't tell you what race she was; but she looked like she could have been Spanish or Latino. As I approached the bar she asked me, "What can I get for you?" with the sweetest accent I have ever heard.

I replied, "What would you suggest Ms. Beautiful?"

At first she just smiled, and then responded by asking, "Well are you planning on getting drunk, or do you want something a little smooth?"

"Personally, I'd prefer to get to know you if that's not a problem. My name is Tj; and you are?"

"Cee Jay, I'm..." she said before I corrected her.

"Not Cee Jay; Tj. Tee as in Tom."

"Oh, I'm sorry Tj. My name is Juanita Maria. Where are you from?"

"St. Louis, Missouri; and you?"

"I'm from Puerto Rico," she said while making me a blue drink. Then she went on and said, "It's not that strong; but it's my favorite," then handed me the drink.

"If you like it and you look like as sweet as you do, I guess it must be pretty good Juanita Maria." She just began smiling again.

I reached in my pocket and pulled out a twenty to pay for the drink, but Juanita said, "You don't have to pay for that, it's on me."

"I don't want you to lose your job behind a drink, I can pay for it."

"Oh don't worry, I own this ship. Besides, after all of the compliments you have given me, I can give you this."

I just said, "Thank you. But maybe when you get some time to yourself, I can get a chance to get to know you better."

"Maybe so."

I didn't want it to seem like I was sweating her, so I said, "I hope so," then left the bar.

I finished looking around the ship to see what else it had to offer, but I was mainly amazed by the color of the ocean as we continue our journey to Puerto Rico. To say this was the first cruise I had ever been on, I was enjoying myself and the day wasn't even over. While I was admiring the ocean view, Temeka walked up behind me and said, "That's a beautiful sunset; if only everyday was as beautiful."

"It is depending on whose point of view you're looking at it from. You might be having a bad day; but somebody else might be having the time of their life. Either way, you have to make the best out of any situation. You feel me?"

"You know you right. I never thought about it like that. Anyway, enjoy yourself. Oh, by the way, I think they're looking for you."

I turned around to see who she was talking about, when Nicole, Rose, and Gold Dee were walking towards me. By the expression on Rose's face, I knew their minds were in the gutter. I didn't have a problem with that either. I figured I'd already snuck out of town, so I might as well enjoy myself to the fullest. They came up trying to play that old innocent role; but I seen straight through it. I knew they wanted to fuck, so I asked, "Where ya'll creeping off too?" once they got close.

"We just were walking around trying to find you. What you doing up here?" Rose replied.

"I'm just chilling, watching the sunset. What ya'll looking for me for?"

Gold Dee answered, "You know what time it is! You ready to do what we talked about earlier?"

Now they had me on the spot. I really wanted to see if they had any other bad bitches on the ship, because I knew I could fuck these three anytime. So I said, "Let's take a dip in the Jacuzzi before we go back to the room."

"I don't have a swimming suit with me." Nicole replied.

"I know you have a pair of bikinis you can go swimming in." I implied.

"All I have are thongs."

"Fuck it, wear that! You don't have anything to be ashamed of. Besides, we're going to be in the water anyway."

"I don't know."

"Girl look, if it will make you feel better, then I'll wear one too." Gold Dee encouragingly insisted.

"Well, what we waiting on? Let's make something happen. I'll meet ya'll there." I responded before anybody could change their minds.

I still hadn't seen Jay Dee or James since we got on the ship; but I figured if they needed me then they'll find me. On the way to the Jacuzzi, I saw Diamond walking by herself. So I walked behind her, covered her eyes and kissed the side of her neck. She turned around quickly, and once she noticed that it was me she then smiled. Her next words were, "Where are you on your way to?"

"I was about to ask you the same thing; and if you wasn't busy, if you wanted to come to the Jacuzzi with me."

"You were probably going there anyway."

"You right on that; but I stopped you. If I didn't want you to go, I could have left you walking ahead of me. You didn't see me. Anyway, I'm going to be there if you decide to come," then I walked off not giving her a chance to say anything. I had a feeling she would come.

Once I made it to the Jacuzzi, I seen it was a few other folks in there already. It was: four Caucasian women that appeared to be in their early thirties; two Puerto Ricans about twenty to twenty-four years old; and an older Black couple sitting to the side by their selves. I was skeptical about getting in the Jacuzzi at this point, but no sooner than I blinked Gold Dee, Rose, and Nicole came walking up. I knew it wasn't any backing out then.

When they removed the towels they had covering them, I was caught off guard. All three of them had on thongs and was looking right. I knew they had to be looking sensational, because everyone was staring. Even the older Black man was looking in lust.

When we climbed into the water, it was just right. We began talking and touching each other on the slick. I can't lie, just by me knowing that I could fuck all of them had my dick hard as a motherfucker! A couple of minutes went by before Diamond walked up. She had on a lime-green two piece. As soon as she entered the water, she said, "I hope I'm not intruding on ya'll." sarcastically.

"We just chilling. I didn't think you were going to come. What made you change your mind?" I asked her.

"When I thought about it, it sounded like a good idea. Oh yeah, Jay Dee said come by his room in about fifteen minutes."

"You know what he want?"

"He just told me to tell you to come by his room," she said with an attitude.

I could tell Nicole, Rose, and Gold Dee didn't want Diamond around; but hey, they didn't say anything. It just got quiet until Diamond broke the silence, "Ya'll didn't have to stop talking because I'm here. Before I got in, it looked like ya'll were having fun. Don't let me stop ya'll!"

"Oh, it's not like that." Gold Dee said. "We're just getting to know each other better. Infact, when we get out of here and make it back to the room, we really planning on getting to know him."

"I heard that girl! Ya'll don't mind if I come then; do ya'll?" Diamond asked.

Nicole answered her, "That's all on you; if he don't mind."

"I don't think he'll mind. Do you?" she said staring at me.

I know damn well, ya'll know I didn't have a problem with her coming too. I was game for that. I was just hoping that I'd be able to deal with them like I wanted to. If not, oh well! I looked her in the eyes and said, "Now you know you can come. How am I going to deny family? It's all good; come and give me a kiss."

When I told her to come and give me a kiss, she didn't have a problem with that. As she came over and kissed me, I reached down and squeezed her soft ass. While she was kissing me, I saw Rose looking as if she couldn't stand Diamond. So when we finished kissing, I just motioned my lips at her and told her, "It's all good."

"I want one too!" Nicole said as Diamond moved away after the kiss.

Gold Dee shouted, "Don't leave me out!"

I knew I had to do something, and quick. I was rock hard. I said, "Hold up, let me go see what Jay Dee want. When I come back, we can do all of that good stuff." and then I hurried up and exit the Jacuzzi.

As soon as I got out of the Jacuzzi and started walking off, James came up to me from out of nowhere and said, "Jay Dee wanted to see you."

"That's where I'm on my way to now." I replied. I was wondering what the hell Jay Dee could have wanted that everybody else knew he was looking for me, but I had the slightest idea. When I got to his cabin, I asked him as I walked in, "Man what's up? What you need?"

"Make sure you lock the door" Jay Dee replied, and then went on, "I need you to count some money for me."

"Count some money for you! What you spent too much on this trip?"

"Naw; it's not nothing like that. I just want to make sure this money right."

"Where's at?"

"In them bags right there."

I noticed that he was pointing at the duffel bags that Diamond, Temeka, Nicole, Rose, and Gold Dee had brought along. The first thing I asked was, "Don't everybody have their own room?"

"Yeah; why?"

"Why is everybody's bag in here?"

"Because all the money I want you to count is in them."

When I unzipped the bags and seen that he was serious, I was fucked up. "Why you bring all of this money with you?"

Jay Dee went clean around my question and said, "It should be two hundred thousand dollars in each one of them bags."

I quickly added up that there was supposed to be a million dollars total between the five bags. It didn't even hit me that he ignored my question completely. I didn't trip off that because this was the first time I had actually ever seen this much money and was able to touch it.

I began counting the money in the first bag. It was all hundreds, so counting it was easy. I just put everything in stacks of thousands, while Jay Dee started on another bag.

In the process of putting all the money in stacks of thousands, I seen that it would have taken up the whole floor before I finished so I began putting the money in stacks of ten thousands. By the time I finished the twentieth stack, damn near an hour and a half done past by. I didn't think counting ten thousand one hundred dollar bills would take that long, but then again I had never counted that much before. The two hundred thousand that Jay Dee gave me when I came home was the most I had ever seen.

We took a small break, and then began counting again. This time, putting the money in stacks of ten thousands, it went by faster. I'd say all together it took us right around three hours to count all the money. When we finished, I lit a Black & Mild, and began talking to Jay Dee, "Now keep it real G; I know you didn't bring all of this money out here with us just to be bringing it. What you really got up your sleeve?"

"Well, let me lay it on the line G. The reason why I got all this money with us is because I'm about to make a major deal. I know you just came home and don't want to get your hands dirty any more than they are, and I been thinking about what you said about chilling out. I figure after we make this deal, I can shut things down. The only reason I asked you to come help me count this money is because I know you ain't gone steal from me plus to put you on point. We not even going to be touching shit! That's why I got them hoes carrying this" he said pointing at the duffel bags full of money.

"You mean to tell me, you got us out here on a business trip; and everybody else already knows about it except for me? What fucking type of shit you pulling? Got damn me, you doing some bad business! I came to chill, not to be on a fucking flunky mission. What the fuck you thinking of? How the fuck you gone get the shit back?"

"Damn Boom, you act like we ain't did this type of shit before! I told you, we ain't gone be touching shit; so what you tripping for? Fuck, if it wasn't for me, we wouldn't have shit!"

"What the fuck you mean I wouldn't have shit? What I'm tripping for? Got damn me, this money don't mean shit to me. You must have forgotten that I'm the one who put you on your feet! I don't owe you a motherfucking thing G!"

"Look G, you got every right to be mad because I didn't let you know what was going on; but don't let this come between us. Besides, we ain't going to be touching anything like I said. We're just going to make sure the deal go through with Jose Iracheta. You with me?"

"I guess I don't have a choice but to be. I'm going to get at you later." I said as I left feeling halfway betrayed.

On the inside, I was past being pissed off. I felt betrayed by everybody. I couldn't believe Jay Dee had me out here like a crash dummy after everything we have done. He knew when it came down to business, I liked to be on top of everything. You never know when something could go wrong, and you going to need a plan B. To top it all off, I didn't even know who the fuck Jose Iracheta was. For all I knew, he might have tried to knock all of us off for a million dollars cash. I knew I would have considered it.

I decided to go back to the ship's lounge, and order me another drink. I felt like I needed it. Just my luck, Juanita was still working. When she recognized me, she said, "You back again."

Without a second hesitation I replied, "I couldn't possibly call it a night without seeing you again. I was just hoping this time, I could get you to have dinner with me and possibly show me around since you are the owner of this ship."

"You're persistent!"

"I hope that don't offend you; but I'm like that, when I want what I want."

"Oh it doesn't offend me. Infact, I was just about to call it a day and grab me a bite to eat. I don't mind you joining me. What do you have a taste for?"

"It really don't matter to me; but whatever you wouldn't mind eating or would recommend."

"I know just the right thing."

Before we made it to go and get the food, Temeka walked by and asked me, "Where is Jay Dee and James at?"

"I just left Jay Dee in his room; and the last time I seen James he was by the Jacuzzi but that was a few hours ago."

"Well, where are you going?"

"I'm about to go have dinner with Ms. Juanita. I guess I'll see ya'll tomorrow." I said after introducing them quickly to each other.

By the time we got our food and began eating, I couldn't help but notice how Juanita stared into my eyes as we talked. It was something about her green eyes that had my full attention. I was starring in her eyes so deep in my own thoughts, that I didn't realize she was still talking to me until she said, "Excuse me, are you alright?"

"Of course I'm alright. I just couldn't help admiring your beautiful eyes."

"Thank you."

"Anyway, it's getting late and I know you had a long day. Maybe we can do this again."

"I would love to. Maybe when we get to Puerto Rico, if you are not too busy, I could have you over for dinner."

"That sounds like a good idea. Hopefully, we can do that. Good night!"

After that I went to my room. I kept hearing Jay Dee's voice in my head saying, "I'm gone make a big deal." He still had me in the blind on how he was planning on getting it back or how he actually planned on getting it. All I knew was after he got it, I wasn't coming back with it. I didn't care how well he thought he had everything planned out. I knew the chances we were taking could cost me my freedom, and I wasn't ready to give it up if something went wrong.

Chapter Thirty-six

$\mathcal{S}$hortly after I laid down, Diamond came knocking on my door. By me knowing she already knew what was going down, I really didn't feel like being bothered with her. I felt like she had been lying to me all along. The only thing I wanted to do with her, was fuck her over until she removed the robe that she was wearing.

"Just because you a bad bitch, you figure you can come over here any kind of way? What if I had company in here, what would you have done?"

"You right; I know I'm a bad bitch! If you had company, I guess you would just have had to choose who you wanted to be with. Anyway, I'm surprised you don't have any hoes in here already. You was the hottest topic after you left us waiting on you in the Jacuzzi. You know they all wanted you."

"Anyway, what you want?"

"Damn! What the fuck wrong with you? You know what the fuck I want, or do motherfuckers just show up like this all the time for you?"

"Got damn me, shut up and come kiss me!"

When she started kissing me, I put it in my heart to fuck the piss out of her. After that, she was going to have to pay me before I put that dick on her again, and I meant that. Once we started fucking, I couldn't help but to trip off how this bitch was trying to play me stupid. I began fucking her harder and harder, then flipping her in different position and pushing her legs as far back as they could bend. I even fucked her in her ass, calling myself taking my anger out on her; but she seemed to even enjoy that.

When we finished, I jumped up and went and took a shower. Once I was done doing that, I seen Diamond was still laying in the bed. Just her presence was making me sick to my stomach, so I lit up a Black & Mild and then said, "Got damn me, you got to get up and take a shower or something. You can't just lay in my bed like that."

I could tell she felt played once I told her that. She jumped up and grabbed her robe, then left. I ain't gone lie, that bitch Angel had some good pussy, but I got my rocks off by fucking Diamond in the ass and hearing her scream. I sat down on the bed, thinking about how I was going to get even with everybody. Next on my list was Gold Dee, Rose, and Nicole; and I planned on doing them all the same way.

I decided to go by Nicole's room first. Once I got there she didn't answer the door, so I figured that she had to be by Rose. I passed by Gold Dee's room next since it was closer, and was surprise to find her there by her self.

Once she let me in, I didn't bother to waste any time making my move. I grabbed her and began kissing her before she could even close the door all the way. I then pinned her to the wall right behind the door, and began removing her clothes. She didn't resist at all. Instead, she unzipped my pants and straight began sucking my dick. It got hard quick. I let her suck on it for about three minutes, and then I laid her on the floor and started fucking her the same way I just did Diamond including in the ass. Once I got mines off, I got up and told her, "I'll see you tomorrow," then went straight back to my room and called it a night.

The next day, I woke up bright and early. I couldn't sleep that good because I had revenge on my mind. As close as Jay Dee and I was, I couldn't accept the fact he was holding back shit from me that could effect my life. I made up my mind though, and decided to play everything cool for the time being.

After I took a shower and got dressed, I wet over to Temeka's room. When she opened the door, I saw that she had been up for awhile. I was like, "Damn! You always up this early? I thought you would have been sleeping."

"I always get up early. What brings you by this morning? Them hoes actually let you leave them?"

I laughed it off and said, "You know can't nobody tell me what to do or when to do it. I came to see if you wanted to go to breakfast."

"Just us; or everybody else too?"

"Just you and me."

"Well, that's cool. I haven't ate yet."

So we went to the ship's restaurant. To my surprise, Juanita was the person who took our order. She gave me a look as if to say, how could you have dinner with me last night and try to holla' at me, but be with another woman this morning; but she didn't say anything. After she took our order and left, Temeka said, "You something else. You mess with her too?"

"What you talking about?"

"You don't have to play stupid! I seen how she was looking at you. I don't know what you be doing to them; but you be having all of their minds gone."

"Somebody got to play that part; besides, that's the owner of the ship. If this deal ya'll about to make goes bad, at least I could have her on our side." When I told Temeka that, her whole face expression changed as if she was shocked that I knew about the deal. That's when I said, "You do think that would be a good idea just in case ya'll slip don't you?" then I stared at her to read her body language.

"What are you talking about?"

"What I'm talking about? Got damn me, you know what the fuck I'm talking about. You know it suppose to go down today. Don't play me stupid!"

"So which one of them hoes told you?"

"Got damn me, that's beside the point! I want to know what all you know about this deal!"

"I don't know much. I just know we are suppose to make the transaction later on today. I don't even know what time or what all we are suppose to be getting."

"For some reason I find that hard to believe. By you being as smart as you are, I know you like to be on top of things. So you just gone sit here and tell me you don't know what all you getting yourself into?"

"I told you everything I know. Jay Dee made this call and I trust he knows what he is doing."

"I'm happy you do trust him; but got damn me, don't be stupid! We all suppose to be family. We're all in this together! Got damn me, I'll ride and die for Jay Dee and anybody else in this family! If you feel you can't trust me, let me know because I ain't with all these secrets amongst us!"

"It's not even like that!" Temeka said before she was interrupted by Juanita bringing us our food.

"If I can get anything else for you all, just let me know," Juanita said.

"Well, I'd like one of you to go, when you get off of work Juanita." I replied.

She just smiled, and then sarcastically said, "I'm sure your friend and you have other plans that don't concern me."

"We're not together like that, we're just friends. Her name is Jo Ann."

They exchanged greetings, and then Juanita said, "I'm pretty busy today, but maybe tomorrow we can get together," then she left.

As soon as she left our table, Temeka asked, "Why did you tell her my name was Jo Ann?"

"Just because I'm flirting with her, that doesn't mean that I trust her. Besides, the less she knows, the better off we are. You understand me?"

She just nodded her head, and then we finished eating our breakfast without any more questions. Once we were finished, we both went to Jay Dee's room. As soon as we got there, he was finishing up a conversation on the phone and writing something down. When he finished he asked, "What brings ya'll by this early, everything alright?"

"You know what time it is! I take it that was Jose E whatever the fuck his name is!"

"Jose Iracheta; yeah that was him. What's up with the attitude this morning?"

"Got damn me, check game and peep play! Got damn me, I could have sworn I taught you better; but it's obvious I must have left something out. How the fuck are you gone have all of us out here and don't nobody knows anything about this fool you got us about to do business with? Nigga', you don't never jeopardize your whole team! Got damn me, you owe us more than that."

"Oh I see you still upset for not knowing what was going down."

"Got damn me, that's what you think this about? Motherfucker, open your eyes! Greed got you so blind, that you ain't thinking. If something goes wrong, what's your back up plan? Are is it gone be everybody go for what they know?"

"G you tripping! Ain't nothing gone go wrong! Want you just go with the flow!"

"Go with the flow! If I'm gone lay my life on the line, you better have some kind of back up plan. What you think Temeka? You haven't said a word."

Temeka quickly replied, "I must agree with you. You never know what can happen, not saying anything is going to happen."

Jay Dee snapped, "Ya'll both talking crazy! Don't ya'll know that this deal is bigger than any other deal we ever made before? It ain't no different than any other deal we made before though; it's just more money for more drugs."

"Say Temeka, go get everybody. Tell them we have a meeting as of yesterday, right now. We got some things we all need to talk about." I said. Once she left, I told Jay Dee, "G you might can't see it right now, but believe me I ain't gone tell you anything wrong. You just slipping right now and I ain't trying to see or let you fall. You know one thing for sure, and that's I'm willing to take six slugs for you and release many more if it comes down to it. You just can't keep me in the blind G; not on a mission like this!"

"Why you tell Temeka to call everybody over here?"

"Put it like this, you feel like I might be tripping; but I want you to see what the whole family thinks."

Right then, everybody started to walk in. James was the first one to ask, "What's going on?"

I waited until everybody was in the room, and then said, "Look got damn me! Everybody in here knows what's about to go down in a few; but how much about this deal do ya'll really know?" Nobody said a word. Everyone was just looking at each other dumbfounded. "Ya'll all don't have to speak at once," I said sarcastically, but still nobody said anything. Out of rage I said, "So all of ya'll are willing to put ya'll life on the line and don't know shit? Say something was to go wrong, what ya'll gone do? Somebody say something! Rose, Gold Dee,

James, Nicole, Diamond."

"I'm gone go all out," James said.

"So you gone go all out huh? You telling me you strapped?"

"Naw!"

"I didn't think so. Even if you was strapped got damn me, what if they got the upper hand and you couldn't pull yours. What you gone do G? Them motherfuckers ain't gone give a fuck about killing you if they want it! Nigga' we coming with a million dollars cash, you better think about that!" I replied then asked everybody else the same thing. After they all seem to be clueless of what they would do or could do, I shook my head and asked them, "Do ya'll want a back-up plan, or do ya'll feel like I'm tripping?"

Rose spoke up and said, "I think we should have a back-up plan just to be on the safe side."

Nobody else said anything and that shit struck my nerves. "Got damn me, don't act like ya'll can't fucking speak now! This some serious shit that we all are in together! What's up?"

Nicole then said, "I agree; we need some type of plan B."

"Well what we gone do?" Diamond asked.

This time I replied, "Check game and peep play got damn me, I need to know everybody in here ain't afraid to put in work if needed. And when I say put in work, I don't mean just going to get whatever or dropping whatever off. I mean if blood got to be spill, it ain't gone be any hesitation. Ya'll with me?" Everybody nodded in agreement except for Nicole. That's when I said, "Got damn me Nicole, I know you use to just doing hair and making drop offs; but I need you to be with us on this. I know you can use a blade. Shit, it ain't hard to cut a motherfucker across their neck if it's gone save your life. Think about it like that. This business, nothing personal! You with us?"

"I don't know about killing. I done witness it, but I don't know," she replied.

"Girl, you know you can cut a motherfucker if you have too. He just saying, we need you to have our backs like we got your back just in case." Gold Dee told her.

"Look, I'm not going to ask you to do anything I wouldn't do for you. Besides, we all are going to be right there with you."

"Okay, I'll do it if I have too!" Nicole replied.

"That's good! Jay Dee, where is the deal supposed to go down at?"

"We gone get a room at a hotel called the Red Lion Inn. That's where it's going down at."

"Do they know who all came out here with you?"

"Naw."

"That's good so check game. Before we even go to the hotel, we need to shop at a store were we can get four walkie-talkies, some switch blades, and razors. I'm assuming Jay Dee, you have a rental car on standby, but we gone need two cars to do this right. Diamond, Gold Dee, and James, ya'll gone be in the room with Jay Dee to make sure the deal go through. Rose once we get to the hotel, you're gone wait in the car. You're gone be our eyes on the outside Temeka and Nicole, ya'll are going to be with me. We gone get a room right across from Jay Dee and them. Ya'll with me so far?"

Everybody nodded their heads in agreement, and then Temeka asked, "What are we going to do with the switch blades and razors?"

"That's a good question. If any of us have to, we gone use them. So before I forget, when we go to the store, make sure we get some latex gloves. That way our finger prints can't be traced back. Now here's the play with the walkie-talkies. Jay Dee, ya'll are going to tie a rubber-band around the talk button so we can hear what's going on in the room, but keep it out of sight. The best place I'm thinking ya'll should put it is on top of the curtains, but when we get there we gone check it out to make sure we can hear ya'll as well. After the deal goes down and they leave, ya'll hurry up and take the rubber-band off so ya'll can hear us. If it looks like they are up to anything outside, Rose you gone have to let us know. That way we can move quickly and won't be caught slipping. If ya'll follow me and don't have any questions or extra input on anything I might have missed, then it's time for us to make our move. Oh yeah, Jay Dee what time do it suppose to go down?"

"Jose said to call him when I get the room; but make sure it's before seven."

"Well let's move; we don't have time to waste." I replied.

Chapter Thirty-seven

𝒯emeka and Jay Dee went and rented the two cars like planned, while the rest of us waited on the ship. When they returned, they already had the switch blades, gloves, and some walkie-talkies, so we just loaded up the cars and shot out.

We ended up driving to a Red Lion Inn hotel, which sat right between San Juan and the valley. I guess Jose choose this hotel because it sat right in the neutral zone. Looking at the structure of the building, it looked like an old red, white, and green Chinese building. It only had one floor, so I knew if any emergency exits were needed we could make any room an exit.

Jay Dee, Diamond, and Gold Dee went in first to get a room. I sent James in right behind them. When James got to the counter, he asked the clerk, "Can I get a room right across from her if possible?" pointing to Diamond who was blowing a kiss at him.

"Oh, that's no problem sir. I see you have good taste" the young clerk replied in his best English accent.

Once we gotten the rooms, we went straight to work. We ended up setting one of the walkie-talkies up on top of the curtains just like planned in the room with Jay Dee and them; and were able to hear everything even the echoes from the room James rented. After that, I put the extra walkie-talkie to B, and then told Rose, "Go ahead and get in your position. Once you get back in the car and see you can hear Jay Dee and them talking, switch your walkie-talkie to B and check to see if you can talk to me."

"Okay," Rose said then left out of the room. Moments later her voice came across the walkie-talkie. "Can ya'll hear me in there?"

"Baby-girl, we can hear you loud and clear. Can you hear what's going on in Jay Dee's room?" I replied.

"Yes, I'm picking them up clear."

"Well check game, all you have to do is watch what's going on out there. If anything looks wrong, switch your walkie-talkie on B and let us know. Other than that, you can keep your walkie-talkie on A to hear what Jay Dee and them talking about."

"Can't I just keep it on B and talk to ya'll since I don't have anything else to do out here?"

"That's cool, but you gone have to talk to Temeka or Nicole while I go tell Jay Dee to make the call so we can get this over with."

"That's cool with me. Put one of them on." Rose replied. I didn't say anything, I just handed Nicole the walkie-talkie and left.

James answered the door as soon as I knocked. Gold Dee and Diamond was just sitting on the bed. When Jay Dee looked me in the face, he knew it was time to make the call. I didn't even have to say anything. The conversation on the phone went by quick. All I heard Jay Dee say was, "Iracheta, 313" and then he hung up.

I knew when Jay Dee said 313, he was giving Iracheta the room number so I asked him, "Is he on his way?"

"I guess so. He just said alright." Jay Dee replied.

On the inside, I was still tripping off how Jay Dee was planning on playing me. I mean, I always kept it straight up with him when it came down to business. The fact that I was the last one to find out what was going down made me wonder what else he was keeping a secret from me. I just said, "Well ya'll, I'm about to go get back in my position. If ya'll need anything, just let me know. I'm going to be able to hear ya'll" and then I left.

When I walked back into the room, I heard Rose complaining about how hot it was outside. I knew she wasn't bitching just to be because on the way to the hotel it felt like it was a hundred degrees with the air condition on. I just told Nicole to tell her, "She got to deal with it for the time being. It ain't gone be that long."

That's when Temeka asked me, "What do we do now?"

"Just wait! That's all we can do."

I stretched out across the middle of the bed anxiously waiting to get this deal over with, when Temeka came and sat next to me and began speaking. "You know you not anything like Jay Dee!"

"What you mean by that?"

"I can see ya'll both are about handling business, but your style is different."

"How is that?"

"You more organize. That's what I like about you. You don't just look at the picture from one point o view."

"You not suppose too. If you do, you just blinding yourself to other possibilities. You never know exactly what's going to happen unless you are watching a movie you already seen before."

"That's what I'm talking about. How did you and Jay Dee end up hooking up?"

"Let's just say, we met up in the same place at the right time. The question is how did you and Jay Dee hook up and you an architect?"

"I met him after I just finish making a business deal and was on my way to eat, when he asked me out to lunch. I accepted his offer, and that was that to make a long story short. Can I ask you a personal question if you don't mind?"

"Be my guest."

"I know you have killed before, but how old was you when you took your first life?"

I just looked at her for a moment. I wasn't expecting her to ask me that out of all the questions in the world. After realizing she really wanted an answer, I told her, "I was sixteen going on seventeen and I accidentally killed my homeboy's baby in a shot out, but it wasn't intentionally." regretting that memory. "Have you ever taking a life?"

"No, but I have stabbed an ex boyfriend of mine." Temeka replied. I just shook my head. I didn't bother to ask her why or what happen.

About an hour and a half went by and Jose still haven't showed up. Rose was saying she had to use the bathroom when a jet Black Range Rover pulled into the hotel parking lot follow by a jet Black Cadillac. "I think they just arrived, but I can't see how many folks are in the truck or car." Rose replied over the walkie-talkie.

I jumped off the bed and told her, "You got to hold tight on using the bathroom right now; just keep watching them."

Jose stepped out of the Cadillac dressed in all Versace. He removed his Versace shades and looked around before reaching inside the Range Rover removing a Black sack, then entered the hotel. Whoever was inside the Range Rover never got out, nor made themselves visible; they just sat in the truck.

Once Jose got inside the room, we were able to hear Jay Dee introducing him to everybody else. After introducing him to everybody, Jose asked to use the bathroom. I knew that was a sign that meant he didn't trust Jay Dee and wanted to see if anybody else was in the room. When he came out, he asked for something to drink. That's when Jay Dee explained to him that the only thing they had to drink was some water. After that, Jay Dee said, "Let's get down to business."

"Let me see the money first." Jose said.

"James, open the duffel bags," Jay Dee commanded. Once the money was revealed, he told Jose, "It's all there."

Jose then opened the sack he had revealing a digital scale and an automatic money counter and said, "I just want to make sure it's all here. It won't take long." It took about forty minutes to count all the money. When they finished, Jose made a phone call and told someone, "Trailo para adento (Which means bring it inside in English)," then hung up.

Outside, Rose was still watching the jet Black Range Rover when both back doors open. She hurried up and switch her walkie-talkie on B saying, "I think ya'll might have some trouble headed ya'll way. Two really big muscular men just got out the truck. Hold on, they grabbing something."

I hurried up and responded back to her, "What's going on out there? What they grabbing?"

"It looks like two large army duffel bags."

"That's it? Do you see any guns?"

"No; but I still haven't seen the driver or who is on the passenger side."

"Just keep watching! The two muscular looking men should be on their way in, and that should be the dope in the bags they carrying. If whom ever left in the cars make a move, then let us know immediately."

By then, we were able to hear them knocking on Jay Dee's room door. It was like going through the same procedures again. Jose asked, "You want to test it? It's pure cocaine. A thousand and eight grams a kilo. See!" and then he put one of the kilos on the digital scale.

When Jay Dee seen it was weighting right, he said, "I don't need to try it."

James interrupted and said, "What you mean you don't need to try it? How you know they ain't trying to sell you no soap? I'll test it for you," he said while removing a fifty dollar bill from his own pocket.

Jay Dee looked at him and said, "Go ahead."

James rolled the fifty dollar bill up into like a straw. Then with the quickness of an experience expert, he spit a razor out of his mouth and cut into one of the kilos. He then began chopping the cocaine up until it became fine. After that, he made two lines out of the cocaine, and snorted one line in each side of his nose. Instantly, his mouth went numb. James then went into the bathroom and ran some water on his hand, and dripped some down his nose. When he came out of the bathroom, he said, "Man, it's good!"

Jay Dee just looked at James then Jose and said, "Well let's get this over with."

Jay Dee started counting the kilos. Every time he got to forty, he put one of the duffel bags on top of that stack that the money came out of. When they finished Jose told Jay Dee, "You real! We have to do more business together," then him and his two men left.

I was still waiting on Rose to tell me if they tried to make a funny move, but as soon as they pulled off her voice came over the walkie-talkie saying, "They gone. Can I come inside now? I still have to use the bathroom, and bad!"

"Give us a few minutes to move that stuff just in case they do come back."

"Alright, but hurry up. I really have to use the bathroom."

Chapter Thirty-eight

*I*t was exactly six fifty by the time we made it back to the cruise ship.

They had so many custom guards patrolling the dock, that my first thought was this got to be a set up. I didn't have the slightest ideal on how we were going to get pass them, but I knew I wasn't carrying a motherfucking thing. Temeka asked the big question that everybody was thinking, "How are we suppose to get pass all of these damn police?"

I co-signed with her, "Yeah Jay Dee, how you planning on getting that shit aboard?"

He had what we call a dick look on his face. Meaning stuck on stupid. He just looked around, and then at his watch and said, "I didn't know the custom guards were going to be out here."

"Well, what are we suppose to do?" Nicole asked in a panicking voice.

"Just relax for a minute and let me think of something, "I interrupted, but was clueless of what to really do. After a quick thought I said, "Check this out! Diamond and Gold Dee, ya'll going to walk together. When ya'll get close to the guards, start talking loud enough so they can hear ya'll talking about shopping. If they try to stop ya'll, Jay Dee going to be right behind ya'll to distract the guards."

"How do I suppose to do that?" Jay Dee quickly interrupted.

"I don't know, make up something! Ask them what time it is. James and Nicole, ya'll walk in like a couple. If they try to stop ya'll, Nicole ask them if they know how to get to the ship's bar before they can finish saying what they want. You got me?"

"Un huh!" Nicole replied.

"Rose and Temeka, as soon as ya'll see Diamond and Gold Dee make it in, ya'll start walking in. Ya'll don't have to be together, but start walking. I'm going to be right behind ya'll. Let's move," I replied with authority.

We all started moving like planned. I could tell everyone was apprehensive just by the way they were walking, but I couldn't blame them. I didn't know if my plan was going to work, but we were about to find out because Diamond and Gold Dee had just reached the boarding dock.

To my surprise, they walked straight in without the guards even acknowledging them. I knew if anything went wrong from this point, we at least had eighty kilos to shake back with. By the time James and Nicole made it up the boarding walk, I figured Rose and Temeka didn't have anything to worry about until I seen damn near all the custom guards walking towards them. I was hoping they would have just kept their cool and continue walking like planned, but Rose stopped on the board walk drawing attention to herself.

"What the fuck are you doing? Keep walking!" I said to myself but it was too late.

One of the custom guards stopped next to her and began speaking to her. I couldn't hear what all he was saying, but I knew it was up to me to do something and quick before they ask to search her bag. When I walked up, I heard Rose saying something about her feet hurt and she had to use the bathroom. The guard said, "You sure you are alright ma'am?"

Before she could respond back I said, "Hello Natilie! I haven't seen you in awhile. Where is your husband John at?"

"Oh, he didn't come with me on this trip," Rose replied.

"Let me give you a hand," I said hoping the guard was buying our act

"Well ma'am and sir, you all enjoy ya'll vacation," the guard said then walked off.

I was thinking to myself that was a close call, when Juanita Maria walked up to me and said, "I see you have a lot of friends," sarcastically.

I thought that was cute, but I couldn't tell you where the hell she came from. I said, "How are you doing Juanita?" admiring her voluptuous beauty.

"I'm alright myself; but I can see you are doing just as fine."

That's when Rose said, "I can see you all have some things to talk about, but thank you for giving me a hand. I'll tell John I seen you," and then I handed her back the duffel bag and she left.

Juanita and me continue walking aboard the ship chatting about different subjects. After a conversation about jealousy came up, Juanita insisted that she wasn't the jealousy type although her actions showed differently. She kept on asking me what I liked about her, when it appeared I could have gotten just about any woman I wanted. I told her, "I'm infatuated with your beauty and accent; but knowing that you are an accomplisher, shows me that you can endue any challenges that may come your way. That's what really makes me want you."

Once I said that, she just kissed me. We must have chilled together for about an hour and a half more before Juanita told me she had to go. When she left, I decided to go get something to eat. To my surprise, Jay Dee and the rest of the family was in the ship's restaurant already. Everyone except for James. I tried not to acknowledge them, but it was too late. "Say Boom, we over here," Jay Dee yelled across the room.

The way they were smiling, I knew they were up to something devious as if this trip wasn't enough; but I kept my cool. The first thing I asked was, "Where James at?"

"He around here somewhere," Temeka answered.

After celebrating and making a toast to a business deal gone good, I had to dismiss myself from the table. It was killing me on the inside to be acting like I was cool with everything that was going down. "You're not going to stay and eat with us?" Rose asked.

"Naw, I'm just gone get me something to eat to go," I replied.

"Damn, what the fuck wrong with you? You been acting funny the whole time we been on this damn cruise," Jay Dee said loudly drawing attention.

"Got damn me, if you don't calm your ass down, you really gone see me lose my cool! Just because you my nigger don't mean the tables can't turn and we can set this motherfucker off in here however you want to! Now what?"

"Ya'll tripping! We family! We got to stick together especially right now," Nicole stated.

Gold Dee, Rose, and Temeka agreed with Nicole. Diamond didn't say anything at first until a waiter came by our table and asked, "Is everything okay over here?"

"Everything is alright. They were just having a difference in opinion. We will keep the noise to a minimum." Once the waiter left she said, "What really seems to be the problem between ya'll? We have too much to risk for ya'll to fall out now. What's the problem?"

I ignored her question and said, "Got damn me, ya'll enjoy ya'll celebration; and I'll see ya'll tomorrow," then left.

I didn't even go to my room. Instead, I went on top of the ship's deck and just stared at the water. I had so much stuff on my mind, that my thoughts were scramble. I knew I had about a hundred and sixty thousand dollars to myself, so I didn't have to be taking this chance. It wasn't worth it to me, but then I didn't have a choice if I wanted in or not. That's what was burning me up. I admit that I like to have the finer things and believe in getting them, but I would've never put myself in this kind of predicament knowing the chances of getting caught over weighted the chances of getting away.

I decided to call Angela just to see what she was doing, but she wasn't there like usually. After the phone just rung a few times, I hung up and called by Keisha's house. I didn't even get an answer there. I figured it was meant for me to be by myself for the night and headed back towards my room.

On the way there, I seen Juanita walking and talking to a man that appeared to be Puerto Rican. She was so heavy into their conversation that she didn't notice me walking towards them. As soon as I got on the side of them I said, "I see you have a lot of friends too!"

I guess my words caught her off guard because she looked around quickly. Once she seen I was the one that said that to her, she smiled and replied, "It's not even like that! Tj, this is my brother Chuey. Chuey, this is Tj."

We exchanged our greetings, and then I said, "Well don't let me stop ya'll from doing as ya'll were. I'll see you tomorrow, and Chuey it was nice meeting you" then continue walking towards my room.

Before I even took three steps, Juanita stopped me and asked, "If you not busy, do you mind taking a ride with me over to my father's house? It won't take long, and afterwards I'll show you around." Now I really didn't want to meet her father, but how could I turn her down after the offer she proposed.

Juanita, Chuey, and me ended up leaving together. I didn't expect Juanita to be driving a BMW, but she was. Just that quick it had slipped my mind that she was the cruise ship owner. Chuey road in the back seat voluntarily. He didn't talk as much, so it was hard for me to figure out what he did for a living. I assumed we had to be around the same age just by his facial appearance, but I didn't question him.

We road for the longest time it seemed like to say this wasn't suppose to take long. The sceneries didn't look anything like the states back home; but I could tell when we were in the slums, and when we reached the counties. Over all it was a pretty site to see. By the time we reached their father's house, I figured he had to be a millionaire.

He had a high electric gate blocking the road off completely, that turned into a light gray brick wall in each direction. Heavy armed bodyguards were visible everywhere I looked. I couldn't help asking, "What do ya'll father do, that he need all of this protection?"

Chuey answered, "Nothing! He just likes to protect what's his" with a look on his face that said not to ask too many more questions.

Once the gate was opened for us, I seen he lived in a huge mansion that had a lake running in front of his home. The closer we got to his house, I seen he had bodyguards securing his entire home. Video cameras covered every piece of ground he owned. Right in front of his house, he had three stretched Bentleys parked. A white one, gray one, and a Black one. I didn't know what type of business he was in, but I admired his taste. Just the outside of his house was more like a house that I could only dream of having, so I couldn't wait to see the inside of it.

As soon as we enter the mansion, I seen it was twelve fourteen on a clock that could have covered a regular size apartment wall by itself. I was so busy looking at the huge room and the exquisite arts that filled it, that I didn't notice Chuey had exit the room we were in. Moments later, an old man with thin gray and white hair came into the room. When our eyes connected, he had an expression on his face as if he caught a theft red handed.

Juanita broke our stare by greeting the old man with a hug saying, "Hi papa. This is my friend Tj. Tj, this is my father; Mr. Calvillo."

I greeted Mr. Calvillo, but I could tell that he wasn't pleased with my presence inside his home. I didn't know how strict he was, or if the fact that it was after twelve o'clock had something to do with anything; but I sensed something was wrong. He walked out of the room, and then called Juanita right behind him. She left me standing in the room by myself to see what her father wanted. That's when I heard what sounded like him going off in Spanish. "Yo no quiero este dedo en mi casa."

I didn't understand a single word he was saying; but when Juanita came back into the room with me she said to me, "We have to leave right now," and that's exactly what we did.

I tried to figure out why we had to leave so soon, but I really couldn't tell you. At first I thought it was because I was Black until Juanita said, "I'm sorry for the way my father reacted towards you; but he doesn't trust anybody he doesn't know."

Now I could tell she was sincere about her apology, but now it was my turn and the perfect timing to fish her on what her father really did to obtain everything he had. Fuck, I just done seen just about everything I ever dreamed about having in a matter of minutes. So how could I possibly past up this opportunity? I couldn't! I started off by telling her, "It's not your fault how your father reacted towards me. Infact, he's not the first person to feel insecure. I guess I might be like that to if I had such a beautiful daughter." Juanita just blushed, and then I went on and asked her, "What exactly did you say your father did for a living?"

She looked at me with an expression of distrust for a moment, and then replied, "He doesn't do anything. Every since I was young, he always had the best; but I never seen my father do any work. He might go on a few business trips as he calls them, but I can't tell you what he does."

I didn't know if Juanita just didn't trust me enough or just wasn't going to tell me what I wanted to know, but from what she did tell me I knew her father was doing something illegal either now or in the past.

Chapter Thirty-nine

*J*uanita ended up showing me around the different parts of Puerto Rico. By it being after twelve o'clock in the morning, it wasn't really any traffic on the roads so we were able to continual our journey in peace. By the time we made it to an urban part, Juanita stopped at a tan brick building with the word "Alas" on top of it. That's when she said, "I should have asked you before I stopped if you were comfortable with going into clubs, but I really need a drink. Besides, this is a nice club."

"Oh, I don't mind! We been riding for awhile now anyway. Let me see how ya'll party," I replied but my real intentions was to get Juanita drunk so that she would open up to me and I could find out what I wanted to know.

When we entered the club, they had a tech mo beat blasting with Spanish words over it so I couldn't understand what was actually being played. Juanita asked me, "Well, how do you like it?"

To be honest I wasn't feeling it at all. How could I? I didn't even understand the music that was being played. They had wings hanging from the ceiling all over the place, with the club's name written on them and everyone was starring as if they were trying to tell me I didn't have any business in this place. I just kept my cool and said, "It's different from home, but why do they have wings on everything in here?"

She smiled then replied, "They have wings everywhere because that's the name of the club. That's what alas means in Spanish. What do you want to drink?"

"I want the same thing that you are having," I responded as we walked towards the bar.

Once we made it to the bar, Juanita told the bar tender what we wanted. When he came back, I reached inside my pocket and gave him a twenty dollar bill. I already knew the blue drink he just brought us wasn't strong at all, so off top the next one I was going to get him to put a couple of shots in it.

We mango around the floor for awhile before I went and got us another round of drinks. By the time I purchase us our third drink, Juanita was real open with me. She was even telling me things that I wasn't even asking her, so I knew she was tipsy.

It was approximately three thirty before we left the Puerto Rican club. A couple of times I seen Juanita staggering on the way to the car, so I decided it was best for me to be the designated driver. She didn't complain at all. She just handed me the keys to the car and said, "I'm sorry! I hope I didn't ruin your night."

I just kissed her on her cheek and replied, "You didn't mess up nothing. I'm still enjoying myself, but you do have to tell me how to get out of here."

Once she showed me back onto the main road, I kind of knew my way back to the ship although I still had other plans. When I recognize the Avalon Resorts Hotel that we past up earlier coming up, I knew we were no more than an hour away from the ship so I pulled into the hotel parking lot and cut the engine off. That's when I woke Juanita up. "Where are we?" Juanita questioned.

"I seen you were sleeping, so I figured I'll get us a room for the night so that you can sleep comfortable. Besides, I don't know my way all the way back to the ship from here."

"Oh that was thoughtful of you, but you didn't have to do that. I have an apartment not that far from here that we can go to."

"You sure? Because it really don't matter to me. I just want you to be comfortable."

"Trust me, I'll be comfortable. All you have to do is make a right at the light, and I'll show you the rest from there."

In the matter of minutes she was telling me where to park. By the look of the outside of the building, I knew it was what we called a shotgun apartment. Meaning when you open the front door, you could see all the way to the back door without going inside; but to my surprise it was much larger when we went inside. The first thing Juanita said was, "Excuse my apartment. I don't usually have company here."

"Oh, don't worry about it. It ain't nothing wrong with your place. Besides, I rather see how you keep your apartment when you are just being yourself, than when you are trying to entertain company," I replied as we began to make small talk. Before I knew it, I could tell the liquor had Juanita in heat because she kept coming on to me. I knew without a doubt in the world I could have fucked, but I didn't want her to feel like I just took advantage of her because she was drunk. So what I did was tell her, "I think we should take things slow. I know everything seems right, but I want to make sure this is what we both really want. Instead of doing something we might regret."

It's not a person dead or living who could tell me I didn't catch her off guard with my reply by how she looked at me. She just said, "You right. Do you want to watch a movie in my room with me?"

"I don't see anything wrong with that. What you got to watch?" I replied really giving a careless about what she put on to be watched.

No soon as she put a movie on and laid across her bed, she was sound asleep. I would have never imagined in a million years, that I would have been in a bed with a pretty, drunk, Puerto Rican chick, that I could have fuck but didn't; who actually snored and loud! I just pulled her cover and sheet over her body, and then went in the living room and made my bed out of her couch.

Later on that day when I woke up, I seen it was already going on three o'clock. Juanita was still sleeping in the bed, so I just let her get her rest on while I went to use the bathroom. I was trying my best not to make to much noise as I rinse my mouth out with some Scope she had on the sink counter when Juanita walked in on me. "Oh! I'm sorry I didn't know you was in here." Then close the door back.

I hurry up and finish rinsing my mouth out, and then walked out of the bathroom and told her, "I'm finish." As soon as she came out of the bathroom I asked her, "How you doing Miss you want to watch a movie with me!"

She just smiled revealing her pearly white teeth, and then she said, "I'm sorry if I felt asleep while watching the movie."

"While watching the movie! As soon as you put it on and got in the bed, you went straight to sleep. I'm surprise you didn't wake up with a head-ache."

"I don't have a head-ache, but my stomach hurt."

"Drink a Sprite or a 7-up; it'll make your stomach stop hurting unless you're just hungry."

"I'm kind of hungry."

"You want me to cook you breakfast; or do you want to go out and have breakfast?"

"You cook breakfast! Come on now, what you want for breakfast?"

"Oh you don't believe I can cook? I can do the damn thang yeah!"

"I'm not going to say you can't cook, but I'll rather be on the safe side," she replied as we both began laughing.

When it was all said and done, we had to go to the store and buy something we could cook to eat because she didn't have anything we could have eaten. We ended up agreeing on making a meal together. I cooked us fried pork chops and French fries; while Juanita made us a salad to go along with it.

By the time we started eating, it started raining hard and the lights went out. We both thought they were going to come right back on, but they didn't. Infact, they stayed off and Juanita had to light some candles. As we continual eating our food and getting to know each other doing that time, it wasn't long before she was telling me her life story and how she ended up being a cruise ship owner. Before seven o'clock that night, I learned that her father, Mr. Calvillo, was the real drug lord in Puerto Rico and her brother Chuey was following right behind him.

A lil' while after I decided it was time for me to get back to the ship. Juanita was cool and all, but I was ready to get away from her for a minute. As soon as we arrived at the ship, Juanita dropped me off at the boarding dock and said, "I'll see you later," and then pulled back off.

I didn't think anything of what she said. Infact, I knew I was going to see her again before this cruise was over. I went straight into my room and began running me some hot bath water when Jay Dee knocked on the door. "G, where you been? We got problems!"

"Man, what you mean we got problems? What you talking about? I just got back!"

"I don't know how to tell you this, but," Jay Dee started before he was interrupted by more knocks on the door.

"Should I answer that?" I asked not knowing what done happen.

"Go ahead."

"Who is it?"

"It's me open up," a female voice replied. When I open the door I seen it was Temeka, but before I could say anything she said, "Where have you been all day? We been looking for you."

"Looking for me, for what?"

"You haven't told him yet?" Temeka questioned Jay Dee.

"Told me what?"

"That's what I was about to tell you. Today, Gold Dee found James dead!"

"Found James dead! How?"

"She said she went to his room and when she went inside, he was leaning forward in the bed as if he were playing asleep. But when she lifted his head, blood just started pouring out of his nose."

They didn't have to tell me any more. I knew James had to be snorting some cocaine before he died and must have busted a blood vessel in his brain which actually killed him. I just shook my head and asked, "Where everybody else at now?"

"Gold Dee is in the room with Nicole, Rose, and Diamond. They're trying to pull her together. As for as James, he still in the room. We didn't know if we should have called the police or not" Temeka replied.

"Call the police! Hell naw don't do that. If ya'll was to do that, they gone search all of us and our stuff because Jay Dee brought all of the tickets together and then we really gone be fucked."

"Well what should we do then?" Temeka asked.

I wanted Jay Dee to answer that since it was his fault we were all out here in the first place, but I just said, "We got to get rid of his body because if they find it on this ship, we all gone be listed as accomplisher to murder in the first degree; and somebody gone have to take the charge. Everybody else gone get accessory and I can't afford that."

"Charge us with murder or accessory; ain't that a bitch!" Jay Dee said unaware that he actually said that out loud.

I couldn't help saying, "Ain't it! Anyway, Jay Dee we need them latex gloves, switch blades, and a ride. I wouldn't give a fuck, if you have to buy a stroller too. We need this shit now while the boarding dock police off. I'm more than sure this ship has a laundry room on it so Temeka, I'm gone need for you to wash all the linen that got blood on them. After that get all of James personal belongings together and put them in a bag. As soon as you finish, make sure you put the room back together as if no one ever had used it. I'll get Diamond to help you, but whatever ya'll do make sure ya'll don't leave behind any clues anybody was in there."

After I said what I had to, I went and turned the bath water I had running off; and then we left. We all walked to Nicole's room where everybody else was. As soon as Nicole seen me, she came and hug me while bursting out in tears. I personally wasn't in the mood nor feeling this sympathetic ass shit so I coldly said, "Look, you're still breathing and living ain't you? So get over this shit! Diamond come on, we got something to do." Everybody looked at me like I was a cold hearted, shrewd, son of a bitch as Diamond followed us back out of the room. When we got in the hallway, I simply told Diamond, "Temeka gone show you what to do when it's time" and we continue walking in silence.

Once we got inside of Jay Dee's room, he past out the gloves and put two switchblades in his pocket. Temeka grabbed some bags and past them to Gold Dee. She was about to say something before I cut her off. "Look, ya'll wait in here until we come back." Then Jay Dee and me left.

I knew where the ship's gift shop was, I was just hoping we could find a stroller or something we could use to move James with. Just our luck, they had wheelchairs for sale in there. On our way back to Jay Dee's room, we bumped into Chuey. I was surprise to see him on the ship again out of all people. I could only assume that Juanita was somewhere around too, but I didn't ask him if he knew where she was. I had one thing on my mind and that was to get rid of James body right and soon. He couldn't help noticing Jay Dee and me was pushing a wheelchair without anyone in it, so he asked, "What's up with the wheelchair?"

I quickly answered, "One of our friends hurt their legs; so we just went and got one for them."

"Are they alright?"

"They fine! Don't worry about them. Before we even make it back home, they won't be needing this wheelchair. Anyway, you be cool and I'll see you later." I replied so that we could hurry up and get this over with.

"Who was that?" Jay Dee asked.

"That's Chuey! He's the ship owner brother."

"How you know him?"

"That ain't important right now! What you need to worry about is what we got to do!" I said sharply as we made our way back to the room. As soon as we entered the room, I told Jay Dee, "Get some different clothes you can put on right quick and put them in a bag."

"For what?" Jay Dee questioned me.

"G, just do it so we can go." I replied.

I had a hunch that we were leaving something that we needed behind, but I couldn't put my hand on it. When we went inside of James room, the first thing I did was observe everything in it. Then I put on my set of gloves and said, "Let's get this over with." As we got closer to the bed, I seen James had one of the kilos on the bed. It looked like he must have been snorting straight out of it, but now it was covered in blood. So I said, "Make sure you subtract that from what you suppose to have, and pass me a big towel to wrap his head in."

Once Jay Dee past me the towel he said, "This nigga' don't even have on any clothes."

"Put him on some. Just make sure they don't get or got any blood on them."

"Who gone put them on him?" Jay Dee said.

"I wouldn't give a fuck witch one of ya'll put them on him! Where his clothes at anyway?"

"They right here," Diamond answered.

"Good! You can give him a hand. Temeka, let's go. I know what we forgot."

When we walked out of the room, Temeka asked, "What you gone do with him?" referring to James.

"I ain't gone do nothing at all. Anyway, I need for you to purchase one of them big straw hats they be wearing out here. They right on the side of the counter in the store. Jay Dee and me just left out of there, so I don't want to go back in there. Infact, just buy three of them."

I could tell Temeka didn't like how I replied to her question, but she wasn't going to question me again about it either. To be honest, I know she wasn't really ready to hear the details of what I had in mind to do with James. When she came out of the store she said, "You know these hats thirty dollars a piece?"

"That's it? That's good! Look at where you buying them from, I know you didn't think they were going to be free. But serious shit Temeka, make sure ya'll don't leave any clues behind. You know Diamond feel like she's made out of princess cuts; but if you have to put her in her place, because we can't afford anymore fuck ups. You feel me?"

It wasn't a need for her to respond back because it was clear about what I meant. When we made it back to the room, I seen they had put James on some clothes so I didn't waste anytime giving Jay Dee a hand putting James in the wheelchair. Once we got James in the chair right, I gave Jay Dee one of the straw hats Temeka purchase and put one on James and myself then said, "Let's go."

We made our way out of the ship and onto the boarding dock without any interruption. Once we got off the ramp, we headed down a dark street that ran along the coast. We kept following the street until the road turned. Right where the road turned, it was a pathway that led closer to the coast and that's the pathway we took.

The farther we walked, the louder we could hear the water splashing off of the coastline. Once we reached a spot that was pitch black I said, "This it; let's go to work."

"What we got to do?" Jay Dee asked.

"Now you got to cut his fingerprints off. If you have to, just cut the whole tip of his fingers off."

"You playing right?"

"Do I look like I'm playing? Got damn me, I'm serious than a motherfucker! Get started." I could tell he wasn't expecting this, but he tried to portray an image as if he was. He removed one of the switchblades from his pocket nervously. When I seen that I said, "It'll be easier for you just to cut the top of his fingers off since you jumpy."

"Is this really necessary?"

"Ask yourself that! This motherfucker was stealing from you and done fuck around and die using what he suppose to be making his paper with; and to set it all off, if they find him got damn me you gone be the one charged with murder. Now is it really necessary?"

What I said was ringing through Jay Dee's head. Within the next couple of seconds, he was chopping James fingers off like he was a Mohican on a slaughtering spree. A couple of times I seen him gag as if he was about to vomit, but he didn't. He just asked, "What's next?" when he finished.

I looked at James ten fingers in Jay Dee's hand and then told him, "You don't need them anymore. You can throw them as far as you can, but now it's time to get rid of his teeth." I reached down and picked up an earth rock about the size of my hand and told Jay Dee, "Just make sure you knock out most of them." and that was a wrap. Jay Dee broke out most of his teeth in one blow, and then we dropped his body in the ocean.

Chapter Forty

$\mathcal{B}$y the time we made it back to the ship, Jay Dee was still kind of shaky; so I whisper to him, "G, go take a shower to get any blood off of you that we don't see. When you finish, come by my room and we can go get a drink together. Besides, we have some things to talk about!"

We went our separate ways from that point. Inside my mind, I really didn't think Jay Dee was really going to have the heart to dispose James the way that he did; especially, by the way that he was shaking. That just goes to show me that I couldn't underestimate him. I just needed him to stay solid.

On the way to my room, I seen Temeka and Diamond coming out of James room. They both were startled when they looked around and seen me. The first thing I asked them was, "Ya'll finish already?"

Diamond looked at me with an old sassy expression as if she wanted to tell me, "Nigga' please! You ain't gone rush me to clean shit up;" but Temeka spoke up and said, "Not quite. We got everything wash down, we just waiting on the linen to finish drying so we can make the bed back and that's it."

"When ya'll finish, don't forget to wipe off the door knob. Ain't nobody else going back in there."

"What you did with James?" Diamond questioned.

"Bitch, I'll break your got damn neck you ever ask me something like that again! Just get finish doing what you got to do," I snapped looking at her dead serious.

Temeka just stared at Diamond like how stupid are you; and then replied, "We'll be finish in awhile."

"Look, when ya'll finish, ya'll can just go chill out. What did ya'll do with his personal stuff?"

"It's all in the duffel bag by the door." Temeka answered.

"Let me get it so I can go."

Once I picked up the duffel bag, I went straight to my room. My bath water had turned cold, so I started running some more. In the process, I decided to see what all James had in his duffel bag. When I opened it up I saw: a few outfits; his identification card; a cellular phone; and two thousand dollars. My first thought was to keep the money, but instead I decided I would give it to Jay Dee. I felt like he deserved it along with the job of getting rid of the rest of James stuff. Then I sat it in the corner and lit up a Black & Mild.

After that, I laid back in the hot water I just had re-ran, reviewing in my mind what all done took place as I watched the clouds of smoke fill the room. The more I viewed the images in my mind, the more I realized I was past being in too deep. It was more like I was dedicated to this game of chance, regardless if I wanted to change or not. For every step I tried to take away from the game, it seemed like I took six more steps even deeper into it.

My thoughts were interrupted by a knock on the door. When I opened it, it was Jay Dee. "You not ready yet?"

"Just give me a second to slide something on," I replied and then began getting dress. "You ate anything?"

"Naw. I really haven't had an appetite for anything."

"G, I got to get me one of them shrimp platters. Oh yeah, you see that bag in the corner? That's for you. Get rid of it wisely."

"What's in it?"

"You gone see."

Once Jay Dee looked inside the duffel bag, he said, "What I 'm suppose to do with this shit?"

"That's on you. Let's go!" Jay Dee lifted up the money inside of the bag, then placed it all back down. When I seen him do that, I told him, "You can bring it along with us now," then I walked out of the door.

We stopped by Jay Dee's room to drop off the duffel bag, and then made our way to the ship's lounge. We ended up getting a table not that far from the counter, and both ordered a shrimp and fish platter. When we tried to purchase a bottle of Hennessey, we were informed that they were out and then was suggested to try a bottle of Puerto Rico Rum.

It was alright if you were a Rum drinker, but I would have preferred the Hennessey. Before our food even much came, we had done already finish the bottle of Rum. I didn't notice the effect of the Puerto Rico Rum until I seen Jay Dee's eyes turn reddish. Neither one of us said anything, we were just lost in our on thoughts for a couple of minutes.

After I noticed we were just sitting at the table like some drunks struck at a bar, I broke the silence. "Got damn me, check game and peep play G! You know I don't know how much you know about everybody on our team, but it's obvious you lacking some knowledge somewhere."

"What the fuck you mean it obvious I'm lacking some knowledge?"

"Got damn me, it don't take a genius to see you slipping. If you was on point, you would have already known your boy would steal from you. Second of all, by he being a dope fiend, you should have never put him in a predicament like this unless it was a must in the first place. You feel me? Now check game, I didn't come here to argue with you, I just wanted to let you know you need to get on point and do your homework on who you got on your team before you make any more moves."

Jay Dee just sat in silence. I could tell that I had pissed him off and he felt played, but on the inside he knew I was right. Our food came right before Jay Dee said, "G, I don't know where I'm really slipping at. Every since this money been flowing in, a lot of shit been happening. If it ain't one thing, it's another. That's why I told you, I wanted you to run shit like you use to."

"Gangster, you caught up in the life style. I told you, I don't want to continue taking these types of chances for nothing. Besides, with the money you make off this trip, you should be able to retiree for good. Just think, if you slang each kilo for eighteen five, you gone make three point seven; and you can't forget each one raw! You can make two out of each one and make seven million and four hundred thousand easily. After you give everybody what you gone give them, you still straight!"

"You right! I didn't even think about that," Jay Dee replied while nodding his head.

"But first thing first. You still got to find out everything about everybody on our team. We ain't got no more room for any mistakes."

"Say no more, that's a done deal! I'm gone know what time each one of them hoes start bleeding even before they do "

I had to laugh because I knew he was about to get on point like he was suppose to been. We continue eating in peace making small talk. All of a sudden, Jay Dee just stop talking in the middle of a conversation we were having. I was waiting on him to continue, but he never did. When I looked up at him, I seen that he was starring across the room so I turned to see what he was looking at. It just so happen to be Juanita.

She had her hair pinned up, wearing a skin tight white dress revealing her figure. I can't lie, her walk by itself was just eye catching. You could see she was wearing some bikini panties, by the way her ass was bouncing. I said to Jay Dee, "I see you like her. Won't you try to pull her."

He said, "You ain't lying! Look at her walk!" and then jumped up and went after her.

You might be wondering why I sent him after her, but I just wanted to see how Juanita would react. If he was able to get her, then I would have to respect his game. I couldn't hate, I would just know how to play my cards with her.

Now I'm watching from a distance and see Jay Dee trying to do his thing. I couldn't hear what he was telling her, but for a second it looked like he had her right where he wanted her. Then I seen her shake her head in a no thank you type of gesture, and I just laughed to myself.

When he made it back to the table, I didn't hesitate to ask him, "What happen? It looked like you had her!" he mumble a few words, and then I said, "Now peep game G. I'm gone show you how to get her," then departed the table.

When I stood up, I felt the liquor kick in. All of a sudden, I was in player mode. I mean the more I looked at her ass, the more I had to have her. When I approached her, I went to speaking so fast and continuously that I made her forget about what she was doing. When I finish speaking, we left together.

I didn't even bother to go back to the table where Jay Dee was. Instead, we went straight to my room. I was telling Juanita some of everything that I thought she might of wanted to hear. I mean I had one thing on my mind, and that was to get Juanita out of that dress. Before long, that's exactly what I did.

We started off slow, as if we were really making love. The more she kiss me, the more passionate we became. The thought of knowing her father was paid to the fullest and she had money herself, only turned me on even more. As we changed positions, I begin hitting her harder. Once she called out my name, it was on. I started fucking her as if she was the last piece of pussy I ever was going to get.

We started in the middle of the bed. Next thing I knew, I had her on the edge of the bed with both of her legs pinned up. Some kind of way, we ended up on the floor. When that happen, she was all in. I let her ride my dick for a few while I caught my breath, and then I flipped her and made her lay down flat on her stomach. I closed her legs all the way, then started dipping in and out of her pussy. When I felt her having an orgasm, I pulled my dick out of her and rubbed it along the crack of her ass.

You ain't got to wonder if I was about to try to fuck her in her ass. To ease ya'll minds, ya'll fucking right I was about to try it. As I continue rubbing my dick against her ass crack to make sure it was nice and wet, Juanita said, "Please don't! It's gone hurt."

I push my dick back inside of her pussy, and then kissed her and said, "It ain't gone hurt. I'm gone take it slow." She was about to say something when I cut her off and said, "Just give it a try. If you don't like it, I'm gone stop."

She let out a sigh as I continue penetrating her. She then barely said, "Go ahead and do it."

I didn't ask her was she sure. I just relubicated her crack again. This time I slowly eased my head into her. She tighten her muscles up so tight, that it was hurting me. I had to be absolutely still and told her, "Relax!"

"I can't it hurt."

I pulled it out and said, "Check this out, lay back down on the bed and suck on my finger."

"Suck on your finger!"

"Yeah, just go along with it."

She put a look on her face that could have only spoken for itself. Then finally she said, "Alright."

When she started sucking on my finger, I begin hitting her form the back while moving my finger back and forth in her mouth as if she was sucking on my dick. As soon as I seen she was relax, I took my other hand and started playing with her purl tongue. She became wetter by the second. Then I just pulled my dick out of her pussy and pushed it all the way in her ass. She let out a loud oh, so I started playing with her pussy even faster and said, "Just relax and keep sucking on my finger."

She started sucking on my finger as if she would be sucking the skin off of my dick. The more I kept playing with her pussy, the more she relaxed. Within a couple of minutes, I was fucking her in her ass as if she been getting fuck like this. Between the tight grip her ass had and hearing her saying "Oh! Oh! O!" only made me come faster. We fucked about four hours straight before we called it quits. As soon as we stopped, Juanita fell straight to sleep and I couldn't help thinking to myself I did that before I called it a night and passed out!

Chapter Forty-one

*T*he next day when we awoke, I seen Juanita was walking funny. In my mind, I was saying, "Yeah, I got her right" but I knew I had to fuck her at least one more time before it was all over.

She went and used the bathroom. When she came out, I pulled her next to me and begin kissing her and rubbing on her breast working my hands down to her pussy. Once I got her wet, I picked her up and push my dick inside of her. I was lifting her up and down on my dick at first, and then I just laid her across the bed and began serving her right.

This time when we finished, I was wore out. I didn't even want to get up to take a shower and I was soaked in our body's moisture. Juanita was just laying on the side of me, staring as if she couldn't believe we just finished having sex. So I asked her, "What's wrong beautiful? Why you staring like that?"

She replied, "Tu me estas asiendo sentir- que me estoy enomorando de ti," fast.

At that moment I knew if I wanted to proceed in any kind of relationship with Juanita, I was going to have to learn how to speak some kind of Spanish. It was starting to drive me not knowing what in the hell she was talking about, although I liked how some things sounded that she would say. I just said, "Now you know I didn't understand nothing you just said, but hopefully it was all good."

"It was all good! I wouldn't say anything bad about you."

I kissed her again and replied, "I hope not my Puerto Rican queen."

"That's what I'm talking about! You're just so sweet. How could I say anything bad about you?"

I just thought to myself, only if you really knew me. We laid back for awhile before Juanita left. She had to get herself together, being that we only had a few hours left before we were schedule to depart from Puerto Rico. I didn't have any plans for the day, so I continue laying back.

All of a sudden, my cellular phone began ringing crazy, and somebody was knocking on the door as if they had lost their mind. I jumped up with an attitude and answered the door. When I opened it, Temeka stood before me. I was actually shock, but by my attitude being fucked up right then I replied, "What the fuck wrong with you beating on my door like you done lost your got damn mind?"

"Excuse me for being concern! I was just checking to see if you were alright. We haven't seen you all day and didn't know if you got left behind or not."

"Damn, my bad! What time is it?"

"It's about eleven thirty."

"Eleven thirty! You act like I been gone all day."

"Nigga', it's eleven thirty at night. You gone let me in or not?"

"You know you can come in!"

"I was starting to wonder if I could. Fix your boxers! You got all of your stuff hanging out, and I don't want to see that."

"Don't act like you never seen dick before. Besides, if you didn't want to see it, then what you looking for? You must see something you like!"

"Don't go there! You gone put some clothes on?"

"Actually, I'm about to come up out of this and take a quick shower. You can chill or come join me if you want, but I got to hit the shower."

"Well you take your shower and I'll see you later. I was just checking up on you to make sure you were alright."

"Well thank you for being concern; but I'm going to be alright. If you don't mind, can you do something for me?"

"What's that?"

"Go and get me something to eat, if you don't mind. I'm hungry as hell!"

"I can do that for you on one account."

"What's that?"

"You got to have on some clothes when I come back."

"That's it?"

"Un huh."

"You got that," I said as I dropped my boxers.

"Boy! What you doing?"

"You said I had to have on some clothes when you got back, you didn't say before!"

"You got jokes huh! What you want?"

"Whatever you bring back."

When Temeka left, I jumped into the shower right quick. I knew if I wanted Temeka I could have gotten her, but I wasn't going to put forth the effort and end up jeopardizing her as a business associate. Although I could tell that she liked what she seen by her action, I felt like it wasn't the time to be thinking with my dick even though I didn't have anything else to do.

When I got out of the shower, Temeka was already back. I didn't even know it, until I came out of the bathroom and she spooked the fuck out of me. She must have seen me jump and said, "It's too late to get scared now; but if you don't hurry up and put on some clothes, I'm going to take my food back."

I couldn't say anything smart right then because I was hungry. I just politely ask, "What you get us," as I put on some clothes.

"I got you the ship's big breakfast. I'm not hungry, I already done ate."

After I finish eaten, we took a walk to the top deck of the ship so we could view the water. While listening to Temeka talk, my mind just drift else where. When I caught a hold of myself, she was telling me about the discomfort she was feeling about this trip. Off top, I was able to feel where she was coming from, but since I found out that we had departed from Puerto Rico safely I told her, "It's all smooth sailing from here." I just didn't know them words were going to come back and hunt me.

When we arrived at the boarding dock for us to depart the ship, I couldn't be any more happier to know that we made it back safely. The sun was still shining, and the wind was blowing just enough breezes to keep it cool. I mean it felt good to be eighty four degrees. I made it my business to get Juanita personal information so that we could keep in touch. Before I left out of the room where Juanita and me was talking she said, "Te amo," and then broke down in tears

Out of all the words she every said to me in Spanish, I could tell what that meant. I didn't know how to respond back right away because I was actually shock to see that I had her right where I wanted her. All I could tell her was, "Don't cry my baby. Everything is gone be alright. You gone hear from me sooner than you think," and then I kissed her and left.

Right when I reached the ramp to get off of the ship, I seen Gold Dee was no more than ten feet in front of me. Her duffel bag strap snapped before she made it off the ramp. By the limousine not being that far, I figured it wouldn't draw too much of a scene if she carried it in both arms. When I seen she was still struggling like that, I told her I'll carry it for her.

Out of the blue, about forty F.B.I. agents rushed the limo as soon as Jay Dee took a seat inside it. He didn't even have time to close the door. I froze up instantly! I knew what time it was and couldn't see me going back to prison. I whisper to Gold Dee, "Something wrong! If we go to the limo, we might as well put the hand cuffs on us our self."

"What we gone do?"

"First thing first, we got to get out of here before they recognize us. I doubt if we can make it to one of the cabs without our faces being seen. The only thing I can think of is to go purchase them Puerto Rican straw hats they be wearing, and then try to make it to a cab."

"Well let's try it!"

After we got the hats, we walked straight to a cab. The feds were still everywhere in sight. I didn't know if they were going to stop us or if they were even looking for us, but I assumed they had to have our pictures by we being affiliated with Jay Dee. I was so nervous on the inside that when the cab driver asked us where to, I couldn't give him a straight reply. Eventually, I told him an address close to Jay Dee's.

When we arrived, I still wasn't quite sure how things went wrong. I waited until the cab pulled off before I told Gold Dee to place the duffel bag in my trunk and get in. I didn't know where to go, but I knew we couldn't hang around Jay Dee's house to long. I wanted to tell Shantay what took place, but I knew if she didn't know yet she was going to find out real soon. I just couldn't see myself going inside their house right then.

I pulled off heading towards the studio, but then realized Jay Dee had rented the building in his name and changed my mind. I asked Gold Dee where she stayed at. After she informed me Nicole and her was roommates, I knew we couldn't go there. I decided the best place for us to go for the time being was a motel.

The first motel that popped in my mind was the Sunset Inn on Manhatten Boulevard. When we stopped at the red light on the corner of West Bank Expressway and Manhatten, Angela pulled up on the side of us. All the way up to this point, I didn't know she even had a car. She started blowing her horn to catch my attention. I knew it was going to be some more shit once I let down my window and she seen Gold Dee. So to cut her short before she even had a chance to get started, I let my window down and told her, "Follow right behind me and don't let anybody else get behind me," and raised the window back up.

Gold Dee asked, "Who is that?"

"You don't know her. Ya'll gone meet in a hot second."

Once I pulled into the motel and parked, Angela jumped out tripping. "Who the fuck is that in your car?"

"Look got damn me, this not the time to be showing your ass; I'm gone introduce ya'll in a minute! But first I need you to go rent us a room."

She looked at me stupid, and then said, "What the fuck do I look like?"

"Got damn me, I ain't got time to argue with you right now. You gone rent the room or not? I'm gone pay for it!"

Once she rented the room and we all made it inside, I introduce them to each other. Angela was still looking at Gold Dee crazy, but we had some business to handle that was more important than her bullshit. To get rid of her, I told her, "Look I need you to go to the store and pick up some thangs and come right back."

"What you need?" she asked. I wrote down on a sheet of paper everything I was going to need to cook the cocaine. Once I gave it to her, she read it and then asked, "What you need with this type of stuff?"

"Look, just go get it! You need anything?"

"Just some money to buy all this stuff!"

After I gave her two hundred dollars I said, "Make sure you come right back."

Once she left Gold Dee said, "You never told me you had a girl friend She cute too."

"Got damn me, fuck her right now. You know Delia number right off hand?"

"I got it in my phone! Let me get it."

"Just get her on the phone."

Within a minute she was handing me the telephone. Delia asked, "What's up? What can I do for you?"

That's when I ran it down to her that Jay Dee, Diamond, Nicole, and Rose just got picked up by the feds and I wanted to get all of them out as soon as possible. The only problem was, they weren't in her computer yet so she couldn't do anything to help me out. When I got off the phone with her, I thought about Paula and called her. That conversation just pissed me off even more when it was all over with. Jay Dee had gotten all the money he had stacked up from her, and spent it on this trip. The only thing I could think of at this point, was to call Chaos and tell her we needed her help seriously. So that's what I did.

When I got off the phone, Gold Dee asked, "What we gone do now?"

To be honest, at this point I couldn't believe Jay Dee made such a stupid ass move. What in the hell was he thinking about, spending everything he had saved? I mean he didn't even keep enough money on standby to bail his self out of trouble. The thought of knowing that I could have been caught to only made me furious. Gold Dee question kept repeating itself in my head. What we gone do now? What we gone do now? I finally made myself answer her and said, "You know we on fire right now! We need to stay low key as much as possible for the time being. I know you were making your drops in Pensacola, but I need to know exactly how many kilos you can get rid of at a time. Other than that, you gone continue working your regular job at the strip club."

"I normally go out there with five kilos. I charge them up to twenty thousand a piece, but all I have to bring back is ninety-two thousand and a half. After that, Jay Dee break me off."

"Over all what you make?"

"About seventeen five!"

"You know right now we in a jam, so this is what we gone do. You gone make your normal trip to Pensacola with five kilos, but you got to bring back the whole hundred thousand you make. Instead of paying you in cash, I'm gone give you a kilo. That's for you to put up for yourself because we gone need every bit of this money to get everybody out. The kilo I'm gone give you is actually more than what you would normally be getting, it's just not cash."

"It's all good, as long as we get everybody out."

Not to long afterwards, Angela came back with everything I sent her out to get. I could tell she wasn't comfortable with Gold Dee being alone with me, especially in a motel room by lil' comments she made. What she didn't know, was that Gold Dee and me had already discussed what to do when she got back and everything was going according to plan. Gold Dee was making conversation with Angela just to help me out while I continue making phone calls.

As soon as I got off the phone, I ran it down to Angela that I needed her to help me out. I needed her to rent a car for me for a week, and while she was at it the room for two more days. She started questioning me as to what I was really up to, but that's when I had to quick talk her. "You know I wouldn't be asking you to do anything for me if I didn't need you too. Besides, I have a lot of stuff to do and a little time to do it in. Baby girl when this is all over with, I'm gone make it up to you. Just work with me right now," I replied and kissed her.

I guess all she wanted was a kiss because after I gave her one, she didn't have a problem with Gold Dee any more. All she asked was, "When do you want me to take you to go rent a car?"

"Just take Gold Dee with you. She can drive it back here for me; I got to make a few more calls before these offices close. I'm gone see you later," I replied as I handed her about eight hundred dollars. "Oh yeah, make sure you go pay for two more days before you leave."

Once they left, I didn't waste any time cooking up the cocaine. By me knowing that it was raw, I decided to make three kilos out of one. If it wasn't grade A, I would've never ever thought about making six kilos out of just two. The only reason I was even doing it now, was because I couldn't see us spending a million dollars four days ago and only had forty kilos to show for. My natural hustling intuition just wouldn't allow me to accept that.

By the time I was finish cooking up the coke, I knew I had to find a safe place to hide the rest for the time being. The only place that came to my mind was a storage, and I knew where the perfect one was that I could go to at any time. It was only about ten minutes away, and I wouldn't have to use my real name to rent it. The only thing that was bothering me was, I was expecting for Gold Dee to be back already. I really didn't want to drive my car anywhere, but in the process I decided to take that ride and come back.

Chapter Forty-two

*I*t was a coincidence that Gold Dee and me pulled into the hotel lot at the same time. Right off back, I noticed they had rented a 1998 Mercury Grand Marquis that was sky blue. Once I parked, I waited until Gold Dee parked and jumped into the car with her. "Where are you coming from?" Gold Dee asked.

"Fuck that! What took you so long to get back?"

"It wasn't my fault! That was your girl friend that had to stop here and there."

"Anyway, what all are you gone need to go to work tonight?"

"Just a few outfits to change into."

"I ain't talking about your clothes! How much coke you gone be able to get rid of while you working? I know you can push something while you're there!"

"I wouldn't be able to tell you if I could or couldn't. I never mixed this business with my regular job."

"Fuck it then! I'm just gone drop you off at work. When you get ready to get off, just call me. I'm gone come pick you up."

"What about what I need for work?"

"I suggest you go get whatever you need now, so when you come back we can leave," I replied getting out of the car.

Once I went inside the motel room, I started wrapping the five kilos together. After every layer of plastic I wrapped around them, I rubbed a layer of Vick's Vapor Rub around it. I then repeated those steps. As soon as I was finish doing that, I cut a slit in the mattress where I hid the kilos. I knew Gold Dee was coming right back, so I put the kilo I had for her inside the dresser draw and just waited on her.

The moment she came back, I jumped into the car with her and told her, "Pull off!" My cellular phone rung no sooner than she pulled off. It was Delia. She was just informing me that no bond was set on Jay Dee or anybody else. After that she hung up. I didn't want to see my dog or anybody else on my team locked up, but it wasn't anything I could do at this point. I just shook my head.

Gold Dee asked, "Who was that?"

I looked at her and replied, "Just be ready to push when you get off of work. Tomorrow morning we're gone roll out." She didn't say anything, she just kept driving. Right before she got out of the car to go to work, something made me tell her, "Just to be on the safe side if anything should happen or go wrong before we see each other again, write down my number and give it to somebody you trust to let me know. If you get into a situation where you can't let me know they already have you, just ask me if I got in touch with silver devil. That's gone be our code. Other than that, just be careful. I'll see you later."

It was already getting late, but I knew that I had to stash the cocaine in the car before we left. The only person I trusted at this point was my baby momma. I knew Tony was going to have a problem with Keisha leaving with me, but he was going to have to respect my mind. I was about to go knock on their door and get her regardless of what he thought. I called Keisha to give her a warning that I was on my way. The first thing she said was, "Don't you know what time it is? I'm married now! You just can't come over here like that."

"Man look, I know you marry and all that, but I just need you to drive my car for me. I'm gone drop you off as soon as we get it where it has to go. It's gone take less than an hour. Tony can ride too! Where he at?"

"He not here, he went out."

"Look, I'm gone have you back home before he gets there. Just handle this for me! You know I wouldn't be asking you if I really didn't need you. So what you say, you gone do it? I can be there in about fifteen minutes."

She hesitated for a moment, and then replied, "What I'm gone do with you? Come on!"

Before she could change her mind, I hung up the phone and was on my way. Right then, it dawn on me that I haven't heard from Jay Dee or Shantay. I was hoping one of them would have called me, but up to this point neither one of them have. I figured I'll wait until it was late before I went by their house and tried to find Jay Dee's key to the storage. I knew if he wanted to save his truck and whatever else he had in there, it was up to me to do it.

Once I reached Keisha's house, I seen she was waiting on me. The first thing I asked was, "Where my son at?"

"He sound asleep, and I don't want to wake him up! You said we coming right back, aren't we?"

"Yeah, but I told you it's gone take about an hour before we get back. I don't want your husband tripping if he beat us back."

"Knowing him, he's not going to be back any time soon. Besides, Tiarell sleep! So let's just go so I can get back."

While we were riding, I couldn't help asking, "Tony treating you right?" because I thought about what she said about him.

"We alright," she replied but I could tell she wasn't telling me the whole story.

I just replied, "You know if you need me, I'm just a phone call away."

"I know; but we're getting along alright."

"I'm serious! Don't let him just fuck over you any kind of way." I said as I turned into the motel lot.

"Don't even think about it! What we stopping here for?"

"Keisha, knock it off! I ain't even coming at you like that. This just where I got my car parked at."

"Oh this is where you and one of your women were?"

"It ain't even like that. You know I don't have a place of my own yet."

"You mean to tell me you brought a car first."

"My car was more like a gift. Anyway, I want you to follow right behind me and don't let anybody get between us."

"Tj, what you're up to?"

"Just don't let anybody get behind me. I don't have insurance on it yet, and I don't want the laws to take it."

"Whatever! Just hurry up." Keisha replied as if she knew I was up to something illegal that I wasn't telling her.

Once I started up my car and pulled off, Keisha trailed me just like I instructed. We made it to the storage within minutes. As soon as we got there, I hurry up and put the car up before she had time to see what else was in there. After I locked it up, I jumped in the passenger seat and said, "Thank you my baby! If you don't want anything while we out, you can drive home."

"I'm alright!"

"You mean to tell me, you don't want anything? Not even a daiquiri?"

"I told you, I'm alright."

"Well can I have something before you get home?"

"What you want?"

"I just want a kiss for old time sake."

"You know it's not like that any more."

"I ain't asking you to tongue me down! I just want to feel your soft lips! You can even kiss me on the cheek!"

"You not going to quit asking until you get one, are you?"

"You know me by now. I don't understand I can't."

"Here," she replied as she kissed me on the cheek.

I would have been satisfied, but she caught me off guard. Before I even thought about it I said, "Now you know you got to kiss the other side. It's feeling jealous."

"I knew that was coming. You so spoil! I don't know why I even started you."

"What can I say," I replied as I turned my head to the other side. Right when she got ready to kiss me, I turned my head to make her kiss me on the lips. For a second I forgot she was driving because she didn't stop kissing me back. When we did stop kissing I said, "Well I see you haven't lost it."

She just shook her head and then replied, "You ain't right. You ain't right at all!"

"What can I say? Can you blame me for wanting to kiss on you?" she didn't say anything. She just had a look in her eyes as if there were still a spark between us.

When we pulled up at her home, she knew that we had beaten Tony back. Out loud she spoke, "Good, he still not home."

"I don't know how good that is, but don't forget what I told you. My line always open!"

"I'm going to remember; but you better be careful. I don't know what you really up to, but you better think about what you doing. Oh yeah, when are you going to come to the Kingdom Hall with me?"

"I can't give you an exact day; but it's gone be soon."

"If you say so! I'll see you later."

Once I left, I thought about what Keisha said about thinking about what I was doing. Her words kept penetrating though my head, as if it was a warning that something could go extremely wrong. My conscious took heed, but my heart was determined to make this happen regardless of the consequences that came along with doing so. I was coming up to a Wal-Mark, when I thought about what tools I was going to need to properly stash the cocaine in my car. So I pulled in.

Right off back I knew that I was going to need: something to cut a hole through metal; a roll of insulation; a dark metal or steel box deep enough to hide the coke in; some screws, and some glue. After I got all the materials that I was going to need, it was time to go to work.

I drove straight to the motel without any more delays. It was a few folks gather on the parking lot when I pulled in, but I didn't pay them any mind. When I got out of the car, one of them said, "What; you don't know me now?" I turned around quick to see who they were talking to, but I still didn't recognize them. I just proceeded going towards my room. This time one of them yelled, "Nigga', what's happening? That's how it is now?"

Again I turned around, but this time I said, "Man what's up; who that is?"

"That's fucked up Boom! You don't know me now?"

When he said my name, I knew that he had to know me, so I started walking towards them even though I was skeptical of whom they were. As I got closer, I seen it was Spanish B and Daniel. "G, what's up? I didn't know who the fuck ya'll was!"

"It's been awhile, but it ain't been that long! What you doing over here?" Daniel replied.

"I'm just chilling right now. The question is, what in the hell ya'll doing here?"

"We just mobbing! (Meaning they were slanging.)"

"Ya'll mobbing! B, you still pushing weed?"

"I'm doing a lil' something right now with the weed; but I'm trying to score some coke."

"How much you looking for?"

"At least a quarter key! My connect got me on hold; and it's rolling now!"

"Man, how much do you want?"

"I got about fifteen I can spend now! Why; what's up? You got a connect?"

"Look, give me fifteen and ten pounds and I'll get you a key."

"You serious?"

"Come on now! You know when it comes to business, what time it is with me."

"4sho! But I got to go pick up the weed."

"That's cool. I'll run and get the key, and meet you by the bowling alley in fifteen minutes. Not a minute later, because I got something else to do. So what's up?"

"Boom, let's do this then! I'm missing out on money!"

"You just make sure it's weighting right, because I ain't coming short."

"I got you! I should be over there in about ten minutes; I'm just going down the street."

"4-sho! But I told you I only got fifteen minutes. Take this number in case you run into any kind of trouble, that way you can let me know something."

"4-sho!"

I waited until they left before I went into the motel room. I was happy I already had a kilo sitting to the side; I just needed for Spanish B to come through on his end. I didn't see a point in coming back to the motel room if Spanish B did come through, so I removed all of the cocaine from the mattress and placed it in a grocery bag. After I had everything ready, I waited for ten minutes to pass before I decided to leave.

When I opened the door, I felt like I seen a ghost and my heart was going to stop. Two police cars were parked on each side of the rental car. I didn't know whether to close the door back and wait on them to leave or just make my move, but I went with my instincts and acted like everything was normal. When I reached the top of the steps, I seen two officers were coming up. As we pass each other, we nodded our heads at each other as a silent greetings. I couldn't help but think this was a close call. If only they knew how many kilos I was holding, walking pass them.

The moment I jumped inside of the car, I started watching the police to see what room they were going to. After I seen they went to the third door down from the room I was in, I pulled off. I knew I wasn't coming back without a female being with me to keep from looking suspicious.

I don't know if the laws just happen to been everywhere I was going or what, but they had a car hemmed up right before I was able to turn into the bowling alley parking lot. I just kept my cool as I rolled pass them. As soon as I pulled in and found a parking spot, I began hoping B would hurry up and come so that we could get this over with.

A couple of minutes later, I saw Spanish B turning in. I flashed my headlights at him, so he could know where I was. The moment he parked next to me, I popped the trunk and then jumped in his car. "Let's get down to business! Where everything at?"

"It's all in the trunk."

"Well pop the trunk so we can get this over with." When he popped the trunk, I got out and looked inside. All I seen was his sound. I quickly said, "Man, where it's at?"

"Reach in front the speaker box; you gone feel it!"

When I reached in front of the speaker box, I felt a bag. I pulled it from behind the speaker box, and with a quick glance began counting its contents. When I seen it was right, I throw it inside my trunk leaving it open. I then walked over to my car window, then reached inside and grabbed the bags containing the kilo. I walked back to my trunk and placed the five kilos inside it, and slid the other one inside my pants. After I got it hid right, I close the trunk, and then jumped back in the car with Spanish B. "Here you go folks! When you need some more, get at me."

"Hold on, let me make sure it's straight."

"Got damn me, you know I ain't gone bring you no bullshit; but check it out."

He made him two lines right quick. Once he snorted it, he said, "Oh yeah! I'm gone defiantly get back at you."

"Yeah, you do that. Anyway, Daniel be cool. You know how to get in touch with me now, so holla'. Let me get out of here."

When I pulled off, they were still parked. I guess they were making them another fix, but I didn't stick around to find out. I drove straight to the storage and went to work. It took me about forty-five minutes to an hour to hook up the stash box right; but when I was finish you couldn't tell what I had did.

I place the two duffel bags in the trunk of my Lexus, and then decided to go by Jay Dee's house. I knew that I had an hour and a half before Gold Dee got off of work; I was just hoping that I could find Jay Dee's keys to his storage, and not get caught up in a jam. Instead of parking in the parking lot in front of Jay Dee's house, I parked on a side street just in case I had to make a run for it. I didn't want the laws to know what I was driving in. I called before I decided to go in, but the telephone just kept ringing.

When I was certain that the house was empty, I rushed inside as if I was breaking in. first I checked all of the spots that Jay Dee normally would have sat his keys down at, but I didn't have any luck in finding them. I looked through every room; draws; shelves, on the tables, but I still didn't find them. The moment I gave up hope in finding them and started walking towards the door to leave, I spotted the keys on top of the television. I said out loud, "Ain't this a bitch! I'm searching high and low for these damn keys, and they been right in front me."

When I said that, somebody knocked on the door and scared the fuck out of me. I mean if I wouldn't have caught myself, I would have jumped clean through the window. The glass and all. Luckily, they didn't hear me inside and quit knocking on the door. The moment the coast was clear, I left running to my car.

Chapter Forty-three

Time was passing by quicker than I noticed it. When I pulled up at She She's where Gold Dee worked at, it was a little after three o'clock in the morning. By Gold Dee never calling me, I assumed everything was alright with her and decided to go in and chill until she got off.

As soon as I took my first step through the door, one of the strippers caught my attention. She was swinging up side down on a pole with her legs spread wide open. On a smaller stage for the strippers, I seen a chick shaken a champagne bottle up inside her pussy until it started shooting out everywhere. I had to light a Black up when I seen that.

A Caucasian stripper came up to me once I got seated and asked, "Can I give you a table dance?"

I had to look at the skinny pale face chick for a second to see if she was really serious before I made any remarks back to her, but the more I observed her I couldn't see me giving her a quarter. So peep how I responded back. "Hey there lil' snow bunny! You look kind of small to be giving table dances; don't you think? What they call you anyway?"

"I'm Winter, but I can do everything everybody else in here can do even better!" she said as if I had insulted her.

"Cool down Winter! That's a pretty name you have and I admire you feel like you do, but give me a reason why I should let you give me a table dance."

She reached down and began rubbing my dick through my clothes, and then said, "You can let me give you a table dance or we can do something else."

"Yeah Winter, well let me tell you something right quick! I ain't no tender dick ass nigger! See how you rubbing on my shit trying to persuade me to do what you want; you got to come better than that. I love my money, and I don't fuck for free. Everything I do, I charge a fee! So if you want to do something with me, its gone cost you cause even this conversation ain't for free."

"What? You think you some kind of pimp or something?"

"Check game snow bunny, I don't know how long you been working here, but I can have any lady in here. Now I don't want to be wasting my time if I'm not getting paid, so peep play. Go make some change while you can and if you think you can afford me afterwards, holla' back," I replied as dismissing her. Winter just stood there as if registering what I told her in disbelief, and then walked off.

I soon spotted Gold Dee, but I didn't interrupt her. I wanted to see how she made her moves at work. From what I seen, she seemed to be doing her thang because she had a lot of money hanging from her garter. I was so busy looking at the strippers doing they thing, that I didn't even notice the waitress talking to me. "Can I get you something to drink sir? Excuse me sir, can I get you something to drink?"

When I turned around and made eye contact with the waitress, I just knew that I knew her from somewhere but I couldn't call it. I just said, "Yeah, let me get a Hennessy on the rocks pretty." She just blushed. When she came back with my drink, I asked her, "What's your name?"

"My name is Peaches, and yours?"

"I'm Tj."

"Tj! Where you from?"

"Saint Louis."

"Didn't you use to hang at Popes on the other side?"

When she said Popes, it dawn on me who she was. "Ain't your real name Natalie, I mean Natasha?"

"Un huh."

"Girl how you been doing? I can see you done got fine as hell!"

"I been doing alright. What ever happen with you and your girl?"

"You know she had a baby for me, but that's about it. What's up with you?"

"I been chilling. I'm just doing me now!"

"I feel you! Well look you blossom Persian fruit, I don't want you to miss out on your money so I guess I'll see you again. You be cool."

"You too, but before you leave I got to get your number and give you mines."

"Well do that! I'm gone be here for a second."

By that time, Gold Dee had made her way by me. "What are you doing in here? I didn't call you yet."

"I'm chilling, just waiting on you so we can go do something."

"I thought you said we leaving tomorrow."

"That's still on, but we got to do something before the sun rise."

"I only have one more dance I have to do before I can leave. It should only be about another thirty minutes."

"Well do you. I'm gone chill until then."

Right then my phone rung and Natasha walked up at the same time. "I see you off the hook, I hope you going to have time for me." Natasha replied.

"You know I make big moves, but let me get this. Hello."

"Where you at?"

"Who this is?"

"You got that many bitches calling you?"

"Got damn me, I ain't trying to hear that shit! Anyway check game, I'm gone call you when I get out of here; I can barely hear you."

"Where the hell you at?"

"I'm gone call you back," click. "Anyway, you came back to bring your number to me?"

"That's what I was planning on doing, but I can see you already have a lot of friends."

"Don't let that change nothing. Besides, most of all my friends are business."

"Business! What type of business you in?"

"Put it this way, I charge four figures or better. The minimum amount I make is eight hundred, and that's just when I'm being nice."

"What you got like that?"

"What you mean what I got like that? Money talks! As long as you can afford it, I got what you need like that."

"I feel you all the way on that. Make sure you give me your number."

"Write it down and get at me. I guarantee I ain't gone waste your time, but don't be just writing it down for the hell of it."

"Trust me, I 'm gone use it! What's the number?"

After I gave Peaches the telephone number and got hers, I finish checking out the rest of the strippers. You could tell just about everybody inside of She She's used some kind of drug whether it was: weed, coke, heroin, ecstasy, or alcohol. I took a walk around the club and seen a light skinned stripper with some strawberries tattooed on her ass giving a lap dance, but the closer I got towards them I seen she was actually fucking the man who lap she was on. I just said to myself, these hoes in here would do anything for the money. That's when Winter walked back up and whispered, "I'll fuck you better than that."

I let out a low laugh, and then said, "When your money right we can do that; but until then, I told you I don't fuck for free no matter how good it might be," and walked off.

I went to the restroom in the back of the club, but it was more like an addict meeting room. All you could see was bags of powder cocaine being past around, and lines being snorted off of the counters. Even a few of the strippers were in the men's rest room getting their nose dirty and participating in sexual activities. I wonder how much coke I could have gotten rid of, but then figured it couldn't have been much.

When I walked back towards the front, I seen Gold Dee had already started dancing. I watched her for a minute enjoying the sight of how she moved her body, but then decided it was best for me to wait on her in the car because she was starting to turn me on. I headed for the door and again Winter stopped me, "How much is it going to cost me?" she questioned.

I was actually feed up of her coming on to me, but then decided to see what I could make this trashy bitch do. I looked at her with a cold stare, and then replied, "Follow me and keep up." Once we reached the rental I let her inside, and then proceeded telling her, "Look bitch, where your money at?" She reached inside a bag she was carrying, and came out with three hundred and forty-seven dollars. I quickly snapped, "Bitch, this all you got? You been fucking with me since I walked in there, and this all you got?" But she began to say before I cut her off, "Got damn me, it ain't no buts. I don't know who administration you were under, but to me anything under four figures is an insult. Just get out of here before I get real pissed off!"

"What about my money?"

"Correct that, that's my money now! I told you even my conversation wasn't free, but now you know it 4-sho. Check game though, this what I'm gone do for you. If you can make me nut with-in a minute, I'll give you some of what you gave me back. The only catch is, you can only use your mouth and you got to swallow it. Do we have a deal or not?" Winter looked at me as if she couldn't believe the predicament I placed her in. so I continual applying pressure on her. "What you gone do? Time ticking!"

"Before I agree or disagree with this, I have a proposition for you."

"Run your mouth then."

"If I agree to this by your terms and can't make you nut with-in a minute, my money for you. But if I can get you off with-in a minute, I want you to give me back double my money since you feel like it wasn't enough."

She had me tipped for a second how she came at me. I didn't believe she could do it, but then again looking at her she had to be good at something. So I accepted her challenge and told her, "Do what you do."

Once she began, I started concentrating on the hands on my watch; instead of allowing myself to enjoy the warm pleasure of her mouth as her head rose up and down while rotating in a circular motion. When I caught myself enjoying it, I had to look at her good and instantly became turned off. I even tried focusing on the folks walking past that were starring, but it didn't seem to be working. She was really doing what she do. I mean I never thought a minute could take so long to go by; it was starting to feel like forever. The second she grabbed my dick with her hand and began jacking me off while she was still sucking it, I then allowed myself to enjoy her service because in my mind I was saying her money gone.

The second I began to shot sperm in Winter's mouth, Gold Dee opened the door. "What the fuck going on in here?" she asked.

I just looked at her. She caught me off guard, but I felt like I didn't owe her an explanation anyway. I simply told her in a calm voice, "Give me a second to finish."

She stood there just starring before she closed the door back. By then, Winter was finish swallowing my sperm. She rose up and said, "I'm so embarrass! Why you didn't tell me you was messing with her? Just give me my money!"

"First of all, you ain't got nothing to be embarrassed about. You was doing what you do! Second of all, I don't owe you an explanation on who I fuck with. You understand me? Now third got damn me, your money gone! The second you put your hand on my dick, your money was spent. So you can have a good day now," I replied dismissing her.

Her mouth dropped open as she digested my un-cut words. Even her eyes began turning watery as she replied, "That's fucked up! How could I be so stupid? I don't even have money to catch a taxi home now. Can you at least give me cab fare, or drop me off at home?"

My conscience quickly became conniving and I instantly thought of using her up to my advantage. Although, something was urging me to tell her to get the fuck out of the car, instead of telling her to get out, I asked, "Who you stay with?"

"I live by myself! Why?"

"Don't question me; I ask all of the question! I'm gone take you home, but it's gone cost you later on."

"It's gone cost me!"

"You want me to take you home or not?"

"Yeah."

"Well shut up then, and get in the back. Why you at it, tell Gold Dee I said lets go. And where in the hell do you stay anyway?"

Gold Dee got in the car and just stared. She didn't say a single word the whole time we were riding until after I dropped Winter off. "I know you don't like to be questioned, but I hope you know what you doing with her. I just don't see what you see in her! Especially after I done seen your girlfriend today!"

I forgot all about calling Angela back. I just said, "Trust me, I'm playing my cards right. Anyway, when we get where we going, I just want you to help me load up whatever we can fit in the truck. Then follow right behind me."

"What truck?"

"You gone see."

While we were driving to Jay Dee's storage, I decided to call Angela back. She was up-set because I hung up on her and took so long to call her back, but I explained to her that I was handling some business and couldn't ta k to her right then. She still fussed for a second before she asked me to come and pick her up; but as soon as I told her I was still handling some business, she began back fussing. I was too tired to even fuss back, I just said, "You have a good night too," and hung up on her again.

We were coming up to the storage, when I seen about four black undercover looking cars pulling in. The way they all turned with persistency, I knew something was wrong and we were too late. I just said, "Fuck! They beat us here." I proceeded to drive forward passing the storage, and that's when I seen what shocked me the most. Jennifer was standing next to a white Toyota talking to who ever that was in the last black car that had just pulled in. That's when I put everything together on why I kept seeing her. Without thinking I said, "That bitch got to die!"

Gold Dee replied, "You saw her too?"

I nodded my head, but my mind was racing trying to figure out how I was going to get rid of her. I couldn't believe that bitch was trying to use me for bait. That's when it had dawn on me that I had gotten her phone number. I already knew that I couldn't call her from my phone without it being traced back to me, but I just had to do something though. I pulled onto a small store parking lot and turned the car back around towards the entrance. That's when I looked at Gold Dee and said, "Look, I need to know how deep in the game are you willing to get?"

She looked at me as if she already knew where I was going with this; then replied, "I been down since day one, and every since then I been getting deeper and deeper. I done experience more than I ever imagine I could, so ncw I feel it's to late to turn back now. What you need me to do?"

"I really don't want to put you in a situation that you really not ready for, but I'm a gangster. I figure if blood gone shed, then let it shed. Show no sympathy, cause I have no pity. As for as religion, may it be with you. Cause place death upon me, and six times worser will be my vengeance. That's something that I'd tell all my enemies as they killing me, and right now I feel it's time we ride."

"I like how you said that."

"Fuck liking how I said it, I want you to remember it because shit real right now. At any giving time we can get caught up. You feel me?"

"Of coarse I do. You have a plan?"

"Naw! The only thing that came to my mind is for us to follow her, but I can't say what to do from there."

"Leave that up to me. I'll deal with her."

"Don't forget she with the F.B.I.! I'm more than sure she had to have some kind of hand to hand combat training."

"I'm not worry about that! I'm going to beat the shit out of her."

"Fuck beating the shit out of her, you got to eliminate that bitch. I don't care how you do it, just make sure it's done and you don't leave anything behind that can be trace back to you."

"Trust me, after being around you I know to make sure I get rid of all the evidence."

I didn't know exactly how we were going to catch Jennifer slipping, but I just couldn't wait to get her out of the picture. All I could think of, was she was trying to send me back to prison. That just made me want to deal with her myself instead of letting Gold Dee, but I had to let Gold Dee earn her strips since she asked.

We must have sat in the car for at least three hours before I seen any of the cars come out of the storage. Day light was just starting to break when Jennifer pulled out. I let her get about a block ahead before I started trailing her. When I seen her get on the highway, that's when I started driving closer to her because I knew the toll point was coming up. For a second I almost lost her while I was paying the toll fee, but I spotted her turning off onto an exit ahead. I began speeding trying to catch back up with her before she was completely out of sight.

She ended up pulling up to a building with a lot of mirror looking windows. I had to pass the place up to keep from looking like I was following her, but then I found an available parking spot that she would have no other choice but to pass when she decided to leave. I was just hoping we wouldn't have to wait all day on her to come out, but we ended up waiting about an hour. As tired as I was, I started feeling my adrenaline building up as I thought about how we were about to deal with her.

We followed Jennifer to an area in the east called Miss U. On the inside I was having doubt about letting Gold Dee deal with Jennifer, but I had to give her the benefit of the doubt. We watched from a distance as she pulled into her driveway and parked. When she got out of the car, she placed a small black case in the trunk and locked it. I assumed her gun had to be what was inside of that, I just couldn't guarantee it. Out of precaution though, I asked Gold Dee, "You sure you ready for this?"

"I couldn't get any more ready!"

"Well get out and handle your business! I'm going to park right where the street turns at, so we can make a clean get away."

Gold Dee started making her way to the house while I parked the car on the corner. I watched to see exactly what Gold Dee was going to do when she reached the house. I seen her knock on the door, but I still didn't think that she was ready to deal with Jennifer by herself up till this point; until the door opened.

Gold Dee didn't hesitate to hit Jennifer with a straight jab. It knocked her inside of her own house, but it wasn't over with. Jennifer retaliated hitting Gold Dee with a monster combination. If this was an ordinary hood fight, I could visualize the would be watching spectators instigating this fight on. The way

Jennifer was starting to demolish Gold Dee, I would have even betted my last dollar on her. I hurry up and ran to Gold Dee rescue before any of Jennifer neighbors might have heard the altercation. With one direct blow I laid her out cold; then carried her all the way inside her house.

The moment we got inside close doors, I said, "It's time to earn your stripes now, but first go and find a couple of towels or something so we can wipe away any extra evidence. But don't use your hands to opening any draws!" Gold Dee took off and came back moments later with some shirts. I took one from her and wrapped it around Jennifer's mouth and nose. After that I said, "You didn't pick up a knife or nothing?"

"I'm already ahead of you," she replied revealing a short handle jagged blade knife placing it against Jennifer's neck.

"Hold on!" I yelled barely stopping her from splitting Jennifer's neck completely.

"Hold on for what?"

"That's why I told you to grab a few towels. Place one of them shirts behind the knife as you cutting her to keep any of her blood from squirting on you. And to make sure this bitch die; cut her wrists when you finish!"

"I got you," she replied as she began to finish what she started. Jennifer released a high pitch squeal for her last words, and then we fled.

Chapter Forty-four

*I*t was going on about nine thirty or ten o'clock in the morning. As bad as I wanted to stay on the highway and shoot out to Florida, I was too tired to make myself even drive that far. Instead, I drove back to the hotel room. Gold Dee asked, "We still leaving today?"

"Yeah, but I got to get a little rest in before we get on the highway. My eyes are starting to burn."

"I can see; they turning red. It looks like you been smoking some weed!"

Until that moment, I didn't realize Gold Dee left eye was a little swollen. The image of Jennifer hitting Gold Dee with combinations quickly replayed in my mind, and I said, "She punched the shit out of you! Your eye starting to swell up! You need to put some ice on that until we get ready to go!"

Gold Dee didn't say anything; she just looked at me as if she wished that I had two black eyes. Out of instinct, when we walked in the room I searched it thoroughly before lying on the bed. I didn't bother to remove any of my clothes, not even my shoes. Before I was able to close my eyes and enjoy a moment of peace, Gold Dee asked, "Before you fall to sleep, what did you do with that stuff?"

"Don't worry about that, I put it up already. But make sure you put some ice on your eye to get the swelling down!" she mumble something, but I didn't pay her any mind.

The next thing I knew, Gold Dee was standing in front of me naked. "You gone answer that? It's been ringing!"

"What the fuck are you talking about," I replied before I realized my phone was ringing. I answered it with an attitude, "What's up?"

"Oh good morning to you too," the caller replied. I quickly realize that it was Keisha and seen what she wanted. Before I even realized it, I had agreed to go to the Kingdom Hall with her. I don't know how I did that; but some kind of way, I did! On the inside I was fierce, I just wanted to get a couple hours of rest. I took a quick shower to try to wake me all the way up, but it instead seemed to have drained me even more. Within about ten minutes, Keisha had pulled into the hotel parking lot blowing the horn. I walked to the car pretending to be happy about going with them. That's when Keisha said, "You not ready yet?"

"What you mean, I'm not ready yet?"

"You can't come like that! You don't have a suit you can put on?"

"Come on now! You got to be out of your mind if you think I'm about to put a suit on! Ain't we about to go to church?"

"Yeah! But," she started before I cut her off.

"Well it shouldn't matter what I'm wearing. My clothes not going to save me! Besides, I thought God said to come as you are!"

"He did! But for me, will you at least put some slacks on and a dress shirt?"

I looked at my son sitting in the back seat wearing a black suit as if he was about to attend a wedding, and then I thought about how many times I told her I was going to go, and figured why not. "I'll wear something to your standards, but you have to take me to the mall to get something on that level."

"We don't have time!"

"Well I guess I'll have to go with ya'll another time."

"Come on, but we gone have to hurry up!"

We went to the mall, where I picked out: a pair of slacks, a pair of snakeskin shoes with the belt to match the shoes, and a casual dress shirt to complete the outfit. I changed clothes in the car on the way to the Kingdom Hall. When we arrived there, the gate that surrounded the place was locked. Keisha said, "I hope you don't mind, but since we are late we are going to have to jump the fence."

I didn't think she was serious at first, until she started climbing over the fence. Out of all the fences I ever had to jump, I never figured I'll be jumping a fence to go to church. Once we got inside of the building, we were able to hear the minister had already begun talking. Most of the seats were occupied, so we ended up having to take seats in the second row towards the front.

It felt like everybody was looking and starring at us by it being my first time there; but I ignored that feeling and tried to follow along with what the minister was talking about. The more I was trying to pay attention, the more I became lost. He wasn't preaching like a preacher at a Baptist church, or any other preacher I have ever heard before. Even to say that I knew a little bit about the bible, I didn't have the slightest ideal on what he was talking about. I looked around to see if I could spot anybody else that seemed not to know what in the hell he was talking about, but everybody seemed like they wasn't paying him any attention except for a small few. I couldn't wait to leave!

After three hours of sitting listen to I don't know what and half way dozing off, I knew that I wasn't coming back again. Before I went inside of there I knew that I believed in God, but I didn't know what or who they really believed in. I didn't even get to ask God for forgiveness.

When we got inside of the car Keisha asked, "What you thought about it?" I looked at her, but I couldn't even begin to put my words together to tell her how I was feeling or thinking. She just said, "I know you didn't like it, but it's not always like that." I still didn't say anything; I just began playing with my son until she dropped me off.

To my surprise, Angela was waiting inside when I opened the door. I looked at her and Gold Dee and just jumped on the bed. I knew I didn't have to say a word before Angela would've started running her mouth, but I beat her to it. "What you doing here?"

"What you mean, what I'm doing here? I been calling you all morning and you haven't been answering your phone, so I decided to come see what you was doing like that. Where you coming from, dressed like that anyway?"

"I was taking care of some business," I replied. I then looked at Gold Dee as if to ask her, why in the world did you let her in.

"What type of business was you taking care of dressed like that?" Angela asked.

I ignored her question and asked, "Are ya'll hungry?"

Angela replied, "I ate before I got here."

That's when Gold Dee quickly spoke up and said, "I was waiting on you to get back!"

I threw Gold Dee the keys to the rental and told her, "Go and get yourself something to eat," so I could have some privacy with Angela. When she walked out of the door, I grabbed Angela by the hand driving her close to me and said in an orderly tone, "You gone stop all that checking to see what I'm doing and getting sassy shit when we talk! I know you be wanting to spend time with me and I be wanting to spend time with you. But when I got business to handle, that comes first unless it's something important. You feel me?" But she began before I cut her off with a kiss, and then replied, "It ain't no buts. Now how my baby been doing?"

She wanted to say something smart by her face expression, but then she changed her mind. With in minutes, we were back to acting like we was when we first met. Slowly but surely, we ended up making out. Her long silky black hair was pinned up, but while she was riding me it came down hanging right above her breast. With the sex faces she was making and hearing her moan, I felt like I didn't want her to ever stop although I knew that eventually every good thing has to come to an end at some point.

After we finish, she got back dressed then said, "Well I have to go now. I just wanted to make sure that nobody else was getting my stuff!"

I let out a laugh, and then it dawn on me that I didn't see her car outside and asked, "Where your car at?"

"That's not my car, it's for my friend. But I parked it on the other side so I could creep up on you and catch you slipping!"

"Girl, get up out of here! I'm gone see you later."

I checked the time. When I seen that it was already three forty, I made up my mind that no matter what we were going to roll out at seven. Not seven fifteen or seven twenty-five; but seven o'clock on the dot. I set the alarm clock for six thirty to make sure I had plenty of time to get ready. Then right before I laid down and tried to go to sleep, I wrote a note for Gold Dee that said, "Be ready at seven. Not 7:01!!!"

I don't know exactly how long Gold Dee had been back; but when the alarm went off to wake me up, it woke her up too. I quickly jumped up and jumped in the shower. The moment I came out I said, "It's time to go!"

We went straight to the storage to pick up my car. As soon as we got there, I said, "The car registration and insurance papers are in the grove box. Oh yeah, can you push some weed out there?"

"Probably so. Why?"

"Because I got ten pounds in the trunk. But if you don't think you gone be able to get rid of them, we can leave them."

"We might as well bring it. 'Cause nine times out of ten, somebody gone want it."

"Well check game. Drive to the gas station and I'm gone be right behind you, but make sure you use your signal lights to avoid being stopped."

After we made it to the gas station and filled up both cars, I reminded Gold Dee, "When we get on the highway, make sure you drive in the right lane unless you passing a car. And whatever you do, don't speed!"

For the next five hours all I could think was, I hope we don't get stopped because I knew the chance we were taking could lead us straight to prison or a grave yard; but it was too late to turn back. Chaos called me while I was still on the highway, "Boom, you heard from anybody yet?"

"Not at all! I was hoping you could deliver me some news on what's going on."

"From what I found out so far, it seem like they all are in a tight situation. I had a chance to talk to Jay Dee."

"What he tell you?"

"He told me to make sure I told you that everything you tried to tell him was true, and sometimes silver devils seem so small when they are on top of everything. Whatever that suppose to mean."

I knew exactly what that meant, but now it was up to me to decide what else was going to go down. I knew the tables could turn at any second, but I had to be ready when they did. I replied to Chaos, "Thanks for the message, but I got a sweet tooth bad! When you gone hook me up with some of your homemade candy?"

The only catch was, I wasn't talking about any regular homemade candy and Chaos knew that. Infact, she knew any time that we spoke about sweets, we were discussing fire arms and said, "I can bring you some this week. I just haven't been having the time to make any."

"Well you gone have to take time out too. I'm gone call you later on this week."

By the time we reached Pensacola, Florida it was already late, so we checked into a Holiday Inn for the night. I didn't know anything about Florida, so I didn't have a choice but to follow Gold Dee's lead while I was there. As soon as we got inside of the room, I checked it thoroughly while Gold Dee went and got straight on the telephone. As soon as she got off she asked, "You want to go to work tonight or tomorrow?"

"That's all on you! However you would normally take care of business, do it! But the sooner the better because we still got a lot of shit to push."

"Well we can rest for the night; and first thing in the morning we can start."

"That sounds like a winner, but let's go and get something to eat. I still haven't ate anything today."

"What you want to eat?"

"I seen a Denny's in front of the hotel; that will be good for now. Infact, we can get it to go."

So off to Denny's we went. After we gotten our food, we stopped at the Shell's gas station down the street before we went back to the room. I grabbed a pint of Hennessy and a frozen slushy; while Gold Dee got herself different kinds of candy and a box of Keep Moving Cigars. When I seen her grabbing the cigars, my desires to get high just hit me hard. I just grabbed two boxes of Black & Mild's because I knew I was all in.

When we got back to the hotel, I told Gold Dee to "Take the food in while I grab that duffel bag out of my trunk," but when I open my trunk I seen that I had forgotten to take the other duffel bag containing the kilos out and said, "Ain't this a bitch, we riding with all this shit! How in the fuck did I slip up like this?" but it was too late to bitch now. I just grabbed both bags and went inside the room.

My mind was racing like ninety going west, trying to figure out how I slipped like that. It wouldn't have been so bad if I knew that we had brought it all with us, but that wasn't the worst part to me. We wasn't strapped with a hand gun at least to begin with if anything would have jumped off. I placed the bags in the closet, and then sat down and began rubbing my head. Gold Dee asked, "What's wrong with you?"

"Look, I'm gone run it with you right after we eat." The moment we finished, I got up and grabbed both duffel bags out of the closet and set them on the table, and then told Gold Dee, "Give me a cigar."

"Then you buy you some Blacks?"

"Yeah I brought me some Blacks, but that ain't what I asked you for!"

"What, you plan on smoking it like that?"

"Hell nor! If that was the case, I wouldn't have asked you for one."

"What about your parole officer?"

"Got damn me, fuck that parole shit. I'll be straight by time I go see him."

"If you say so!"

After she gave me the cigar, I opened the duffel bag and removed a pound of weed. Just by unzipping the bag, you could smell that the weed was potent. I twisted up a blunt, and then rubbed some of the Hennessy around it. After that, I fired it up. The first hit I took, was like being reunited with a long lost love one. I took another puff, and then told Gold Dee, "Go and get you a cup."

When she came back with the cup, she said, "That smell like that's that fire!"

"Believe me, it is!" I replied while pouring half of the slushy and Hennessy I brought in the cup for her. I passed her the blunt and mixed my drink up; then replied, "Check game boo! You already know that I don't know what's popping down here so I got to follow your lead, but um. We riding with more than I thought."

"What you talking about?"

"I fucked up and forgot to remove the rest of the cocaine out of my trunk before we left, so we been riding with all of it."

"How did you do that?"

"It's too late to try to figure that out now. All I'm saying is that I want to see where you make your drops at before we make any moves because I don't know these folks. You feel me?"

"They cool! I go straight to their house and do business there. They practically consider me family now."

"That might be so; but I don't trust, not nam motherfucker that I don't know!"

"I understand, but like I said they damn near consider me family. If it's going to make you feel better though, we can ride pass there now."

"That's exactly what we gone do; but first lets roll up the rest of these blunts, and then we can roll."

It took us about thirty minutes to reach the neighborhood where everything was supposed to go down at. The house itself sat right in the middle of the street, so if anybody happen to be outside they would be able to see when anybody else was coming down the street. After I was satisfied seeing all I could see, Gold Dee took us to what they called, "The Strip." It was basically just a hang out spot for everybody.

Gold Dee recognize someone in a money green Nissan with gold trimming and gold rims, and then pulled next to them. She said, "Let me holla' at him for a minute. He liable to buy all the weed from you."

"Well do what you do," I replied watching her make her move.

When she approached the dude, he greeted her with a hug. I could hear him asking her where she been, but I still didn't trust him for a second. I fired up another blunt while watching them; and then a couple of minutes later, Gold Dee came back to the car. When she got inside of the car she said, "I told him to meet us in thirty minutes at the Denny's. He wants five of them for a G a piece. That's straight?"

"Off top! Let's make that money!"

After we made the transaction at Denny's, we went back to the room and chill until the next day. Around nine o'clock, Gold Dee made a phone call to make sure everything was straight. Then we left.

When we pulled up at the house, it felt like we just left there. The only difference was now it was a few more cars parked outside. I asked Gold Dee, "Is it always this many cars over here at this time in the morning?"

"Pretty much, but you don't have anything to worry about!"

When we got out of the car, we didn't even make it to the door before a man came greeting Gold Dee. She quickly introduce him to me as Ricardo Luna; then he invited us in. As soon as we walked inside, Ricardo asked, "Are you all hungry? I can cook up some breakfast right quick."

That's when I spoke up, "Thanks for the offer, but we came just to do business."

Ricardo looked at me as if trying to read a book; then replied, "Tell me about yourself."

I knew when he asked me that question, that he didn't trust me and wasn't comfortable doing business in my presence. But, I didn't blame him though. Infact, if the shoes were on the other feet, I would have felt the same way. "Ricardo," I replied, "I know you don't know me and I don't know you, but I already feel where you coming from. Infact, I don't blame you a bit, but I'm as solid as one can get. If you don't trust me, I don't know what else to do but this," then I started removing all my clothes until I was naked, then replied, "I don't work with the mother fucking laws! I'm already a two time loser! I ain't even strapped right now! But if you don't want to do business, I'll be more than happy to leave your home and never return."

"Get dressed! I'm sorry if I offended you in any kind of way, but I just don't know you. By your reactions though, I can see I'll be more than satisfied doing business with you."

"Well let's get down to business!"

"Gold Dee, what you have for me?" Ricardo asked.

"I have the five I normally bring you and five pounds of hydro if you want that too."

"How much is the hydro going to cost me?"

"Fifteen a piece."

"I think I can find an extra five laying around here. What can I get for that?"

That's when I spoke up and said, "I'll let you have four of them for that, just to show you I'm real with it."

"Well go ahead and bring it in."

"You sure you don't want to go and get it with me, because it is in a stash spot?"

"You mean to tell me you have a stash spot on a Lexus?"

"I wouldn't have it no other way."

"I got to see this! You can pull it in the garage."

"If it will make you feel more comfortable, you can pull it in the garage yourself. Here the keys!"

When Ricardo opened the garage, I seen that he had a burnt orange 1964 Chevrolet Impala with hydraulics; sitting on some gold and silver Player Wire Wheels. I couldn't picture Ricardo driving a car like that, but I could have seen myself inside it.

When Ricardo got out of my car he said, "It sounds like it drives smooth. I didn't hear it start up. By any chance, you wouldn't want to sell it, would you?"

I took one look at my car, and then at his six four and said, "I tell you what, I'll trade you if you think your car can make it on the highway."

"I know for a fact my car can make it anywhere. Everything under the hood is new. Check it out, it even have a couple of stash spots. The keys are inside there."

When I got up close and actually seen inside of the car, I saw that even the interior was customize. I instantly fell in love with it. I barely turned the key, and it started right on up. I popped the hood and seen that everything under there was chrome. I could only hope he really wanted to trade, and said, "So far I like what I see. It's all on you if you want to trade or not. I have my papers in the glove box where you can see it's a clean title."

"First let's wrap up this other business, and then we can do business with the cars."

"That's all good!"

After we made exchanges with the dope and the money, I showed him how to get into my stash box and he showed me where his was. Next thing I knew, we were trailing each other to a notary to do the paper work on both cars. Right after that, Gold Dee and me went back to the hotel and smoked a couple of blunts before we rolled out.

Chapter Forty-five

*I*t felt like it didn't take us any time to get back to New Orleans. The first place we stopped at was at the storage to avoid being caught with all the cocaine we had left. While we were there, I grabbed three keys and the last pound of weed we had, and brought that along with us back to the hotel.

When we got back inside of the room it was just like we left it, but I still checked it all the way out. After that, I called Chaos to see when she was going to be able to come through. When she told me she wouldn't be able to make it for another two days, I just told her to call me when she made it down here. I then told Gold Dee, "Go buy a fifty box of cigars, while I start cooking up this coke. When you get back, knock on the door two times before you come in."

When she walked out of the door, the first thing I did was put the fifteen thousand I made with the hundred thousand we just made, and then began cooking up the cocaine. By the time she made it back, I still had a long way to go. Gold Dee already knew what time it was with the cigars and just began rolling them up. The way she was rolling blunts and I was rocking up the coke, it seemed like we were at work for a drug assembly line because neither one of us broke our rhythm for awhile.

When Gold Dee finished rolling up all of the blunts, she asked, "What we doing today?"

"As soon as I finish cooking up this shit, we can hit the lake front or what ever. You don't have to go to work tonight?"

"Un-un. I'm off tonight, but I can go in if I want to."

"Well check game! You can light up one of them blunts, but we need to discuss where we gone stay because these hotels ain't gone get it. Me personally, I think it's time for me to move back up north. I don't know what your intentions are or how you feel about moving out of town, but you know that you are more than welcome to move any where I lay my head at."

"That's cool, but what about your girlfriend?"

"I'm gone tell you like this; if she ain't ready to move on when I'm ready to leave, then life goes on. I'm not about to put myself in a predicament where I feel I'm bound to go back to prison to please anybody except for my son! If my own momma abandon me, then I know 4-sho that the next bitch will do it too! Let me hit that weed!"

Gold Dee remained quiet for a minute, and then said, "I don't know anything about up north! I don't even know anyone up that way! If I go with you, you gone have to promise me that you ain't gone leave me struck out!"

Now when she said that I felt insulted and replied, "Got damn me, I ain't left you stuck out in all of this time. What you ain't learned by now that if I fuck with you, I fuck with you and I'm all the way down with you? Loyalty means everything to me! That's just like that prayer I shared with you; you remember it yet?"

"It's something like: If blood gone shed, then let it shed. Show no sympathy. Cause death upon me and six times worse will be my revenge. Ain't that it?"

"Not quite! It goes like this. If blood gone shed, then let it shed. Show no sympathy, because I have no pity. As far as religion, may it be with you. 'Cause place death upon me, and six times worser will be my vengeance. I told you I wanted you to remember that, because I meant it. What I probably didn't tell you was why I wanted you to remember it. I feel like we share a bond and as long as you stay loyal, I'll go out in the deepest water for you and behind you. I could careless about who you decide to sleep with or who you give your feelings too, as long as they know where we stand. So think about what you gone do; time ticking!"

Without a doubt time was ticking! Infact, it was moving so fast that before I even realized it, two days had past and Chaos was calling me to meet her at the airport. I knew we only had two more days that we could keep the rental, but I decided that it was time to turn it in to save a little money. Besides, I didn't know how long I was going to be wrapped up with Chaos and I was already laying next to Angela.

When I jumped up and began getting dressed, Angela asked as if she felt offended, "Who was that, that got you having to move so fast?"

"Got damn me, don't fuck up a good moment with that bullshit! Anyway, this is what I need for you to do. Take the rental back and I'm going to pick you up."

"Where is your car at anyway?"

"I'm about to go pick it up now. Just go drop that car off."

"How are you going to go pick up your car if I leave you here? I know you ain't got another bitch coming to get you!"

"Quit tripping! I'm gone catch a cab! Infact, you can call one for me."

When I tell you she called one, you can believe she did. Infact, when the taxi picked me up, I spotted her trying to hide to see if I really was going to wait on it or someone else. I was pissed off at first; but then just shook my head at the whole situation. Instead of going straight to the storage, I had the cab pull up to a close by Rally's and then I walked from there.

As soon as I got inside of the storage, I made sure I removed all of the cocaine and money this time. After that, I shot straight to the airport to pick up Chaos. I informed her that I had to pick up Angela as well, and that all of our business was to be kept private. She didn't question me, instead when she met Angela she said to her, "So you are the one he's going crazy about; it's good to meet you."

Angela didn't know how to respond back; she just began blushing. We all made small talk until I dropped Angela off, after that I knew it was time to get down to business. I couldn't help wondering if Chaos was going to be able to shake something for the rest of the crew, so I asked her, "What you think are the possibilities that you can beat this case we having problems with?"

"You know it's always a fifty / fifty chance that things can go either way; but in this case and I don't want to lie to you; they are in a real bad situation! Without a doubt, I know one of them is going to have to take the charge if not all of them. I'm going to look more into it while I'm down here. Anyway, you didn't tell me exactly what kind of guns you wanted or how many, so I'm just having a few of them delivered."

"Delivered! How in the hell are you going to be able to do that?"

"Don't panic! A good source of mine is bringing them. Infact, he will be here by tomorrow night. Anyway, where my girl Gold Dee at?"

"Oh she went to gather her belongings. She should be back at the hotel by the time we get there."

Right when I said that my cellular phone went off. When I answered it, Shantay quickly replied in a highly upset voice, "Where the hell you been? What in the fuck going on?"

I didn't say a word. I quickly hung the phone up in fear that her phone might have been tapped. Within seconds she was calling back, but I didn't answer it. Chaos said, "That's a shame! You want me to tell them to quit calling?"

"It's not like that! That's Jay Dee's girl; but I'm not about to take a chance, on talking to her on this phone." I replied; and then at the first pay phone I seen, I pulled over and called her back. As soon as she answered the telephone I snapped, "Got damn me, don't say no names just listen! I know you want to know what in the hell going on, but I can't run it all down to you right now. You just gone have to be cool; I'm working on getting Jay Dee out now. By any chance if my parole officer come there, just tell him I just left and you don't know what time I'm coming back. One more thing, don't call my number again! I'm gone talk to you later" then hung up not giving her a chance to say a word.

When I got back in the car Chaos asked, "Did you get things straight with her?"

"Yeah; but I can tell this is effecting her bad."

"That's normal; but don't worry about a thing. First thing tomorrow, I'm going to see what's going on and what all I can do. Anyway, what you plan on doing with the guns that's coming?"

"Come on now; look at how we living! Look at what I'm driving! You don't think a nigga' will try to knock me for this? But before I let a motherfucker play me or them laws send me back to prison, I'll go to war with them! Real talk! Then how things been going, I'll rather be strapped then caught slipping needing one. You feel me?"

"I can see your point on things; but you gone have to chill and be careful! I don't want to have to be getting you out of jail too!"

"Believe me, you ain't gone have to do that! Just try to help Jay Dee and them. The money good! Whatever it's gone cost!"

When we made it to the hotel room, Gold Dee was sitting on the bed watching television. I let her and Chaos get into their girl talk, and then shot out on them. I went by Angela's house with the intention to discuss us moving out of town together, but before I was even able to speak about what was on mind she said, "It's something I need to tell you; but I don't know how you are going to take it."

"Well lay it on the line; and don't sugar coat it! What you have to tell me like that?"

"Since I met you I haven't been quite honest with you; but I can't keep lying to you."

"You what?"

"Before you get upset, I want you to know it's not what you thinking."

"How do you know what I'm thinking? Just tell me what you got to tell me."

"I love you from my heart, but I'm not as innocent as I appear to be. I never once cheated on you. Infact, you are my first and only sexual partner, so you don't have to worry about anything like that. What I have to tell you, is what you don't know about me. I know you might look at me like the house wife or jealous type, but I'm really bout' getting it."

"Getting it! What you mean by that?"

"I'm bout' hitting licks to get paid!"

"Come on now! You know you ain't bout' dirtying your hands or breaking a nail!"

"I'm for real!"

"You can tell me anything; but I'm from the Show-Me-State! You gone have to show me before I'll believe that."

"Well come on then, I got something set up now."

We left my car parked in front of her house, and jumped into her friend's white Geo Metro that she was driving. I really thought that Angela was just talking shit, so I didn't have a worry in the world. I lit up a Black & Mild, and then let down the top while she was swirling in and out of traffic. This was the first time I seen her actually drive like a professional. She stopped at an apartment complex and then said, "I'll be right back. I have to pick up my friend." I climbed into the back seat while she was gone. When she came back to the car she said, "You didn't have to get in the back; I could have gotten back there."

"It ain't a biggie! Besides, that's your friend you picking up."

Angela took a seat on the passenger side, and then said, "You still think I'm playing huh?"

"Hey, I'm not going to say a thing! I'm just gone see what you bout'."

When her friend finally came to the car, I took a good look at the Spanish chick and figured she wasn't a day more than eighteen. She introduced herself as Ivory, and then took off driving. The way she drove and knew how to operate everything inside of the car, I knew it had to be hers. She made all types of turns on streets I never been on. Eventually she turned onto a short street that had a meadow field on one side, and a grayish white building on the other side. Once she reached the stop sign, it was nothing but trees in front of us causing us no other choice but to turn left or right. She made a left turn, and then parked not that far from the building. Ivory raised the top back up, and then told Angela, "Everything is in the purse."

Angela didn't say a thing. She just got out of the car as if everything was normal, and then began walking towards the grayish looking building. I still didn't know what type of business it was, but I really didn't care. I seen Ivory kept looking in the mirror, so I turned around trying to see what she was seeing. When I didn't see anything that looked strange besides us being parked on the street instead of the small parking lot connected to the building, I asked her, "I don't want you to take this the wrong way, but do I make you feel uncomfortable or do you see something that I don't see because I see you keep looking in the mirror?"

Ivory removed her eyes from the rearview mirror for a quick second, and then placed them back. After that she said, "Don't mind me; you alright!"

"I'm happy we got that clear. I was starting to think that I was tripping." A couple of minutes after I said that, Angela came running towards the car along with a guard that she looked like she was holding hostage. The first thing that came to my mind was, what the fuck is this bitch doing? I opened the back door up just so she could jump in the car when I seen another guard running towards them. "Ivory, what the fuck you waiting on? Start up the motherfucking car!"

Instead of Angela jumping in the door I opened for her, she went around to the front passenger door and got in. I was about to close the door I had opened when the guard Angela looked like she was holding hostage began to get in. They had me all the way fucked up then. I looked up and seen the other guard had his gun drawn and out of instincts I grabbed for the guard's gun that had just got in the car with us opening fire. The guard died instantly; but his gun went off sending pieces of the other guard inside of the car brains flying. Blood quickly started filling up the floor and Ivory let out a loud scream. I snapped, "Shut up bitch and drive; or move out the way!"

By then we could hear the building alarm system going off and police sirens coming our way. Ivory still didn't pull off. That's when I jumped out of the car and was about to drive it, until I spotted a police car turning onto the street that we were on. Angela said to nobody in particular, "Everything going wrong "

As pissed off as I was for not knowing what Angela had did, I still told her and Ivory, "If ya'll want a chance in getting away, ya'll better start walking now" then I wiped my fingerprints off the gun as I dropped it next to the guard in the back seat, and began walking down the street the way the car was facing.

When the police officer in the car coming towards me was about to pass me up, we made a strong eye contact with each other but I kept walking. I had a feeling that he wanted to stop me, so I started walking faster. Right before I made it to the street that turned into the street that I was on, I heard gun shots followed by a high pitch scream. I looked back and seen Ivory was stretch out not that far from the car in the middle of the street. That's when I took off running.

I had the slightest ideal of where I was trying to run to, I was just running. While I was running I heard someone say, "Fool where you running to?" that only made me run faster. A few seconds later I heard a horn blowing followed by a familiar voice saying, "Boom! Quit running! Where you going?" When I heard my name, that's when I stopped running to see who it was calling me. Out of everybody in the world, it was a Mexican that I got cool with in prison. I thought I was tripping at first, because I knew he had thirty years and had to do at least fifteen. He replied, "Ese you just going to stand there; or are you going to get in fool?"

He didn't have to ask me again; I got in! "What's up Adoffo? When you got out?"

"Ese I been out for a minute now. What's been up with you? You look like you were running from them pigs!"

"I ain't gone even lie to you; I am!"

"You know I owe you for looking out for me up that road; how can I help you out?"

"Right now, just get me out of this neighborhood if you can."

"Fool, you were running the wrong way to say you want to get out of this neighborhood! What you did anyway?"

"I ain't did nothing!" I replied. Then I began running it down to him about what just took place.

When we reached the street that everything took place on, all you could see was police cars. Adoffo said, "You wasn't lying ese! Look at all them pigs down there!"

"You can look all you want, just get me from back here!"

"You think they caught your girl friend?"

"I don't know, but if they didn't I'm gone kill her and you can bet that. I mean how in the fuck this bitch gone put me in a situation like this and my feelings involved."

"You don't have to kill her, you have enough problems! Let me do it ese, if she didn't get caught. That way you can see I really get a trill off of killing."

I thought about what he said, and really didn't want to kill Angela myself. I don't know how I fell weak behind her, but I knew if she got away she had to go without a doubt. I couldn't let her have the benefit in turning against me. We turned down another side street and that's when I spotted Angela. All I could say was, "That's her right there!"

"Ese you want me to get her, or you gone do it?" I couldn't say anything. I was just stuck looking at her. Before I knew it, Adoffo had pulled over the car and walked up to Angela shooting her multiple times.

Chapter Forty-six

I had Adoffo quickly drop me off at my car because the whole time we were riding he kept bragging about how he killed Angela. I still couldn't believe what had happen in what started off as a beautiful day, but I had to accept it to get over it. The thought of moving out of town was really ringing in my head now; regardless of who came with me. To be honest, how I was feeling, I didn't know if I wanted anyone to know where I was going to be.

When I arrived back at the hotel room, Gold Dee and Chaos were lounging around in their panties and bras. They looked surprise when they seen me and said at the same time, "We didn't expect you to be back so soon."

"I wasn't expecting to be back so soon either, but I had to come back to take ya'll to get a better room then this. So get all of ya'll stuff together so we can leave, and don't leave anything behind."

After we got all of our things together, I drove Chaos to Queen and Crescent Hotel while Gold Dee followed behind us. Chaos checked the room out for a week, and then I helped them get settle in. While talking to them, I must have replayed Angela falling and the sound of Ivory scream a hundred times in my mind without noticing it. "Boom!" Chaos replied but I didn't even hear her. So she called me again and said, "Are you alright? You need to get you some sleep because you just drift off in your own little world in the middle of our conversation."

"My bad, but I got to go! I'm gone get back at ya'll tomorrow." I replied because she had me right.

While I was driving and reviewing what happened in my mind, my mind quickly register that I needed a place to duck off until I was ready to leave. The best and only place that came to my head was by Winter's house since I knew that she was easy to manipulate. Besides, I just couldn't think of any where else that would have been a better place than that! I didn't know exactly how I was going to get her to go along with allowing Gold Dee and me to move in; but I was going to come up with something by the time I reached her house.

When I pulled up at Winter's house, my mind was made up. I wasn't taking no for an answer. I figured if I had to fuck her until she started bleeding, then that's what I was going to do. I walked up to her door with confidence, but right before I got ready to knock it sounded like she was watching a porno flick. I thought for a second to myself, this bitch told me she lived by her motherfucking self until I heard other voices. My temperature started flaring and before I knew it, I barged through her door.

All I seen was assholes and elbows. For all of ya'll folks that don't know what that mean, that mean they were having one big as motherfucking orgy. Everybody froze up and looked at me. All I could hear people saying was, "What the fuck! Who's that? I'm caught," followed by, "I'm sorry!" then motherfuckers started grabbing for their clothes and even running out the house naked.

That's when I spotted Winter and said, "What the fuck going on in here bitch? All these motherfuckers in here butt ass naked! How much money you made?"

"I...I...I."

"Bitch don't get to stuttering now! Got damn me check game and peep play, I don't even want to know what you was doing. Go take your ass a bath."

When she came out of the bathroom, I had already put together my next parts to my plan. I was counting some money just to show her that I had plenty of it, and then just stopped in the middle of counting it and snapped, "Got damn me, I don't know where your mind at, but you better catch your head and real fucking quick. You under my administration now! And bitch you bet not never disrespect me like that again!"

"I told you I was sorry! I was just having fun."

"Having fun! You don't choose when you want to have fun; you do what the fuck I tell you to do. Infact, I'm moving in and gone teach you exactly what I want you to know and do."

"What you mean you moving in?" Winter asked as I quickly cut her off.

"Bitch what I tell you about questioning me? You heard what the fuck I said! Matter of fact, Gold Dee going to be staying here to just to teach you how to carry your got damn self around me." Now Winter just had what we call a dick look on her face. Which means she just froze up staring in extreme shock and disbelief of what I told her; but I didn't pay that no mind because I knew what I had to do. I took a good look at what had just became my new home, and then I told her, "All that motherfucking fucking that was going on in here, and all you got is a bedroom set. Bitch clean this place up from top to bottom and when you think you finish let me know!"

It took her about forty minutes before she came telling me that she was finished. While she was cleaning up I figured I'll take her out and make her feel like I was wining and dining her, and then maybe dick her down when we returned. Instead I took her out; but when we returned and got ready to call it a night, I stripped down to just my boxer but didn't allow her to touch me. That fucked her all the way up!

Ya'll probably wondering why I played my cards the way I did, but that just put my whole game plan into play. I had to let her know without words being said that I didn't need her for her pussy. Throughout the night she tried repeatedly to turn me on, but I didn't give in. I simply said cold blooded, "Bitch you need to be letting your pussy get all the rest it can before I send you out on a whore stroll," then went to sleep.

The next morning when I woke up, I was rock hard. Even after I used the bathroom, I was still rocked up. That's when I figured what the hell; I might as well make Winter satisfy my sexual needs before I put her to work.

When I tell you she satisfied my needs, believe me she did the damn thing. She might have been: a small, pale, petite, snow bunny to me; but I couldn't complain at all. I could just hear the change building up from her that I was going to make.

Afterwards, we sat back and she ran it down to me her total cost of living and how much money she made. I personally didn't really give a care about how much her total living cost was; I just wanted to know exactly how much money she was playing with. After I gave her instructions to change the telephone number and to go pay all of her bills up to date, I shot out to go meet Gold Dee.

When I pulled up at the Queen and Crescent Hotel, I didn't see Gold Dee's car parked anywhere. For a second I thought she was gone; until I called her cellular phone and she told me that she was inside of the room. I just told her to get dress and to come meet me outside. By the time she came to the car, I pretty much had my next steps to my plan together and was ready to run it down to her. Before I did though, I asked her, "Where Chaos at?"

"I let her use my car so she can see what she can do for the rest of the family!"

"You know when she gone be back?"

"Not really, but she is going to call if we are not back by time she make it there. Where are we going anyway?"

"Check game, I told you to think about moving out of town, but for the time being I got us somewhere to stay. Now peep play! You might not like it, but we'll be well ducked off for a minute."

"Where in the world did you find a place at?"

"You remember your friend from the strip club Winter?"

"Hell Nor! I know you ain't about to tell me that you got that nasty trifling bitch to agree to let us stay with her. What, you must have fucked her real good!"

"How I got her to agree with it ain't the point. I told you anywhere I lay my head at; you can consider it your home! It isn't going to be permanent, but it's gone have to do for now. I already told you all these different hotels ain't gone get it. So it's up to you. What you gone do?"

"Fuck it! I'm gone roll with you."

"That's what I'm talking about!"

"Don't get no ideals though. It ain't gone be any threesomes going on!"

I let out a laugh, and then told her, "I feel you! That thought didn't even come across my mind. We about to go and get a sofa bed set. When we finish getting what we gone get, you gone have to wait at the apartment for them to drop it all off. I got to get our next shipment ready! You can call me when everything gets there. If Chaos calls you first, just have her call me. Oh yeah; and under no condition what so ever, let anybody know where we living."

After we finished picking out what furniture we wanted and I dropped Gold Dee off, I went to the storage and did an inventory on how much cocaine, weed, and money we had altogether. We had a total of: thirty-six kilos, two hundred and twenty thousand dollars in drug money, and fifty pounds of weed. That wasn't even including the hundred and something thousand that I had for myself. I placed ten thousand to the side to pay for the guns Chaos had coming even though I didn't know exactly what they were going to cost me. Then I removed six kilos, and put everything else back up. After that, I placed the six kilos and the ten thousand dollars inside my car stash spots, and then drove to a nearby store to get everything that I was going to need to cook the cocaine. After that, I went and rented a room at Best Western and went to work.

A few hours went by before Gold Dee called me with the news that they had delivered the furniture and Winter had returned. The first thing I told her was, "Make sure you keep her ass in line, and don't let her do shit I wouldn't go for. Oh yeah, find out do she have to go to work tonight."

"She said she do. She suppose to go in at seven."

"What about you?"

"Unfortunately, I do too!"

"Well peep play; I'll swing through in a little bit. I'm almost finish here. Chaos haven't called you yet?"

"Not yet; but when she do, I'm gone tell her to call you."

"Off top do that! Well let me wrap up things here."

As soon as I finished rocking up the cocaine, Chaos called me and informed me that she had gotten a speedy trial set up for Jay Dee and the rest of the family. I didn't know if that was a good ideal or not until Chaos told me, "The way the reports are wrote up, they all are going to get convicted."

"It ain't nothing you can do to beat this case?"

"I'm afraid not."

"Well if I give you the money, can you at least get all of them bonded out?"

"That would be a waste of money in a sense because as soon as they all get out the feds are going to wonder where all that money came from and then link it back to you. Then you are going to be going under for conspiracy."

Damn, she made a good point. All I could ask her then was, "You can put some money on all of their books for the time being?"

"Of coarse I can do that. You just can't put a whole lot of money at once."

"I should be able to drop them off a thousand dollars a piece without it being a big deal; shouldn't I?"

"That would be good."

"Well I'm going to bring you that money in a little bit. I got to swing by there so Gold Dee can get her work clothes. What time does your source suppose to make it here?"

"Around eight or nine o'clock."

"Well I'll be there shortly."

After I got everything stashed away in the car, I checked out of the hotel and went straight to pick up Winter and Gold Dee. To my surprise, the furniture we had picked out looked even better set up in our living room. Winter was still overwhelmed with joy. As soon as she saw me, she approached me with open arms and happiness congratulating me on making her house look move presentable. I quickly set her straight and corrected her in a serious tone. "First of all, I made our house look more presentable to call home. Second; as long as you stay in your place and do what I tell you to, it can get better than this. Anyway, Gold Dee I'm going to take ya'll to pick up your car; that way we don't have to make any extra trips for you to get all of your things."

"4-sho" Gold Dee replied. "But I guess that mean we won't be seeing you any more tonight after you drop us off."

I just looked at her as to say, you already know what time it is. Finally I replied, "You know you can never know when I'm going to pop up. Anyway, let's go!"

When we pulled up at the Queen and Crescent Hotel, Winter asked, "Why did we come here?"

I quickly snapped, "Can you go anywhere without asking questions? You just make sure you make more money than you made when I first met you. Now get up out of here! Gold Dee, I'll see ya'll later."

I waited until they pulled off before I went up to the room where Chaos was. She was dressed in a business suit, with some small pretty eye glasses that matched. "Oh you made it here earlier than I expected. Where Gold Dee at?" Chaos asked.

"She already took off to go to work."

"How did she leave and I still have her keys?"

"I guess she had another set. Anyway, what's the latest we can go drop that money off on everybody's account?"

"We can go do that now, if you don't have anything else to do."

"Well let's go handle that. I got the money with me for that. Infact, you can take my car and go handle that by yourself."

"Why you don't want to come?"

"You know my car draws a lot of attention; and I don't even feel like putting myself in a situation where the laws can even catch up with me. Besides, I still haven't had a chance to get a little rest in. I been running around like I'm going crazy. If you do get stopped, just don't let them search the car because I got a lot of money stashed in there. All of the paper work is in the glove box though."

Finally Chaos agreed to drive my car by herself. While she was gone, I laid back and watched television. I felt funny watching television being that I haven't been able to just lay back and do that. Then all of a sudden while I was flipping stations, I ran across a sketch that looked like Adoffo on a crime stoppers commercial. I started paying close attention to the commercial to find out what he was wanted for. That's when they revealed that he was wanted for questioning connected to an arm robbery and homicide. I immediately became jittery. I mean my nervous became so bad, that all I could do was light up a blunt as I paced back and forward. Even though I knew Adoffo from prison, I couldn't help but hope that he wouldn't indicate me in any kind of way if the laws caught up with him.

Chaos came back shortly after I began to calm down. The first thing she said was, "Damn, you have it smelling loud in here! I thought you were supposed to be resting!"

"This is my way of relaxing, but accept my apology because I didn't mean to disrespect you in any kind of way. You know we bigger than that."

"It's cool! I understand! Anyway, your package should be here in about thirty minutes or less. He called me while I was dropping that money off, so if you are going to leave then don't go to far."

"You don't have to worry about me going anywhere. The sooner the better!"

It wasn't even close to thirty minutes before Chaos connection was knocking on the door. Chaos introduced him to me as Cali. For some reason I felt like I already knew this dark skinned cat standing in front of me. The only thing that kept throwing me off was that he spoke real fucking proper; but he didn't waste any time asking me, "Are you ready to get down to business?"

"Off top G! Let's do this."

Cali, Chaos, and me went down stairs to his car. Cali had a 1983 Fleetwood Cadillac equipped with hydraulics sitting on some thirteen inch Daytons. When I seen his car, I was surprise he even made it with the guns without having to kill anyone. Unless he did, and I just didn't know it. He popped open the trunk and just pulled out a sub-machine gun. Chaos rapidly replied, "Fool, what you doing? You can't just pull that out right here!"

"Where are we supposed to do business at then?" Cali asked.

"Check game, I know where a spot at were we won't have to worry about a thing. Just follow me, it ain't far."

I lead them to Andy's Self Car Wash. That's when Cali got to running it down to me on what he had. "Say cuzz, this right here is a Germany Machine pistol. A MP44. It has a 7.92mm caliber; feeds 30-round box, and sights is 875 yards. If you want something smaller, then I have a twin set of Israel Uzis."

"Got damn me, it don't matter if they big or small! So far, I'm liking what I see."

"Say cuzz, where you from?"

"I'm from the Lou!"

"Saint Louis! What part you from?"

"I was raised in the Pea Bodies! What, you know some folks out there?"

"Do I? I use to stay in Saint Louis too. Infact, I have an aunt that use to stay in the Pea Bodies."

"What's her name? I might know her."

"They call her Sparkle."

"Sparkle!"

"Yeah! She have two kids name Precious and Tj. They should be around twenty something."

"Man you got to be kidding me! The only Sparkle I know is my momma, and her name is Sparkle Green. When she supposed to have lived there?"

"Cuzz, that been some years ago now. I just seen her about a week ago when I was in the Lou."

"What's your momma name?"

"LaTonya."

"LaTonya! G, your real name Robert?"

"Chaos must have told you that."

"I didn't tell him anything." Chaos interrupted.

"Got damn me, you my cousin! My momma name is Sparkle. My sister name is Precious, and I'm Tj. When I was going to Gun Lock, you use to come visit us until you moved to California. That's why you look familiar!"

Right then Cali couldn't help but to show me love. The thought of doing business had completely slipped our minds until Chaos said, "I'm happy to see you all reunite, but don't forget what we are doing out here is illegal! Let's get this over with first."

I quickly shook back and replied, "Check game, you right. How much you want for all the guns you brought or do you want some dope?"

Cali answered, "For you cuzz, just give me five thousand."

I went inside my car stash spot and gave him that at ease. After that I asked him, "How long are you going to be down here?"

"I'm going to be staying down here. I'm just waiting to get an apartment before I move the rest of my things down here."

"So you going to be staying at the hotel where Chaos at until then?"

"I guess so, unless Chaos have something else she want me to do" he replied looking at Chaos as if expecting her to respond.

Chaos just hunched her shoulders as if to say her business was done as far as she was concerned. When I seen that, I said, "Check game and peep play cuzz! I can't promise you that I'll be able to hook back up with you tonight, but 4-sho by tomorrow I'm gone get at you. We got a lot to catch up on!"

Chapter Forty-seven

I never did get a chance to catch back up with Cali and Chaos that night. Infact, when I did catch back up with them the next day, it was time for Chaos to fly back to California. I thought Cali was going to shoot out as well, but he didn't. He kept the hotel room Chaos rented for the next three days until his apartment became available.

Over them three days, Cali filled me in on how his life has been since the last time we saw each other. After listening to some of the stories he told me, he reminded me of myself before I ever went to prison. I mean he was out there fifty-one fifty! Pretty much, the only difference I seen in our life styles was: I done been to penitentiary twice, chose to sell dope, and preferred to be with a light skinned female over all. On the other hand, it didn't matter what type of female a woman may have been to Cali; and he had a thing for pulling robberies. That only made us click tight.

I introduced him to Gold Dee, Winter, and my son. As soon as he saw my son, Cali said, "Damn Tj, he look just like your mother."

Up until this point I didn't have a desire to see my mother again; but by me knowing Cali knew how to find her, I had to see her. As much resentment I felt towards my mother, I just had to look her in the face and ask her why she left me. It wasn't the fact that I expected her to explain why she abandon me, because I grown to understand the life of an addict. I just wanted to hear it from her in her own words of why she left me. Instead of letting my true feelings be reveal I said, "Maybe we all can get together soon; I'm about to take a trip to the Lou. You can roll with me if you want."

"We might just be able to do that! I don't have anything planned for the next few days."

After that, we began discussing the possibility of combining some business opportunities together by us both liking each others styles. Shortly afterwards, we came to an agreement to start selling used cars after we fixed them up. All we had to do was find a spot to paint them and actually find some used cars. We both agreed as long as they weren't beat up with dents and started right on up; then they were ready to go. We continual chattering for a moment before I told him, "Just get ready G! I'll be back in a couple of hours to get you so we can take that trip."

Once I departed Cali, I called by the house and asked Gold Dee if she wanted me to bring her packages since I was going by the spot. She just replied, "You can bring me my medication, because this bitch getting on my nervous!"

I knew that meant she wanted some weed and bad. The only thing I could tell her was, "Look, don't let her get the best of you. She's only going to be around temporary. Besides, I don't want to see you with another swollen Black eye from a petite snow bunny!" then I began laughing.

"Fuck you bastard!" she said enraged.

I quit laughing at her then replied, "Don't worry about nothing; I got you. Let me talk to Winter." When Winter came to the phone I told her, "Check game! I know you and Gold Dee not seeing eye to eye; but just try to stay out of each other's face and get along."

"I'm trying!"

"Well try harder! Anyway, I got some business to take care of; but I'll be there in a little while. When I return, I expect for you to have at least three thousand dollars waiting on me."

"How do I suppose to make that much money? How long are you planning on being gone?"

"How you suppose to make it is on you. You just better come up with it! And when I say come up with it, you bet not bring a motherfucker to the house! You understand me?"

"Yes daddy!"

"I'll see ya'll in a little bit."

I drove to the storage, and then began filling my car stash spots up. I placed the twin Uzis in the front stash spot just in case anything jumped off; and twenty pounds in the back next to the two kilos I already had stashed. After that, I counted five thousand dollars out to bring with me on this trip and left the rest.

Next, I swung by the discount cigarette store and purchase two fifty boxes of cigars. After that, I went by the house to get things right with Gold Dee and Winter. Gold Dee barely allowed me to make it through the door before she harshly snapped, "Did you bring me my medicine?"

"Got damn, calm down! I told you I had you cover." I replied as I reached her the package and the two boxes of cigars. "By the way, I need for you to roll one of them boxes up for me. I'm gone come help you in a minute! The rest of that is gone be for you."

When I walked into the room where Winter was, she replied, "I'm happy to see you finally made it here; but can I ask you a question?"

"Run your mouth! What's on your mind?"

"Was you for real about what you said over the phone?"

"Was I for real? I couldn't get any more serious! So I suggest when you walk out the door today, that you get started." Winter didn't say anything else. She just began moping around as I gather some outfits to bring with me. Before I walked out of the room I told Winter, "I hope you mumbling about how you gone make that money before I get back."

"But I don't know how to make that much money; and I don't even know when you're coming back, or where you're going."

"I don't want to hear all of your I don't know how shit! As long as bread sells, pussy sells! So you better make something work. I told you as long as you play your part, then everything gone be all good. Just keep that in mind and you gone make it." I replied as I walked out of the room.

Gold Dee had the whole living room smoked out, and she was even speaking to herself. I just stood still and watched her. She was going off talking to herself. "This bitch don't know who she really fucking with!" she replied and then hit the weed. When she looked around and seen me, she said in shocked, "Oh, I didn't know you was right there. I'm about to start rolling them blunts up for you. I just had to get right first!"

"I can see that! You talking to yourself and shit! Shake back my baby; you got me not wanting to ask you to pass the weed if it's gone make me do all that!"

"I didn't even realize I was talking out loud. How much did you hear?"

"I heard enough! Anyway boo, I'm about to go out of town. I don't know exactly how long I'm going to be gone, but I need you to hold down everything here while I'm gone."

"Where you going?"

"Me and Cali about to go to Brooklyn."

"Brooklyn! Who ya'll know in New York?"

"He got some folks out there that buy weight. I'm just about to see what type of dealings we can make."

"Just be careful out there, and call me if anything goes wrong." And then she mumbled under her breath almost at a whisper, "I can't believe he gone leave me along with this crazy bitch."

"You know I'm gone do that. Besides, I can't leave you with my crazy bitch too long; ya'll might just kill each other."

Ya'll probably wondering why I flat out told her a bold face lye; but the truth is, I didn't want her to panic and think I was just about to abandon her. Anyway, we continue with our conversation while we rolled blunts until I got ready to leave. Once I left, I went straight to pick up Cali; and then we hit the highway.

After ten and a half hours of straight driving, we finally made it to Saint Louis. It was something about just being in Saint Louis that made me feel good, even though I was tried as hell! I rented us a room at a Days Inn Hotel for a week because I wasn't sure how long we were going to be in town. By it being kind of early we decided to get some rest before we made any moves, but my mind wouldn't allow me to get any rest without thinking about my childhood. The more I thought about it, the more furious I became until I felt asleep.

After a couple of hours of sleep, Cali and me woke up fully energize. The first thing Cali said was, "Say cuzz, you plan on dropping that dope off first; or do you want to go by your mother's first?"

"We can pass by mom's crib first. If she ain't doing anything, we can take her out to eat." I replied hiding how bad I really wanted to see her. "But first I got to smoke something!"

"I feel you on that! I can't even think about eating anything before I get my head right."

"Well fire one up before we make any moves."

After we both got on cloud nine as we call it, we left. I didn't know how to begin to locate my mother, so I let Cali drive to keep from asking questions. He drove us to the north side to a street name Hebrew. I knew from the surroundings that it wasn't a real good neighborhood, and figured I could find her in a neighborhood like this if not in the projects. Cali pulled up to an apartment building on the corner, and then parked the car. He then said, "Cuzz go see if she there!"

I didn't want him to know that I had the slightest ideal which apartment was hers and said, "I wanted you to knock on the door so I can surprise her. She hasn't seen me in a minute!"

"Oh that's cool, I got you." He replied as we both got out of the car.

When he knocked on the door, I heard a woman voice ask, "Who is it?"

Cali replied, "It's Robert. Is Sparkle here?"

The door swung open and then a lady replied, "Oh she not here baby! She should be back in a few hours. I'll tell her you came by, or you can just come back when you think she has made it back."

"I'll pass back in a few. Just tell her I'm looking for her, and have a surprise for her if you don't mind." Once we made it back outside, Cali asked, "Where do we go from here?"

I answered him in a disappointed tone, "G, I don't know! You still want to go and get something to eat?"

"I'm really not hungry myself; but if you are we can stop somewhere."

"I don't have much of an appetite either. We can ride around if you want. Other than that, I have to go on the south side to get rid of the dope, but I'm not planning on doing that until tomorrow."

Since we were already on the north side, we decided to hit the main strip and floss for a minute. I mean we rolled down Kingshighway turning heads. Folks were giving us compliments on the car at just about every stop light that we came to; but my mind was somewhere else. Before long, Cali had us on the river front shining. I could tell that he was enjoying all of the attention we were getting, but all I could do was smoke blunt after blunt.

I can't even begin to tell you how many folks asked Cali if he wanted to sell my car. I just shook my head no each time that happen. After awhile Cali told me, "Say cuzz if you even think about getting rid of this car, then let me get it. I been trying to find a six four!"

"I'm not really trying to get rid of it yet; but we might be able to work something out. I like your Cadillac! Does it run good?"

"Do it? She runs like a champ!"

"When we make it back to New Orleans, I'm gone have to check it out. I might just swap you." I replied as we continue down the river front. I spotted some of my folks from Far Side and told Cali, "Pull over next to them."

As soon as Cali pulled up next to them, I heard one of them say, "G shit clean, it's just the wrong color."

When Cali heard that, he asked me, "Cuzz, you know them?"

"Off top; them my folks! You don't have to worry about a thing G! Besides, if anything do kick off them twin Uzis I got from you right here." After I told him that, I yelled to my home boys, "What's up gangsters? What the fuck are ya'll doing out here?"

They all looked at me as if trying to figure out if I was starting some beef; but once they recognized that it was me they yelled out, "What's up gangster? What's popping?"

I got out of the car and showed them all some love; and then quickly told them, "Ya'll get ya'll money together, and tomorrow I'm gone meet ya'll in the park to bring ya'll some work."

"Gangster, what you working with like that?"

"I got some coke and some weed! Ya'll just meet me in the park around noon. Keep ya'll heads up G."

"Before you leave, throw us some weed. You smelling like a pound and shit!"

"Ya'll got that," I replied as getting back in the car with Cali to get them a couple of blunts. Once I gave the blunts to them, I told them, "Don't forget at noon, and watch out for them laws. One love!"

As we were pulling off, the munchies had kicked in and I told Cali, "G stop by White Castle's so I can get something to snack on before we go back to see if my momma made it home."

"Which one you want to go to because I got the munchies too?"

"It don't even matter! The first one you get to or see you can stop by it!"

We ended up going to a White Castle off of Washington Street. The whole entire parking lot was packed when we pulled up. I mean we were barely able to pull onto the parking lot without holding up traffic on the street. By the grace of luck. it only took us about thirty minutes to get something to snack on; but as soon as we got ready to leave, that's when all the drama kicked off.

Chapter Forty-eight

"*S*ay Tj, look at them bitches cuzz!" Cali said as he nudged me with his elbow, and then pointed to his right where the pair was starting towards a car.

"Damn G, them hoes fine as hell." I replied and that was all I had time to say because just at that moment, somebody came stumbling and slammed into me from behind.

"What the fuck!" Cali replied as I caught my balance before I damn near fell.

My first thought was, I was being hacked up by the police. When I realized it wasn't the cops and was just some white boy, I got mad as a mother fucker! "What the fuck wrong with you fool? You better watch where the fuck you running got damn me!" I said looking at the white guy get up, look around wide eyed, and then take off running again.

"You alright cuzz?"

"Yeah! That bitch just pissed me off for a second. He around here running like he Forest Gump or somebody!"

"Forest Gump!" Cali repeated then bust out laughing as if he was being tickled. "Cuzz, you stupid; but he did look like him!" and began laughing again.

The sound of folks shouting had caught our attention, so we turned and looked towards the shouting and seen four individuals arguing over something. We caught a little of their conversation as the closer we got towards them. I know some of you readers would wonder why we would walk towards the chaos, but there was no other choice but to go towards the scuffle by it being right by the car. Three of the four folks were guys. The female that was with them, was mostly what Cali and me was paying attention to at first.

"Motherfucker I told you that I don't give a damn about how you got jacked, I just want my damn money!" One of the guys said to another, and then hit him.

Up until this happen we were getting ready to get in the car, but the guy that got hit fell against the car. "Whoa got damn me, uh-un! I don't give a fuck about what ya'll do, but ya'll got to get the fuck off my ride!" I spoke up.

Cali backed me up telling the dude that fell onto the car, "Cuzz, you didn't hear him? Get the fuck off the car!"

The guy that got hit, slide off the car and stayed down. The other two dudes had the nerves to turn and confront us as if we were in the wrong. "Say fuck you! Ya'll want some too, bitch?" one said as they started towards us.

Cali was closer to all three of the dudes and the chick, by him being on the passenger side where everything was going down at; but as soon as the one that was mouthing off got in Cali's arm reach, Cali hit him with a quick left jab followed by a right cross knocking him out cold. I quickly made it around the car, and then my cousin and me began beating the shit out of the other dude.

"Bitch huh! Who the bitch now?" Cali snapped as he kicked the dude in the side as he was trying to get up. The chick that they were with started screaming by now, and the guy they was about to jump on some how vanished. That's when we heard sirens. "Damn Tj, I knew they were going to come, but let's do like Forest Gump did and get the fuck cuzz." Cali said as grabbing and dragging the guy that was still out cold him from blocking the door.

Just as we were pulling out of the parking lot, I spotted a black and white police car making the corner with its lights flashing. "Damn Cali, that's the last thing we need, is to get involved with the cops. I hope nobody got my license plate numbers." I said swirling through traffic. The first block I came to I made a right; went down two more blocks, then took a left. "You see any sign of the cops?" I asked Cali.

"Naw they gone, but that was close cuzz! That would have been a dumb ass way to get busted, especially behind another idiot's mess. We got enough shit in here to get us life."

"I feel you G! But like a man, I wouldn't have let them take me back to prison without opening fire on them. I done lost enough of my life behind bars and walls, lock down in blocks. I'm just happy I didn't have to put you in a fucked up situation like that." I said in a tone that told my cousin I was dead serious.

"Cuzz, I want you to know that I'm down for whatever; we family! If things ever reached that level I want you to know, that I'm going all the way out with you!" Cali said as he leaned back letting out a relieved breath, and turned on the sound to break the mood.

We rolled the rest of the way to my mother's house in silence. The whole while, while we were riding, I was preparing myself for the moment that I would actually meet my mother; but I wasn't sure what I wanted to ask her first or even tell her. I came to the conclusion that I'd just wait until the moment we would meet, and go off however I would feel at that time. That moment came quicker than I realized it though.

It was like déjà vu having Cali knock on the door and hearing the same woman that answered the door the first time ask the same question again. She even opened the door right after Cali asked for my mother. I thought she was about to tell us that my mother still haven't made it back until she told Cali, "Come in." Cali looked back at me, hunched his shoulders, and then walked in. I was just standing at the bottom of the steps clueless of what to do until the lady looked down the stairs at me and said, "Baby, you can come in too! You don't have to wait out here." Once I walked in, the lady closed the door behind us and said, "Ya'll can have a seat while I go get her for ya'll."

My body began letting off perspiration by the seconds as we waited on the lady to go get my mother for us. All kinds of thoughts and questions flashed before my mind distracting me from even noticing my mother had walked into the room until Cali said, "Hello aunt Sparkle."

At that moment I looked up at the woman he was talking to and now embracing with a hug, but that was all I was able to do. The young pretty woman I use to call momma had aged quite a bit. She now even had scars across her forehead as if she had been in some type of accident some years ago and was still healing. Before I even realized it, I was standing up walking towards them. When we made eye contact, I just stopped and froze up. I was confused, mad, and glad all at the same time.

All of a sudden, she just began crying and said, "Baby! My baby!" and began crying even harder.

Cali stepped back revealing a smile on his face, and then said, "Cuzz give your momma a hug. We surprised her so good that we got her crying!" but I still just stood there though. Even after he pushed me towards her, I just stood there staring at her.

Finally she just grabbed and hugged me saying, "It's my baby! Thank God!" while still crying.

I was in total disbelief; unable to believe that a single tear of hers was real. My mind just kept telling me to say, "What the fuck are you crying for? You was the mother fucking one that left me sitting on a stranger's porch in the middle of the fucking winter crying" but I didn't. As much hatred and resentment as I felt towards my mother over the years, I all of a sudden didn't feel none of that. Instead, I felt sympathetic. As if what she done to me as a child, didn't even much matter now that she was embracing me in her arms. I even found it inside of me somewhere to hug her back and say, "Momma don't cry! It's really me. How you doing?"

By then the other lady had walked back in the room where we were and said, "Is everything alright in here?"

Sparkle answered her stuttering, "This…This… This my… My baby!"

"Your baby! What?" the woman replied as if she thought Sparkle was lying. "I didn't know you had a son."

That's when I said, "Yeah, she my mother. My name Tj!" and pulled away from my mother with extended hands greeting the lady. "By the way, what's your name? I didn't catch it!"

"Baby just call me Dimples!" she replied in a sexy voice much softer than when she previously spoke.

"That's a very unique name you have! I can see why you were named that." I said ending our conversation.

Dimples then excused herself from the room by saying, "Well let me quit interfering in ya'll business! It was nice meeting you Tj."

"The pleasure was mines." I replied and then looked at my mother and harshly said, "I can see you living pretty good now! By any chance, do you have time for me to take you out to eat or something? We got a lot of catching up to do."

My mother was looking at me as if she really couldn't believe that I was standing in front of her. Then she replied with glossy eyes, "Baby we can go anywhere you want to go! What about Robert?"

"What you mean, what about Robert? He coming too!"

I guess Cali picked up the hint that she wanted us to be along because he replied, "Oh don't worry about me. I can chill here if that's cool with Dimples and you. Cuzz, go and take your mother out! I can see she wants to spend time with you alone. We can go out later. Auntie Sparkle, go see if it's cool with Dimples if I stay until ya'll get back."

My mother hurried up and walked out of the room where we were. That's when I told Cali, "G I'm gone make this up to you, but me and moms got a lot to catch up on. If you want though, I can drop you off somewhere else. You don't have to chill here if you don't want to."

"Cuzz, I'm going to be straight. I know Dimples!" Cali said with a smurf on his face.

"Man you sure?"

"Just handle your business."

My mother and Dimples came out of the backroom right behind each other. Dimples was staring at Cali as if she had sexually plans for him as soon as we would leave. My mother then asked me, "Are you ready to go?"

"Whenever you are" I replied. I didn't have the slightest ideal on where I was going to take her; we just got in the car and began riding. "Where do you want to go and eat?" I asked her looking away.

"Where ever you decide to take us will be fine" my mother replied. Then it became quiet as a church house mouse.

I tried to break the silence between us by asking, "Well, what do you have a taste for?" but that really didn't do any good because all she did was hunched her shoulders as if saying she didn't know. I knew where a real good seafood place called Mother's was and decided to stop there.

I could imagine ya'll thinking out of all the places we could have went, why would I go to a place called Mother's. At least that's what came to my mind as I viewed the big bold red sign.

"Mother's! What you know about this place boy?"

I sharp and harshly replied, "When you left me as a child, I came to this place thinking they would give you back to me; but I didn't know any better then. Second of all, let's get one thing understood about this term boy. It's only three such things as a boy: a white boy; a cowboy; and them homosexuals locked up. So don't you ever refer to me as a boy again!"

"I'm sorry if I offended you, but I didn't mean any harm by that."

"I just had to let you know that so you wouldn't think it was alright for you to call me that again."

We sat down inside the place for about three hours straight, running it. Half of the time I didn't know whether I should have left her sitting inside the place by herself, or to hug her extremely tight. Before it was all over with though, I think that we both found a long overdo closing peace bond between us. Now it was simply time for Cali and me to get down to business and make some moves.

After all of our arrangements; connections, and persistence in making moves, we started doing good. Even the cars we were selling were flying, so it wasn't any telling of what type of car you might have been able to get from us. Our specialties seem to have been, painting all our cars bowling ball colors and changing the tires and rims to Daytons and lows; but that's what was in. Sometimes we even went as far as adding switches to make sure our cars stayed flossed out and were off the chain. But damn, even more fucked up trouble came as if we didn't have enough bad luck and competition. My lil' cousin got popped!

Chapter Forty-nine

Cali was telling me that he had a lick he wanted to do and asked me if I wanted to get in. I thought about it, but after listening to what he was planning on doing I declined. To me, he didn't have it well organized; but I couldn't make him see it any differently. Besides, I knew if we were to get caught, we weren't going to see the streets for a long time if we were to see the streets again; but Cali was convinced that this was going to be an easy lick. I had to break it down for him like this, "Cuzz, you know I don't knock you for shit you decide to do, but you need to plan this one out a little more in my opinion. Right now, over half of my main team already locked up so I can't take this chance and Sabotage everything we have built! Besides, we're doing pretty good with these cars and the music."

Greed had Cali so blind to the point that I knew he wasn't trying to hear me out. Instead, all he kept on saying was, "All you have to do is drive and I'll break you off!"

Cali almost sounded convincing, but I couldn't see me taking that chance. I told him, "Since we been little kids, you know I ain't never told you nothing wrong; but something about this lick ain't right."

He just blew me off right quick replying, "I-ight. I'm gone find someone to do it with me."

When Cali told me that, I knew it wasn't anything I could do to make him change his mind. He had already put it in his heart, so it was only a matter of time before he took his chances.

We separated around about seven that even after we finish painting a two-door Cutless we had just got. His lil' brother kept on asking can he get the

Cutless, and we both kept on saying, "It's not ready yet, it's not ready yet" to him. He comp an attitude and must have thought that we were just telling him no because we didn't want to see if he could drive or not; but it wasn't nothing like that.

Anyway, Cali told me he was about to go to his gal crib and we was going to go shopping for his kids and my son Saturday morning before we start messing with any cars so not to plan anything. I was cool with that, so all I replied was, "We gone do that!" and then I left to go and get my son.

I thought to myself on the way to pick my son up, *I hope Cali keep his head up* because I had a funny feeling that he was about to fuck up. While I was driving, I was like: *Cool, we'll go shopping early in the morning; and then set the cars we had ready for sale on display, out in front of the strip club that was going to be getting off later on that night. If we didn't sell any of them, oh well; but at least folks would have seen them and would have a number to get in touch with us if they wanted to do business.*

The moment my son got in the car, I had to admit that he was starting to look more and more like me without a doubt. He was even starting to act like me. I asked him, "What do you want to do?"

He replied, "Play the video games!"

"Play the video games! Alright!" then took him to the arcades. We stayed in the arcades until nine o'clock. After that, I took him to get something to eat; then dropped him back off at home.

The next morning when I woke up, I knew something was wrong because it was ten thirty to be exact. I knew one thing for sure. If Cali said he was coming in the morning, you could count on him being there around seven; no later than seven ten, as if he was going to miss something if he came any later. I paged him about six times myself; and even had Winter and Gold Dee call him repeatedly, but he never did hit me back or even answer the phone. I called by the spot where we painted the cars, and nobody answered. The same thing happened at the studio as well. I tried his cellular phone again, but after so many rings it went to the answering machine. At this point I was like fuck it. Let me get ready so at least if he showed up, I'll be ready to roll.

I got dressed and then checked my beeper and phone to see if I had any missed calls; but unfortunately, the only unanswered number that I missed was from a number that I didn't want to bother by anyway. Finally, I called by his girl's crib and nobody answered the phone there. I knew something was definitely wrong now.

I told Gold Dee and Winter I'll be back, and then went and jump into my Cadillac. I stopped at a Danny & Clyde gas station to fill up and while I was pumping my gas, Cali little brother came running up to me out of nowhere damn near out of breath. I quickly asked him, "What you running from; and where in the fuck is your brother?"

Cedric replied between breaths, "Cali locked up! Him and La'Trice!"

"What? Locked up! What happened?"

Cedric begin, "I don't know! They went out somewhere last night; but as soon as they came into the house, the laws came running in the house right behind them. I don't have the slightest ideal of what happened though."

Come to find out, his very own bitch, La'Trice, snitched. I couldn't believe his baby momma! La'Trice even told the police how he planned and pulled off certain capers that they couldn't even link him to; but that wasn't the worse part. When it was time for him to go to court and face his charges, out of all the people in the world, I couldn't believe who took the stand against him. Cedric! Yeah, his own baby brother turned out to be low down bad dirty. Ain't that a bitch! Family can be a mother fucker! The truth be told, I still believe that he told on him behind not letting him drive that Cutless he wanted so bad that day. My cousin Cali ended up getting sentence twenty-five years and had to do eighty-five percent of that.

Now in the mix of all this shit, you know times started getting hard. Gold Dee and Winter were bumping heads it seemed like every fucking day. It got to the point that I had to just kick Winter and Gold Dee to the curve to end some of the dumb shit that they stayed into over just to focus. I still haven't heard anything new on what was going on with Jay Dee and the rest of the gang. It was like I had the weight of the world on my shoulders trying to maintain for us all. So you know me, I went to doing what I felt like I knew how to do best. Hustle.

What can I say; I refuse to endure in the struggle when I knew how to over come it. I sold the few cars Cali and me had invested in: broke bread with Cali to make sure that he was straight; and then I invested the rest of my time and money into the drug business. Money was flowing right, but I got caught up in the life style again. I was slanging all out of the studio running shop like it was legal, but that's when it happened to me. I ended up getting popped.

I couldn't blame it on anybody but myself. I knew what I was facing and the chances that I was taking. I just didn't believe that it would have happen to me like everybody else that has ever been caught up. Anyway, I took a plea bargain to serve seven more years behind bars because I knew it was my shit and didn't need a jury passing judgment on me. They had already labeled me a code six in their eye sight; and if they found me guilty, I knew they were going to deal with me. Besides, I didn't want to go through all of the waiting frustration, when I knew that they actually had me right in this situation. All I wanted to know was what was they proper cause in stopping me; because it wasn't like I was hanging on the corner or even speeding when they jumped out on me. I was simply going to the store to get some more blunts and Black & Milds. They couldn't even say that they had seen me because I was inside the studio from about ten o'clock that morning to about ten o'clock that night smoking, drinking, and recording a song called "Life."

The way the song was going, actually describe how my next eighty-four months was gone be like. Just picture this if you could. *Could you ever imagine the same water you shit and piss* in, *would be the same water you wash your fucking clothes in. Would be the same water you keep your milk from going bad. That's how it is my nigga' when you caught up from doing bad. Life…*The only difference was that I didn't have life and actually had a roll out date as long as I lived to see it.

So far my reality was waken up early in the morning for role call, getting feed two pieces of bread and syrup and having to roll with it because didn't anybody want to stick together to get at least treated like the adults that we were suppose to be. I mean, can you imagine for a television you just hoping: looking out of your cell through some bars; just hoping, that somebody would walk past, so you could at least say that you seen something for months. Twenty-three months had passed by the time I made it to population. In prison population only mean to live and be around other offenders without individual cells keeping you all separated.

The truth be told though, I had got to a point that I preferred to be isolated than to be apart of population. As funny as that sound, it was just a lot of fake as shit going on, on the compound as they called it, that I just preferred not to even much be apart of. Everyday it was some type of bull shit going on. It didn't matter who was wrong are right; or was something fair or not. It was like, everything was a gamble that could be gambled on. Just like it goes in jail or on the streets in this matter though, you might see something; but you don't see anything, especially if it didn't have anything to do with you. You feel me? In other words, mind your own business and don't get caught snitching if you choose to go that route.

On another note though; today I saw a couple of dudes get into it over some juice. I didn't pay it any mind at first, because I didn't have anything to do with it. Besides, I had mines already, so it wasn't a big deal to me what they got into about. Apparently though, this juice was a big deal to these two other individuals. They past a few words as we begin to eat, but I'm still not knowing that the tension amongst them had built up so, so, deep. One of the dudes went and strap up his tennis shoes. I figured he was just being on his P's and Q's and continue eating until I also noticed the stare in other dude eye as he walked pass me; towards the lil' dude. Now me being me, I don't know about you; the way the conversation was going as he was getting closer to lil' homie, should have told him to swing first and save the chattering for later. Now I'm watching as this lil' dude sizing the other one up (In other words, he plotting on where he is about to hit him at.) but before I could even much swallow, all I seen was lil' homie getting snuck. Boom! He fell across the bed and your boy that hit him then pinned him down so he couldn't get back up. By the time that he did let him get up, (Ya'll that was there, already know.) lil' homie was fucked up! His face had knots everywhere and was swollen like a balloon ready to burst Black and Blue. Nobody said a word about it; instead, everyone minded their own business even though we all know that everybody was thinking the exact same question, "What did he hit him with because nobody believed that your boy could be hitting that hard." After that, things that day went on as if nothing ever took place.

By the time I started working in the fields, I knew we were just modeling day slaves. The only difference we showed amongst ourselves was how we mentally escaped our realities. Some sang, some rapped, some preached, some prayed. Some, well we not even much going to say. No matter how much we all might have wanted to escape our reality, from my point of view of working in the fields, it was hopeless. I mean just hopeless; but, not everyone agrees with me.

If you never been to a prison in the south, then let me give you a brief description of the prison that I'm being housed in is so you can easily visualize the prison and the situations that I'm going to take you through. Surrounding the entire prison are three huge rolls of razor barbwire fences. These fences are every bit of at least fifteen feet high. You have what they call, "*Gun-guards*" (Which are simply prison-guards who are armed with shotguns; sitting around in what they call "*Watch-towers / Gun-towers*", just hoping that you try to run so that they can legally shoot you down with no questions asked. If any questions happen to get asked, they all will be concluded as clearly being justified when they finish explaining what supposed to have happen.) These *Watch-towers / Gun-towers* are scattered throughout the entire prison grounds so it would just plan oh stupid to try to escape. Now outside these prison grounds are nothing but flat fields outlined by tall trees as far as you can see in any direction that you may choose to look.

Anyway, this one particular day that we were working in the field, it was hot as hell without a moment of a cool breeze blowing. The guards were on some bull shit! They kept trying to make us keep up with the horses they were riding on, as they lead us the long way to wherever we were going to be working at. They must have walked us an hour and a half straight before we even made it to the place where we started working. When we did start working, they swung us down almost every six to eight minutes. (Meaning they gave us a new place to start working at.) Some folks weren't even finish with the cut that they were working in. The more quicker that they tried to make us work though, only made us that was working in the field want to ride out. The only problem with riding out was didn't nobody want to go to the cell blocks right now. It was eighty-seven degrees outside; but if you were in the cell blocks, it felt more like a hundred and twelve degrees at ease.

Anyway, back to the escape. They had just called *head-line* being that we had so far to walk back to the prison. (Head-line means to line up, paired off; and get ready to go back in.) But on the way back in, the guards wasn't really paying attention to us prisoners like they were supposed to have been. I guess in their minds they figured that they had us well trained and didn't have to worry about us doing anything; but they were wrong. A prisoner by the name of Timothy decided that he had enough of being incarcerated. While walking, he started dragging back until he made it to the end of the line and came across an opening in the fence. Nobody thought nor had an ideal of what he was really up to; but without second thoughts, he took off running with his work hoe and all.

I peeped him, but I didn't say a word. I just kept on walking while looking at him through the corner of my eye saying to myself, "Damn, he look like he running slow to be trying to escape; but I hope he get away for his sake!"

He damn near made it to the middle of the field before he would have reached the halfway point to get in the woods before anyone else noticed him. All the chattering in the line is what brought attention to him and got him busted. "Look at him out there!" that's what damn near everybody started saying until the guards took notice of him.

I quickly but quietly thought to myself, *I hope he get away because I wouldn't want to be around all of these snitches if I got the chance to break.* By looking at him though, I knew that he wasn't going to make it. The only thought and question that came across my mind was, "Are they going to kill him or not?"

The gun-guards shot off warning shots. Boom! (Click clack) Boom, as they begin taking off towards him on their horses! I said to nobody in particular, "That's ten dollars gone out of his account when we get back in."

One of the gun-guards took aim at Timothy from no more than twenty feet. I thought to myself, *well at least he tried*; but the gun-guard missed. I don't know if he intentionally missed on purpose, because in my opinion he was too close to have had missed.

The other guard watching the line now had already called in back-up. With-in what seemed like seconds later, all you could see was White GMC Blazers, Jimmies, and F150's coming across the fields. The previous gun-guard that just had missed shooting Timothy took another aim at him; but this time the other gun-guard intervened telling him not to shot him and that he was going to run him down. Upon hearing that, I couldn't help but wonder if this redneck would have told him not to shot the inmate down if he was Black; or even if the other gun-guard would have missed when he took his first shot.

Still watching the guards though, I witness him run over Timothy with the horse. He not only did it once; but he did it twice. By then, the guards that came across the fields in the trucks had him surrounded. They beat the shit out of Timothy unmercifully as they begin trying to block our view with the trucks; but we were partiality still able to see them. When they finally picked Timothy up so that we could see him in a clear view, he had blood all over him and looked as if they had hog tied him. I kept thinking and saying to myself, *"At least he tried! At least he tried!"*

Chapter Fifty

*I*t must have been about three hundred and sixty days later, when three young inmates and me had some differences. The killing part about this whole situation was that it was all over some water. Yeah, you read me right; some motherfucking water!

I was using the phone when these three lil' youngsters by the names of Kobey, Chad, and Red began horse playing in the dorm. It wasn't a big thing to me, because I was being entertained on the telephone. Now in the mix of this conversation I was having, Kobey, Chad, and Red horse playing than lead up to them throwing water around the dorm. All of a sudden, splash! Some water almost hit me. I interrupted my conversation on the telephone and told the young cats, "Watch that water!" Meaning where they threw it at and who they hit with it. That's when Red and me pass some words.

I can't tell you what all was said word for word or exactly what was said, but Red's last comment to me was, "You got to be ready to die and go all out for words."

I looked straight at him and told him, "It don't make me no difference; we all got to die someday!" and left it at that.

He didn't say anything else; but I continue watching all three of them because I knew that I couldn't trust them a hundred percent, or put anything passed them. I been in here to long to just go for anything and not acknowledge the tension in the air once it was sparked; but didn't anything else jump off that day, or the next day. Infact, a couple of days went by as if nothing ever took place, so the little incident was clean out of my mind.

You don't have to say a word; I know that I fucked up by letting my guards down especially being in prison, but I thought that the little bullshit was over. Boy was I wrong. After last feed up, the mother fucker they call Chad snuck me. *Pow!* I was shocked at first because I couldn't believe this lil' cat just stole on me. Without another thought though, we went into a quick mix. When it was all over I ended up busting all of his mouth opening sending him to the infirmary. I came out without a mark on me, but I still felt played because he stole on me first.

His lil' partner Red that I had exchange words with, yelled out his cell, "Yeah, I did that! I sent him at you." as I walked pass him.

I looked at him through the bars that separated us and replied, "Yeah, that's why he gone to the infirmary; you lucky it wasn't you!" and left it at that.

By now his other lil' partner, Kobey, must have gotten the word on what happened; because now, every time we cross paths I peeped that he keeps on slick-side mugging me. In prison it doesn't take a genius to know when it's tension in the air and is about to go down, so I'm on my P's and Q's waiting on him to act like he want to do something so I can run on him. Somehow we never did cross path on that level.

A week passed now and I see that Chad mouth starting to heal. Kobey and Chad have been hanging real tight. From time to time, I catch them both staring, but that's about as far as it goes. Picture one day Chad tried to play me. He came by me one day just before last feed up, talking about, "Lets put this behind us." as if I haven't noticed all of the slick-side mean mugging that he been displaying towards me.

So of course, you can imagine in my mind I said fuck that because I know he go to be trying to play me. I said, "You sunk me once, you want to try your luck and do it again?" at the same time I'm thinking about sneaking him now, but he steady trying to comp a plea. Eventually, I was like fuck him because I seen that he wasn't bout it; but I'm steady watching him just incase.

Now it's feed up time. I see Kobey and Chad back hanging together, so I'm just watching them both being on top of my shit. That's when I peeped Kobey wrapping something white around his hands. It didn't take a convict or a genius to figure out what time it was. That was the giving sign in prison that something was about to go down regardless. I got my food and sat down with my tray, but at the same time I'm steady watching Kobey trying to ease close by me. As soon as he got close enough to me, I jumped up and hit him first. I was right on point too; because the little motherfucker was just about to try and sneak me, but I caught him by surprise.

"*Boom, boom, boom*" was all you heard as we were exchanging them dogs violently. I ain't going to lie, I feel like this lil' young motherfucker was getting the better of me than I was getting of him; but neither one of us were bleeding. Infact from the spectators point of view, it was a good live fight going on.

With a quick jab fake, I side-step him; and "Crack!" my finger sounded off instantly swelling up. I don't know how in the hell I did that; but my finger was hurting like a motherfucker! Now with this throbbing pain in my hand, I couldn't help but to think that I fucked up now because we were still mixing. All of a sudden, he caught me back with a nice side-step. "*Bam!*" I fell back against a wall surprise and a lil' shook up at that, but I see him trying to rush me so I'm prepared for him. When he swung, I ducked and he hit the wall. "*Boom!*"

How his hand looked after the impact, I could tell that he had broken it. I figured that about even the fight so I didn't let that stop anything. Instead, I came up with an upper-cut, followed by multiple hooks. It seemed like the more that I hit him though, the more I was only hurting myself. After a few more hits, I stepped back and looked at him and could easily see that he didn't want any more. I ain't going to lie, I didn't really want any more neither. I felt like it was a draw, even though I could have taken advantage of the situation and fucked clean over him. It was so tempting too because everybody that was around watching was cheering it on.

"Fuck over him! Fuck over him! If he had the upper hand he'll do it to you!" is what some spectators shouted.

Even though I knew they most likely were right, I had enough myself and let him make it. I felt like if he wanted to fight all over again, he'll have to wait until his hand healed unless he was going to try and sneak me with a cast on. Either way, I'll be ready.

Chapter Fifty-one

I say now it's about a year later. Shit has been happening, but not too much over all. All of my so called friends have either gone on with their lives; or I just don't hear from them anymore. Some ended up dead; others just in different jails. As for as Jay Dee and the rest of the family, I just don't know whatever had happened with them. It was like everybody was just separated without any way of being connected. After awhile, it was just like the saying goes, *"When you're out of sight, you're out of mind."* I only say that because rarely did I found myself thinking about them as time passed on. Other than the typically basic stuff in prison, I gained a little weight along with a few tattoos. I figured everything was going to be smooth sailing from here on out. Shit had died down. I had exactly four months left before I was schedule to go home; but I guess I was wrong.

I was using the bathroom; when out of nowhere, somebody ran up behind me and started stabbing me. He stabbed me about twelve times before allowing me fall to the floor. Even though I was in pain, I couldn't help thinking to myself; *I never figured I would get killed like this in prison.*

Moments out of my whole life seemed to be quickly displaying before me. I mean from the time that I was a little: moving from place to place; sleeping in car-shop garages; to even jumping in the game running from police. All of these scenes seemed as if I was actually re-experiencing each event, but with the exception of knowing the outcome. The shoot-outs; the murders; the robberies; my son; I mean everything. I couldn't believe it! I couldn't even move; and the fucked up part about the whole situation was, it wasn't a doctor or a guard anywhere in sight. I was assed out with nothing to look forward to accept for death.

When I woke up, I could tell that I had been through surgery. I had a bunch of sticky pads stuck all over my chest, sides, back, and arms. Whether I was bless to have another chance or my purpose here on earth wasn't finished yet, I don't know. I was just lucky to be living. I never did find out who stuck me up, but I had feeling that it had to Red even though I couldn't prove it.

By the time I got out of the infirmary, it was time for me to be release. After eighty-four months of being incarcerated, I couldn't believe my roll-out date was finally here; but it was. After all of the years that have gone by and me anticipating my release, it was finally real. I was finally on my way home.

Two prison guards dropped off me and three other inmates that were being released at a Grey Hound Bus Station in Alexandra, Louisiana. From there I had to catch a bus back to New Orleans. I didn't give a fuck about what another person might have thought about seeing me riding on a bus; I was just so happy to be free.

On the bus ride back to New Orleans, I was tripping off how so many things looked different. Cars, roads, even buildings were in places I could remember where just woods. I said, "Damn, a lot of shit has change!" to nobody in particular. It was mind blowing to me on how much the city and technology had developed, but not everything changed in a good way. Infact, when it was time for me to get off the bus, I knew some things didn't change.

The bus-stop was right in front of a neighborhood convenient store. Instead of appearing to look like a normal convenient store, it looked like we had pulled up to a neighborhood dope set were drug sells were in transaction. Everybody that was out in front of the store, were either selling drugs; or trying to buy some. Despite some of the new faces that were out there, it was quite a few folks out there that I use to have dealings with before I got sentenced to prison.

Those that knew and remembered me instantly asked me the same questions, "Where you been? You still got that work?"

My only reply was, "Un-un lil' homie; I ain't even with that no more. I just came home, and just trying to see my lil' one." Then I pushed.

When I crossed the street, I was hoping my eyes were deceiving me; because the visible picture I was seeing, I just couldn't believe it. Cali lil' brother, Cedric, was posted up kissing Shantay. Yeah, Shantay! Jay Dee's girlfriend! As bad as I wanted to know how in the world that could possible happened, I just shook my head and figured somebody was going to snatch her. I just would never have figured that those two would have hooked up.

When they saw me, they both looked as if they had just seen a ghost and froze up. They didn't know what to say or do. I just looked at them with a stare that could have spoken for itself. I eventually nodded my head at them, but kept it moving leaving them wondering what was on my mind. I didn't even ask about Jay Dee or the rest of the gang.

A few days after getting settle in, I decided it was time for me to get started back on my own music if I was planning on doing anything with it. I didn't know where to start because I had so much stuff running across my mind. I kept thinking about all of the years that I spent incarcerated, and all of the planning I had made; but what was bothering me the most, was I couldn't get the picture out of my mind of Cedric kissing Shantay. It was driving me to the point that I couldn't stay focus regardless of what I tried. I wanted to know what had happen to my boy and the rest of the crew; and how in the hell Shantay ended up with Cedric. To clear my mind, I decided to go visit my son.

We started off playing video games, and then decided to walk around to the neighborhood park before it got dark. I could tell something was bothering him; so I began to talk to him, in hope that it would get him to open up to me. It eventually worked; because as we continue to communicate, he started telling me how much he been missing me.

Cortez was mainly mad at me because he felt as if I had just left him, and stayed gone away for him for so long. I had to explain to him about the decisions that I had made, which overall caused us to be separated for as long as we have been. At first, it didn't seem like he was truly understanding the consequences that came along with of some of actions that I had taking; but he eventually got it. He just didn't want me to go away like that again; which I understood. Right then and there I made Cortez a promise that no matter what, I wasn't going back to prison or was going to leave him alone as long as I did again.

Cortez let out a genuine smile that only an innocent kid could have, and then he asked me, "You promise?"

I replied, "I promise" and then took him back to my house so that he could send the night.

That night after Cortez had fallen asleep, I decided to go club hopping just to get a vibe of what type of music folks were overall listening to. At first, the night started off slow; but the later it got, the more cooler it got. After the third club, I was easy able to identify what types of songs majority of the people seemed to be enjoying. This helped me make up my mind on which songs of mines that I wanted to go and record at once. After I was sure of my decision, I decided that it was time for me to make it back home just incase my son woke up.

I remember checking my watch and seeing that it was only 1:32 a.m.; but I kept getting this bad feeling that something was wrong, or was about to go wrong. You know how you be watching a movie and can predict what's about to happen even though you are not exactly sure of what's going to happen; that's how I was feeling.

It started lightly sprinkling right when I made it home and parked my ride, but I decided to run across the street to store to pick up a pack of Black & Milds before calling it a night. I wasn't even three minutes away from my home, when a dark color mini-van came speeding from around the corner with the side door open. I didn't think anything of it at first; but before I knew it, it was too late.

Two people were in the back of the mini-van with ski masks on and had guns pointed at me. I was fucked out of luck. I wasn't even home a good week and had guns pointed at me. The trip part about this whole situation to me was, that I didn't even know why. The first thing that came to my mind was run. I couldn't see me getting away before they could have shot me down or even hit me with the vehicle that they were in; but my adrenaline was pumping so hard that before I even knew it, I kept on slipping on the pavement. I didn't realize that I had already broke out running. Infact, I never even heard the gun shots. The last thing I heard was a voice that sounded a little bit familiar, but I wasn't sure of whom it was.

That's when it felt like the mini-van must have hit me head on and I fell; but this time I couldn't get back up. I felt like every bone in my body was broken until they couldn't be broken any more. The pain started at the top of my shoulder and seemed to spread rapidly. When I looked at my shoulder, I saw that it was still there; but I had a hole in it now that was gushing out blood as if it wasn't going to stop. I didn't know was I going to bleed to death or not, but I still tried to get up.

All of a sudden, I caught another bullet. This time I seen my whole hand look like it was just snapped out of place. I just closed my eyes because I heard a voice saying, "We got him! We got him!"

I felt one of them put a gun to my head as I tried to remain motionless. I didn't know whether they were going to finish me off with a dome shot, or even if they had too. I was in so much pain, but they weren't making it any better as they kicked me over rambling through my pockets.

After all of the things that I have done, this was the first time that I feared death. I didn't know how many times I was shot, but I acted like I was dead so they wouldn't shoot me any more until I heard them pulling off. Once I knew that they were gone, I was trying with all my might not to pass out and to get back on my feet; but I still couldn't. I had pain running through my right leg that I just couldn't bare. I kept telling myself to hold on and things was going to be okay; because I knew that if I passed out, that was going to be it.

I was in so much pain that I started to pray for death; but I wanted to be there for my son. I didn't want to break my promise that I just made to him, so I had to hold on; but what was I suppose to do? I was stretched out, soaked in my own blood; only minutes away from where I lived.

Prologue

*A*pproximately six minutes had past and I was still stretched out in the middle of the streets. I was sure the shooters were long gone; but what was bothering me besides the pain that I was in, was the fact that I still didn't hear or see a police or ambulance. I knew from that moment that if I was planning on surviving, then it was going to be up to me to get to a hospital.

I struggle effortlessly to stand up, but with the burning pain in my legs and hand I just continue to fall. Having no other choice, I dragged myself out of the streets to a nearby parked car for support to lift myself up; but I still was unable to do so. All that kept replaying in my mind was how I was caught slipping and left for dead. Those thoughts quickly came to an end when a young boy appeared out of nowhere. I just knew he was about to finish me off! So I replied the only thing that came to my head. "If blood gone shed, then let it shed. Show no sympathy, because I have no pity. As for as religion, may it be with you. 'Cause place death upon me, and six times worser will be my vengeance."

The young boy just stood and looked in disbelief. Then he replied, "I didn't come to hurt you. My name is Elijah. I came to help you. I know who you are."

Even though Elijah looked as if he could have been innocent, I was still defensive; but could you blame me? I was just shot down and robbed by three youngsters. All I could manage to ask him was, "How do you know me?"

Elijah quickly responded, "Everybody knows you. You the man they call Boom with the tricked out cars. Besides, I know your son." At the mentioning of my son, my mind flashed out. All that kept replaying in my head was the promise that I made to Lil' Threat about never leaving him. Now here I was dying not too far from the crib. Elijah spoke again, "You don't look alright!"

Indeed he was right. I knew if I didn't hurry up and make it to my feet, I would surely die. I weakly asked the little youngster, "You think you could help me stand up?" He just nodded his head as he began trying with all of his strength. Once I was standing I thanked Elijah, and then told him, "Now you go ahead and get in the house, and make sure you take a bath first before you do anything else. Anyway, it's too late for you to be out here," with that being said he ran off.

I struggle to reach my car as I kept my balance on other park cars. When I reached mines, the alarm went off and Cortez came running out the house saying, "Daddy, I see you trying to creep out! Where you think you going?" but then froze in his tracks when he saw me bleeding and screamed.

"I'm okay son; just open the door for me."

Cortez replied while crying, "What happen to you?"

"I just got to make it to the hospital and everything is going to be alright." I replied as I got in the car.

"I'm coming too; but what happen?"

I didn't see any sense in being argumentative with him; besides I knew this could very much have been the very last time that I might have been able to share anything with him. Once he got inside the car, I told him, "First, put on your seat belt. You never know when it might be able to actually save your life." As he fasten his seat belt, I lower the music so he could hear every word that I was about to tell him clearly. "Now Lil' Threat, I want you to listen to me real good because what I'm about to tell you can make a difference in the rest of your life."

"I'm listening" he replied with a sincere expression on his face.

"When you get older, I don't want you to be like me. I want for you to be better than me. So learn all that you can about anything and everything that you get involved in beforehand. Knowledge is your most important tool son. Second, always remember that anything possible is always possible even when it don't seem like it. So never count anything out as impossible." I replied as I swirled across the highway causing a state trooper to turn on their bubble gum lights in pursuit of me.

"*Ooh* dad! The police got they lights on behind you!"

I continue driving ignoring the state trooper. Then said with sharpness in my voice, "I hope you paying attention to me; because it's a lot of stuff that you are going to have to watch out for, and the police are one of the main things! Never believe them a hundred percent; and never ever under no means give them information concerning anything or anybody even if they promise to help and protect you!" Feeling a little more weaker, I swirled towards the exit ramp and then continue, "Never trust anybody completely son. You never can know what's exactly on someone else's mind; but you can always be positive about what you say, and what you do. That's it. Always keep your word son! Your word should mean everything! So whenever you give your word to someone, keep it! You understand me?" Cortez just nodded his head so I continue. "Son no matter what, always finish what you start. That way you won't be caught sleep by anyone that feels like you are too much of a threat to them. The last thing I want you to know before we make it to the hospital son, is to always remember where you lay your head at."

"I know both your address and my momma's too."

"That's not what I'm talking about. What I mean is never do any dirt close to where you stay and sleep. But the most important thing I want you to always remember, is always think before you react. You got that?" but before I could hear his answer I lost control of the car and crashed into a parked car in front of the emergency room side of the hospital.

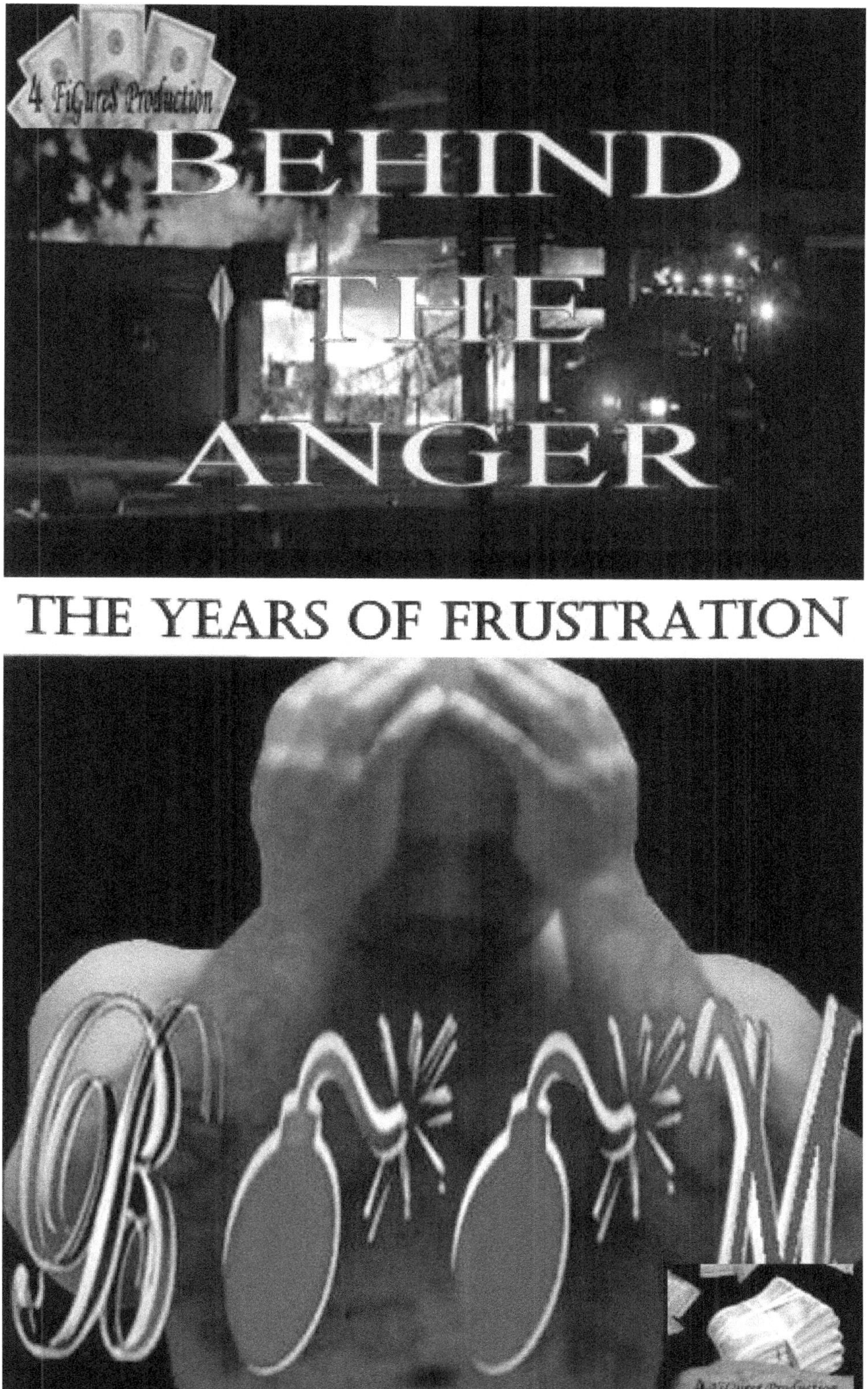

THE YEARS OF FRUSTRATION

If you like this urban novel, then you should also check out my next release.
Here's a sneak peep inside of it.

Chapter One
(A New Start)

$\mathcal{N}$ow here it was six years later, and I was still waking up in cold sweats recalling the last hours that I spent with my father. For some reason, I just couldn't seem to erase the memory of seeing my father bleeding as he sincerely gave me a lecture on the principles that he wanted me to live by. You couldn't have convinced me that that's how our relationship would've ended as I recalled the nurses and doctors scrambling trying to revive him. Blood was everywhere. At the time, I didn't quite fully understand how seriously injured my father was when I heard the nurses yelling out, "Hurry up, we're losing him!" I just knew everything was going to be alright and my father was going to pull through even though the hospital staff refused to allow me to enter into the surgery room with him. How wrong was I?

Life quickly had changed for me after my pop's funeral. Things just weren't the same. Although my mother was already married to Tony at the time of my father's death, she still took it hard. On several occasions, my momma would look at me and then just out of the blue break down crying saying, "You look just like your father."

I knew that was true. I looked like a splitting image of him; so I didn't know how to console her. She constantly would burst out in tears, and that led to Tony and her constantly getting into it. One day, my mother was going through one of her emotional break downs and Tony snapped out on her.

"Bitch, you sitting around here crying about another nigga'; when ho', you suppose to be my motherfucking wife! Keisha, if you don't stop this shit, I swear to fucking God you going to be joining that nigga' since you love him so fucking much!" At least that's how their last argument went that I witness before they physically began to fight.

They must have fought every other day; at least three times throughout a week. Their relationship became so full of domestic violence, that it led to them filing for divorce. I was glad when I found out that they were serious about getting divorce; because hearing Tony talk the way he talked to my mother and about my father, only made me want to brutally murder him. I knew if my father was still living, that he wouldn't have said a single word out of line about him; and most definitely not in front of me. He wouldn't even be putting his hands up with the intention of fighting my momma; but what could I do? I just use to think to myself, *His time coming, he just don't know it yet; but soon enough, he going to get his.*

Once the divorce was finalize Tony went his separate way, and mom and me were on our own. The first week, moms kept mentioning that it was time for a new start; but being that we where in the slums, I didn't see how much change we were going to be able to make in New Orleans. Besides, New Orleans was all we knew. I guess my mother had more faith than me, because moms kept on talking about it was time for us to meet new people; go to new places, and just do new things.

I overheard her talking on the telephone to her sister, auntie Keniesha who stayed in Saint Louis, Missouri about the divorce being finalize; but I didn't really pay it any mind until I notice how excited mom seem to have gotten. "Sis, are you for real? I don't know! It's just Cortez and me now. I was just telling him we need a new start; but I don't want us to be a burden to you! I'll think about it. If anything, it'll be temporary. Okay. I love you too sis! Talk to you later." My mother said, and then hung up the telephone.

From what I got out of their conversation, I figured auntie Keniesha must have been trying to convince my mother to bring us up there like she usually did; or at least until she knew that we were situated. Either way, I personally felt like if we were going to get a fresh start, then moving out of town would have been our best option. I didn't want my momma to know that I was somewhat ease dropping on her conversation; so I played it off once I heard her set the telephone down, I yelled out of the room that I was in, "Momma, tell aunt Keniesha I said hello!"

"Cortez, you are a second too late. I just got off the phone with her; but you can call her back if you want. Come here anyway; before you do anything eles, I need to talk to you first."

I walked into my mother's room not knowing exactly what she was about to say, and quickly replied, "Huh momma. How auntie Keniesha doing? I see you been talking to her a lot lately."

"She's doing just fine; I told you that you could call her back if you want too, but first I want to talk to you. Have a seat." Keisha said patting on the bed next to her.

Instead of sitting on her bed though, I took a seat in the blue lazy boy recliner chair that sat in the corner in her room and asked, "What's wrong? Is everything alright?"

"Ain't nothing wrong boy; just listen up! Anyway, now I know that you are probably tired of hearing me talk about we need a fresh start; but today your auntie and me were talking, and she invited us to come stay with her in Saint Louis until we get ourselves situated. I didn't want to make that big of a decision until we sat down and talked about it; because it's important to me to see how you would feel about a change like this."

"I don't know momma! I don't know nothing about Saint Louis besides my father was from there. Have you ever been there?"

"Nope; but that's the beauty of it! I've never been, and you've never been; so it will be brand new to both of us. Then from what my sister tells me, it's quite a few good job opportunities there for me and kids your age along with good schools." Keisha said as if she had pretty much had already made her mind up about the whole ordeal.

"All of that sound good to me momma; but what about all of our stuff? How are we going to get it all there?"

Keisha looked around her room slowly in disappointment; and then replied, "Things are going to be tight baby; so we can only take our clothes, and you can bring your video game system because I know how much you love that thing."

I was like, "That's it!" with what I imagine was a total look of disbelief expression written across my face.

"Yeah baby, that's it! We going to start all over and get everything brand new!"

Three days later, we were on the Greyhound Bus headed to Saint Louis, Missouri.

Chapter Two
(Da Move)

*W*hen we first enter Missouri, I saw a sign that read, "Welcome to Missouri the Show-Me-State." I don't know what it was about that sign, but it stuck out to me. I wanted to know why they called Missouri the Show-Me-State.

As we continue heading towards our destination, I just looked out of the bus windows in excitement thinking to myself, I *hope it ain't going to be country where we going,* as we passed a field full of all Black cows. It was about the thirty-six one I had seen. I was starting to lose hope, as we continually passed fields after fields for awhile. I thought to myself, *I can't believe we had came this far to be getting ready to move on a farm. Auntie Keniesha or momma ain't never mention nothing about a farm, cows, chickens, and sheeps to me.* I felt like they played me for a fool.

It seemed like it was getting worse until I saw a sign that read "St. Louis City Limits." At that moment I knew that we were in the city and shouldn't have been seeing any more farms. As the bus driver switched highways and approached his exit, I saw some tall shinny grey thing that looked like reflecting mirrors going high up into the sky and coming back down to the ground. I became full of excitement and said, *"Ooh* momma, you see that?" pointing at this new object. "You know what that is?"

She looked in the direction of this object in amazement as well; but at the same time, my mother nor me knew what it was until another passenger who overheard me asking about it informed us. "It's called The Gateway Arch. It's the third tallest monument in the world. Isn't it a beauty?" the older lady replied. I just nodded my head in agreement.

Within minutes, we had arrived at the Saint Louis Greyhound Bus Station. My auntie Keniesha was already there waiting on us sitting inside her platinum gray Chrysler 300C. After a brief exchange in greetings, hugs, kisses, and getting our luggage settle into the trunk of her car, my auntie said, "I know ya'll probably hungry as hell after that long as ride! What ya'll want to eat?"

"I could go for an ole shrimp poor-boy." Cortez answered.

"A shrimp poor-boy! Boy we don't have that up here. What else do you got in mind?"

"Ya'll don't have shrimp poor-boys up here; aw man auntie! Ya'll sell crawfish up here; don't ya'll?"

"We do; but not anywhere around here. I got a place for ya'll. Ya'll want some pizza for now?"

"Sure, I can go for some!" Keisha calmly said.

"Can we get some with hamburger on it?" Cortez questioned.

"We sure can! Bacon, extra cheese, and hamburger is my favorite kind." Keniesha replied.

Within moments, we were pulling up to a building with the letters IMOE'S on it. "I-Moes! I never heard of this. Is they food good auntie?"

"First off, it's pronounced E-Moes; and their pizza is the best! You can only get it here in St. Louis. Wait until you taste it, you'll see." We finally entered the restaurant and I saw that it was quite a few people inside of there already. My auntie looked at me and asked me, "Cortez, what do you want to drink?"

"It don't matter to me auntie; I'm not choosy."

"Okay then, well go find us a table." Auntie Keniesha instructed me to do. I chose a table that set in the corner, but near the window. After a couple of minutes, both my mother and auntie joined me. Once they got seated and comfortable, Keniesha said in a serious tone, "I think that this would be a good time to discuss the house rules with ya'll before we even much get there." She then paused until she knew for sure that she had both of our undivided attention before carrying on. "I don't really expect much. All I ask of ya'll is: Whatever ya'll mess up, clean up. We all are old enough to clean up behind ourselves, and don't neither one of us sitting here have a maid. Second, don't leave anything on in my house if you are not using it because my bills are high enough. Third, I don't mind ya'll having company from time to time, but lets keep it to a minimum. I really don't want and I don't like having a bunch of people running in and out of my house. Overall, just respect the house; that's all I ask. Ya'll don't feel that I'm asking too much of ya'll, do ya'll?"

"Not at all!" momma replied.

"What about you Cortez?"

"Nope! Momma had way more rules than you do." I truthfully answered causing all of us to burst out laughing.

After we all got a good laugh in, momma asked her sister, "How are we going to split the bills? Cause as of right now, I have eight hundred dollars."

"As far as the bills go, as long as ya'll do what I asked and keep everything off when ya'll are not using something, then everything should be just fine. I make enough money at Southwestern Bell to cover the household bills. Remember this is about me helping ya'll; not ya'll helping me." Auntie Keniesha replied.

As soon as that conversation was established, the food arrived. We had pizza and hot wings. Off the flip, I was tripping off how thin the pizza was; but at the same time, it looked good as hell! The wings didn't look bad either. They were smoother in an orange color sauce. Auntie Keniesha said, "Don't just sit there and look at it, dig in!"

We all grabbed a piece and began eating. Momma was the first one to break the silence by saying, "Damn this pizza good!" and grabbed another slice.

Aunt Keniesha smiled and then asked, "What about you Cortez? What do you think about it? Do you like it?"

"Un huh! They should sell this in New Orleans!"

"Well that's good ya'll like it because I eat this all the time. We have one right by the house, but you can't go in there and sit down and eat in that one; it's only pick-up or delivery." She then said in between bits, "I'm happy ya'll came up here; I haven't seen my lil' sister and nephew in awhile now. I thought I was going to have to come down there and kidnap ya'll!" she said jokingly. "When we get to the house, I have a surprise for you Cortez."

"Well what we waiting for, we finish eating ain't we?"

"I'm just waiting on ya'll to say ya'll ready to go."

"Well I think I speak for both of us when I say we ready to go auntie." I held the door open for both my auntie and mother and ran to the car to open up the doors for them both again so we could hurry up and leave. I was so excited and couldn't wait to find out what my surprise was going to be, but I soon learned that auntie Keniesha drove like a bat out of hell as we flew down the highway passing cars.

We were all pretty quiet as if we all where in each of our own world until my auntie Keniesha broke the silence. "Keisha, you ready for tonight?"

"What do your crazy ass got up your sleeve?"

"You'll see!" aunt Keniesha responded with a smurf clearly visible on her face.

As we got off the highway, I noticed a big white tower was built in the middle of the street as cars drove in a circle around it. "What is that place called auntie?" I questioned eager to learn more about my new surroundings.

She said, "Oh that place been closed probably more than a hundred years now; but it's called *The Water Tower*. That's one of the places they sold slaves out of back in the slavery days. You see this street right here," she said pointing to a street that sign read 20th Street "everybody here in St. Louis calls this street *The Dub!* It's very dangerous over here, so stay from over there."

"I hear you loud and clear auntie"

My momma just being herself had to say something as If I didn't understand what auntie Keniesha just explained. "Your ass better! 'Cause Keniesha he likes to roam all over the place."

I just kept my mouth shut. We went down two or three more blocks and I noticed the streets signs read Grand Blvd. and Lee Ave., as we made a right turn onto Lee. I was happy to see so many kids my age outside playing and then all of sudden, the car started to slow down as auntie Keniesha made a U-turn and pulled in front of a nice house that looked better than most of all the other ones on this part of the street. She cut the car off and said, "Well, this is it! It ain't much, but its home!"

I said, "It looks good to me." as I opened the car door.

My momma said, "Yeah girl, this is a nice ass house. It looks like it was just built."

"It was; it's only about five years old." Aunt Keniesha said. "Wait until I show ya'll the inside." she continued as she popped the trunk so I could retrieve our luggage.

In the process of doing so, an older lady in the next house over from us yelled over the fence to my auntie, "This must be your handsome nephew and his momma?"

"It sure is!" auntie Keniesha responded back to her. "Ain't he a cutie pie? "

The older lady said, "He gone have all the girls calling all times of the night!" We all laughed as she came across the yard so my auntie could properly introduce us.

"This here is my sister Keisha and my nephew Cortez." My auntie Keniesha said.

"Well how are ya'll doing? My name is Rosemary; but just call me Rose. I stay next door, and just wanted to introduce myself. By the way, welcome to St. Louis. If ya'll need anything, just knock on my door; I'm always home."

As we entered the house, Keniesha said, "Just sit ya'll bags by the crouch so I can show ya'll around the house real quick. This house has: two bedrooms, one bathroom, a dinning room, and a big kitchen."

I must admit that it was a nice house. She showed us her bedroom first, and than showed us the other bedroom. Upon seeing it, I said, "Momma, I want to sleep on the side by the window! "

Auntie Keniesha intervene and said, "You ain't sleeping with her; you got your own space down in the basement! I got it set up real nice just for you; plus you got a few gifts waiting on you down there."

"The basement! What the hell is that?" my mom asked as the exact same question ran through my mind.

Sensing the concern in her sister's voice, Keniesha answered, "It's the lower part of the house that people usually use for storing things. But instead of that, how I got it set up, it's going to be like Cortez own lil' apartment." All I could do was smile because I felt super special. We walked into the kitchen, and she opened what I thought was just a closet door. Instead of it being a closet though, it was the entry way to my room. The basement. As we walked down the steps, the rest of the room came into view. I thought this hidden room was off the chain even though it wasn't much in it. Auntie Keniesha said, "Now this is your room! I know it's not much in here right now, but next week I'll take you to get a few more things to make you feel even more comfortable. But for now, you got a brand new bedroom set, and a few more gifts that I know you going to love. As a matter of fact, go ahead and open your gifts and tell me if you like them or not. They right there in the corner."

I turned around and seen a television stand with no television on it; but sitting next to the stand was two nice size boxes. One was wrapped in some Christmas paper wrapping; while the other one was wrapped in some happy birthday design wrapping paper. I asked, "Which one should I open first?"

"Which ever one you want!" auntie Keniesha replied.

Keisha then said, "You should open the smallest one first."

I grabbed the smallest box first. I noticed that it had a nice bit of weight to it, as I picked it up and set it on the bed. Once I begin opening it, I saw the words play station; and out of excitement I yanked the rest of the paper off as fast as I could. "Look momma!" I yelled "Auntie Keniesha got me the brand new PS3 that I been asking for."

Auntie Keniesha said, "Opening the next one."

The next box was two times the size of the first one and weighted more too I quickly pull the paper off and underneath was a brand new Sony 32" flat screen television. I was out done. "Thank you! Thank you so much auntie Keniesha! I love them!" I said and gave her a hug and kiss.

"Why you spoiling him like that Keniesha?" my momma asked.

"Because I missed my nephew sixteenth birthday; and Christmas. Plus, he's my only nephew. Anyway, I'm glad that you like your gifts; but now I have somewhere I want to take your momma, and I need you to stay here and hold the house down cause you the man of the house now."

"I got you!" I said.

"Okay. It's late, so stay in the house and play your game. Don't go anywhere Cortez, because we won't be gone long."

"I'm about to play my game auntie. I ain't going outside, not tonight."

"Okay. Your momma and me are about to go get dress. If you want something else to eat or drink, the refrigerator is always full and some snacks are in the closet. We'll yell down here and let you know we gone before we leave."

As soon as they began walking back up stairs, I began hooking up my new video game system and began playing Grand Theft Auto as I sat on my brand new queen size bed. I guess about thirty minutes later, momma and auntie Keniesha came back down into my room to get my opinion on how they looked. I took a quick glance at them both and said, "Ya'll look good." Which they did, but turned my focus back on my game.

"He ain't paying us no attention; he all up in that damn game!" My mother said.

"Oh well, we gone! If you need to reach us, I wrote my cellular phone number down on a piece of paper on the dinning room table."

"Okay." I replied but kept my focus on the television screen.

Chapter Three
(Ladies Night)

"Girl, where in the hell are we going anyway?" Keisha questioned Keniesha.

"We about to go to the *Royal Palace*; so we can have a few drinks, and a lil' fun sis. From our conversation we had over the phone, it sounded like you needed a change of pace. Plus with all the extra hours I've been working, I need this break too! Besides, I seen you had your hair and nails done already, so I said fuck it; we out here tonight! Anyway, when was the last time we kicked it? It's been a hell of a long time!"

Thinking about that, I knew she was right and said, "I really feel like this is a good ideal. I should've been and came up here when you first asked."

"Well you don't need to worry about it now, cause ya'll here now; and you know big sis got some shit lined up for you already as far as work goes, but we can talk about that shit tomorrow. Tonight, we are just going to have fun!"

We arrived at the Royal Palace and the parking lot was packed with all kinds of brand new cars. I was excited to go in because I could hear the music jamming. When we finally got in, I could see the place was jammed packed, considering that it was pretty small on the inside. I quickly looked passed that after I down my first drink and my song *Step in the name of love by R. Kelly* came on. "This is my shit!" I said feeling the vibe.

"Girl, you look like you ready to start stepping. You still know how to dance, don't you?"

"Hell yeah! I can still get down!" I said with confidence. That's when I noticed that this spot was full of nice looking men. I told Keniesha, "Watch my drink while I get my step on sis."

"Okay girl, don't break a leg."

"Yeah right!" I said over my shoulder as I stepped my way onto the dance floor. I couldn't help thinking it felt good to be dancing and having fun with my big sis without all of the extra drama.

I noticed this fine ass nigga' looking at me from across the room. I assumed he had to be every bit of six feet, and two hundred pounds. He had a light brown skin complexion; sporting a wavy low hair cut just like I like. His outfit looked as if it was made just for him. He was the hottest nigga' in the whole damn club from my point of view.

He started walking towards me and I could feel this shyness hit me like a ton of bricks, because I just knew that he was coming to introduce his self. I tried to play it off like I didn't notice him, but it was too late. He approach me saying, "Excuse me Ms.; how you doing tonight? I don't mean to cause you any trouble, but I've never seen you in here before. My name is Quincy, but everybody calls me Que. What's your name?"

I quickly pulled myself together and answered, "My name is Keisha."

"Damn Keisha, I love your accent. Where are you from; and are you in here by yourself? If so may I dance with you?"

"No I'm not in here by myself, I'm with my sister; but I would love for you to dance with me, and by the way I'm from New Orleans." Just as soon as we started to dance, the song went off. Thank God it did because I felt a tingle between my legs as he brushed up against me and I smelt his cologne. I said, "It was nice meeting you." and turned to walk away.

"Hold up sweetie, can I at least buy you a drink since we didn't get to finish our dance?"

"Only if you're planning on buying my sister one too!"

"I'll buy the whole motherfucking bar if I have too! Just say whatever it's going to take for me to get to know you. Ms. Keisha from New Orleans!"

She blushed as she began walking back towards the bar where her sister was watching her from the side line, with Que right on her heels. "Oh shit, I see you! You ain't been here twenty minutes and already found somebody to talk too!" Keniesha said teasingly; and then turned her attention towards Quincy who was revealing his perfect even white teeth and smile. "Now who the fuck are you, trying to talk to my lil' sister?" she said jokingly.

"Calm down big sis; they call me Que. I hope it's okay with you for me to talk to your sister."

"Girl quit bullying him; he came over here to buy us a drink!" Keisha interrupted saving Que from being interrogated on the spot.

"Us!"

"Yeah, us!"

"Bartender." Quincy shouted over the blaring music.

The bartender quickly made his way over and asked, "What can I get for you today Que?"

"You already know what I want; but I want you to give these two beautiful women whatever it is that they want."

"No problem Que! Well ladies, what can I get for you?"

Keisha responded, "I would like a Long Island Ice Tea. Keniesha, what do you want?"

"I'll take the same thing she's having." Keniesha replied to the bartender who was checking her out.

"So you must come here all the time; you got the bartender calling you Que and shit." Keisha said striking up a conversation.

"Yeah, I do actually. I love the music and the food here. Speaking of food, would ya'll like something to eat? If so, order whatever ya'll want. I got ya'll."

"We straight; we already ate before we got here."

"That's cool. How long ya'll been up here?"

"I just got here today, but my sister been living here for a few years now." As Keisha was answering Que's question, their drinks arrived.

"So you just got here today; well how long do you plan on staying up here before you leave?"

"I'm here for good. My son and me needed a change in environments."

"So you have a son; how old is he?"

"He sixteen; going on twenty-six! His name is Cortez and he's my everything."

"That's good to hear; but you know that I have to ask you, are you still with his daddy because you are too beautiful to tell me that you are single unless something is wrong with you and I just don't know it?"

"Que, ain't nothing wrong with me boy; but for real, my son father past away a few years ago."

"Oh I'm sorry. I'm sorry to hear that."

"It's okay."

"Well, I'm single; with no kids. I just help my sisters with their kids. I have three nephews and one niece. My oldest nephew is sixteen like your son. Maybe, one day they might get a chance to meet each other."

"That might be possible; but anyway Que, what do you do for a living?"

"I'm a." just as he began to answer Keisha's question, someone interrupted their conversation by calling out his name. It was an older guy who had on more gold than the law should allow.

"Que, I need to talk business with you as soon as possible." The older guy said.

"Give me a second, and I'll be right with you. Say Blue, take care of these two! Whatever they want give it to them and it's all on me. Excuse me Keisha; I'll be back in a minute."

"I got you bro." Said the bartender. "Ladies, my name is Blue. Do ya'll need anything?"

"We good right now!" Keniesha replied.

"Well, whenever ya'll change ya'll minds, let me know. Just give me a holla'!"

While Blue was talking to us, I noticed Que and the older gentleman walked into a room behind the bar; and shut the door behind them. From what I could see, Que was a pretty well known guy; which is good most of the time, I was just hoping he wouldn't be gone too long.

"So what do you think about him sis?" Keisha asked Keniesha.

"Since you asked me, I say he's worth trying to learn more about. Now you can stop smiling so hard love bird!"

"I want another drink; what about you?"

"Hell yeah!" Keniesha replied and then said, "Say Blue!"

"How can I help you sweetie?" Blue asked as he came over.

"I would like another Long Island Ice Tea please."

"And you honey?"

"Another Long Island as well."

"I get that right away ladies!"

"Anyway Keniesha, I'm really feeling Que right now; if he ask me out, do you think I should say yes or would I be moving too fast?"

"Hell nor you wouldn't be moving too fast! That is what I brought you here for; to have fun and meet new people. So far you doing good at that, but I ain't telling you to go fuck him tonight that'll be on you."

"Girl quit playing; you know he ain't ready for none of this pussy. His sexy ass wouldn't know what to do with all this." Keisha said but briefly allowed her mind to wonder on how fucking him would feel before Blue came back with their drinks. "Thank you Blue."

"Anytime ladies."

"I know one thing, you got the hottest nigga' in here." Keniesha begin before Keisha cut her off.

"Oh shit, he's on his way back over here girl."

"I hope I didn't take too long; is everything going okay? Blue been getting ya'll whatever ya'll needed?" Quincy said as he returned.

"You straight; and Blue is one of the best bartenders I've ever seen." Keisha answered trying not to reveal how much she was anticipating him coming back.

"As long as ya'll are having a good time, then I'm good. Are you ladies driving home tonight? Do ya'll stay near by?" Que asked out of concern because he notice Keniesha appeared to be a lil' tipsy.

"We stay close by, so we gone be okay." Keisha answered.

"I was just asking because I wouldn't want ya'll to get too drunk and couldn't make it home safely." He replied honestly. That scored him a couple of more like points in Keisha's book. Then he continue, "I'm really feeling you Keisha, and really would like to see you again after tonight. I personally be all over and busy a lot, but I would love to show you around the city. I know a lot of places we could go."

"Oh yeah; like where?"

Before Que could answer, his cellular phone rang. "Oh shit!" he said out loud and then told me, "Give me one second." as he took the call walking away. It had to be something important because he came back with a whole different expression on his face. "Look Keisha, something just popped up and I have to go. I'm sorry I have to leave like this, but can I at least get your number so we can talk more?"

Keisha firmly said, "No; but I'll take yours!"

"Fair enough! Blue, I'm out; but I need you to make sure these ladies make it to their car safely for me." Then he dug into his pocket and pulled out what had to be at least ten thousand dollars in all one hundred dollar bills. He peeled off five crispy bills and then handed it to Blue saying, "Three of that put in your pocket; the other couple of hundred should cover my tab."

"Thanks Que!" Blue said then turned around and began walking off.

Que then peeled five more hundred dollar bills off his knot and tried handing it to Keisha while saying, "Take this right here, just in case ya'll end up needing to catch a cab or anything else."

Keisha quickly decline his offering saying, *"Naw*; we good!"

As soon as I said that, Keniesha elbowed the shit out of me saying, *"Naw*; we ain't good!"

That was my clue to get the money as I said, "Thank you Que."

"You welcome. Get my number from Blue and call me whenever you get ready." We hugged and then he left.

"Keniesha, he wants your sis!" I said feeling myself just a bit.

"You better make sure you get his number and call him then."

"Okay I plan too, trust me."

"And just for future reference sis, when a man offers you that kind of money with no strings attached, you don't ever turn it down!"

"Since when did you become an expert in men? Where's your man at?"

Feeling insulted and all in her feelings, Keniesha snapped, "I ain't got one, and I don't need one. I've been having fun just dating around; but tonight was all about you. Whenever you ready to go, just let me know."

"I'm ready now! Let me get this phone number from Blue and we can go."

I called Blue and asked for Que's phone number. He wrote it down for me, and asked, "Can I get anything else for either one of you?"

"Naw, we about to go; but thank you for everything."

"Well hold up one moment and let me get security to escort ya'll out to ya'll car."

"Cool!"

Security came and walked us to the car, opened the doors for us, and even watched us pull off safely. We were quiet the whole ride home which was only about six minutes if that. Infact, we actually made it home at 2:46

a.m.

When we went inside the house, I said, "I'm about to check on Cortez." but Keniesha didn't say a word. She just straight into her room and closed the door. I got halfway down the stairs that led to Cortez's room, and heard a low snore coming from him. I thought to myself, *Ain't this cute; my baby sound asleep.* Then I went to my room, undressed and fell out thinking, *I'll call Que tomorrow!*

ALSO

COMING

SOON

THIS COULD BE YOUR PAGE!

Interested in getting a book publish?

Then give us a try.

4 FiGure$ Production

Contact Us At 314.585.5733

Email Us
4figuresproduction@Gmail.com

U.S. Postal Services
4 FiGure$ Production
5050 Clayridge Drive suite#213
Mehlville, Missouri 63129

THIS COULD BE YOUR PAGE!

SPECIAL THANKS

TO ALL WHO HAS
SUPPORTED
THIS BOOK

AND MAY YOU KEEP ON SUPPORTING
MY FUTURE PROJECTS

4 FiGurS Production

www.ingramcontent.com/pod-product-compliance
Lightning Source LLC
Chambersburg PA
CBHW052017020726
47501CB00004B/1105